LAUREN KEELY

STORY
SCRIPT

JONATHAN LUNA

STORY
SCRIPT ASSISTS
ILLUSTRATIONS
LETTERING
DESIGN

Please return/renew this item by the last date shown on this label, or on your self-service receipt.

To renew this item, visit **www.librarieswest.org.uk** or contact your library

Your borrower number and PIN are required.

Libraries**West**

SPECIAL THANKS

Dave Hanson

Tim Ingle

Nicole Mitrocsak

Guy Nicolette

William Rockabrand

David Spence

Rebekah Spence

Linda Wyatt

Richard Wyatt

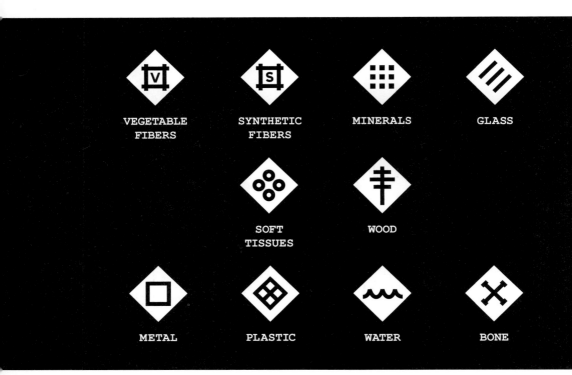

VEGETABLE FIBERS

SYNTHETIC FIBERS

MINERALS

GLASS

SOFT TISSUES

WOOD

METAL

PLASTIC

WATER

BONE

IMAGE COMICS, INC.

Todd McFarlane: President • **Jim Valentino:** Vice President • **Marc Silvestri:** Chief Executive Officer • **Erik Larsen:** Chief Financial Officer • **Robert Kirkman:** Chief Operating Officer • **Eric Stephenson:** Publisher / Chief Creative Officer • **Shanna Matuszak:** Editorial Coordinator • **Marla Eizik:** Talent Liaison • **Nicole Lapalme:** Controller • **Leanna Caunter:** Accounting Analyst • **Sue Korpela:** Accounting & HR Manager • **Jeff Boison:** Director of Sales & Publishing Planning • **Dirk Wood:** Director of International Sales & Licensing • **Alex Cox:** Director of Direct Market & Speciality Sales • **Chloe Ramos-Peterson:** Book Market & Library Sales Manager • **Emilio Bautista:** Digital Sales Coordinator • **Kat Salazar:** Director of PR & Marketing • **Drew Fitzgerald:** Marketing Content Associate • **Heather Doornink:** Production Director • **Drew Gill:** Art Director • **Hilary DiLoreto:** Print Manager • **Tricia Ramos:** Traffic Manager • **Erika Schnatz:** Senior Production Artist • **Ryan Brewer:** Production Artist • **Deanna Phelps:** Production Artist

IMAGECOMICS.COM
JONATHANLUNA.COM
LAURENKEELY.COM

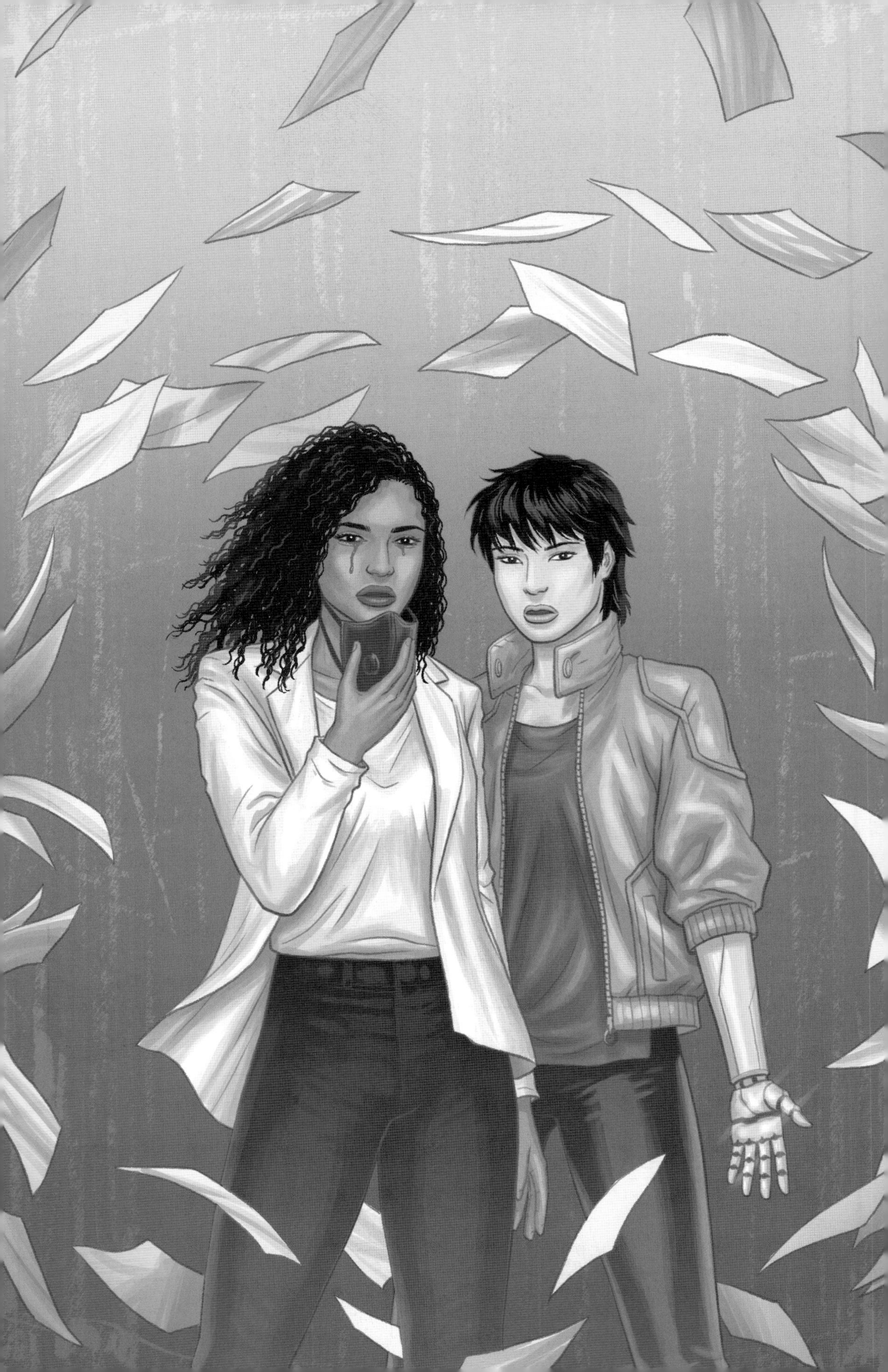

Everyone believes they're so goddamn special.

Every day, they're bombarded with the threat of death-- mass shootings, freak accidents, cancer, killer bugs.

And still, they feel safe--exempt from the awful realities that fall on other people.

They say to themselves, "not my town, not my school, not me."

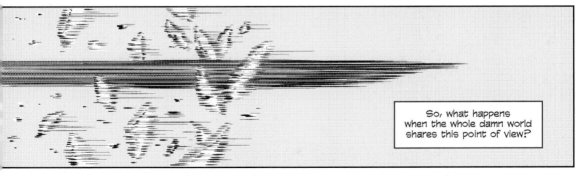

So, what happens when the whole damn world shares this point of view?

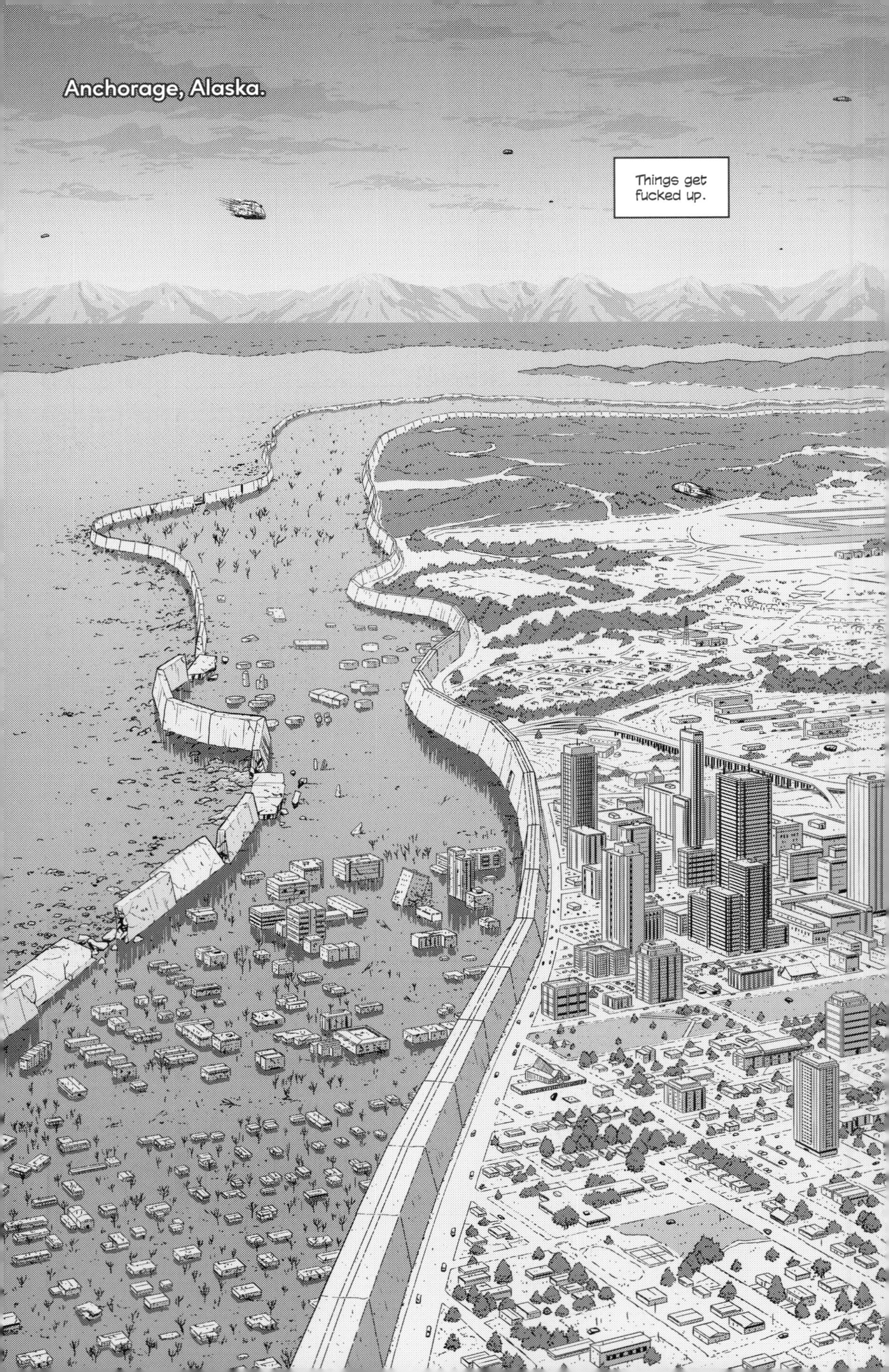
Anchorage, Alaska.
Things get fucked up.

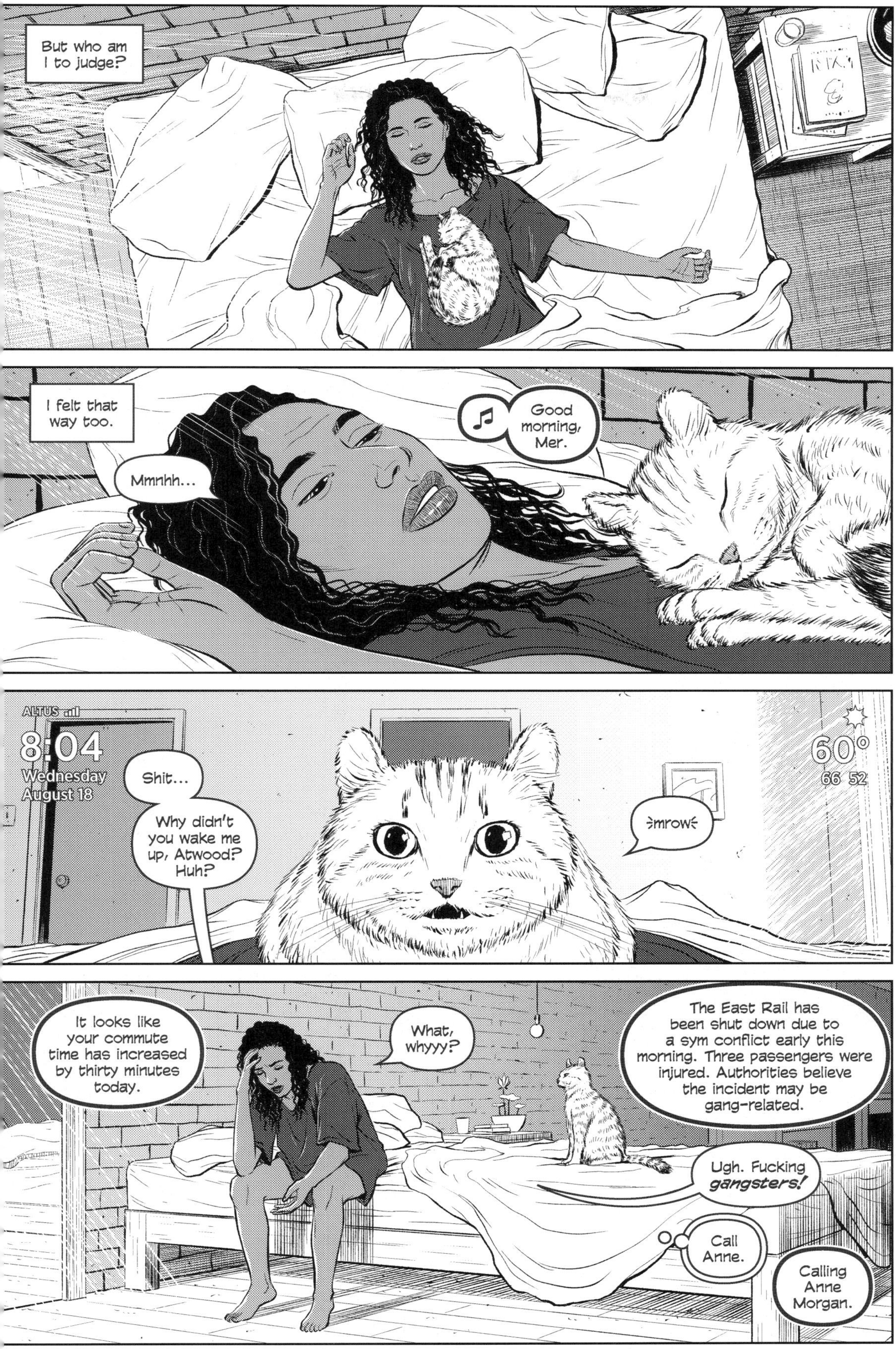
But who am I to judge?
I felt that way too.
♪ Good morning, Mer.
Mmhhh...
ALTUS
8:04
Wednesday
August 18
60°
66 52
Shit...
Why didn't you wake me up, Atwood? Huh?
mrow
It looks like your commute time has increased by thirty minutes today.
What, whyyy?
The East Rail has been shut down due to a sym conflict early this morning. Three passengers were injured. Authorities believe the incident may be gang-related.
Ugh. Fucking *gangsters!*
Call Anne.
Calling Anne Morgan.

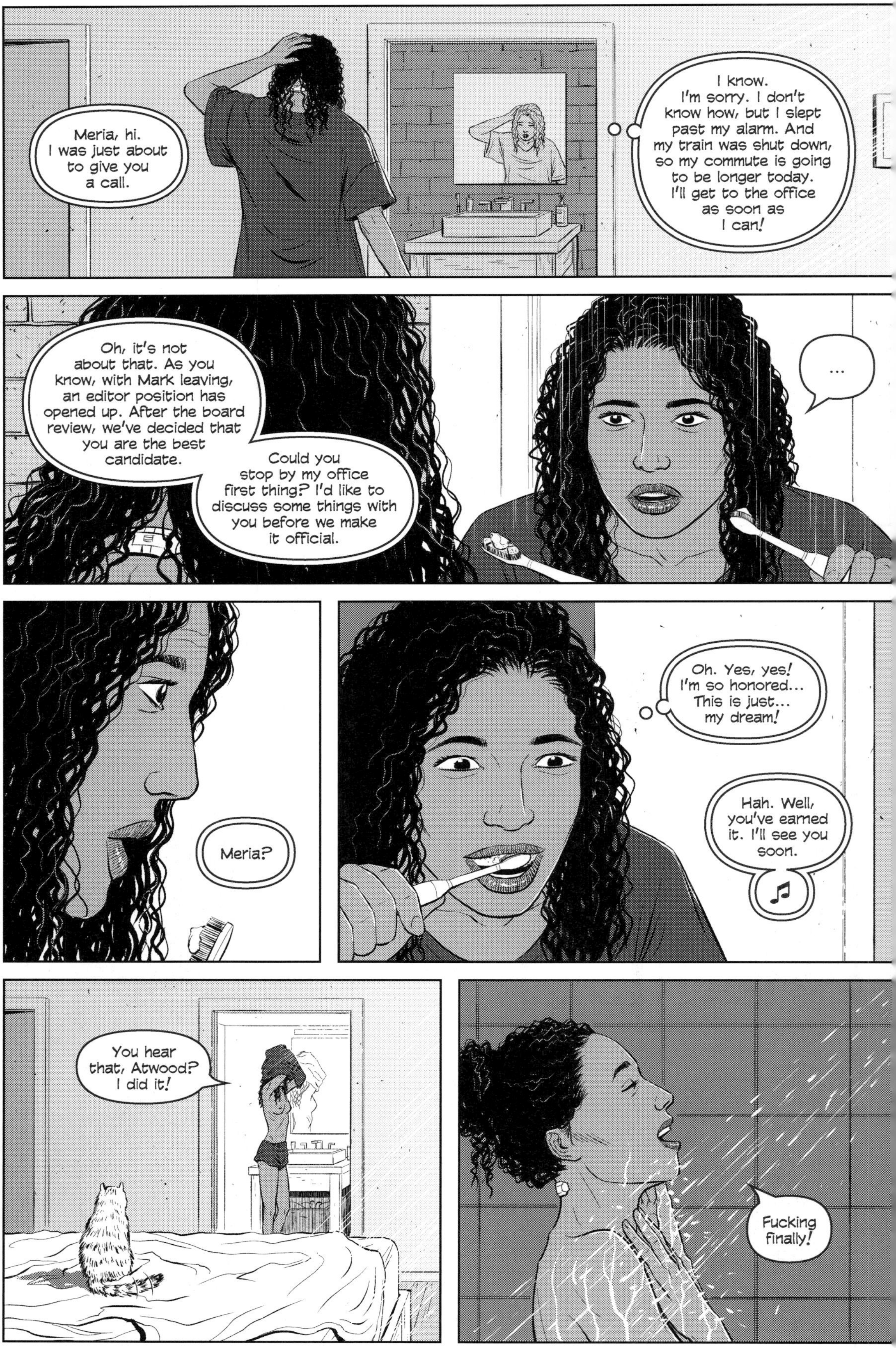
Meria, hi.
I was just about to give you a call.
I know. I'm sorry. I don't know how, but I slept past my alarm. And my train was shut down, so my commute is going to be longer today. I'll get to the office as soon as I can!
Oh, it's not about that. As you know, with Mark leaving, an editor position has opened up. After the board review, we've decided that you are the best candidate.
Could you stop by my office first thing? I'd like to discuss some things with you before we make it official.
...
Meria?
Oh. Yes, yes! I'm so honored... This is just... my dream!
Hah. Well, you've earned it. I'll see you soon.
♫
You hear that, Atwood? I did it!
Fucking finally!

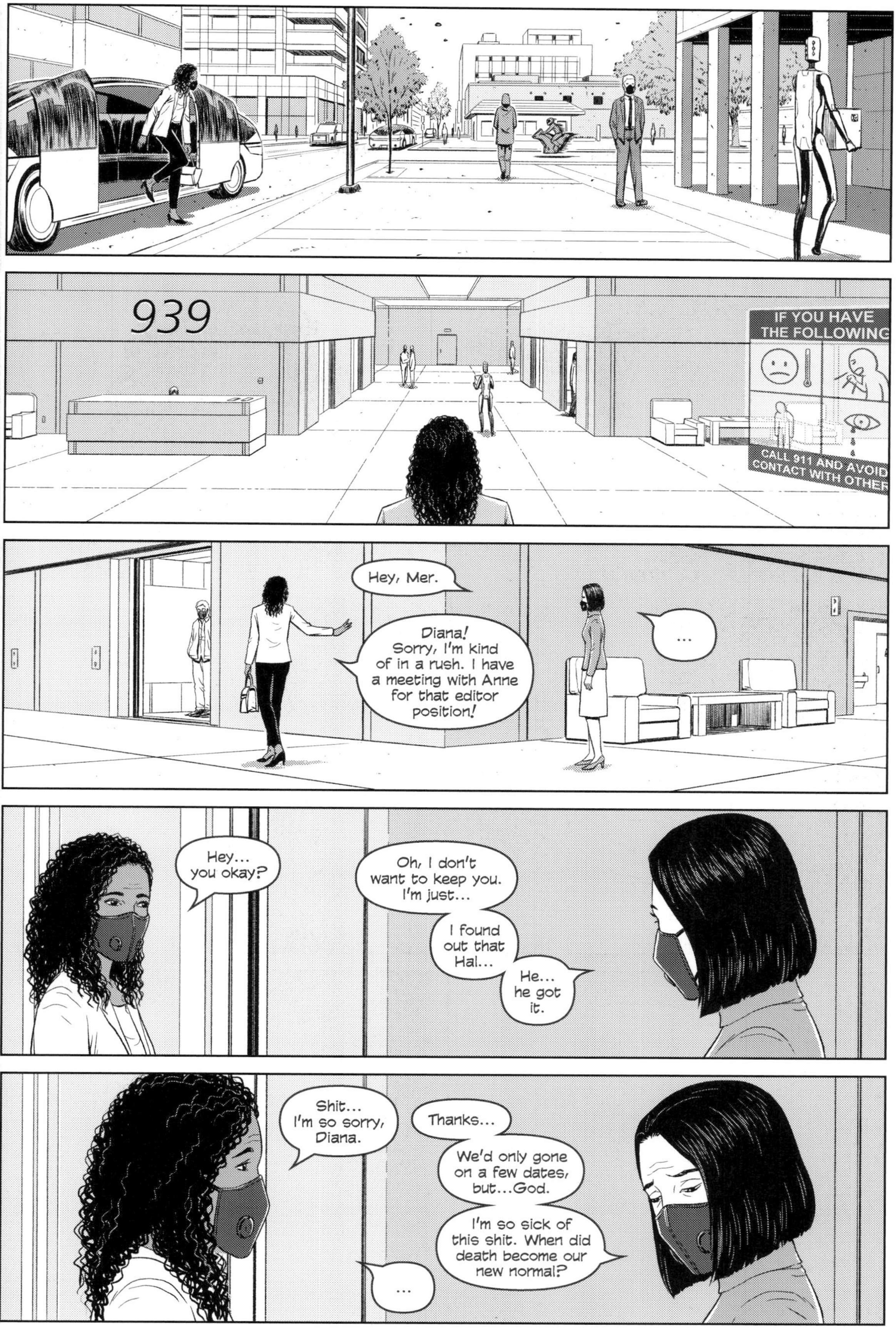
939
IF YOU HAVE THE FOLLOWING
CALL 911 AND AVOID CONTACT WITH OTHER
Hey, Mer.
Diana! Sorry, I'm kind of in a rush. I have a meeting with Anne for that editor position!
...
Hey... you okay?
Oh, I don't want to keep you. I'm just...
I found out that Hal...
He... he got it.
Shit... I'm so sorry, Diana.
Thanks...
We'd only gone on a few dates, but...God.
I'm so sick of this shit. When did death become our new normal?
...

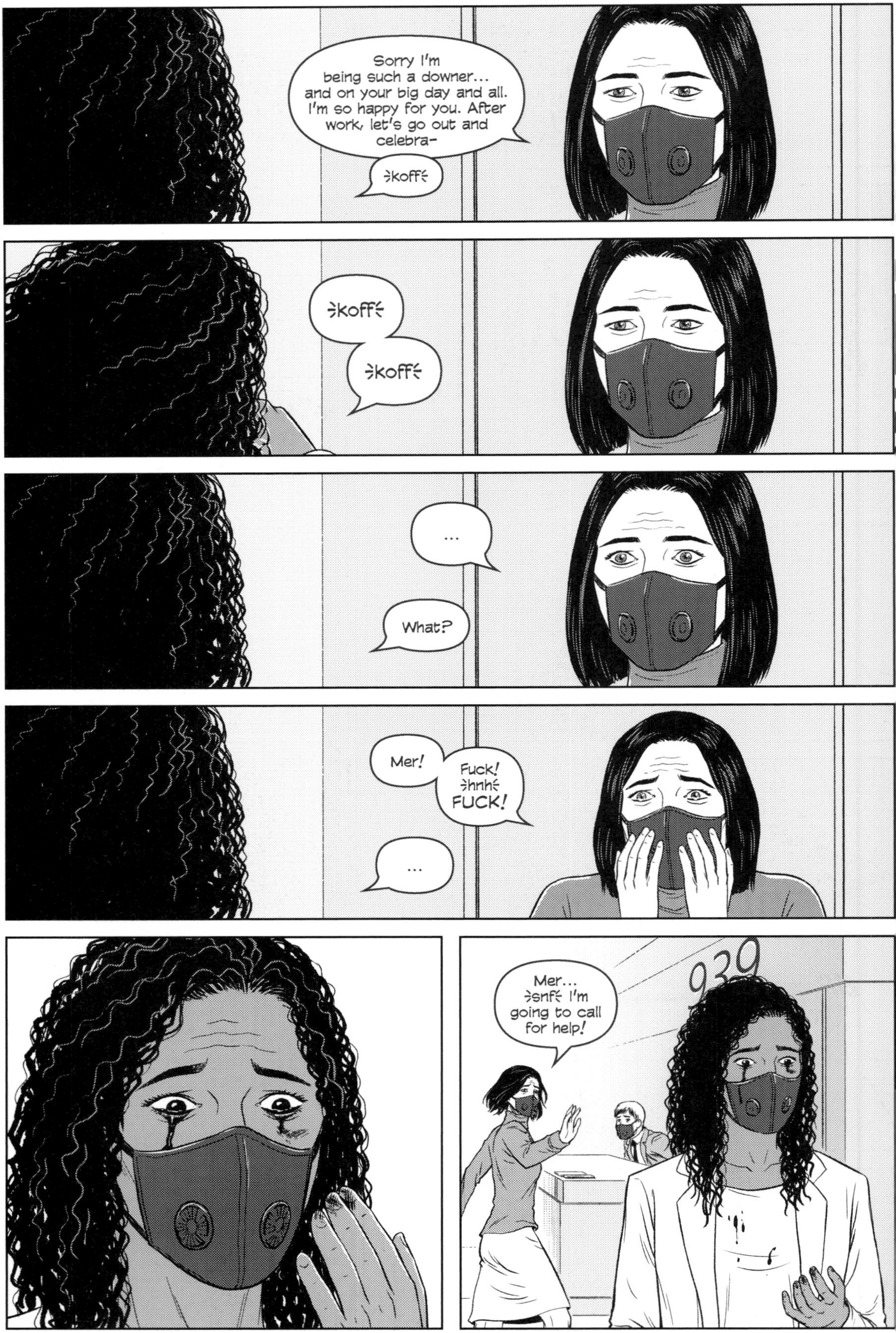
Sorry I'm being such a downer... and on your big day and all. I'm so happy for you. After work, let's go out and celebra-
koff
koff
koff
...
What?
Mer!
Fuck! hnh FUCK!
...
939
Mer... snf I'm going to call for help!

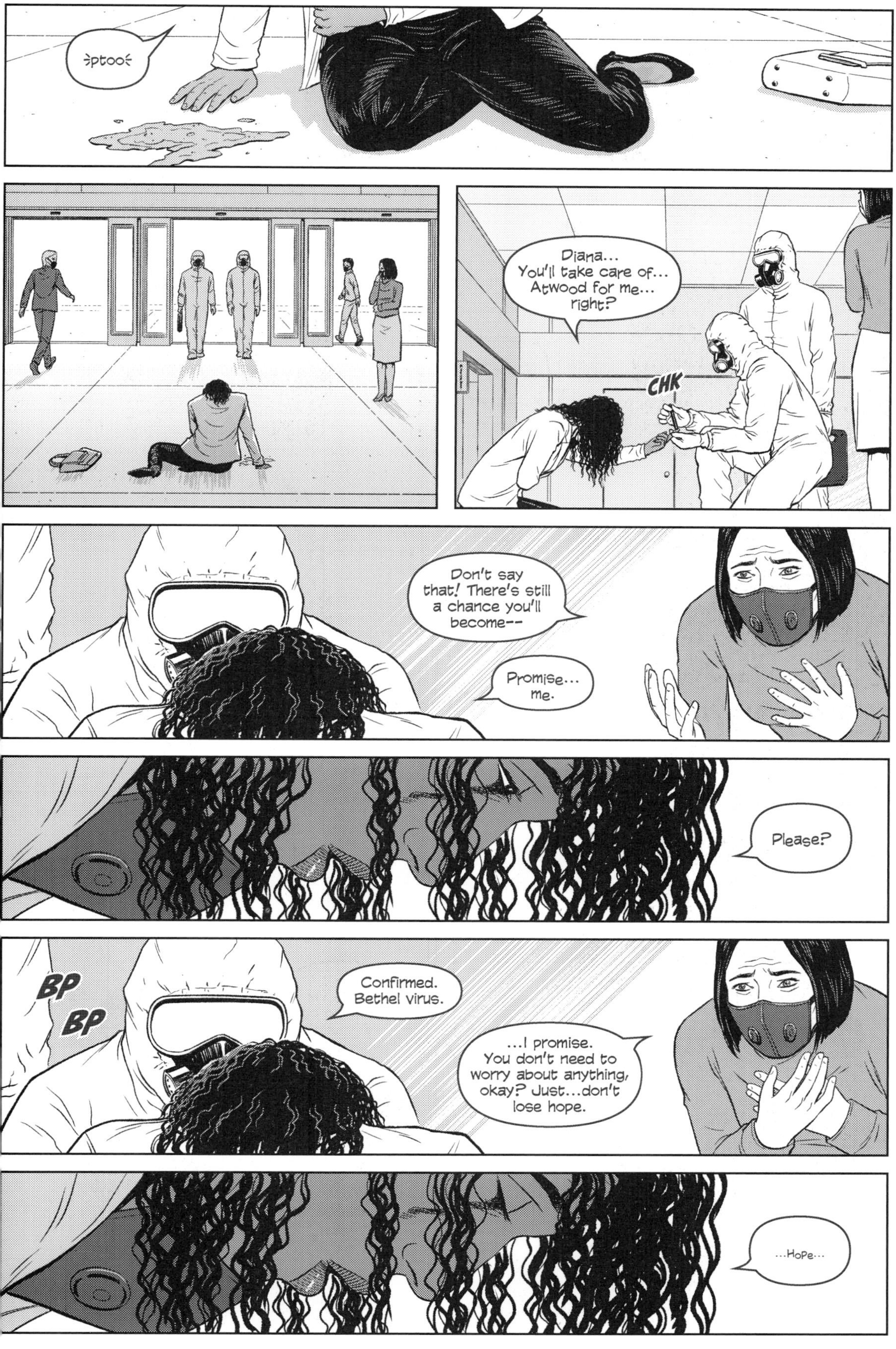
ptoo
Diana... You'll take care of... Atwood for me... right?
CHK
Don't say that! There's still a chance you'll become--
Promise... me.
Please?
BP BP
Confirmed. Bethel virus.
...I promise. You don't need to worry about anything, okay? Just...don't lose hope.
...Hope...

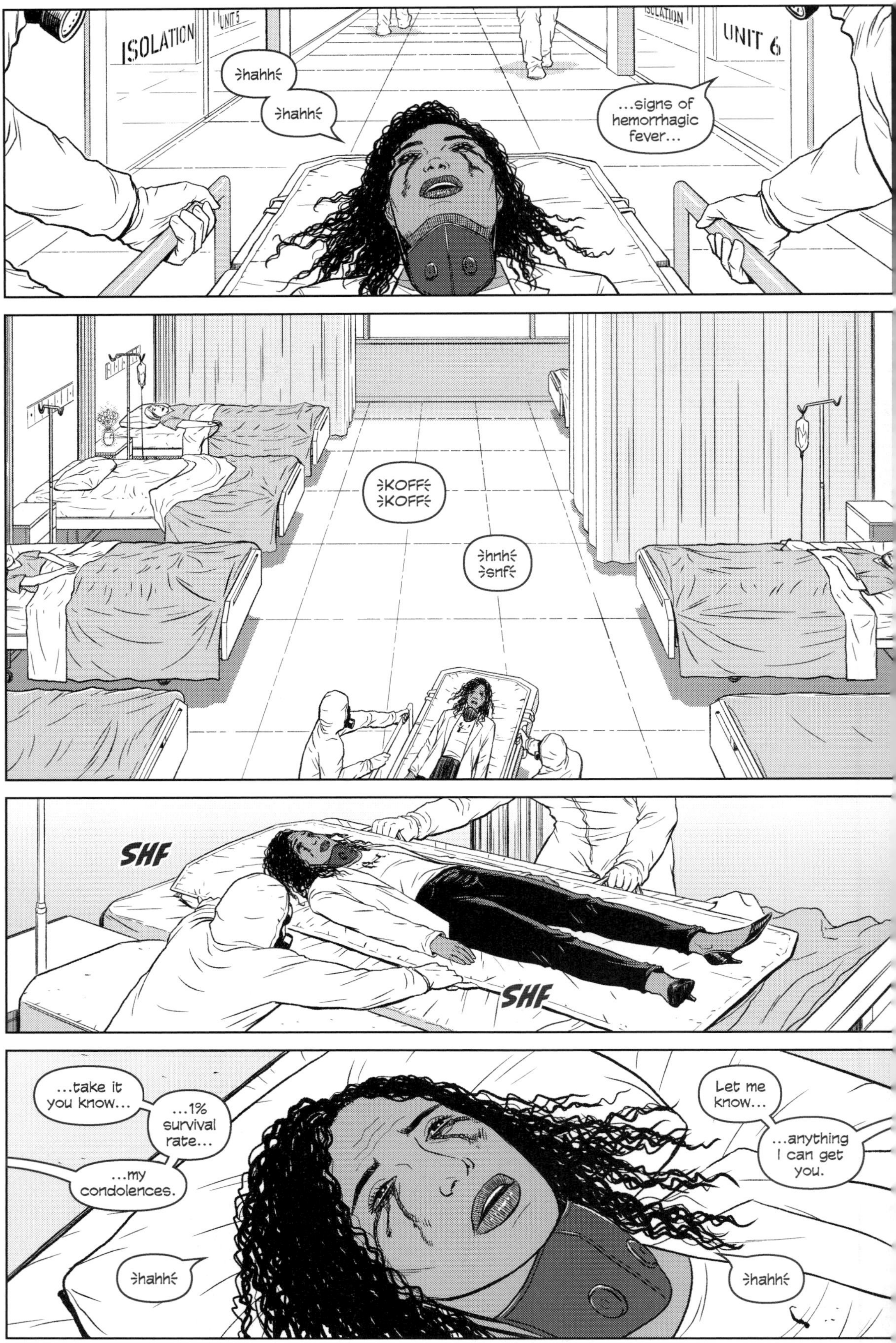
ISOLATION
UNIT 5
ISOLATION
UNIT 6
hahh
hahh
...signs of hemorrhagic fever...
KOFF KOFF
hnh snf
SHF
SHF
...take it you know...
...1% survival rate...
...my condolences.
Let me know...
...anything I can get you.
hahh
hahh

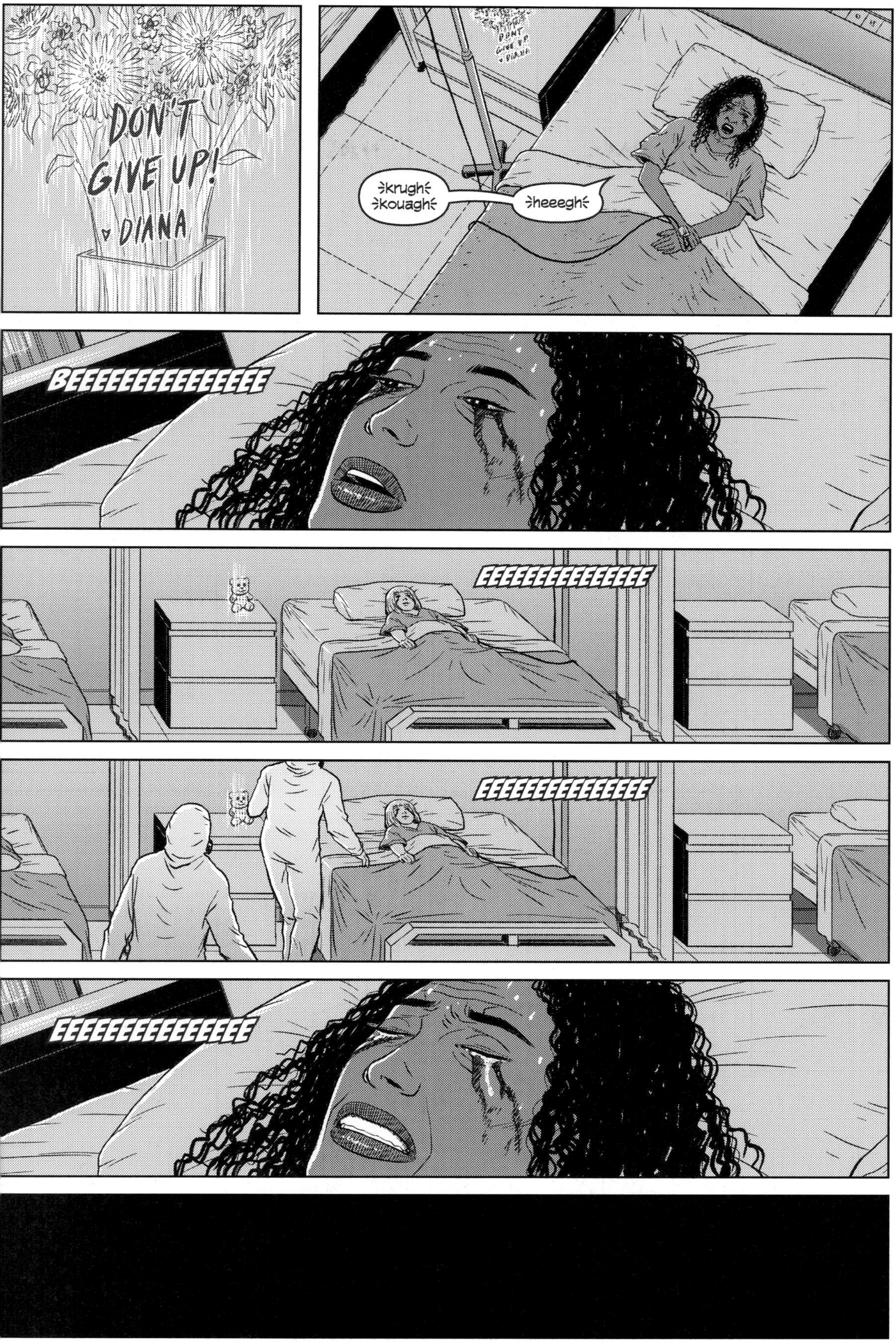
DON'T GIVE UP! DIANA
krugh kouagh
heeegh
BEEEEEEEEEEEEEEE
EEEEEEEEEEEEEEE
EEEEEEEEEEEEEEE
EEEEEEEEEEEEEEE

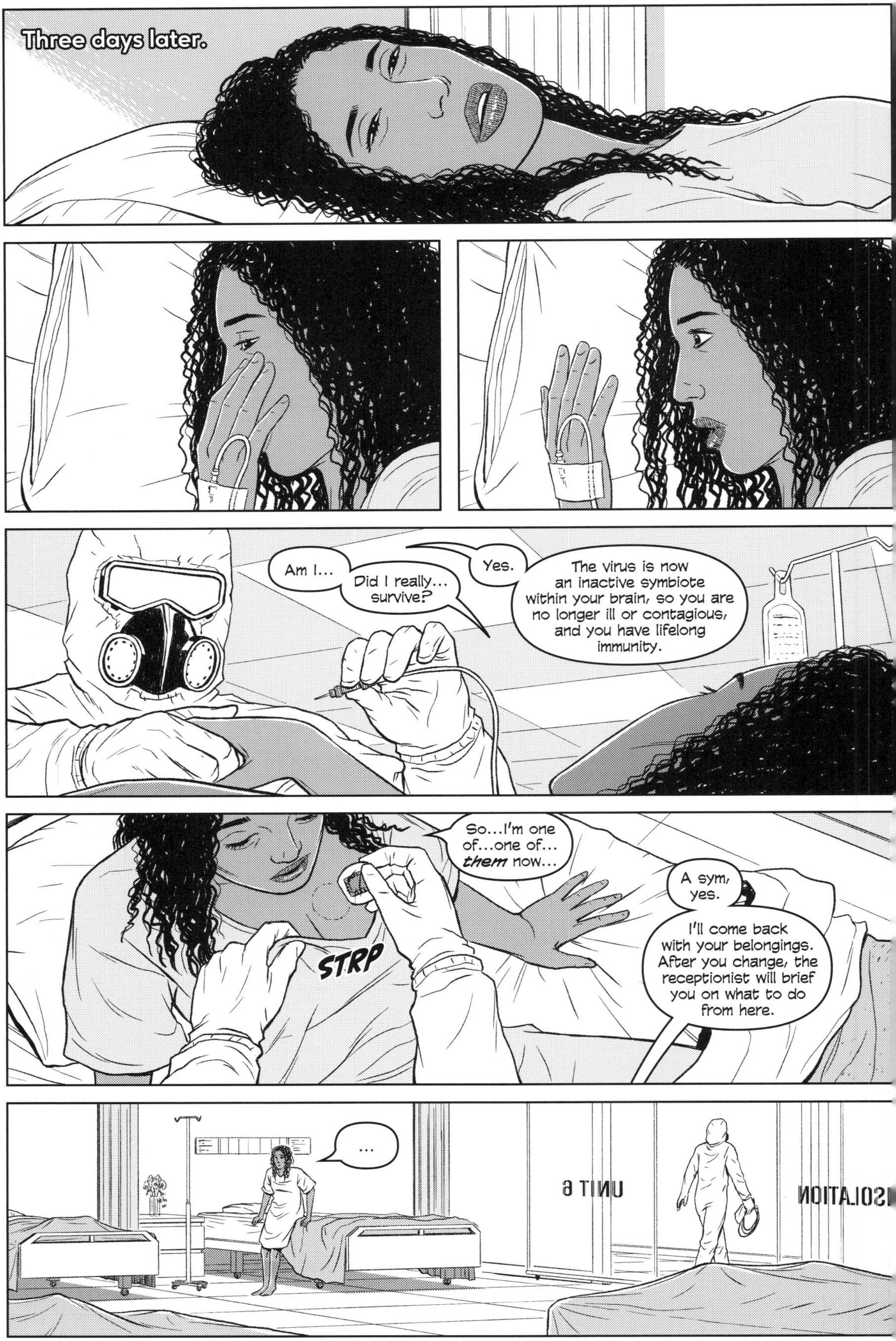
Three days later.
Am I...
Did I really... survive?
Yes.
The virus is now an inactive symbiote within your brain, so you are no longer ill or contagious, and you have lifelong immunity.
So...I'm one of...one of... *them* now...
STRP
A sym, yes.
I'll come back with your belongings. After you change, the receptionist will brief you on what to do from here.
...
UNIT 6
ISOLATION

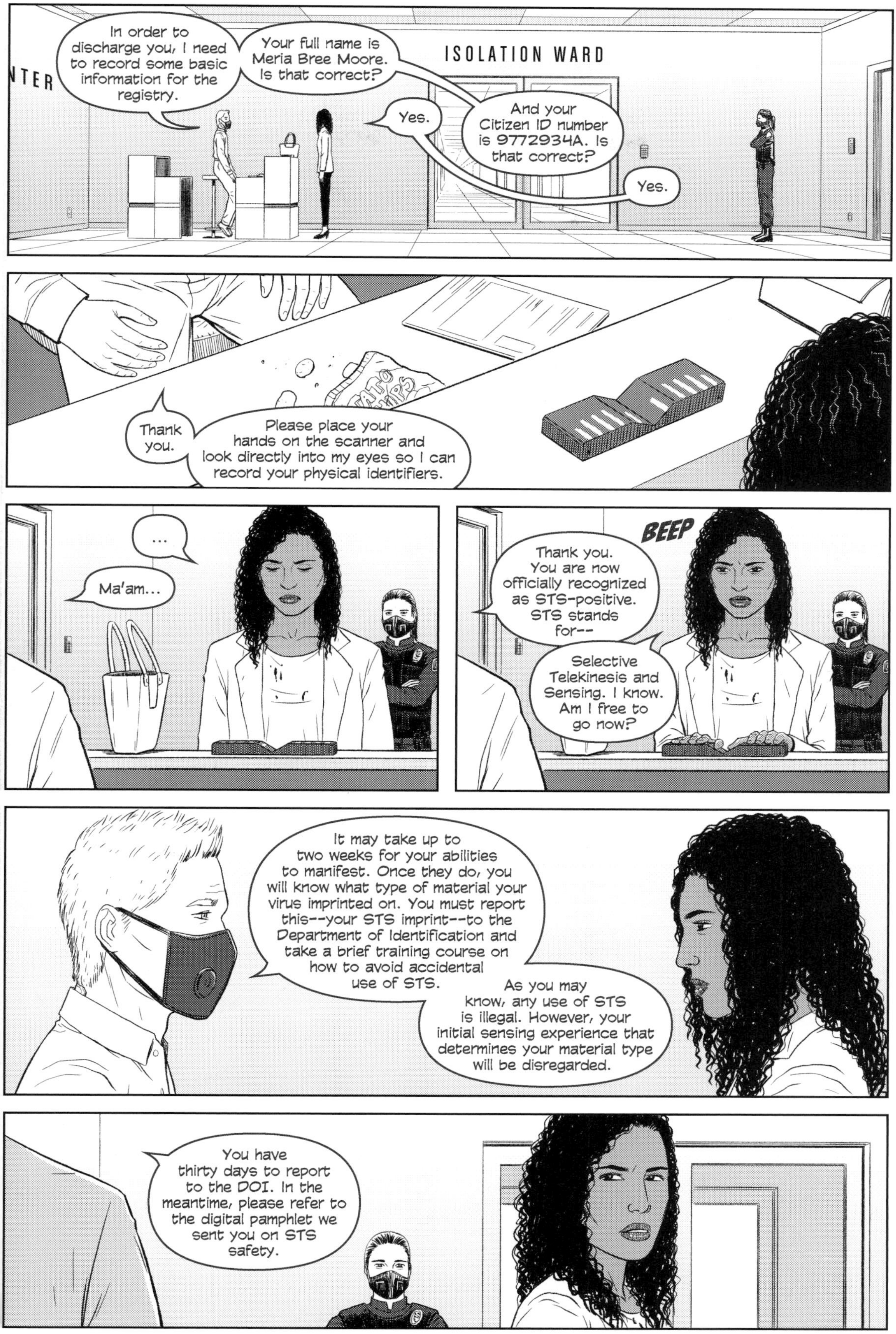
ISOLATION WARD
NTER
In order to discharge you, I need to record some basic information for the registry.
Your full name is Meria Bree Moore. Is that correct?
Yes.
And your Citizen ID number is 9772934A. Is that correct?
Yes.
Thank you.
Please place your hands on the scanner and look directly into my eyes so I can record your physical identifiers.
...
Ma'am...
BEEP
Thank you. You are now officially recognized as STS-positive. STS stands for--
Selective Telekinesis and Sensing. I know. Am I free to go now?
It may take up to two weeks for your abilities to manifest. Once they do, you will know what type of material your virus imprinted on. You must report this--your STS imprint--to the Department of Identification and take a brief training course on how to avoid accidental use of STS.
As you may know, any use of STS is illegal. However, your initial sensing experience that determines your material type will be disregarded.
You have thirty days to report to the DOI. In the meantime, please refer to the digital pamphlet we sent you on STS safety.

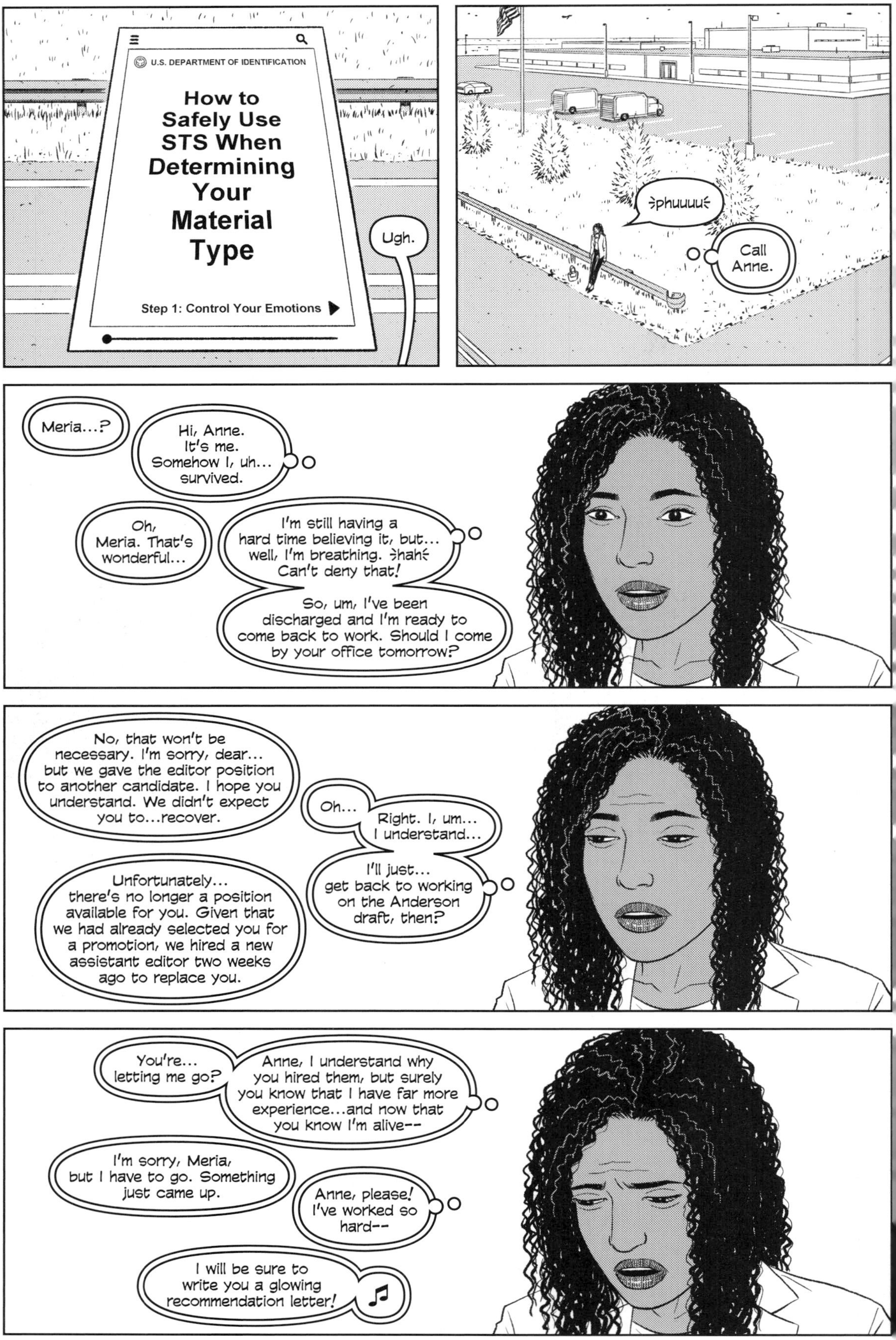
U.S. DEPARTMENT OF IDENTIFICATION
How to Safely Use STS When Determining Your Material Type
Step 1: Control Your Emotions
Ugh.
⫘phuuuu⫗
Call Anne.
Meria...?
Hi, Anne. It's me. Somehow I, uh... survived.
Oh, Meria. That's wonderful...
I'm still having a hard time believing it, but... well, I'm breathing. ⫘hah⫗ Can't deny that!
So, um, I've been discharged and I'm ready to come back to work. Should I come by your office tomorrow?
No, that won't be necessary. I'm sorry, dear... but we gave the editor position to another candidate. I hope you understand. We didn't expect you to...recover.
Oh...
Right. I, um... I understand...
I'll just... get back to working on the Anderson draft, then?
Unfortunately... there's no longer a position available for you. Given that we had already selected you for a promotion, we hired a new assistant editor two weeks ago to replace you.
You're... letting me go?
Anne, I understand why you hired them, but surely you know that I have far more experience...and now that you know I'm alive--
I'm sorry, Meria, but I have to go. Something just came up.
Anne, please! I've worked so hard--
I will be sure to write you a glowing recommendation letter! ♫

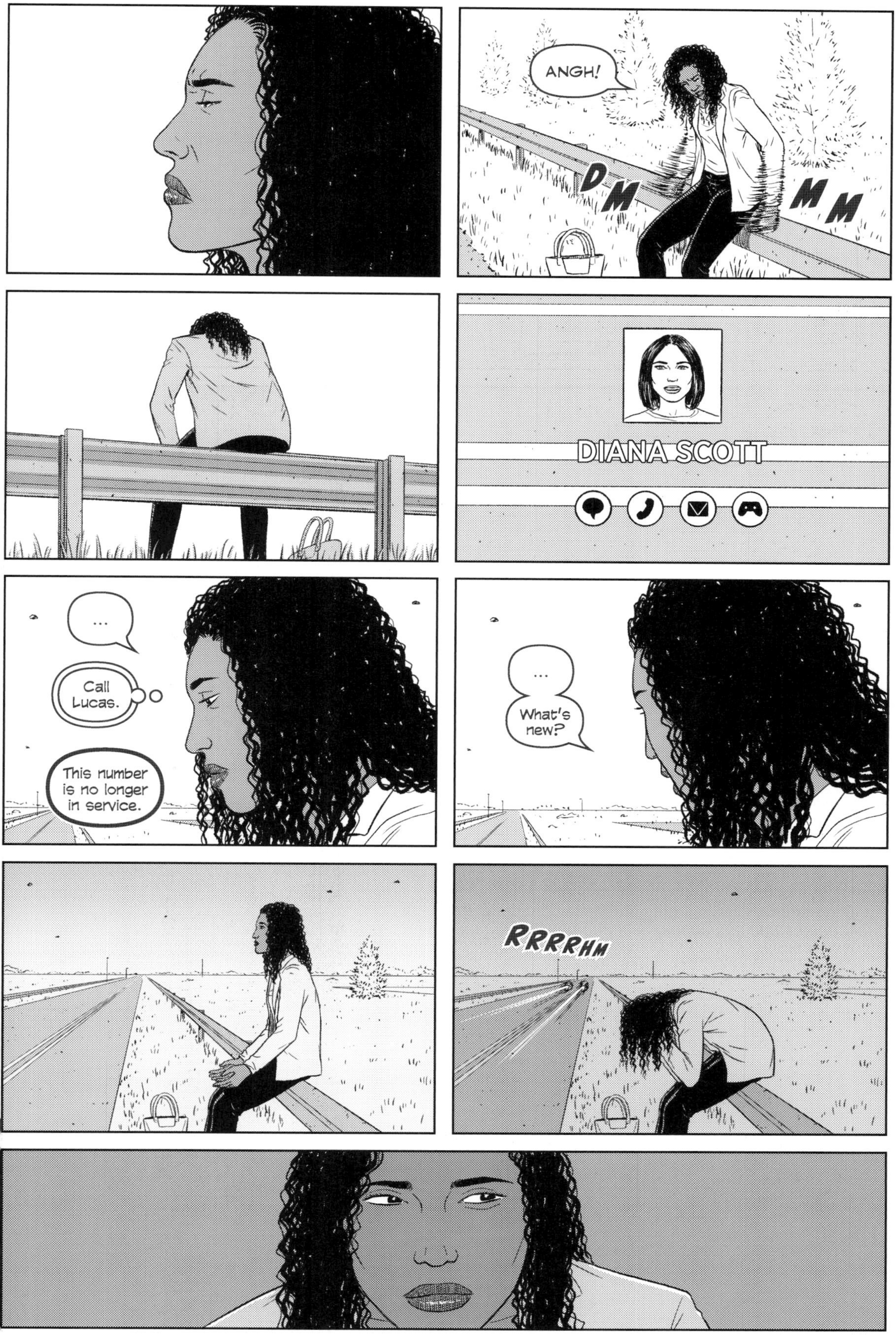
ANGH!
DMMMM
DIANA SCOTT
...
Call Lucas.
This number is no longer in service.
...
What's new?
RRRRHM

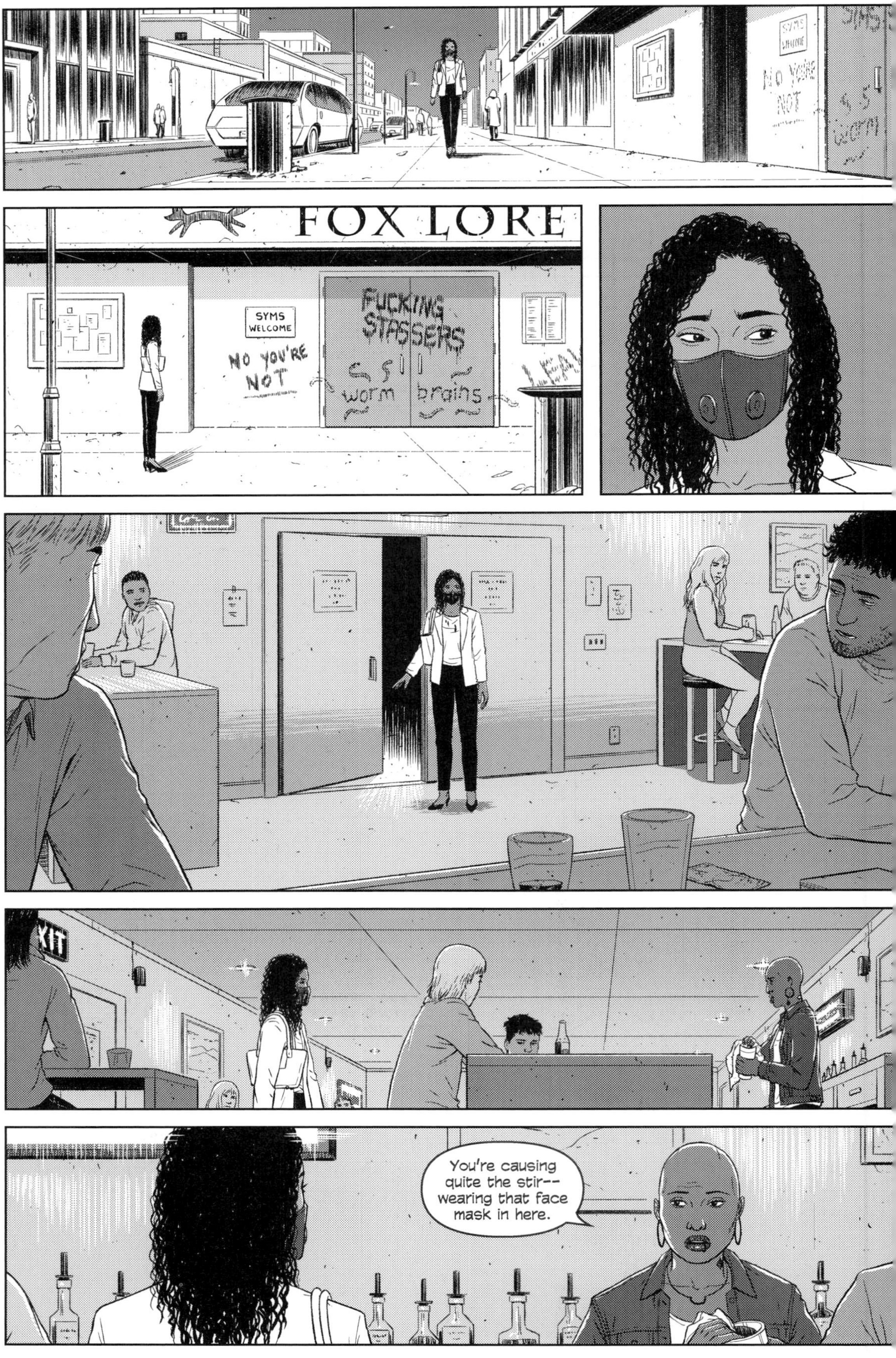
FOX LORE
SYMS WELCOME
NO YOU'RE NOT
FUCKING STASSERS
worm brains
EXIT
You're causing quite the stir-- wearing that face mask in here.

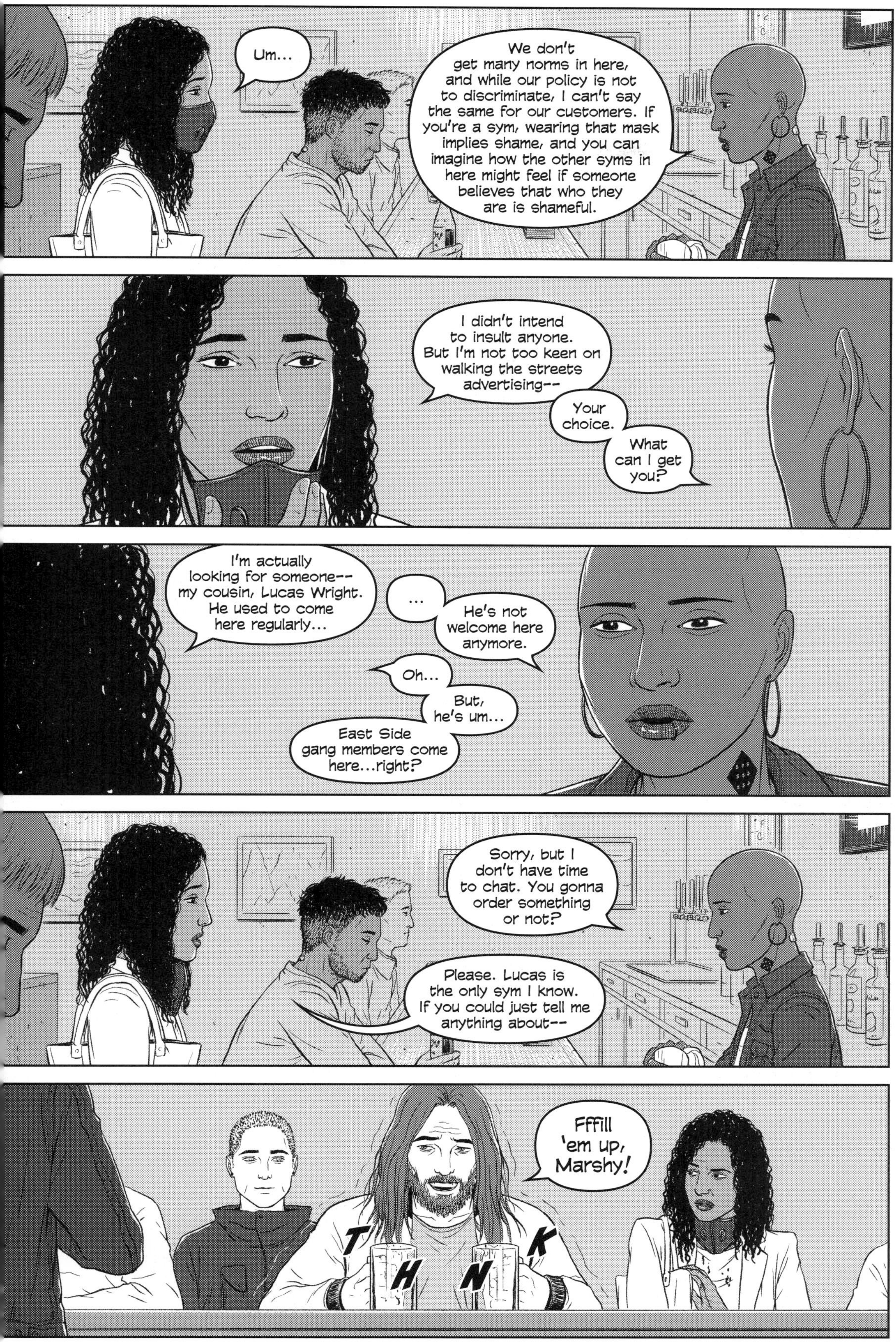
Um...
We don't get many norms in here, and while our policy is not to discriminate, I can't say the same for our customers. If you're a sym, wearing that mask implies shame, and you can imagine how the other syms in here might feel if someone believes that who they are is shameful.
I didn't intend to insult anyone. But I'm not too keen on walking the streets advertising--
Your choice.
What can I get you?
I'm actually looking for someone--my cousin, Lucas Wright. He used to come here regularly...
...
He's not welcome here anymore.
Oh...
But, he's um...
East Side gang members come here...right?
Sorry, but I don't have time to chat. You gonna order something or not?
Please. Lucas is the only sym I know. If you could just tell me anything about--
Fffill 'em up, Marshy!
THNK

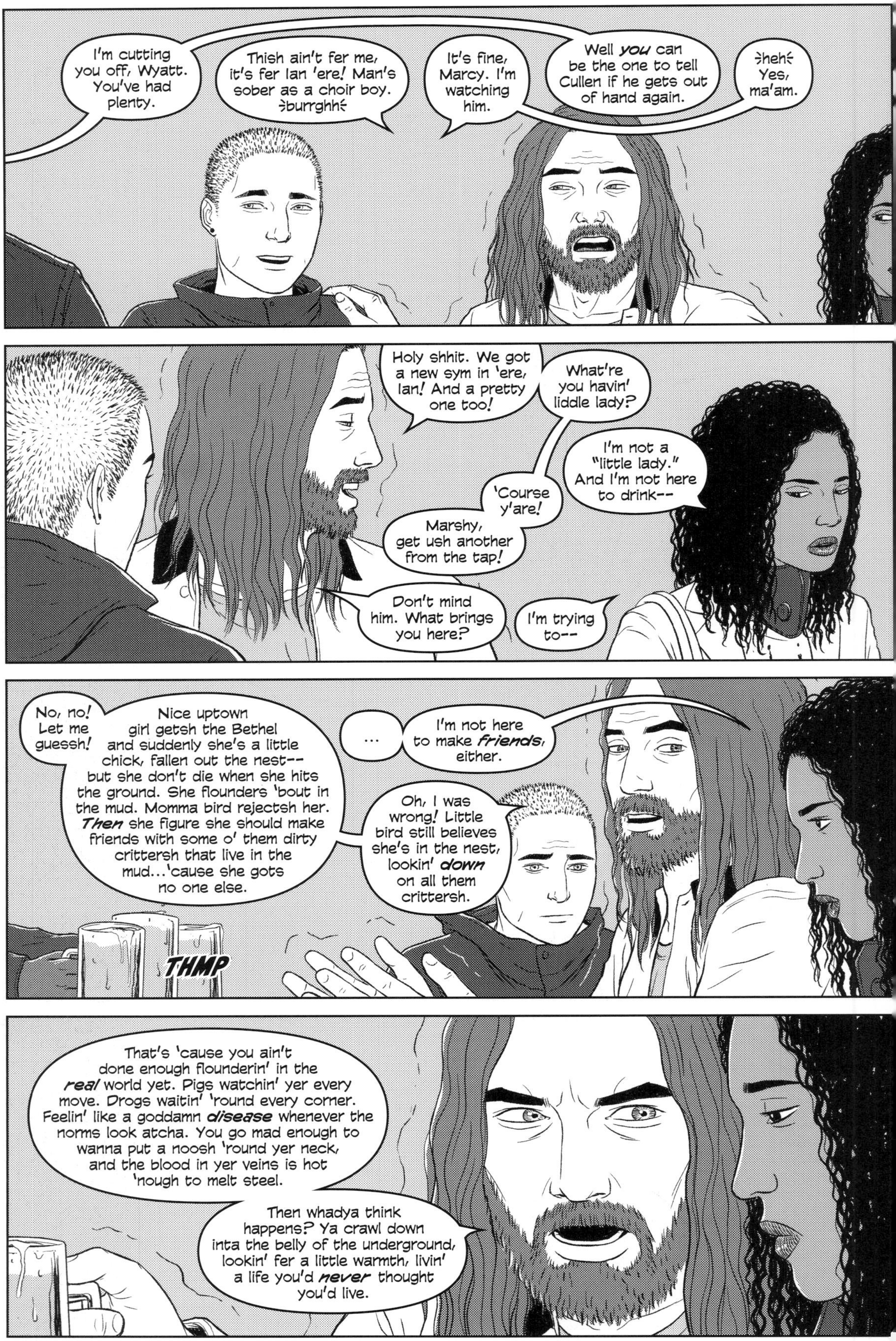
I'm cutting you off, Wyatt. You've had plenty.
Thish ain't fer me, it's fer Ian 'ere! Man's sober as a choir boy. ⸗burrghh⸗
It's fine, Marcy. I'm watching him.
Well *you* can be the one to tell Cullen if he gets out of hand again.
⸗heh⸗ Yes, ma'am.
Holy shhit. We got a new sym in 'ere, Ian! And a pretty one too!
What're you havin' liddle lady?
I'm not a "little lady." And I'm not here to drink--
'Course y'are!
Marshy, get ush another from the tap!
Don't mind him. What brings you here?
I'm trying to--
No, no! Let me guessh!
Nice uptown girl getsh the Bethel and suddenly she's a little chick, fallen out the nest--but she don't die when she hits the ground. She flounders 'bout in the mud. Momma bird rejectsh her. *Then* she figure she should make friends with some o' them dirty crittersh that live in the mud...'cause she gots no one else.
...
I'm not here to make *friends*, either.
Oh, I was wrong! Little bird still believes she's in the nest, lookin' *down* on all them crittersh.
THMP
That's 'cause you ain't done enough flounderin' in the *real* world yet. Pigs watchin' yer every move. Drogs waitin' 'round every corner. Feelin' like a goddamn *disease* whenever the norms look atcha. You go mad enough to wanna put a noosh 'round yer neck, and the blood in yer veins is hot 'nough to melt steel.
Then whadya think happens? Ya crawl down inta the belly of the underground, lookin' fer a little warmth, livin' a life you'd *never* thought you'd live.

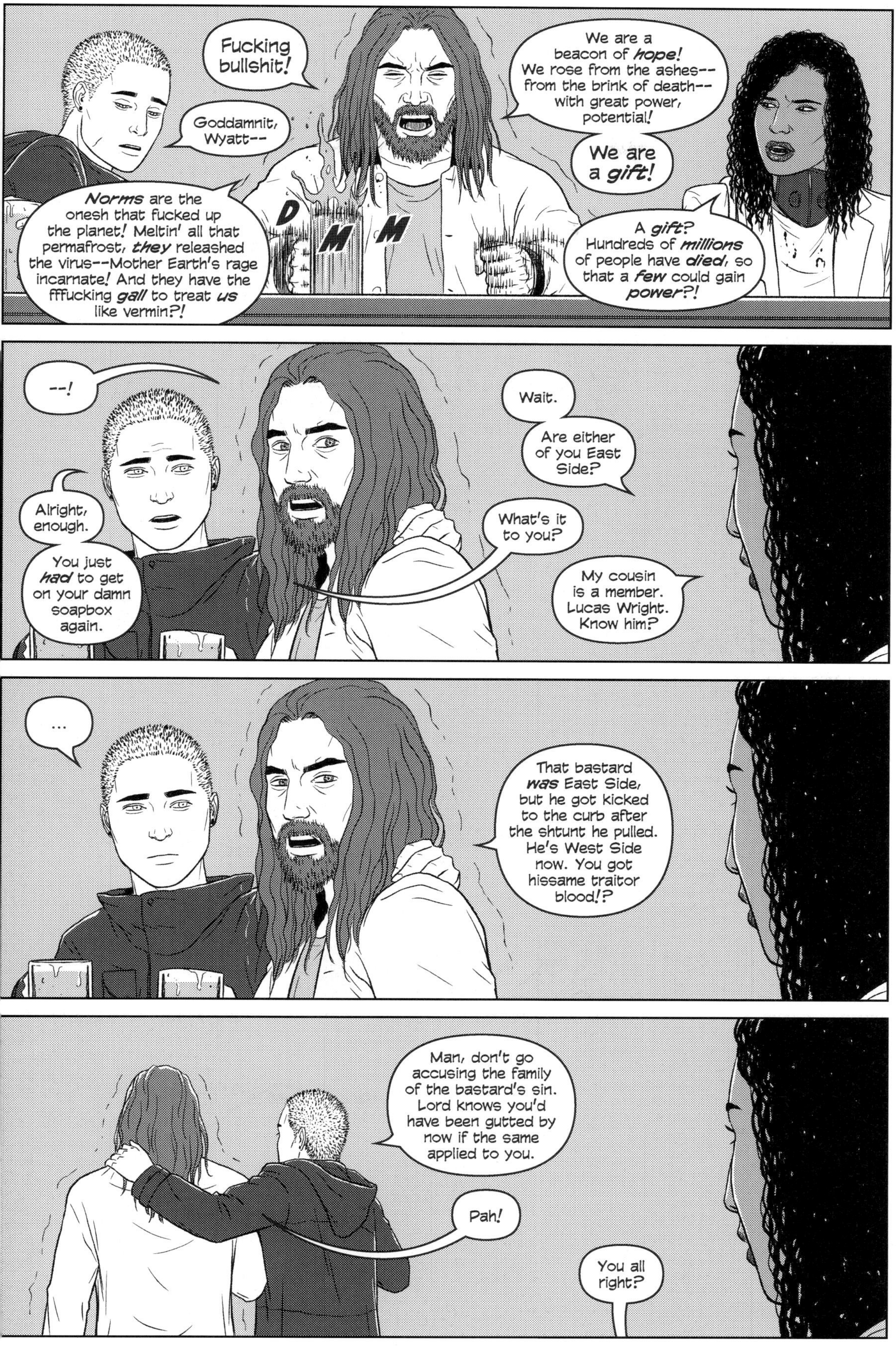
Fucking bullshit!
Goddamnit, Wyatt--
We are a beacon of hope! We rose from the ashes--from the brink of death--with great power, potential!
We are a gift!
Norms are the onesh that fucked up the planet! Meltin' all that permafrost, they releashed the virus--Mother Earth's rage incarnate! And they have the fffucking gall to treat us like vermin?!
DMM
A gift? Hundreds of millions of people have died, so that a few could gain power?!
--!
Wait.
Are either of you East Side?
Alright, enough.
You just had to get on your damn soapbox again.
What's it to you?
My cousin is a member. Lucas Wright. Know him?
...
That bastard was East Side, but he got kicked to the curb after the shtunt he pulled. He's West Side now. You got hissame traitor blood!?
Man, don't go accusing the family of the bastard's sin. Lord knows you'd have been gutted by now if the same applied to you.
Pah!
You all right?

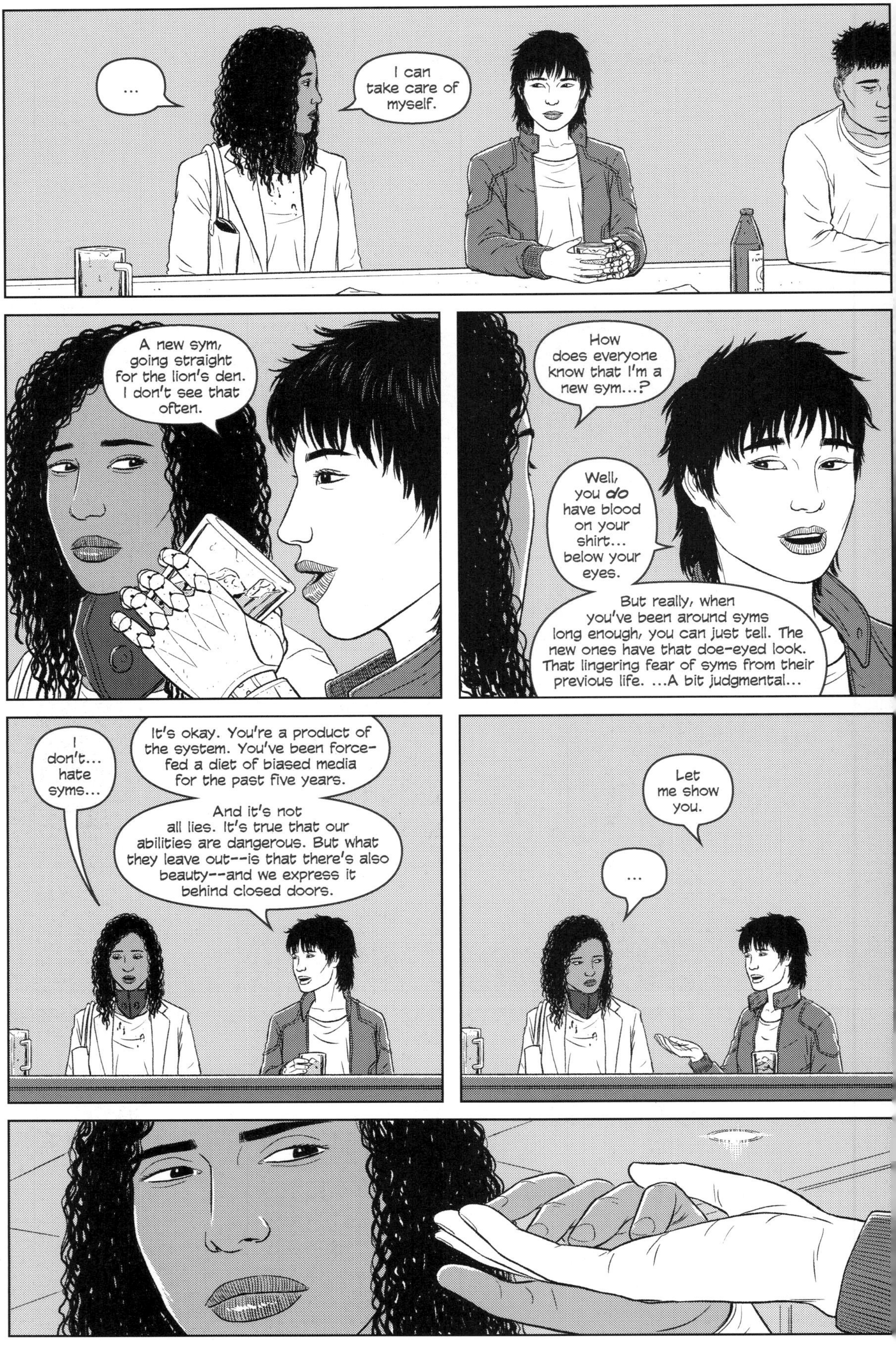
...
I can take care of myself.
A new sym, going straight for the lion's den. I don't see that often.
How does everyone know that I'm a new sym...?
Well, you *do* have blood on your shirt... below your eyes.
But really, when you've been around syms long enough, you can just tell. The new ones have that doe-eyed look. That lingering fear of syms from their previous life. ...A bit judgmental...
I don't... hate syms...
It's okay. You're a product of the system. You've been force-fed a diet of biased media for the past five years.
And it's not all lies. It's true that our abilities are dangerous. But what they leave out--is that there's also beauty--and we express it behind closed doors.
Let me show you.
...

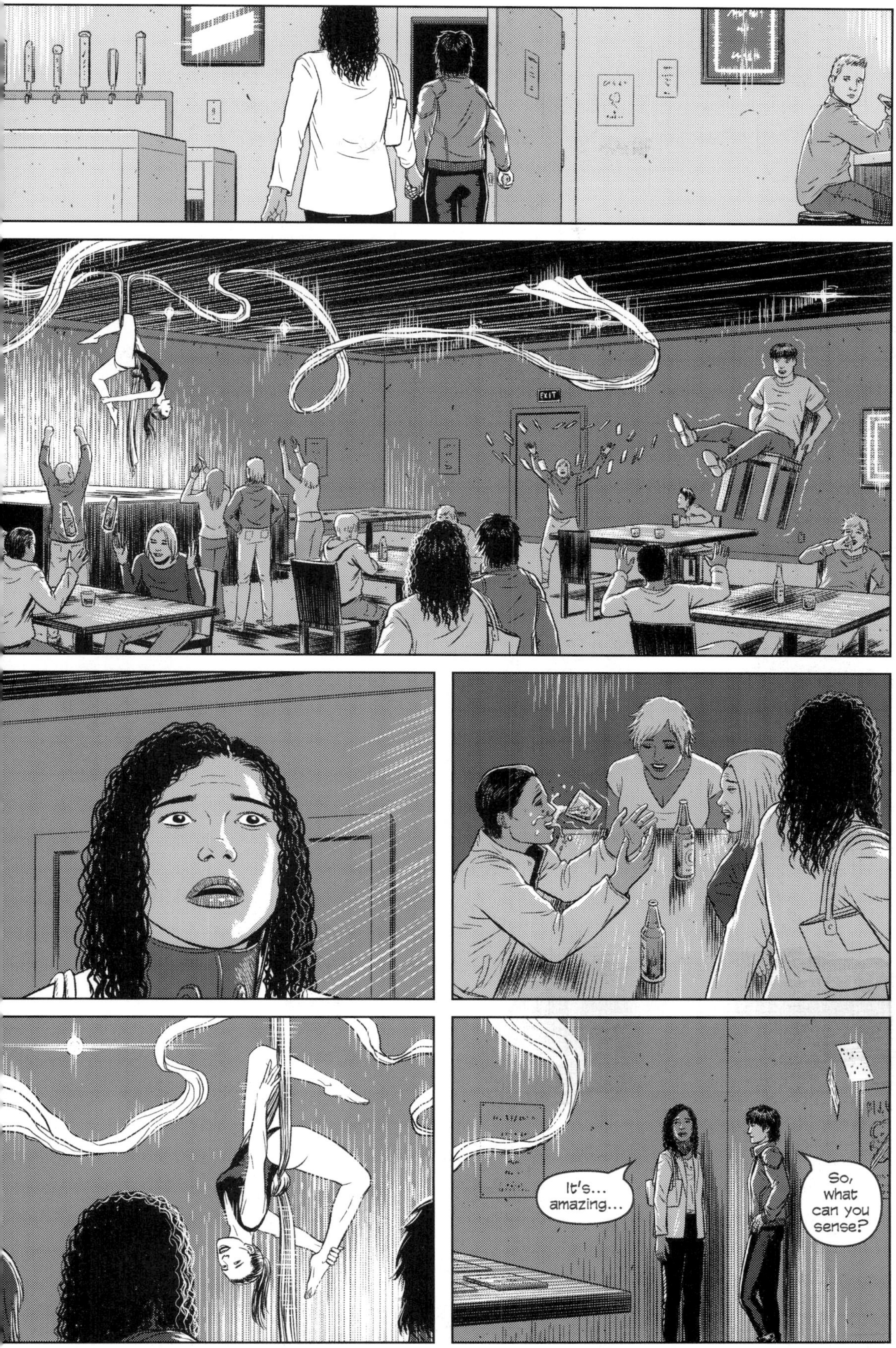
It's... amazing...
So, what can you sense?

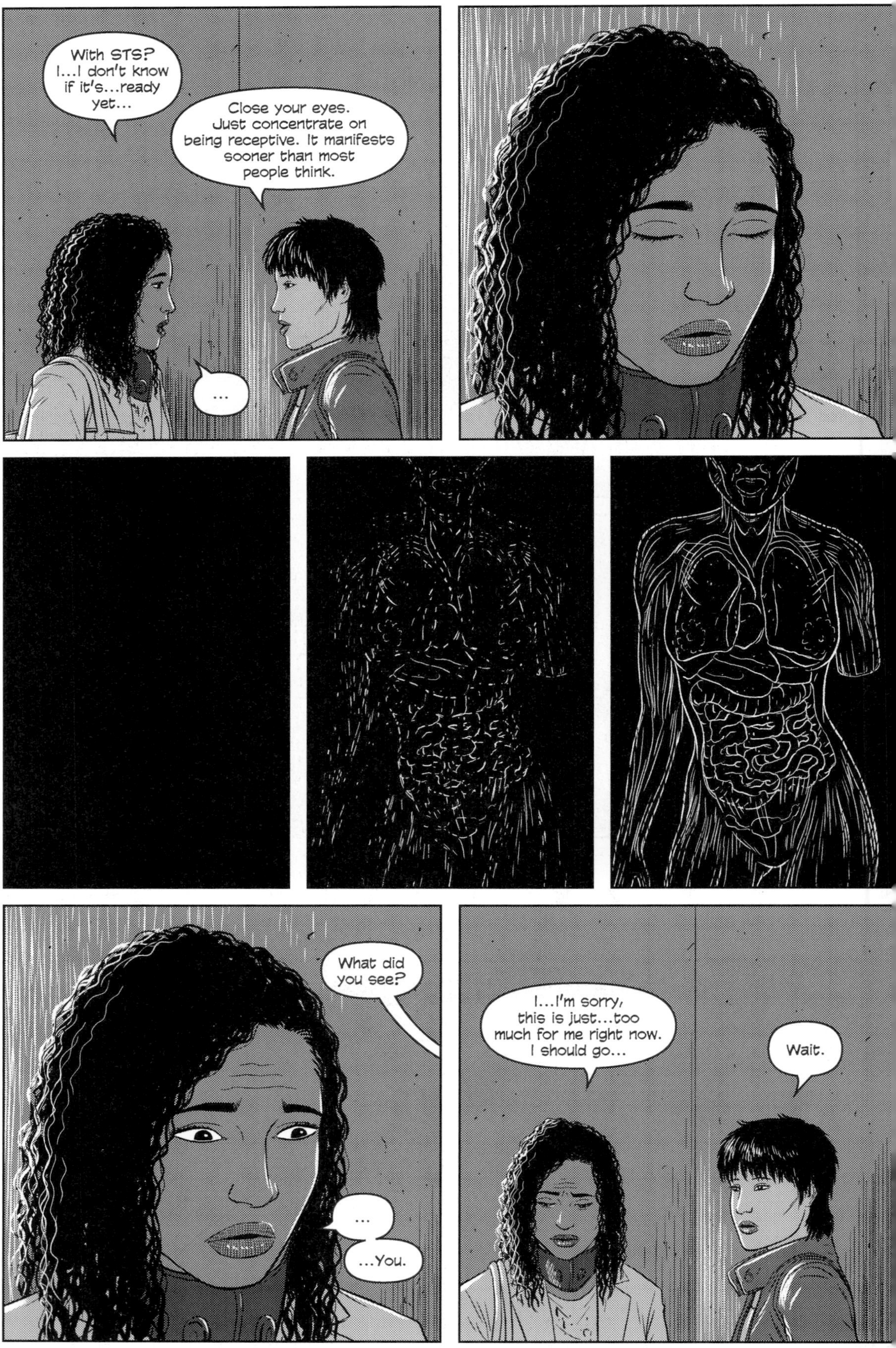
With STS? I...I don't know if it's...ready yet...
Close your eyes. Just concentrate on being receptive. It manifests sooner than most people think.
...
What did you see?
...
...You.
I...I'm sorry, this is just...too much for me right now. I should go...
Wait.

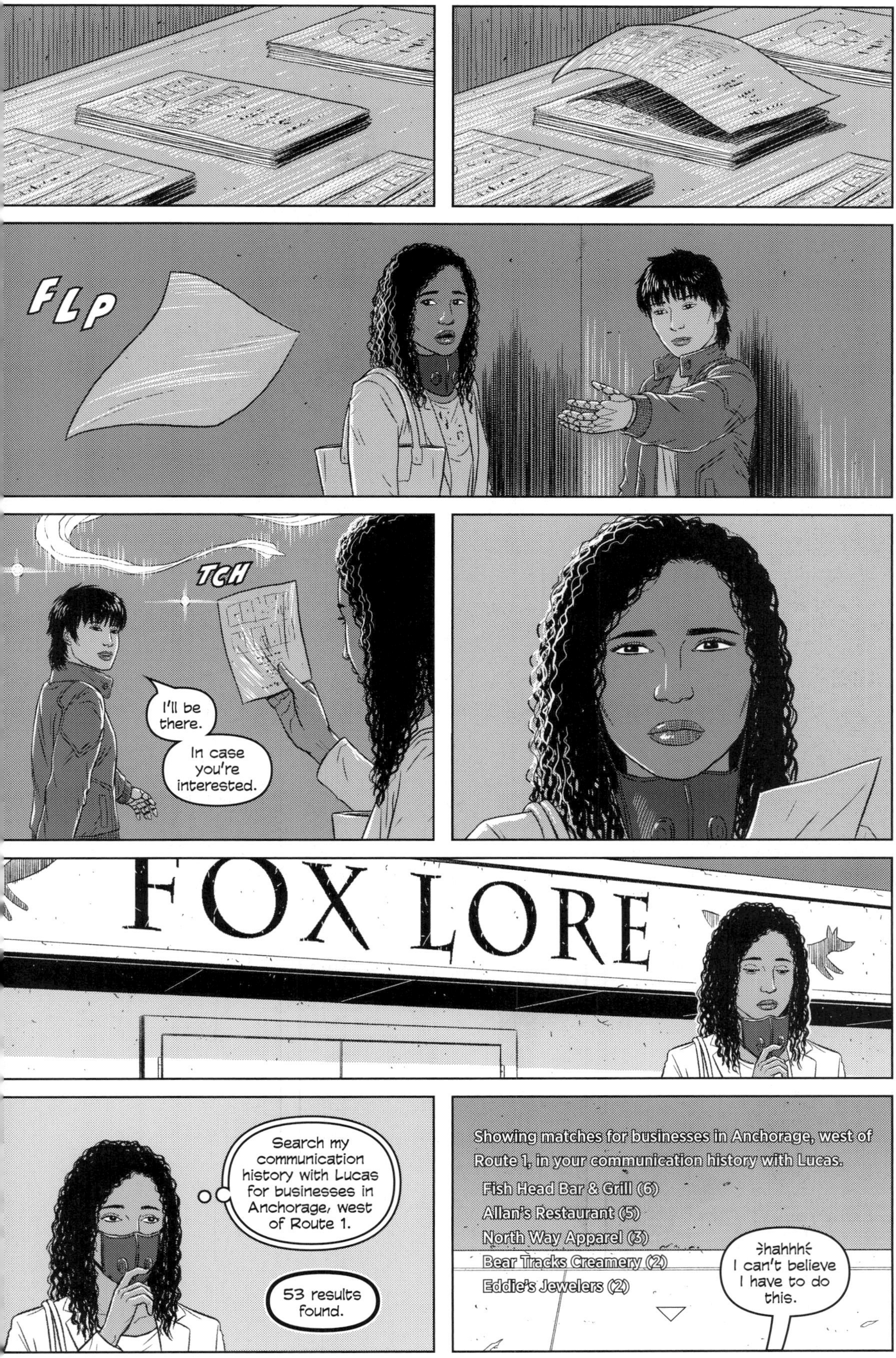
FLP
TCH
I'll be there.
In case you're interested.
FOX LORE
Search my communication history with Lucas for businesses in Anchorage, west of Route 1.
53 results found.
Showing matches for businesses in Anchorage, west of Route 1, in your communication history with Lucas.
Fish Head Bar & Grill (6)
Allan's Restaurant (5)
North Way Apparel (3)
Bear Tracks Creamery (2)
Eddie's Jewelers (2)
hahhh
I can't believe I have to do this.

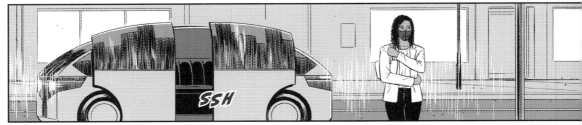

‡tch‡ Just because we're syms doesn't mean we know any gangsters.

No one by that name here.

428

THINHORN BAKERY

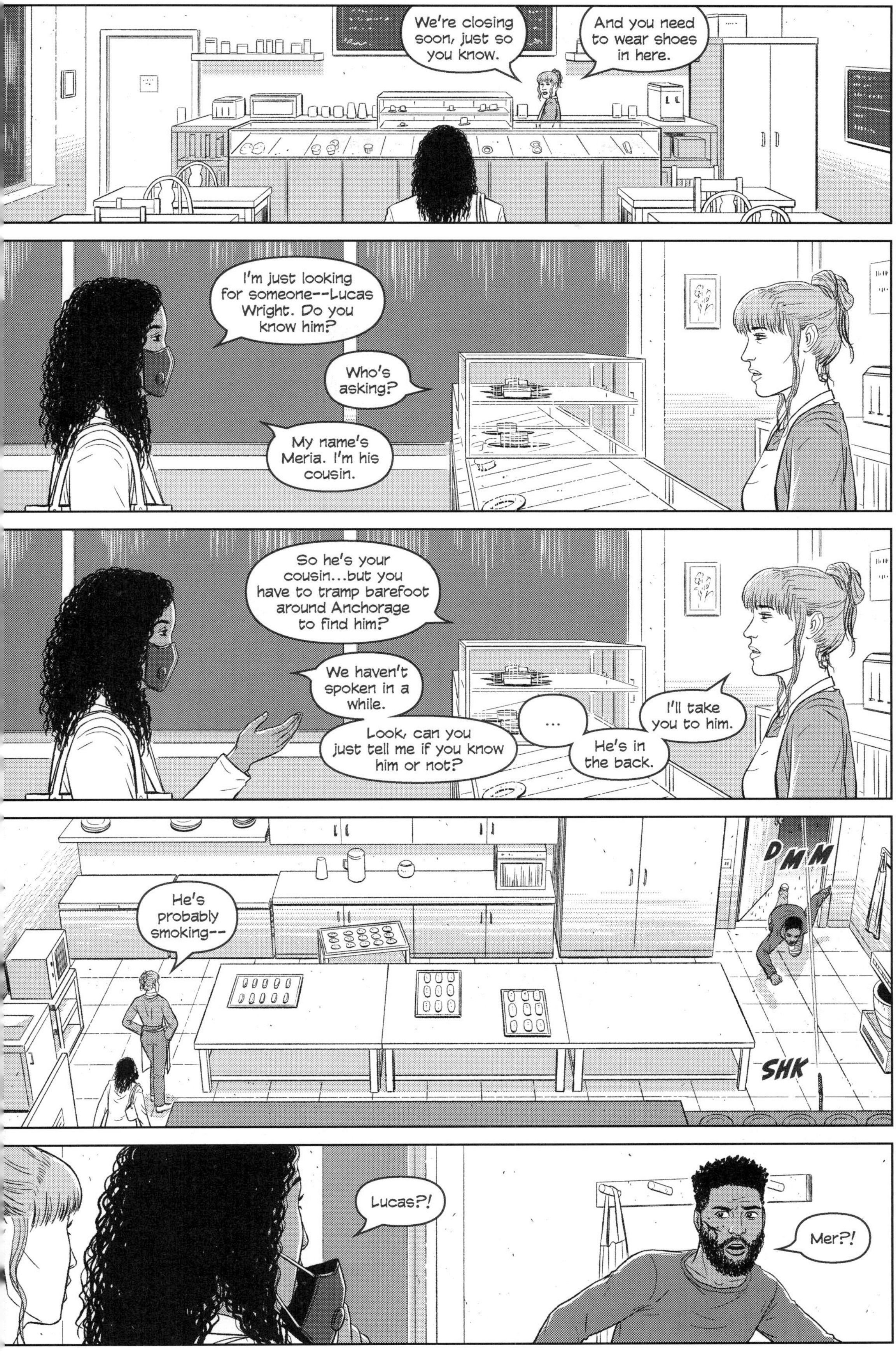

We're closing soon, just so you know.
And you need to wear shoes in here.
I'm just looking for someone--Lucas Wright. Do you know him?
Who's asking?
My name's Meria. I'm his cousin.
So he's your cousin...but you have to tramp barefoot around Anchorage to find him?
We haven't spoken in a while.
Look, can you just tell me if you know him or not?
...
He's in the back.
I'll take you to him.
He's probably smoking--
DMM
SHK
Lucas?!
Mer?!

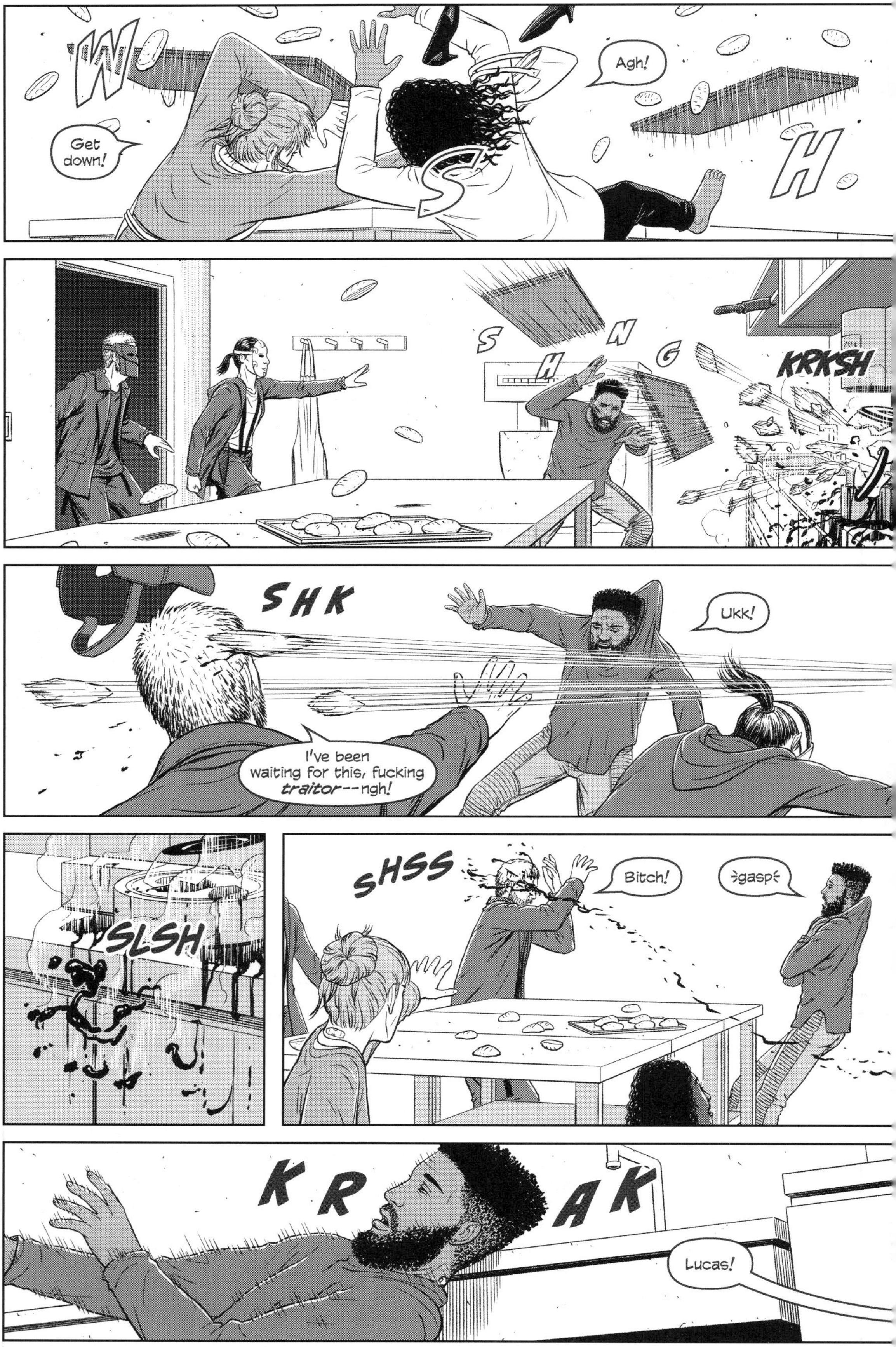
WHOOSH
Get down!
Agh!
SHNG
KRKSH
SHK
Ukk!
I've been waiting for this, fucking *traitor*--ngh!
SLSH
SHSS
Bitch!
⸗gasp⸗
KRAK
Lucas!

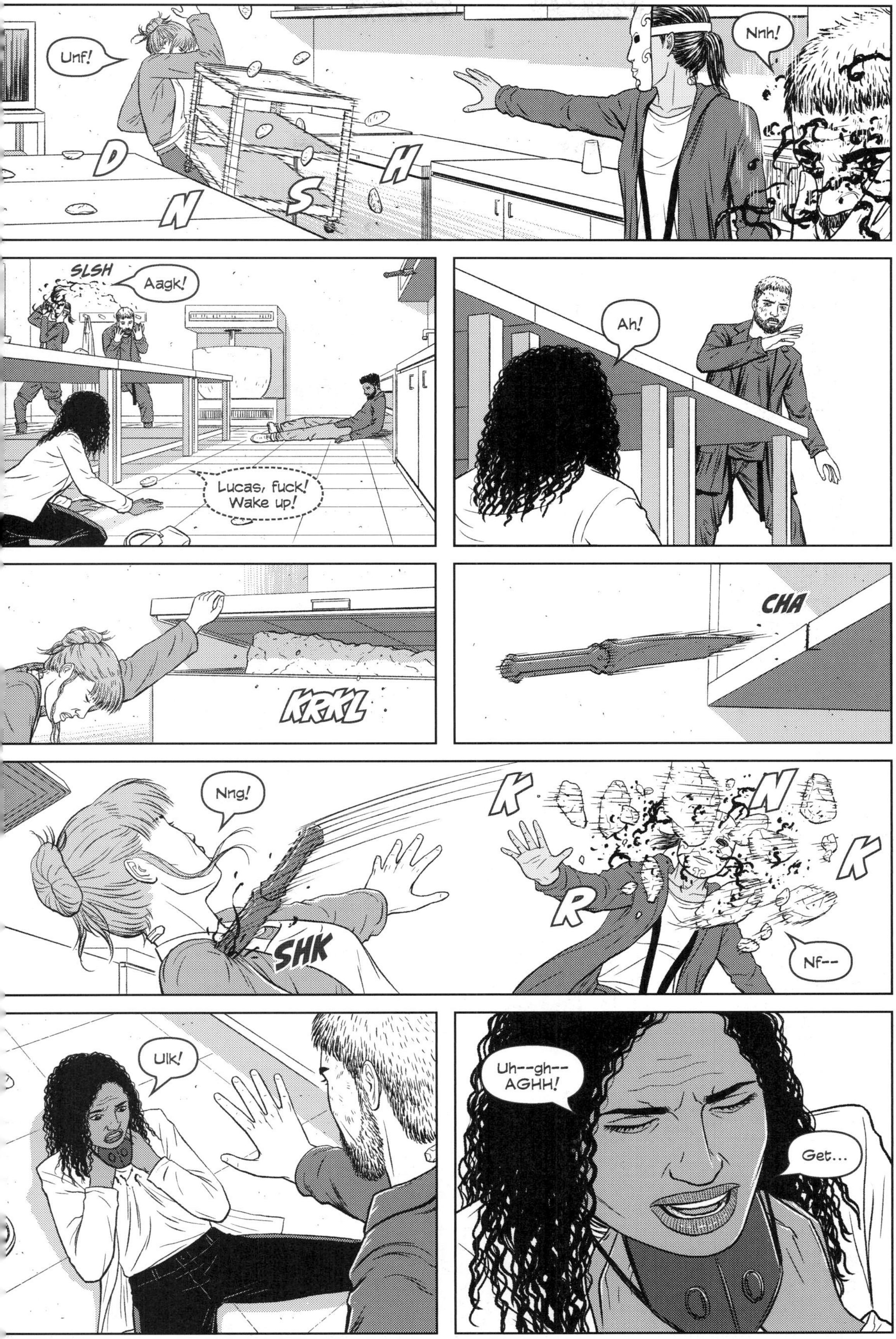
Unf!
D
N
S
H
Nnh!
SLSH
Aagk!
Lucas, fuck! Wake up!
Ah!
KRKL
CHA
Nng!
SHK
K
R
N
K
Nf--
Ulk!
Uh--gh-- AGHH!
Get...

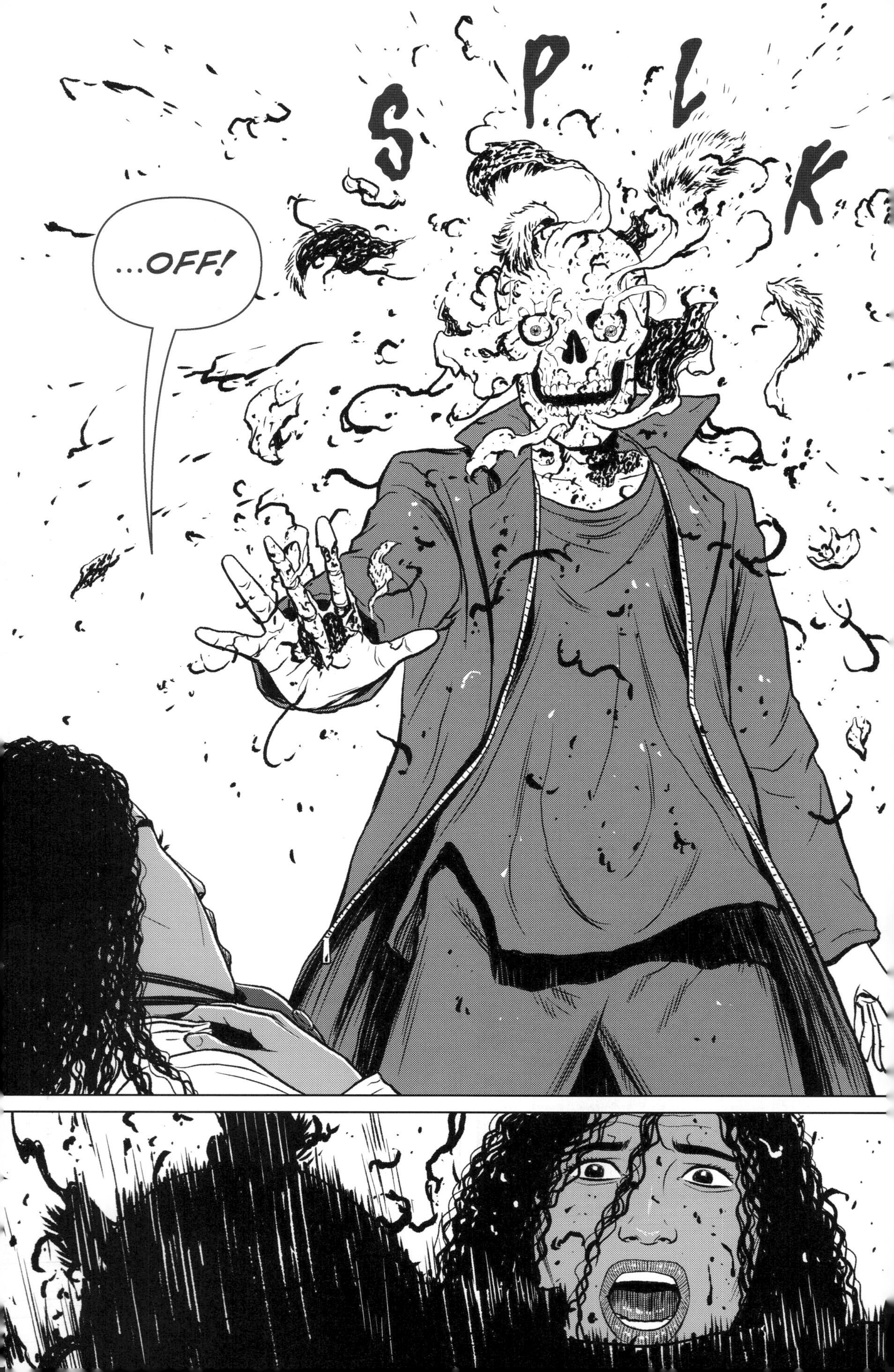

...OFF!
S P L K

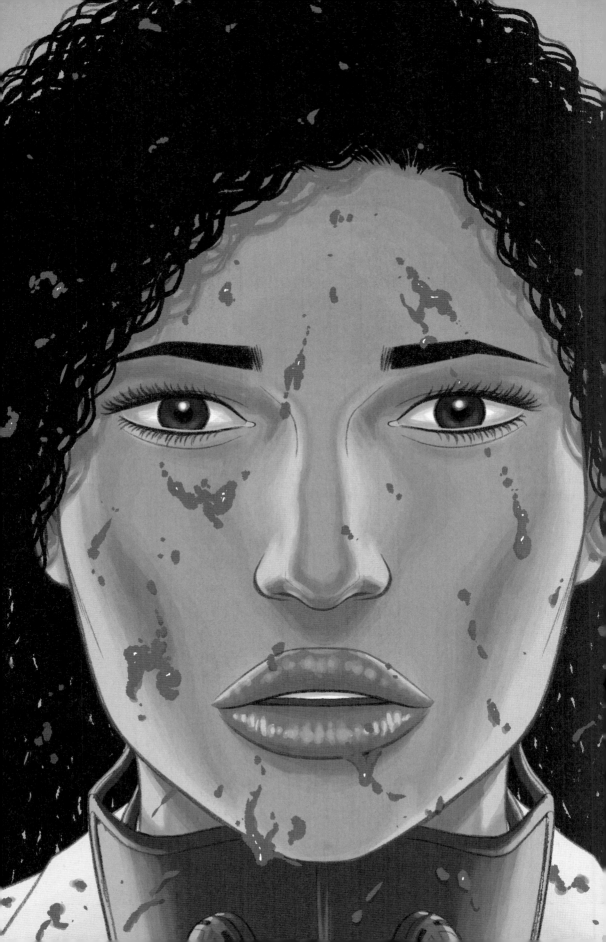

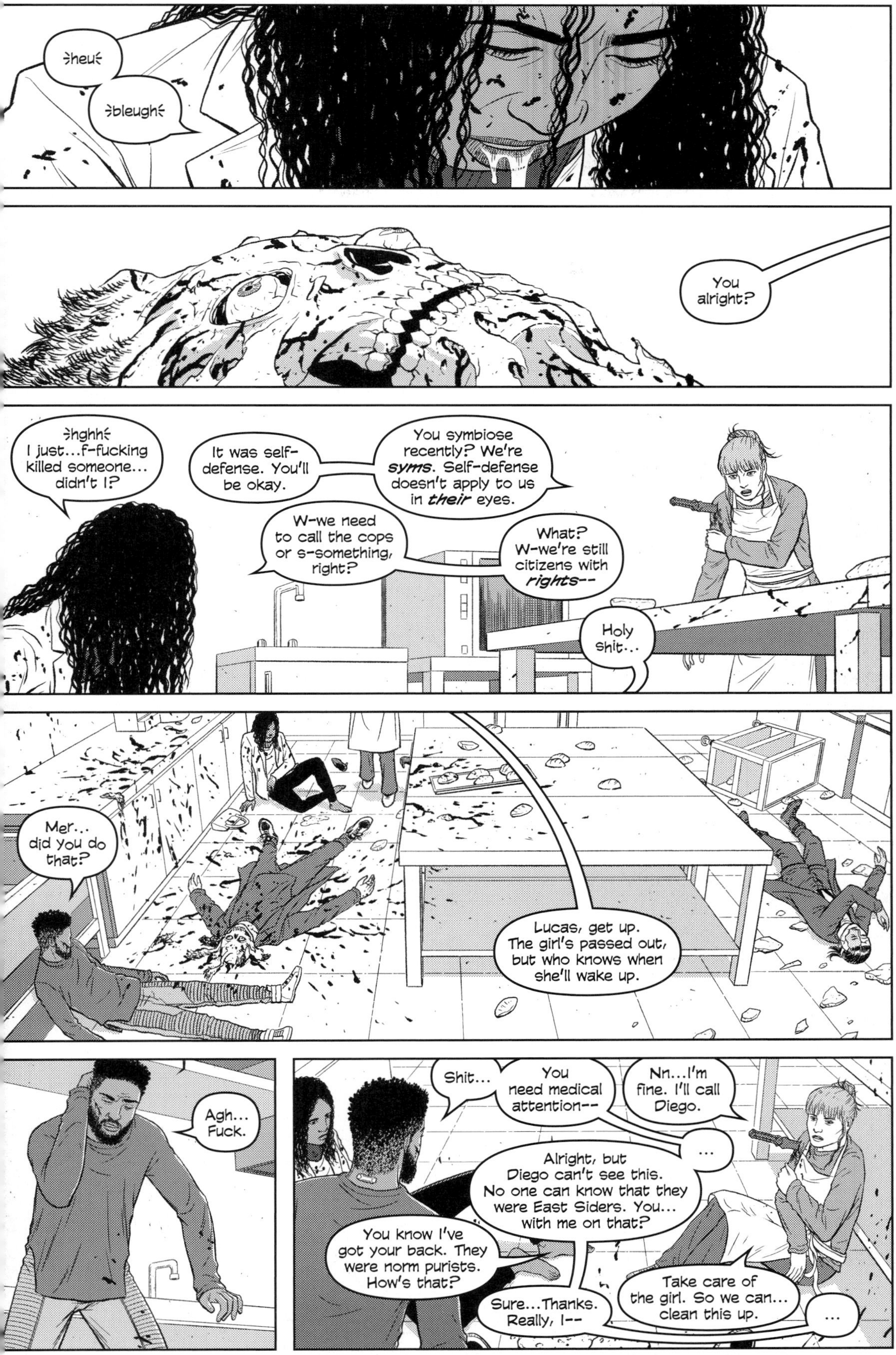

≑heu≑
≑bleugh≑
You alright?
≑hghh≑ I just...f-fucking killed someone... didn't I?
It was self-defense. You'll be okay.
You symbiose recently? We're *syms*. Self-defense doesn't apply to us in *their* eyes.
W-we need to call the cops or s-something, right?
What? W-we're still citizens with *rights*--
Holy shit...
Mer... did you do that?
Lucas, get up. The girl's passed out, but who knows when she'll wake up.
Agh... Fuck.
Shit...
You need medical attention--
Nn...I'm fine. I'll call Diego.
...
Alright, but Diego can't see this. No one can know that they were East Siders. You... with me on that?
You know I've got your back. They were norm purists. How's that?
Sure...Thanks. Really, I--
Take care of the girl. So we can... clean this up.
...

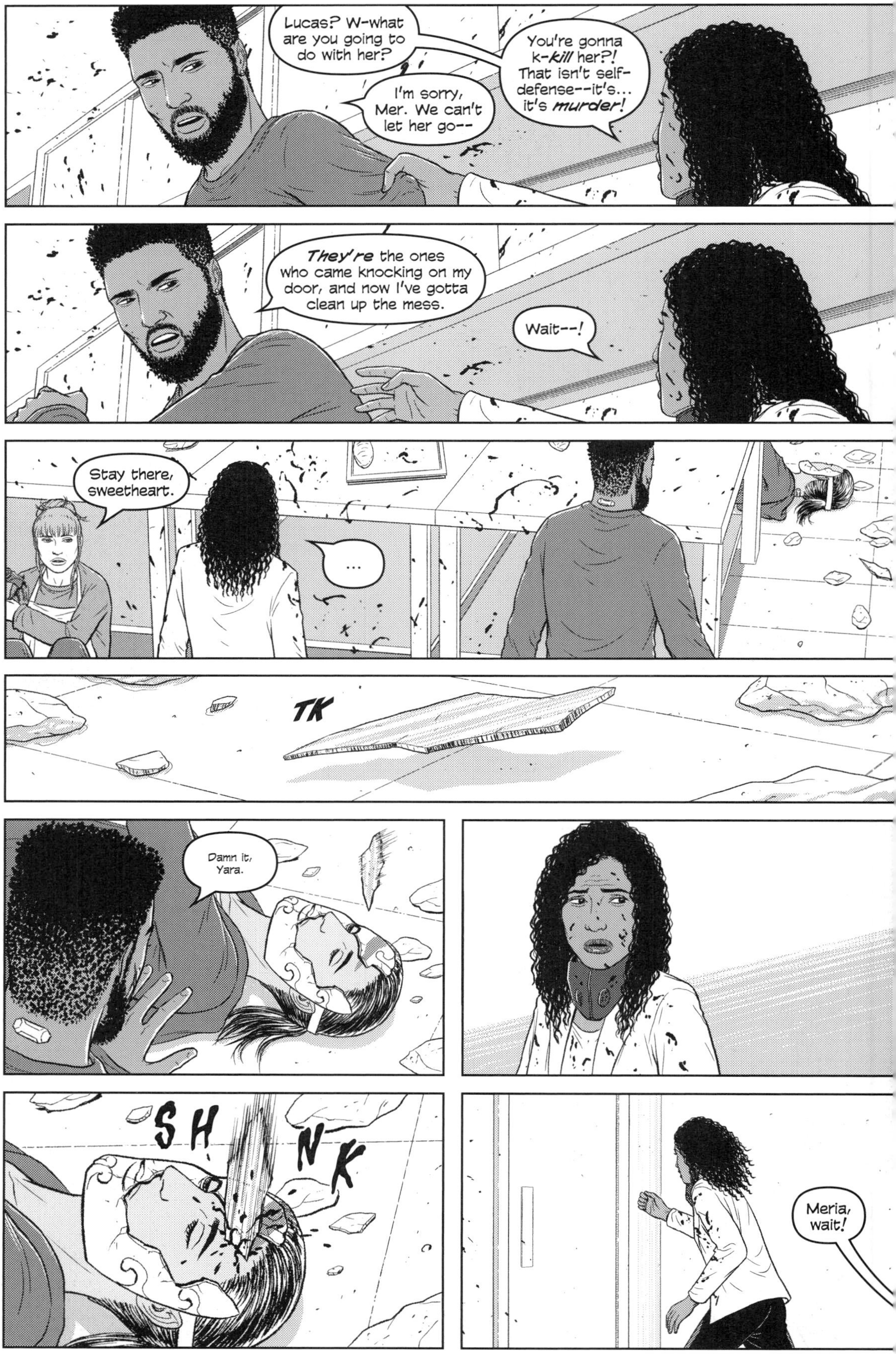
Lucas? W-what are you going to do with her?
I'm sorry, Mer. We can't let her go--
You're gonna k-*kill* her?! That isn't self-defense--it's... it's *murder*!
They're the ones who came knocking on my door, and now I've gotta clean up the mess.
Wait--!
Stay there, sweetheart.
...
TK
Damn it, Yara.
SHNK
Meria, wait!

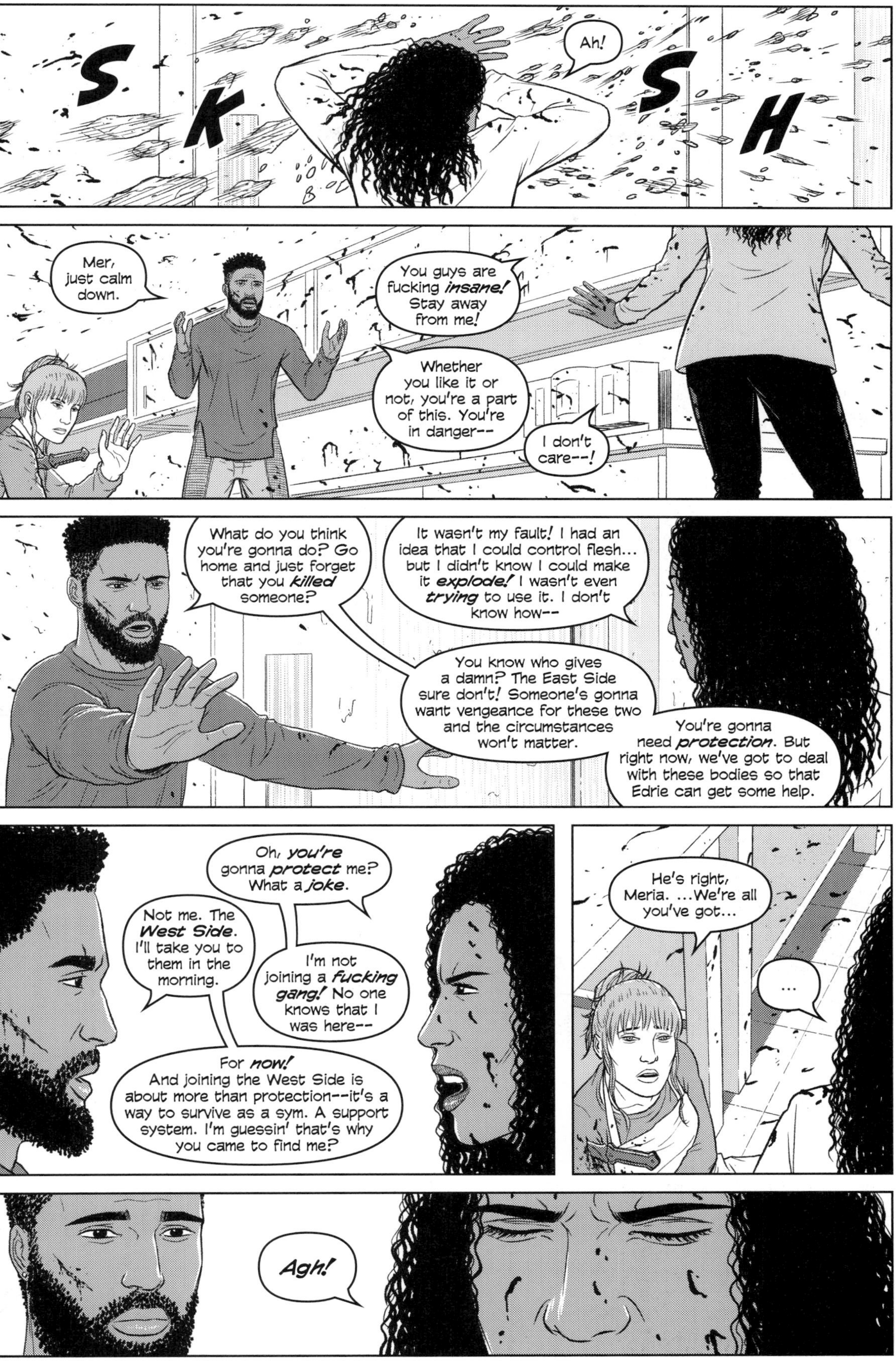
S K
Ah!
S H
Mer, just calm down.
You guys are fucking *insane!* Stay away from me!
Whether you like it or not, you're a part of this. You're in danger--
I don't care--!
What do you think you're gonna do? Go home and just forget that you *killed* someone?
It wasn't my fault! I had an idea that I could control flesh... but I didn't know I could make it *explode!* I wasn't even *trying* to use it. I don't know how--
You know who gives a damn? The East Side sure don't! Someone's gonna want vengeance for these two and the circumstances won't matter.
You're gonna need *protection*. But right now, we've got to deal with these bodies so that Edrie can get some help.
Oh, *you're* gonna *protect* me? What a *joke*.
Not me. The *West Side*. I'll take you to them in the morning.
I'm not joining a *fucking gang!* No one knows that I was here--
For *now!* And joining the West Side is about more than protection--it's a way to survive as a sym. A support system. I'm guessin' that's why you came to find me?
He's right, Meria. ...We're all you've got...
...
Agh!

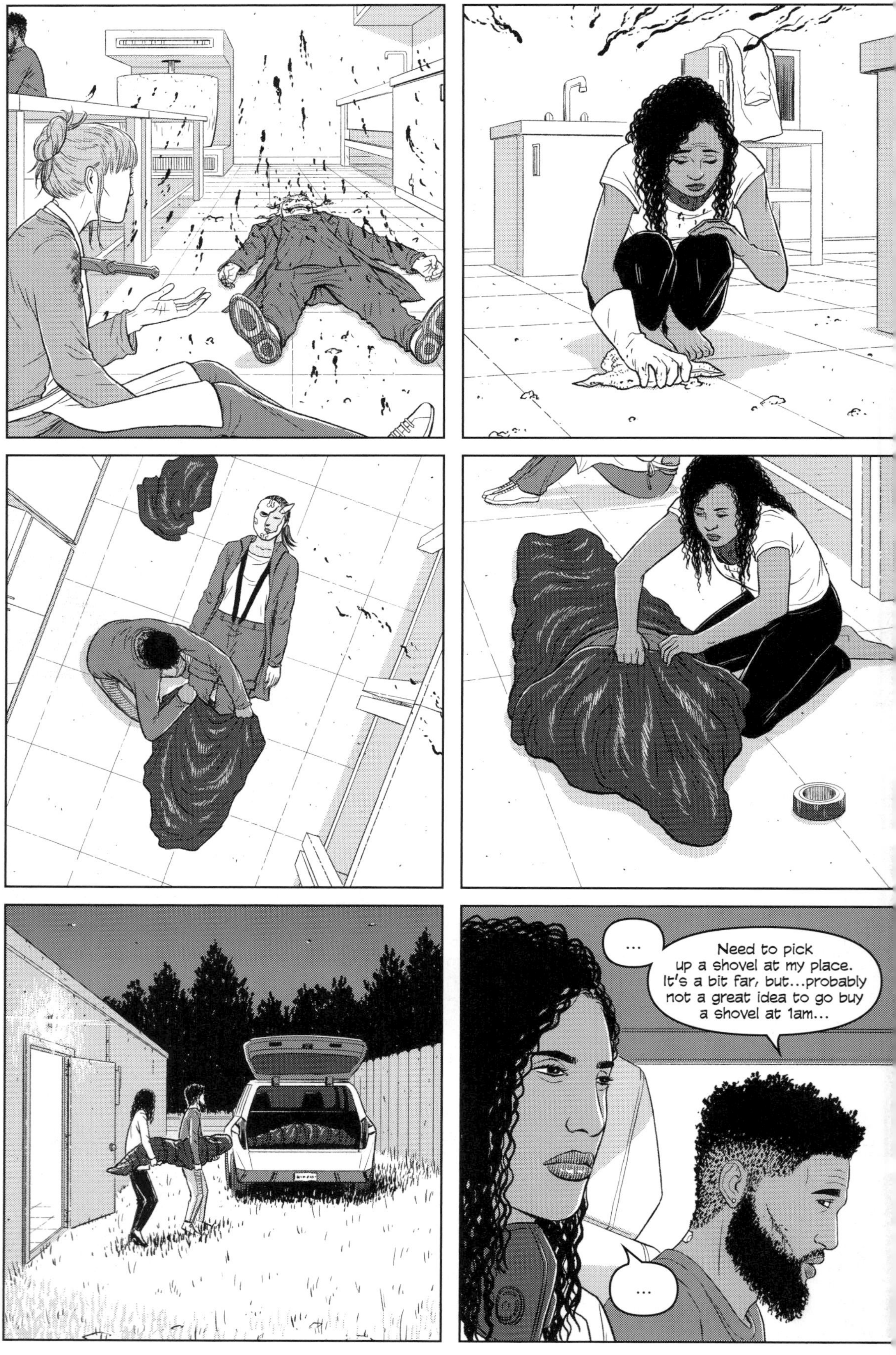
...
Need to pick up a shovel at my place. It's a bit far, but...probably not a great idea to go buy a shovel at 1am...
...

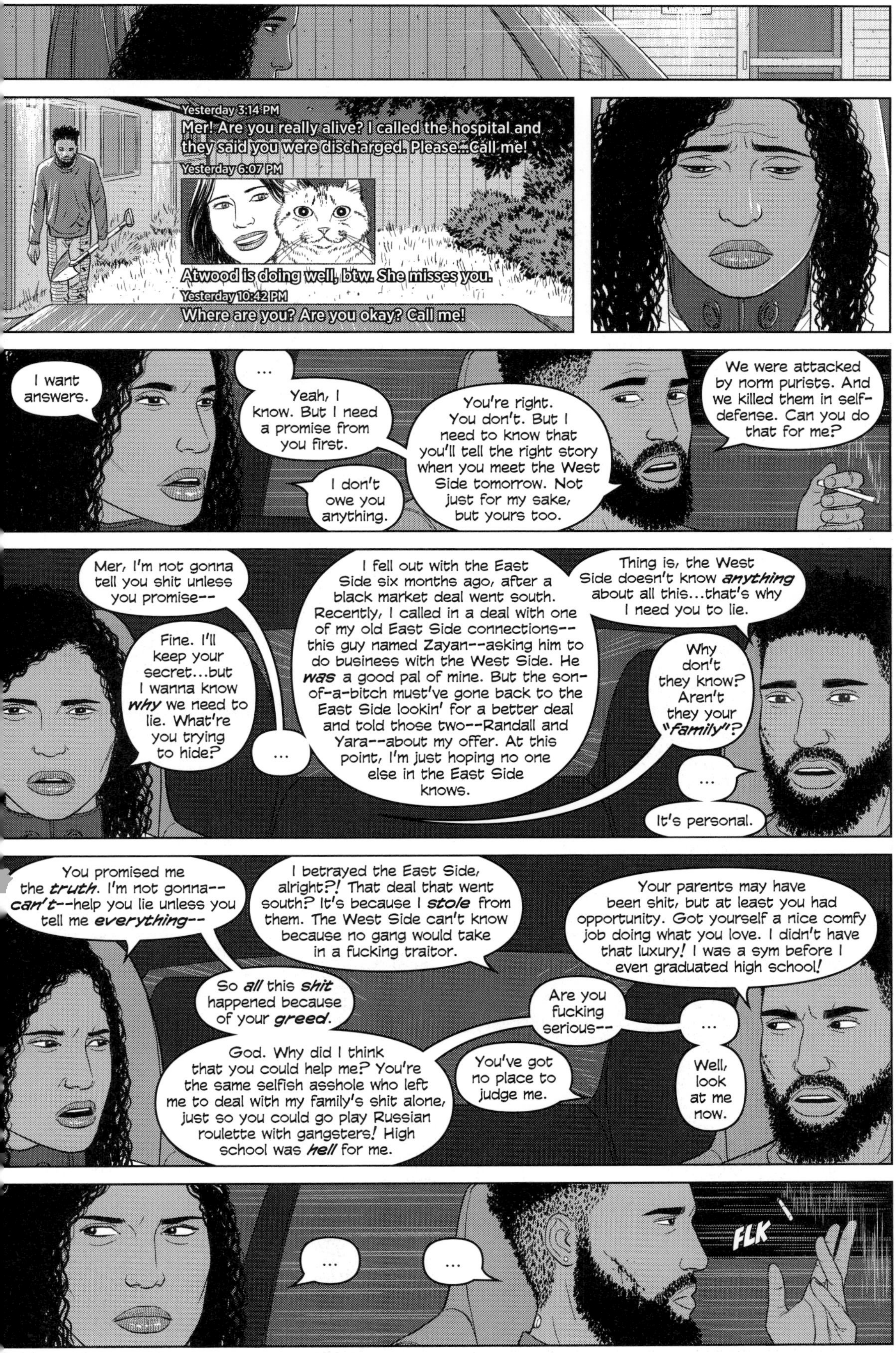
Yesterday 3:14 PM
Mer! Are you really alive? I called the hospital and they said you were discharged. Please...Call me!
Yesterday 6:07 PM
Atwood is doing well, btw. She misses you.
Yesterday 10:42 PM
Where are you? Are you okay? Call me!
I want answers.
...
Yeah, I know. But I need a promise from you first.
I don't owe you anything.
You're right. You don't. But I need to know that you'll tell the right story when you meet the West Side tomorrow. Not just for my sake, but yours too.
We were attacked by norm purists. And we killed them in self-defense. Can you do that for me?
Mer, I'm not gonna tell you shit unless you promise--
Fine. I'll keep your secret...but I wanna know *why* we need to lie. What're you trying to hide?
...
I fell out with the East Side six months ago, after a black market deal went south. Recently, I called in a deal with one of my old East Side connections--this guy named Zayan--asking him to do business with the West Side. He *was* a good pal of mine. But the son-of-a-bitch must've gone back to the East Side lookin' for a better deal and told those two--Randall and Yara--about my offer. At this point, I'm just hoping no one else in the East Side knows.
Thing is, the West Side doesn't know *anything* about all this...that's why I need you to lie.
Why don't they know? Aren't they your *"family"*?
...
It's personal.
You promised me the *truth*. I'm not gonna--*can't*--help you lie unless you tell me *everything*--
I betrayed the East Side, alright?! That deal that went south? It's because I *stole* from them. The West Side can't know because no gang would take in a fucking traitor.
So *all* this *shit* happened because of your *greed*.
Your parents may have been shit, but at least you had opportunity. Got yourself a nice comfy job doing what you love. I didn't have that luxury! I was a sym before I even graduated high school!
Are you fucking serious--
...
God. Why did I think that you could help me? You're the same selfish asshole who left me to deal with my family's shit alone, just so you could go play Russian roulette with gangsters! High school was *hell* for me.
You've got no place to judge me.
Well, look at me now.
...
...
FLK

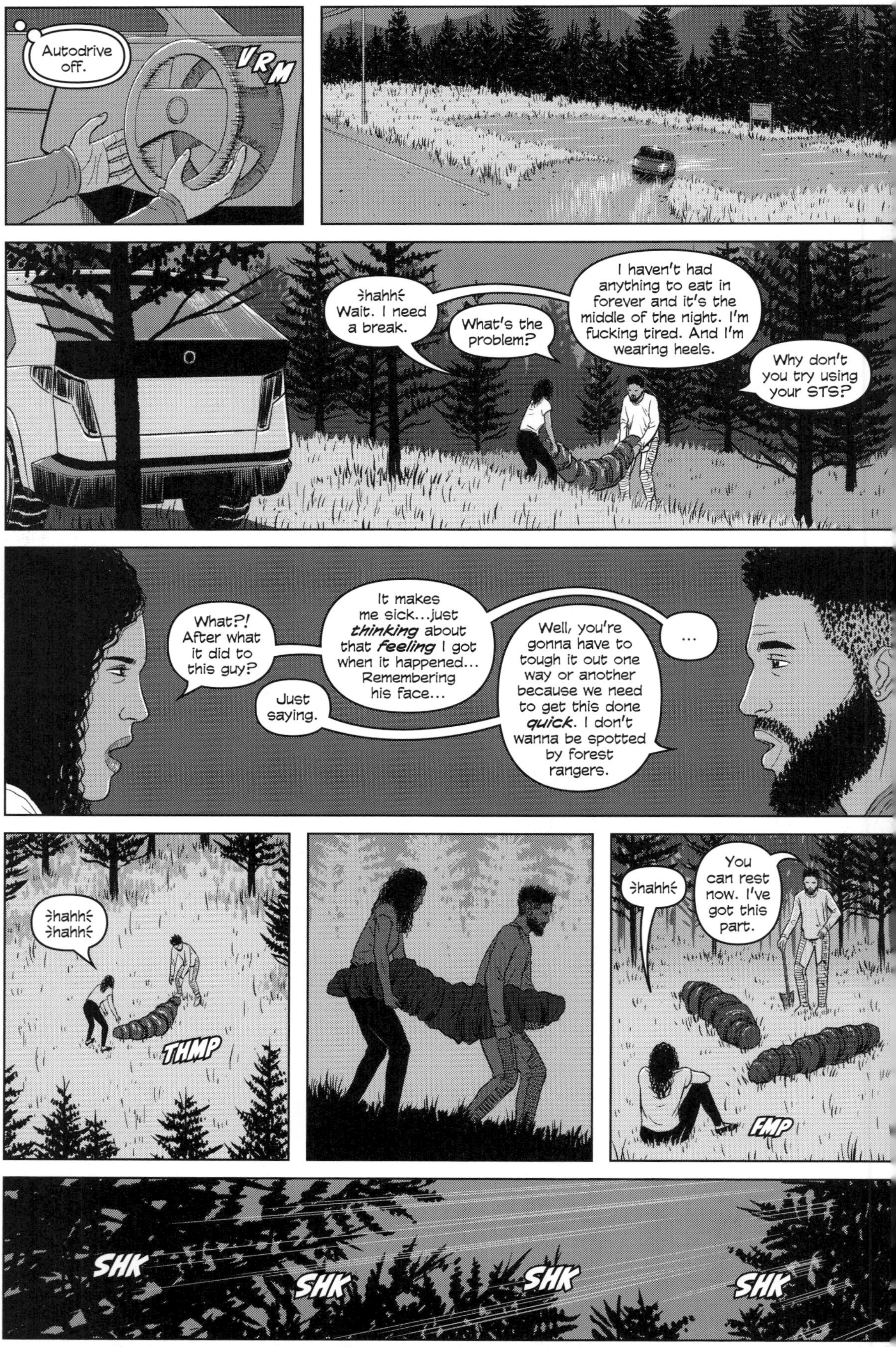

Autodrive off.
VRM
≯hahh≮ Wait. I need a break.
What's the problem?
I haven't had anything to eat in forever and it's the middle of the night. I'm fucking tired. And I'm wearing heels.
Why don't you try using your STS?
What?! After what it did to this guy?
Just saying.
It makes me sick…just *thinking* about that *feeling* I got when it happened… Remembering his face…
...
Well, you're gonna have to tough it out one way or another because we need to get this done *quick*. I don't wanna be spotted by forest rangers.
≯hahh≮ ≯hahh≮
THMP
≯hahh≮
You can rest now. I've got this part.
FMP
SHK
SHK
SHK
SHK

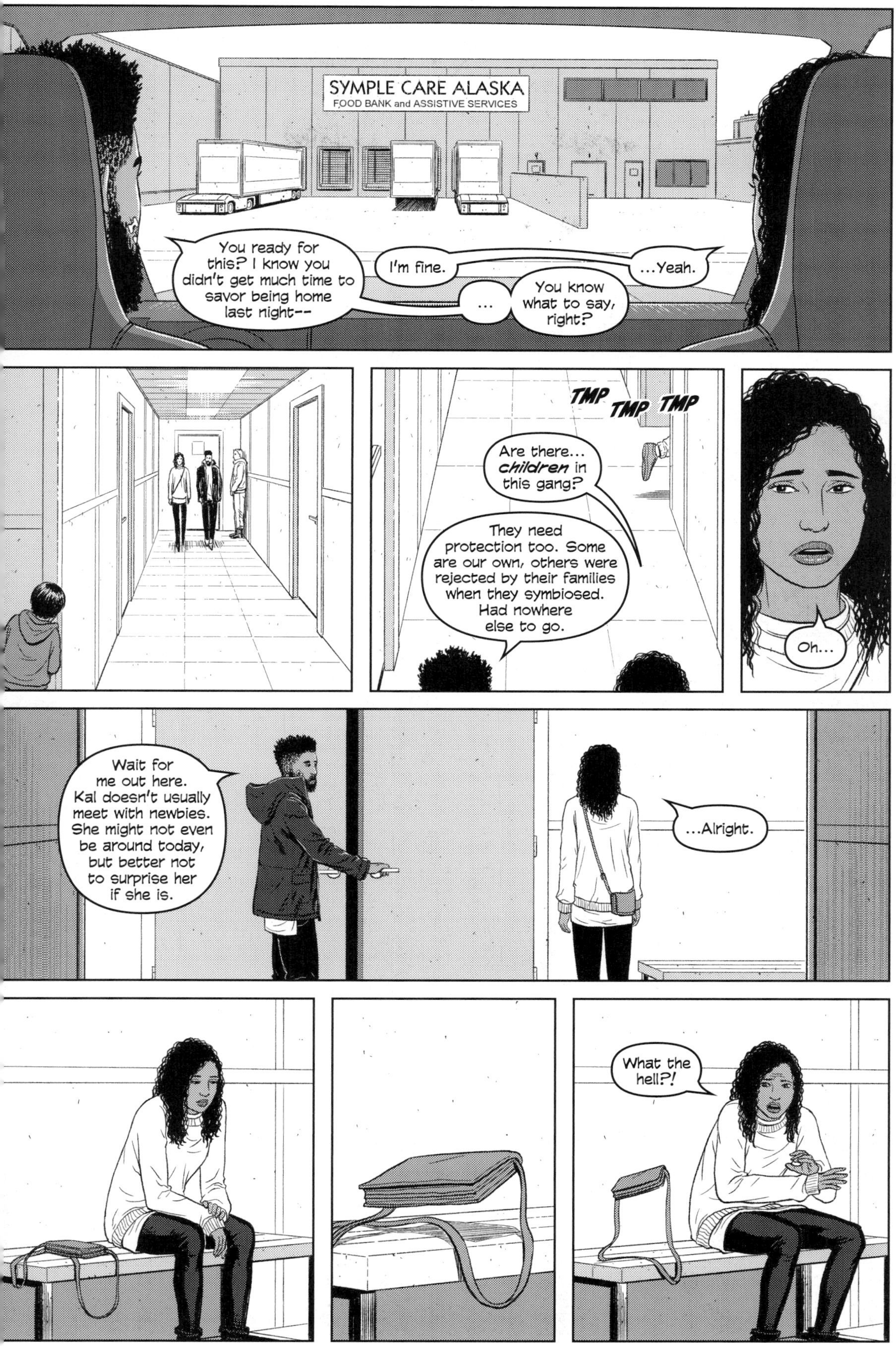
SYMPLE CARE ALASKA
FOOD BANK and ASSISTIVE SERVICES
You ready for this? I know you didn't get much time to savor being home last night--
...
I'm fine.
...Yeah.
You know what to say, right?
TMP TMP TMP
Are there... children in this gang?
They need protection too. Some are our own, others were rejected by their families when they symbiosed. Had nowhere else to go.
Oh...
Wait for me out here. Kal doesn't usually meet with newbies. She might not even be around today, but better not to surprise her if she is.
...Alright.
What the hell?!

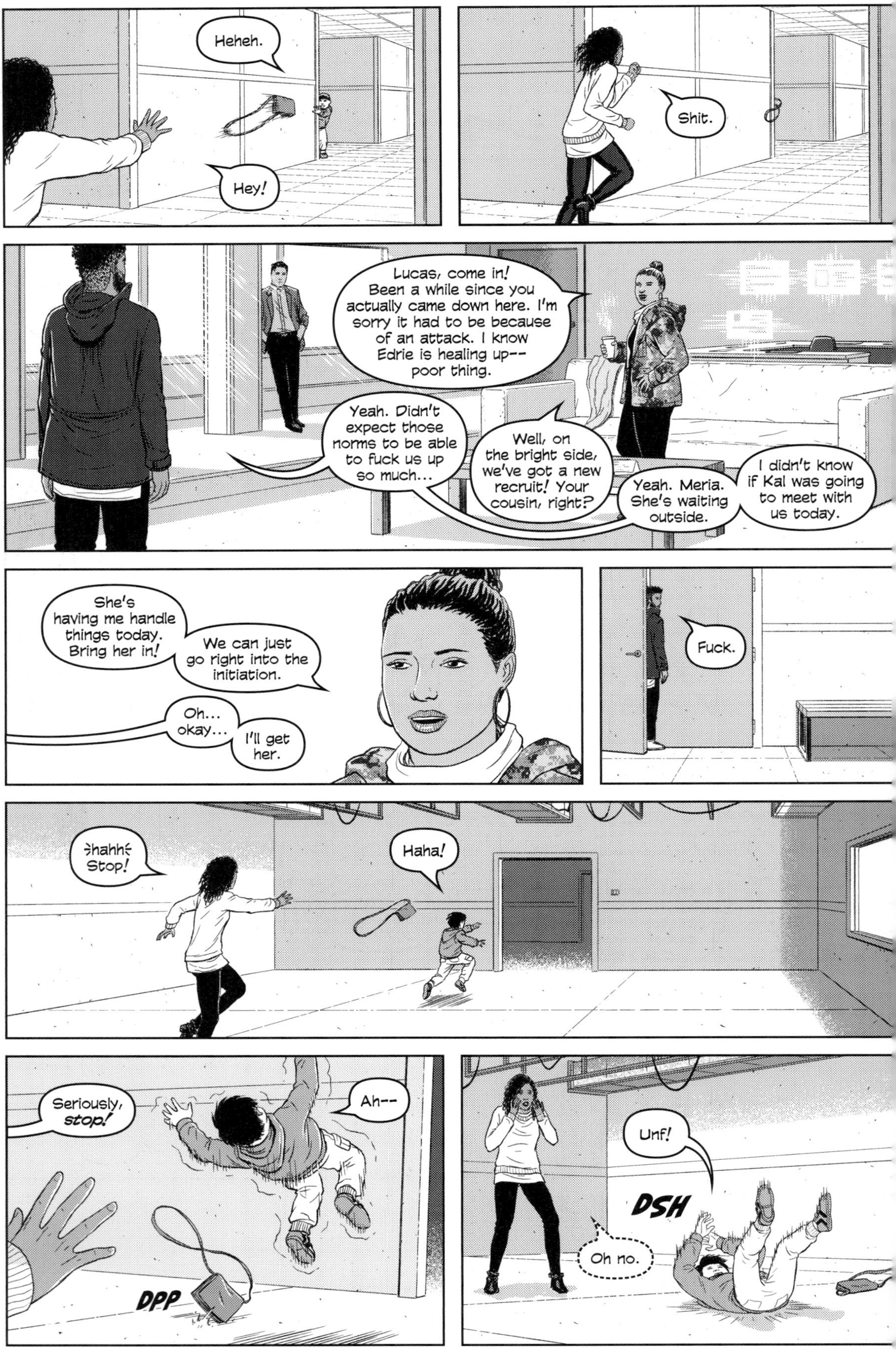
Heheh.
Hey!
Shit.
Lucas, come in! Been a while since you actually came down here. I'm sorry it had to be because of an attack. I know Edrie is healing up-- poor thing.
Yeah. Didn't expect those norms to be able to fuck us up so much...
Well, on the bright side, we've got a new recruit! Your cousin, right?
Yeah. Meria. She's waiting outside.
I didn't know if Kal was going to meet with us today.
She's having me handle things today. Bring her in!
We can just go right into the initiation.
Oh... okay...
I'll get her.
Fuck.
hahh Stop!
Haha!
Seriously, stop!
Ah--
DPP
Unf!
DSH
Oh no.

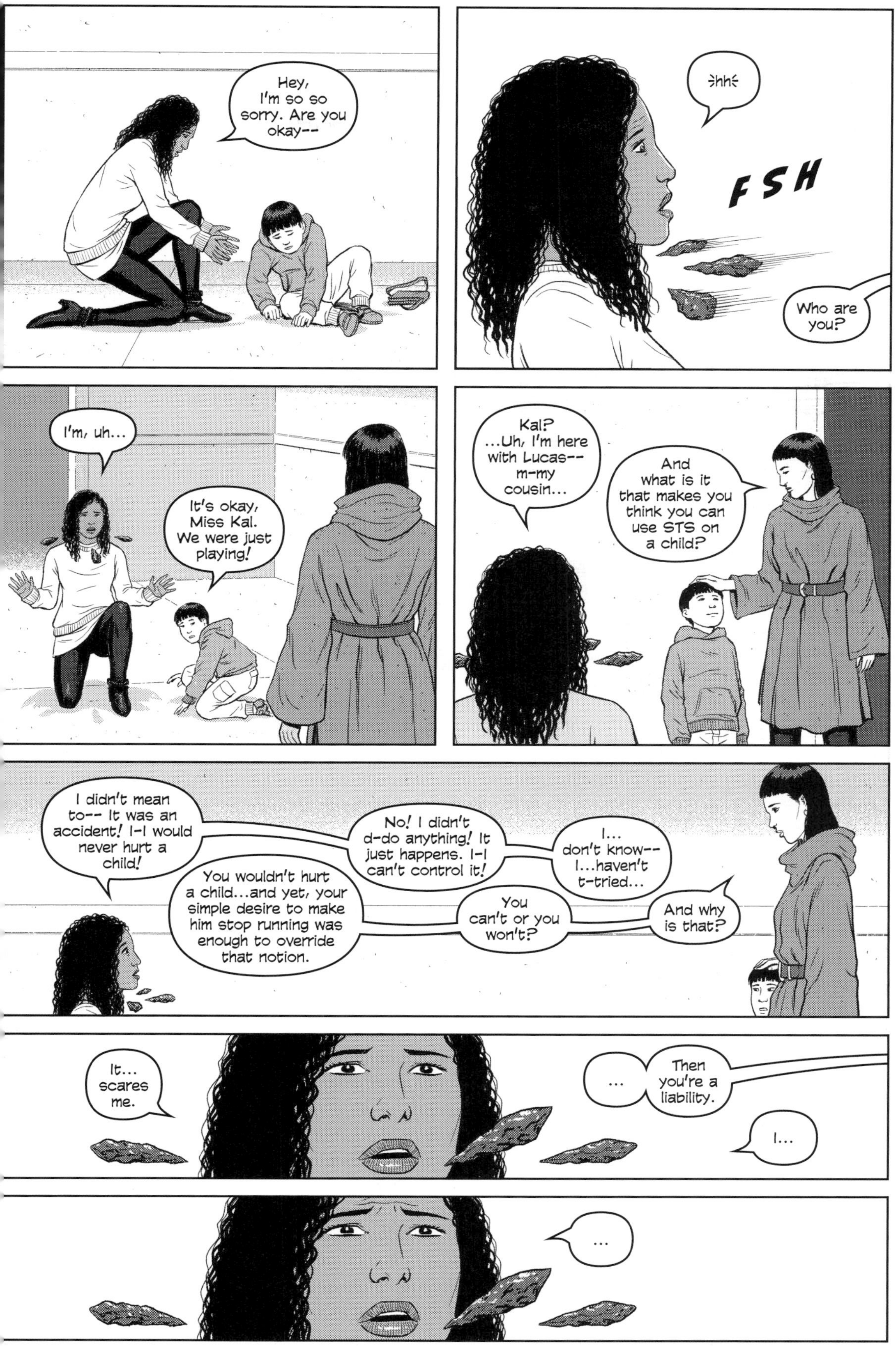
Hey, I'm so so sorry. Are you okay--
shh
FSH
Who are you?
I'm, uh...
It's okay, Miss Kal. We were just playing!
Kal? ...Uh, I'm here with Lucas-- m-my cousin...
And what is it that makes you think you can use STS on a child?
I didn't mean to-- It was an accident! I-I would never hurt a child!
You wouldn't hurt a child...and yet, your simple desire to make him stop running was enough to override that notion.
No! I didn't d-do anything! It just happens. I-I can't control it!
You can't or you won't?
I... don't know-- I...haven't t-tried...
And why is that?
It... scares me.
...
Then you're a liability.
I...
...

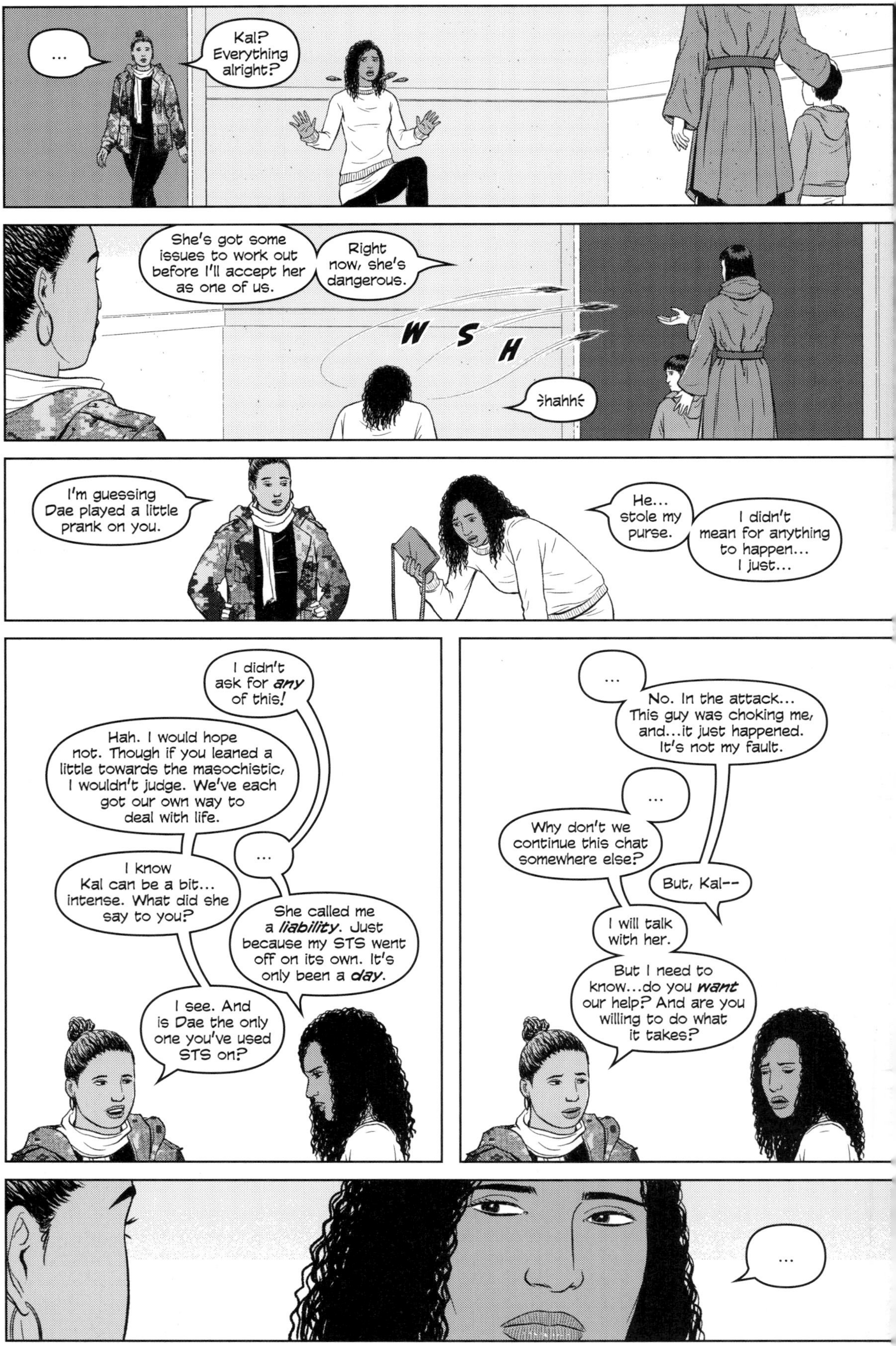

...
Kal? Everything alright?
She's got some issues to work out before I'll accept her as one of us.
Right now, she's dangerous.
WSH
hahh
I'm guessing Dae played a little prank on you.
He... stole my purse.
I didn't mean for anything to happen... I just...
I didn't ask for *any* of this!
Hah. I would hope not. Though if you leaned a little towards the masochistic, I wouldn't judge. We've each got our own way to deal with life.
...
I know Kal can be a bit... intense. What did she say to you?
She called me a *liability*. Just because my STS went off on its own. It's only been a *day*.
I see. And is Dae the only one you've used STS on?
...
No. In the attack... This guy was choking me, and...it just happened. It's not my fault.
...
Why don't we continue this chat somewhere else?
But, Kal--
I will talk with her.
But I need to know...do you *want* our help? And are you willing to do what it takes?
...

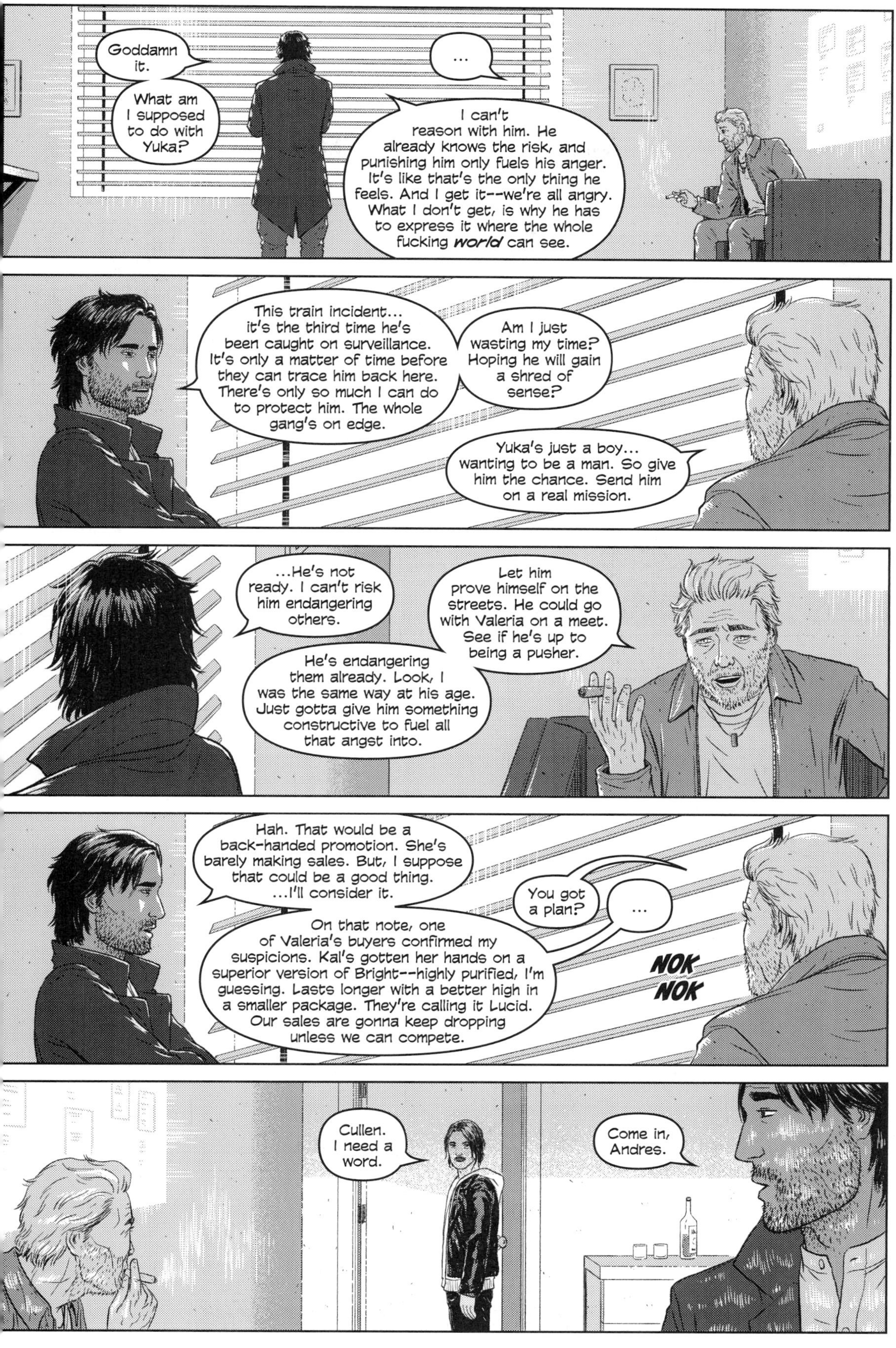
Goddamn it.
What am I supposed to do with Yuka?
...
I can't reason with him. He already knows the risk, and punishing him only fuels his anger. It's like that's the only thing he feels. And I get it--we're all angry. What I don't get, is why he has to express it where the whole fucking *world* can see.
This train incident... it's the third time he's been caught on surveillance. It's only a matter of time before they can trace him back here. There's only so much I can do to protect him. The whole gang's on edge.
Am I just wasting my time? Hoping he will gain a shred of sense?
Yuka's just a boy... wanting to be a man. So give him the chance. Send him on a real mission.
...He's not ready. I can't risk him endangering others.
He's endangering them already. Look, I was the same way at his age. Just gotta give him something constructive to fuel all that angst into.
Let him prove himself on the streets. He could go with Valeria on a meet. See if he's up to being a pusher.
Hah. That would be a back-handed promotion. She's barely making sales. But, I suppose that could be a good thing. ...I'll consider it.
You got a plan?
On that note, one of Valeria's buyers confirmed my suspicions. Kal's gotten her hands on a superior version of Bright--highly purified, I'm guessing. Lasts longer with a better high in a smaller package. They're calling it Lucid. Our sales are gonna keep dropping unless we can compete.
...
NOK NOK
Cullen. I need a word.
Come in, Andres.

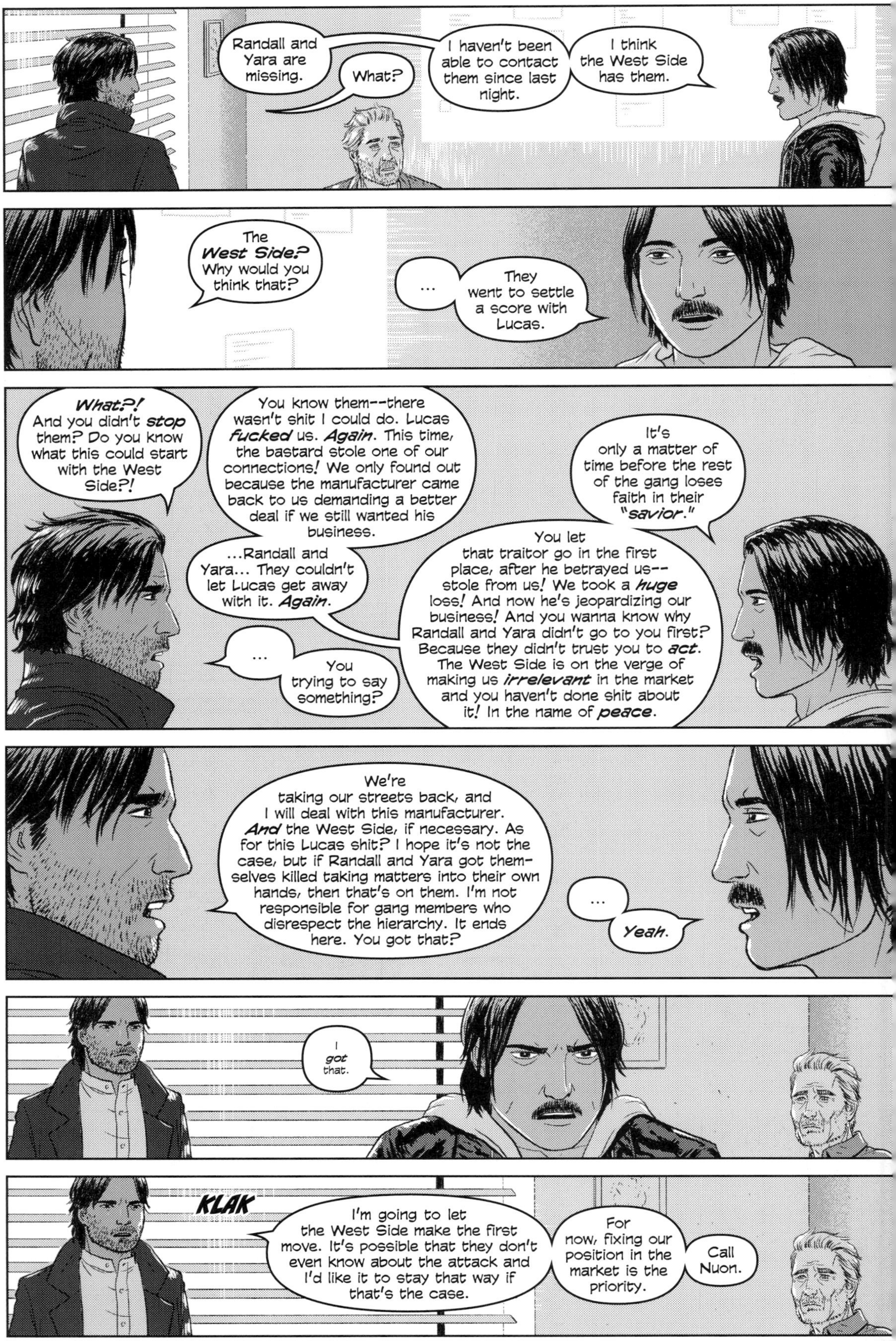
Randall and Yara are missing.
What?
I haven't been able to contact them since last night.
I think the West Side has them.
The West Side? Why would you think that?
...
They went to settle a score with Lucas.
What?! And you didn't stop them? Do you know what this could start with the West Side?!
You know them--there wasn't shit I could do. Lucas fucked us. Again. This time, the bastard stole one of our connections! We only found out because the manufacturer came back to us demanding a better deal if we still wanted his business.
...Randall and Yara... They couldn't let Lucas get away with it. Again.
It's only a matter of time before the rest of the gang loses faith in their "savior."
You let that traitor go in the first place, after he betrayed us--stole from us! We took a huge loss! And now he's jeopardizing our business! And you wanna know why Randall and Yara didn't go to you first? Because they didn't trust you to act. The West Side is on the verge of making us irrelevant in the market and you haven't done shit about it! In the name of peace.
...
You trying to say something?
We're taking our streets back, and I will deal with this manufacturer. And the West Side, if necessary. As for this Lucas shit? I hope it's not the case, but if Randall and Yara got themselves killed taking matters into their own hands, then that's on them. I'm not responsible for gang members who disrespect the hierarchy. It ends here. You got that?
...
Yeah.
I got that.
KLAK
I'm going to let the West Side make the first move. It's possible that they don't even know about the attack and I'd like it to stay that way if that's the case.
For now, fixing our position in the market is the priority.
Call Nuon.

Call from Leo.

Ah!

Shit.

Accept.

Nuon. I've got a job for you. You're not gonna like it.

I'm good. Thanks for asking, Leo.

Thought you weren't one for all that small talk. And you never tell me how you're really doing anyway.

I'm fine... I just don't hear from you much outside of business lately.

...And I miss our impromptu rides.

SHF SHF

I do too. Seems like we're always waitin' for shit to blow over. But there's always more shit.

So, what is it this time?

Cullen has a mind to find out how the West Side is sourcing a superior product. We need intel from the inside.

And how am I supposed to do that? They know who I am.

Any way you can.

And it goes without sayin', but...don't get caught. We're walkin' a fine line as it is.

Why am I the first one Cullen thinks of whenever he wants something impossible?

Sounds sappy, but he believes in you, Nuon.

So do I. ♪

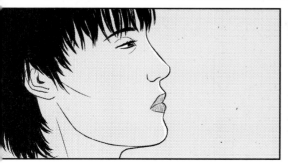

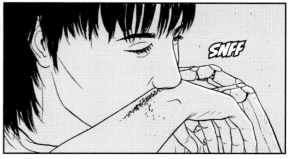

SNFF

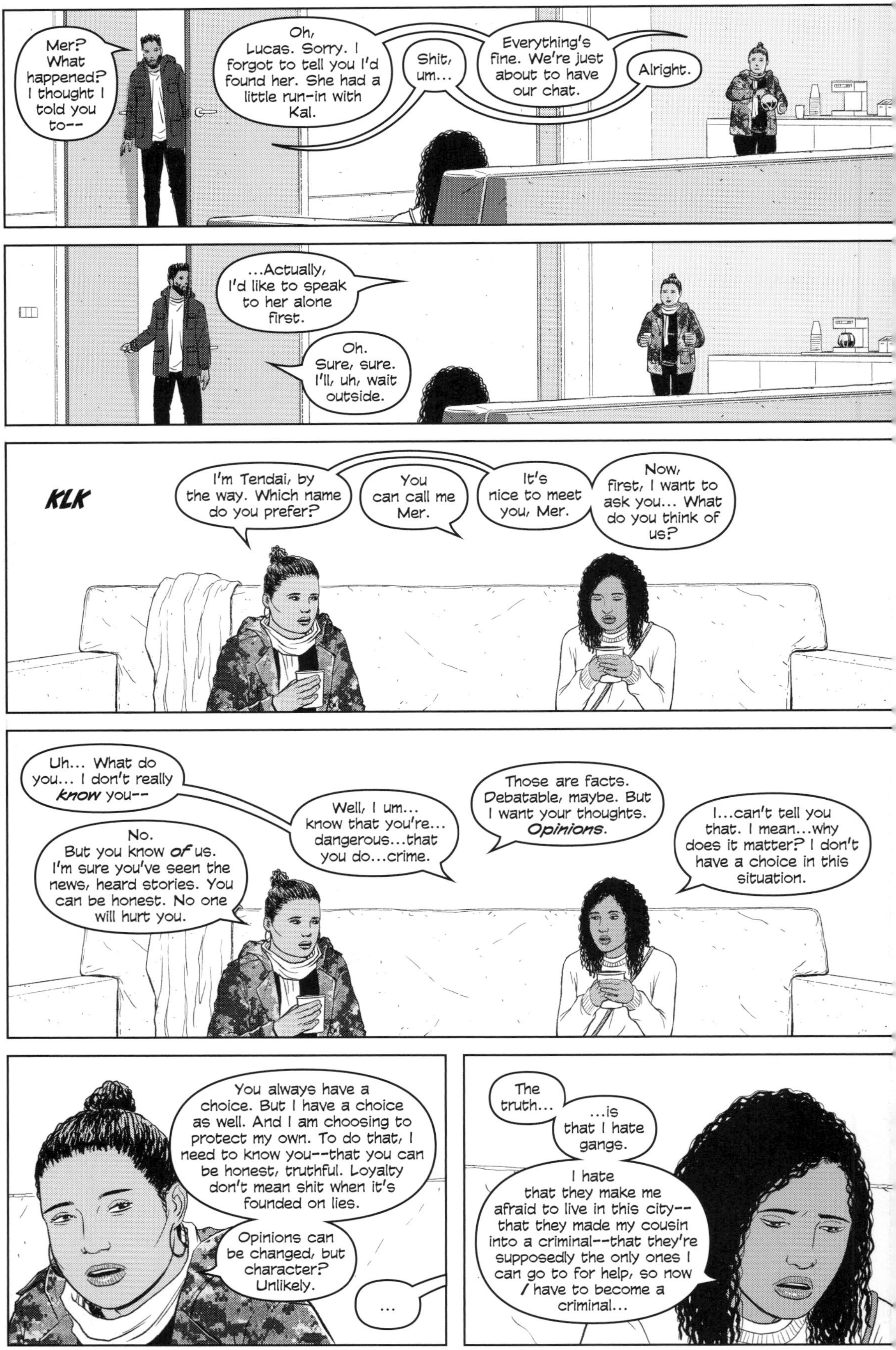
Mer? What happened? I thought I told you to--
Oh, Lucas. Sorry. I forgot to tell you I'd found her. She had a little run-in with Kal.
Shit, um...
Everything's fine. We're just about to have our chat.
Alright.
...Actually, I'd like to speak to her alone first.
Oh. Sure, sure. I'll, uh, wait outside.
KLK
I'm Tendai, by the way. Which name do you prefer?
You can call me Mer.
It's nice to meet you, Mer.
Now, first, I want to ask you... What do you think of us?
Uh... What do you... I don't really *know* you--
Well, I um... know that you're... dangerous...that you do...crime.
No. But you know *of* us. I'm sure you've seen the news, heard stories. You can be honest. No one will hurt you.
Those are facts. Debatable, maybe. But I want your thoughts. *Opinions*.
I...can't tell you that. I mean...why does it matter? I don't have a choice in this situation.
You always have a choice. But I have a choice as well. And I am choosing to protect my own. To do that, I need to know you--that you can be honest, truthful. Loyalty don't mean shit when it's founded on lies.
Opinions can be changed, but character? Unlikely.
...
The truth...
...is that I hate gangs.
I hate that they make me afraid to live in this city--that they made my cousin into a criminal--that they're supposedly the only ones I can go to for help, so now *I* have to become a criminal...

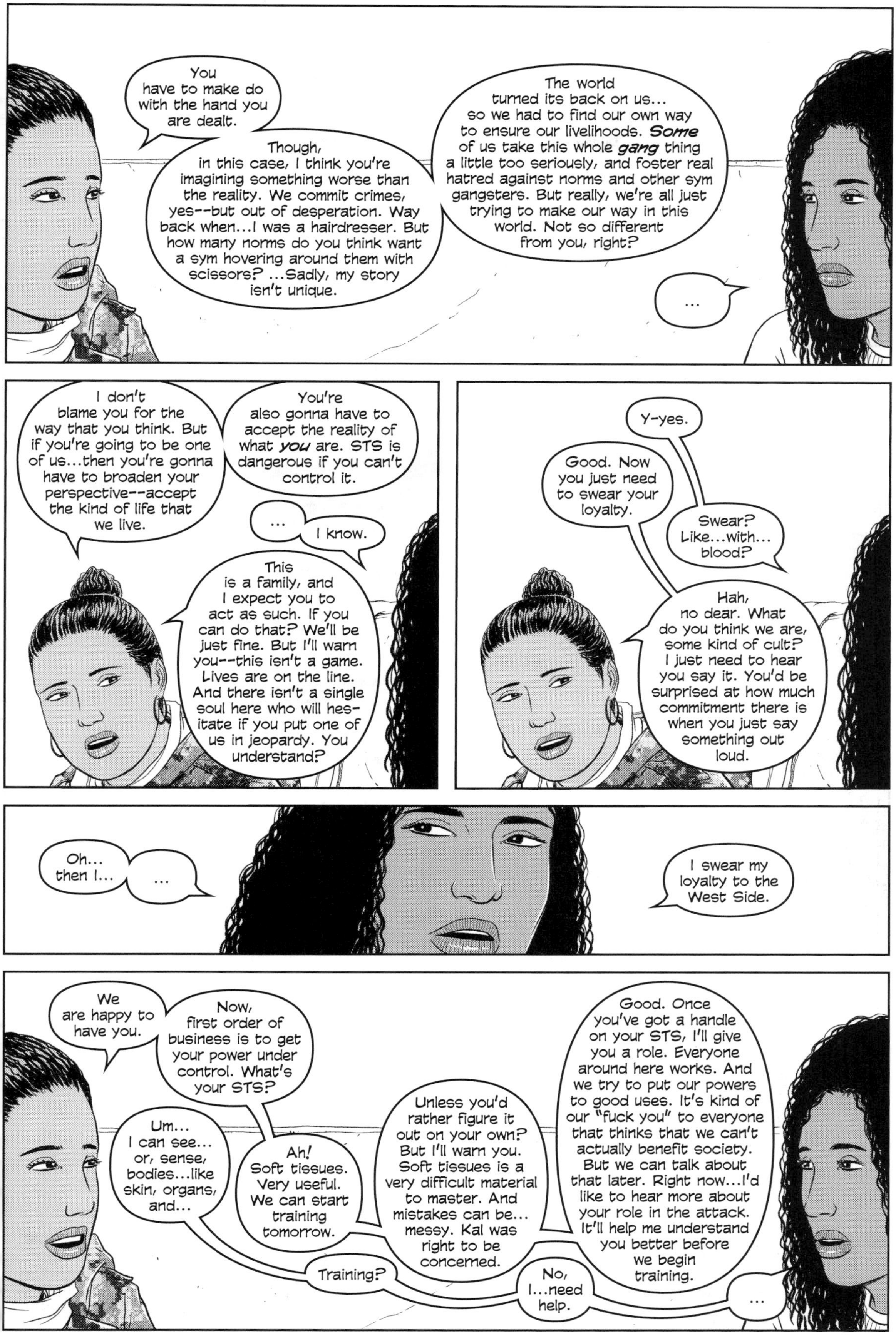
You have to make do with the hand you are dealt.
Though, in this case, I think you're imagining something worse than the reality. We commit crimes, yes--but out of desperation. Way back when...I was a hairdresser. But how many norms do you think want a sym hovering around them with scissors? ...Sadly, my story isn't unique.
The world turned its back on us... so we had to find our own way to ensure our livelihoods. *Some* of us take this whole *gang* thing a little too seriously, and foster real hatred against norms and other sym gangsters. But really, we're all just trying to make our way in this world. Not so different from you, right?
...
I don't blame you for the way that you think. But if you're going to be one of us...then you're gonna have to broaden your perspective--accept the kind of life that we live.
You're also gonna have to accept the reality of what *you* are. STS is dangerous if you can't control it.
...
I know.
This is a family, and I expect you to act as such. If you can do that? We'll be just fine. But I'll warn you--this isn't a game. Lives are on the line. And there isn't a single soul here who will hesitate if you put one of us in jeopardy. You understand?
Y-yes.
Good. Now you just need to swear your loyalty.
Swear? Like...with... blood?
Hah, no dear. What do you think we are, some kind of cult? I just need to hear you say it. You'd be surprised at how much commitment there is when you just say something out loud.
Oh... then I...
...
I swear my loyalty to the West Side.
We are happy to have you.
Now, first order of business is to get your power under control. What's your STS?
Um... I can see... or, sense, bodies...like skin, organs, and...
Ah! Soft tissues. Very useful. We can start training tomorrow.
Training?
Unless you'd rather figure it out on your own? But I'll warn you. Soft tissues is a very difficult material to master. And mistakes can be... messy. Kal was right to be concerned.
No, I...need help.
Good. Once you've got a handle on your STS, I'll give you a role. Everyone around here works. And we try to put our powers to good uses. It's kind of our "fuck you" to everyone that thinks that we can't actually benefit society. But we can talk about that later. Right now...I'd like to hear more about your role in the attack. It'll help me understand you better before we begin training.
...

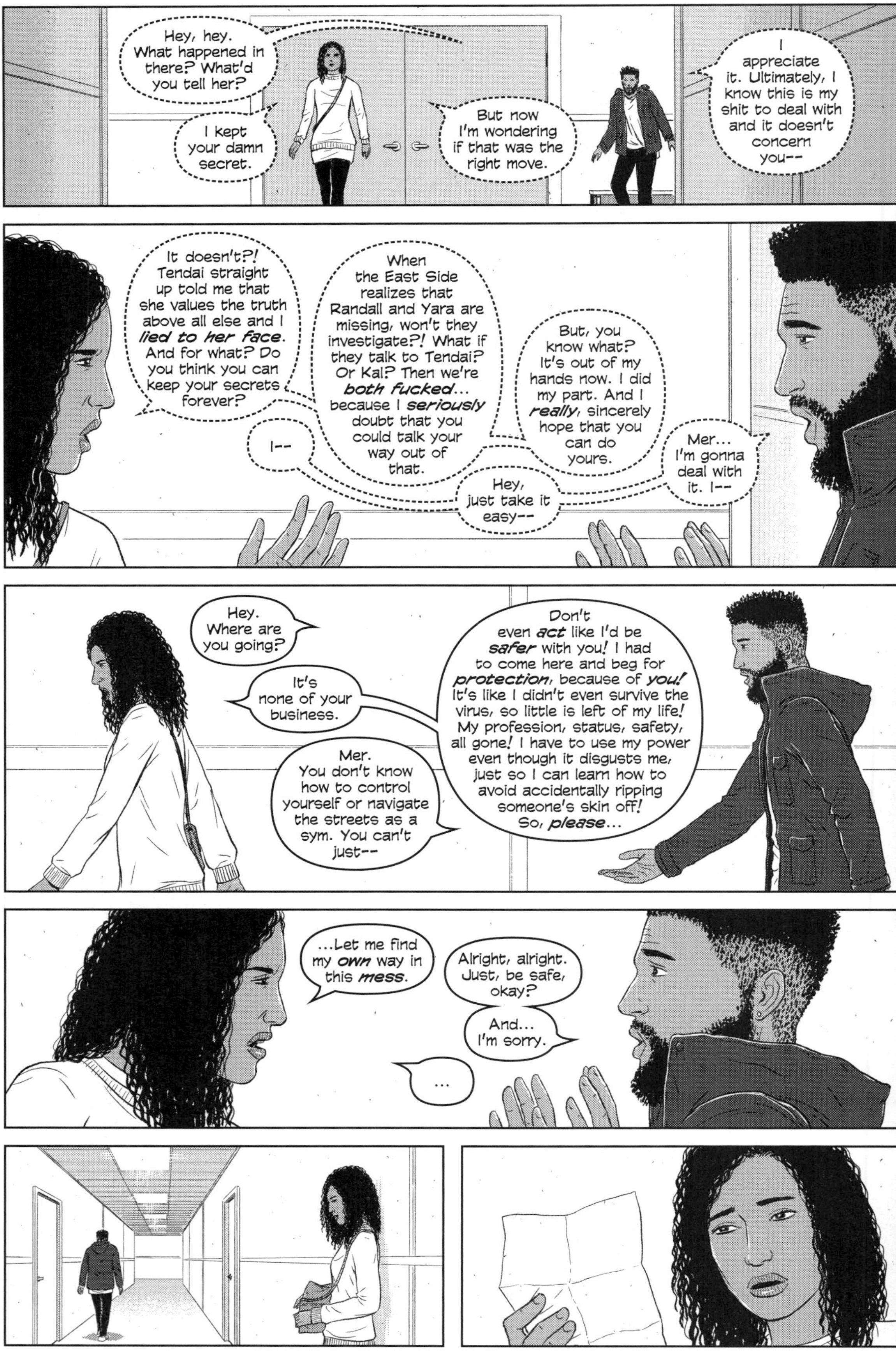
Hey, hey. What happened in there? What'd you tell her?
I kept your damn secret.
But now I'm wondering if that was the right move.
I appreciate it. Ultimately, I know this is my shit to deal with and it doesn't concern you--
It doesn't?! Tendai straight up told me that she values the truth above all else and I *lied to her face*. And for what? Do you think you can keep your secrets forever?
I--
When the East Side realizes that Randall and Yara are missing, won't they investigate?! What if they talk to Tendai? Or Kal? Then we're *both fucked*... because I *seriously* doubt that you could talk your way out of that.
Hey, just take it easy--
But, you know what? It's out of my hands now. I did my part. And I *really*, sincerely hope that you can do yours.
Mer... I'm gonna deal with it. I--
Hey. Where are you going?
It's none of your business.
Mer. You don't know how to control yourself or navigate the streets as a sym. You can't just--
Don't even *act* like I'd be *safer* with you! I had to come here and beg for *protection*, because of *you!* It's like I didn't even survive the virus, so little is left of my life! My profession, status, safety, all gone! I have to use my power even though it disgusts me, just so I can learn how to avoid accidentally ripping someone's skin off! So, *please*...
...Let me find my *own* way in this *mess*.
Alright, alright. Just, be safe, okay?
And... I'm sorry.
...

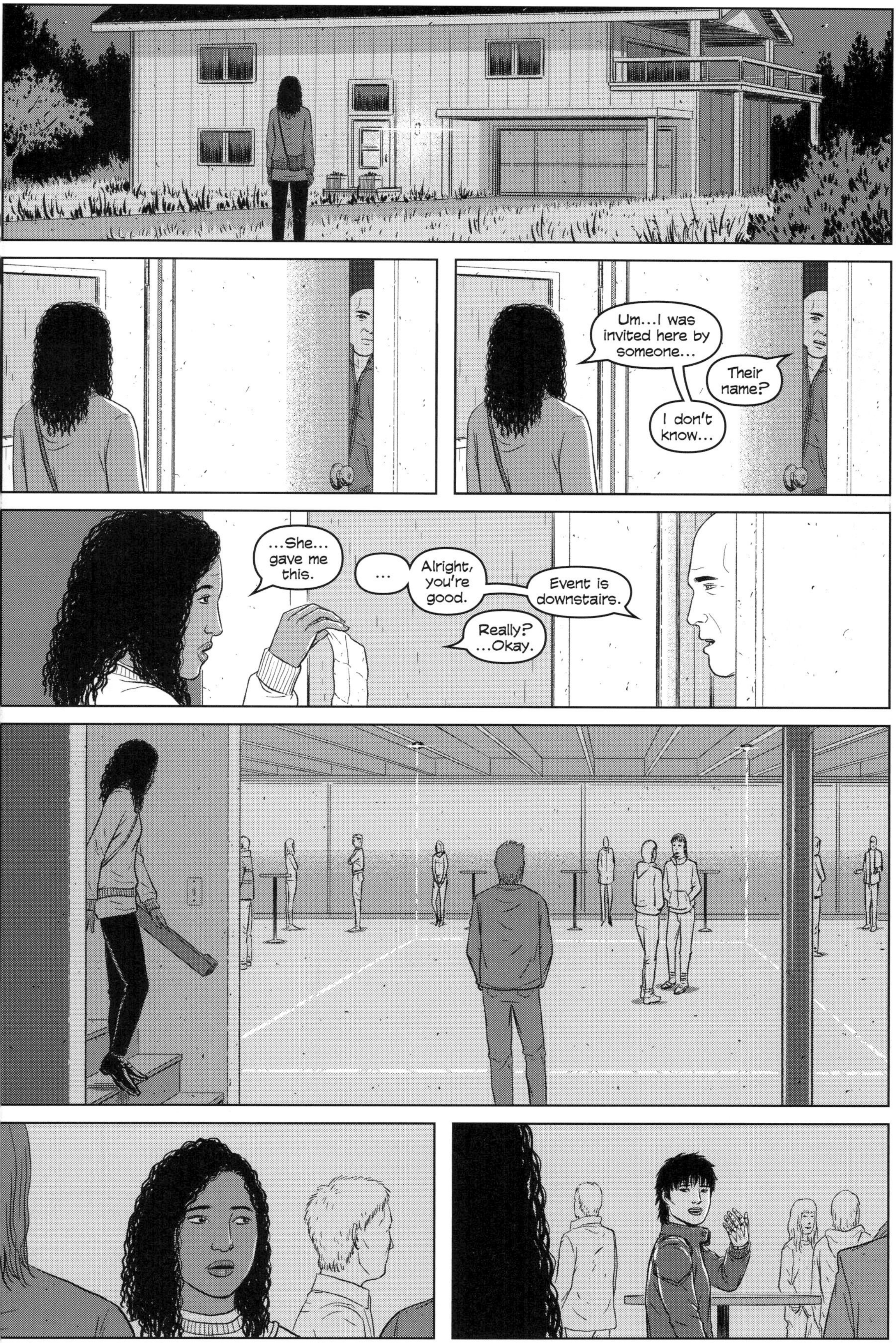
Um...I was invited here by someone...
Their name?
I don't know...
...She... gave me this.
...
Alright, you're good.
Event is downstairs.
Really? ...Okay.

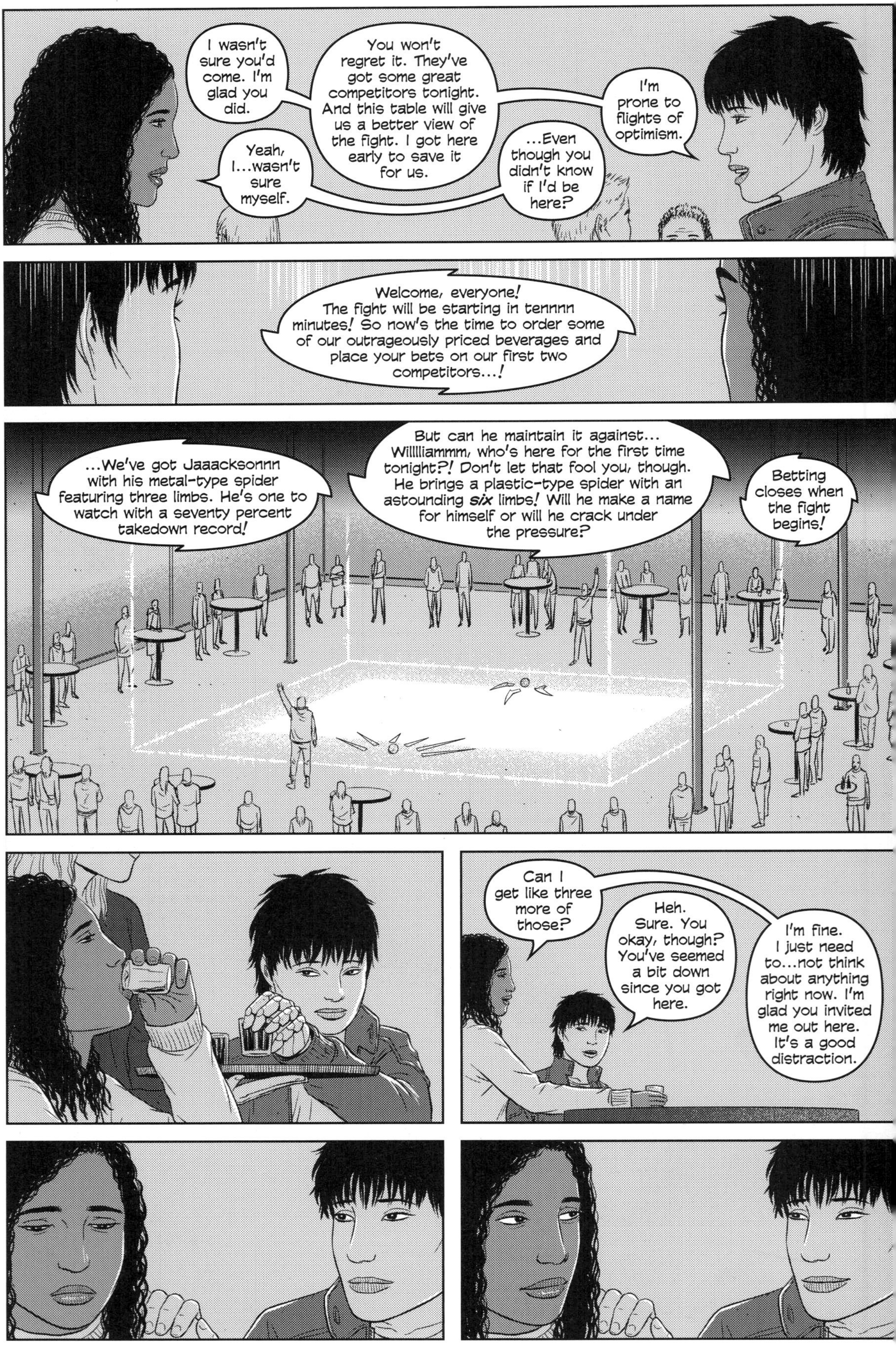
I wasn't sure you'd come. I'm glad you did.
Yeah, I...wasn't sure myself.
You won't regret it. They've got some great competitors tonight. And this table will give us a better view of the fight. I got here early to save it for us.
...Even though you didn't know if I'd be here?
I'm prone to flights of optimism.
Welcome, everyone! The fight will be starting in tennnn minutes! So now's the time to order some of our outrageously priced beverages and place your bets on our first two competitors...!
...We've got Jaaacksonnn with his metal-type spider featuring three limbs. He's one to watch with a seventy percent takedown record!
But can he maintain it against... Willlliammm, who's here for the first time tonight?! Don't let that fool you, though. He brings a plastic-type spider with an astounding *six* limbs! Will he make a name for himself or will he crack under the pressure?
Betting closes when the fight begins!
Can I get like three more of those?
Heh. Sure. You okay, though? You've seemed a bit down since you got here.
I'm fine. I just need to...not think about anything right now. I'm glad you invited me out here. It's a good distraction.

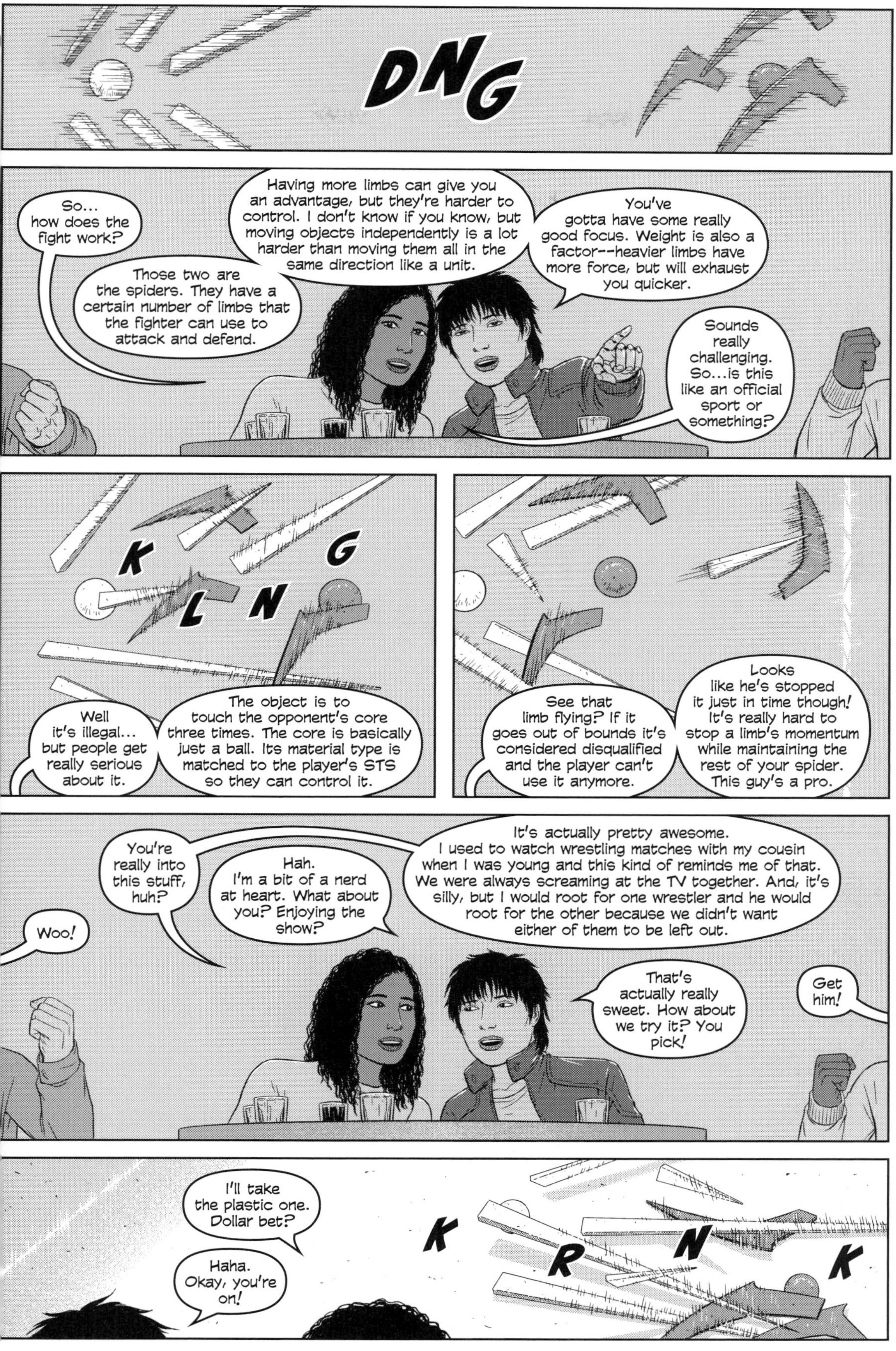
DNG
So... how does the fight work?
Having more limbs can give you an advantage, but they're harder to control. I don't know if you know, but moving objects independently is a lot harder than moving them all in the same direction like a unit.
Those two are the spiders. They have a certain number of limbs that the fighter can use to attack and defend.
You've gotta have some really good focus. Weight is also a factor--heavier limbs have more force, but will exhaust you quicker.
Sounds really challenging. So...is this like an official sport or something?
KLNG
Well it's illegal... but people get really serious about it.
The object is to touch the opponent's core three times. The core is basically just a ball. Its material type is matched to the player's STS so they can control it.
See that limb flying? If it goes out of bounds it's considered disqualified and the player can't use it anymore.
Looks like he's stopped it just in time though! It's really hard to stop a limb's momentum while maintaining the rest of your spider. This guy's a pro.
Woo!
You're really into this stuff, huh?
Hah. I'm a bit of a nerd at heart. What about you? Enjoying the show?
It's actually pretty awesome. I used to watch wrestling matches with my cousin when I was young and this kind of reminds me of that. We were always screaming at the TV together. And, it's silly, but I would root for one wrestler and he would root for the other because we didn't want either of them to be left out.
That's actually really sweet. How about we try it? You pick!
Get him!
I'll take the plastic one. Dollar bet?
Haha. Okay, you're on!
KRNK

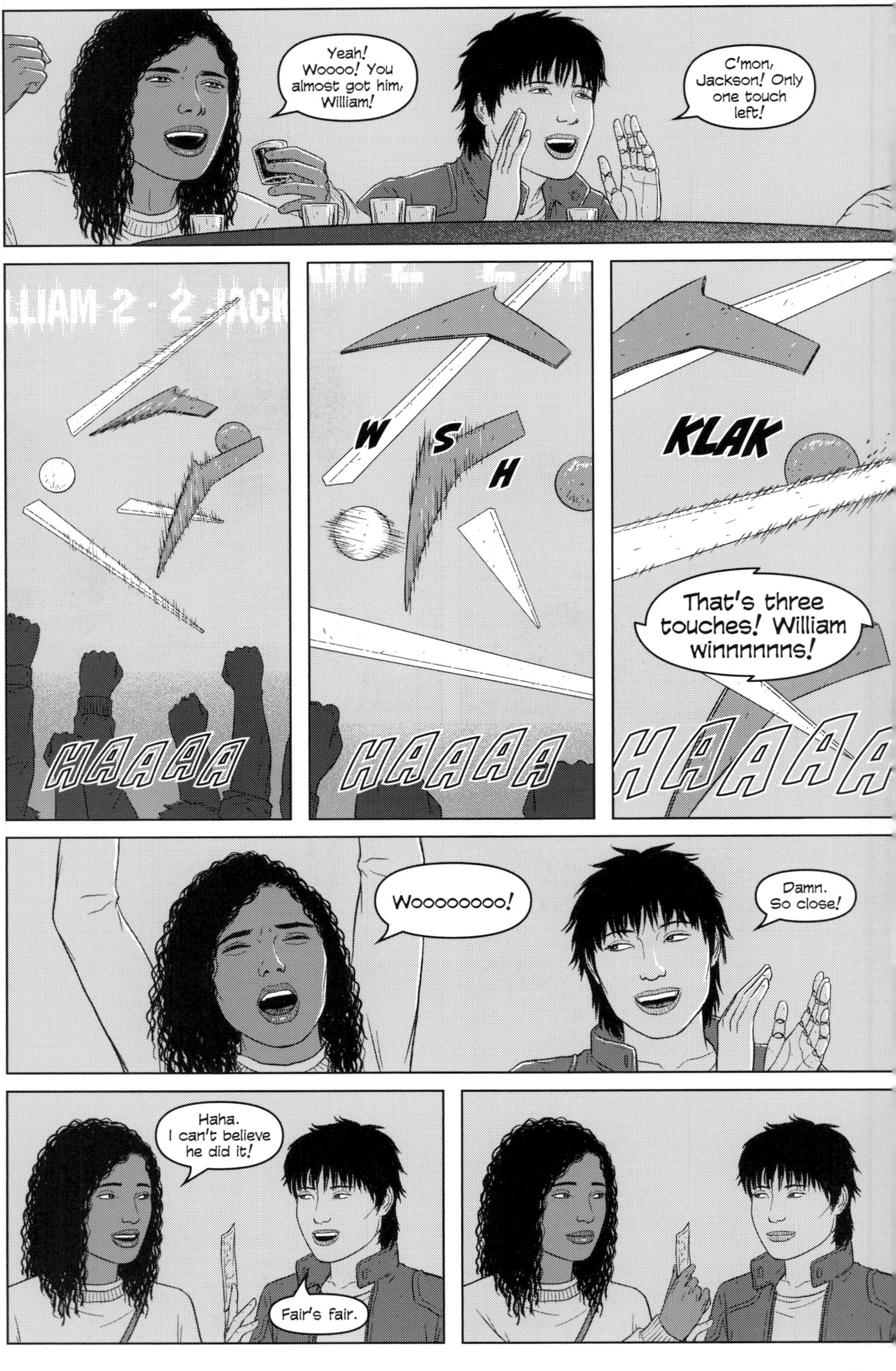
Yeah! Woooo! You almost got him, William!
C'mon, Jackson! Only one touch left!
LLIAM 2 - 2 JACK
HAAAA
W S H
HAAAA
KLAK
That's three touches! William winnnnnns!
HAAAA
Woooooooo!
Damn. So close!
Haha. I can't believe he did it!
Fair's fair.

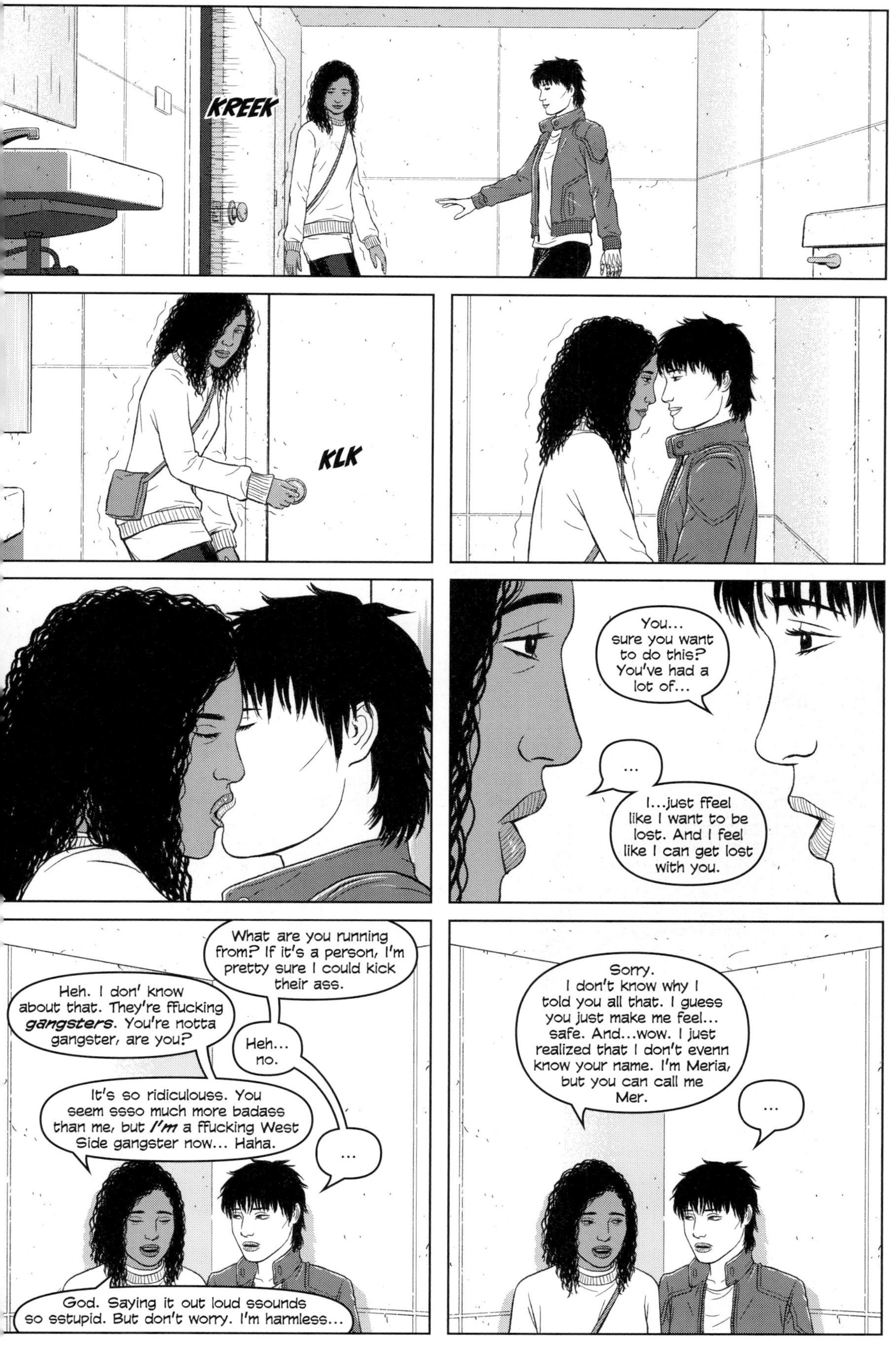
KREEK
KLK
You... sure you want to do this? You've had a lot of...
...
I...just ffeel like I want to be lost. And I feel like I can get lost with you.
What are you running from? If it's a person, I'm pretty sure I could kick their ass.
Heh. I don' know about that. They're ffucking *gangsters*. You're notta gangster, are you?
Heh... no.
It's so ridiculouss. You seem ssso much more badass than me, but *I'm* a ffucking West Side gangster now... Haha.
...
God. Saying it out loud ssounds so sstupid. But don't worry. I'm harmless...
Sorry. I don't know why I told you all that. I guess you just make me feel... safe. And...wow. I just realized that I don't evenn know your name. I'm Meria, but you can call me Mer.
...

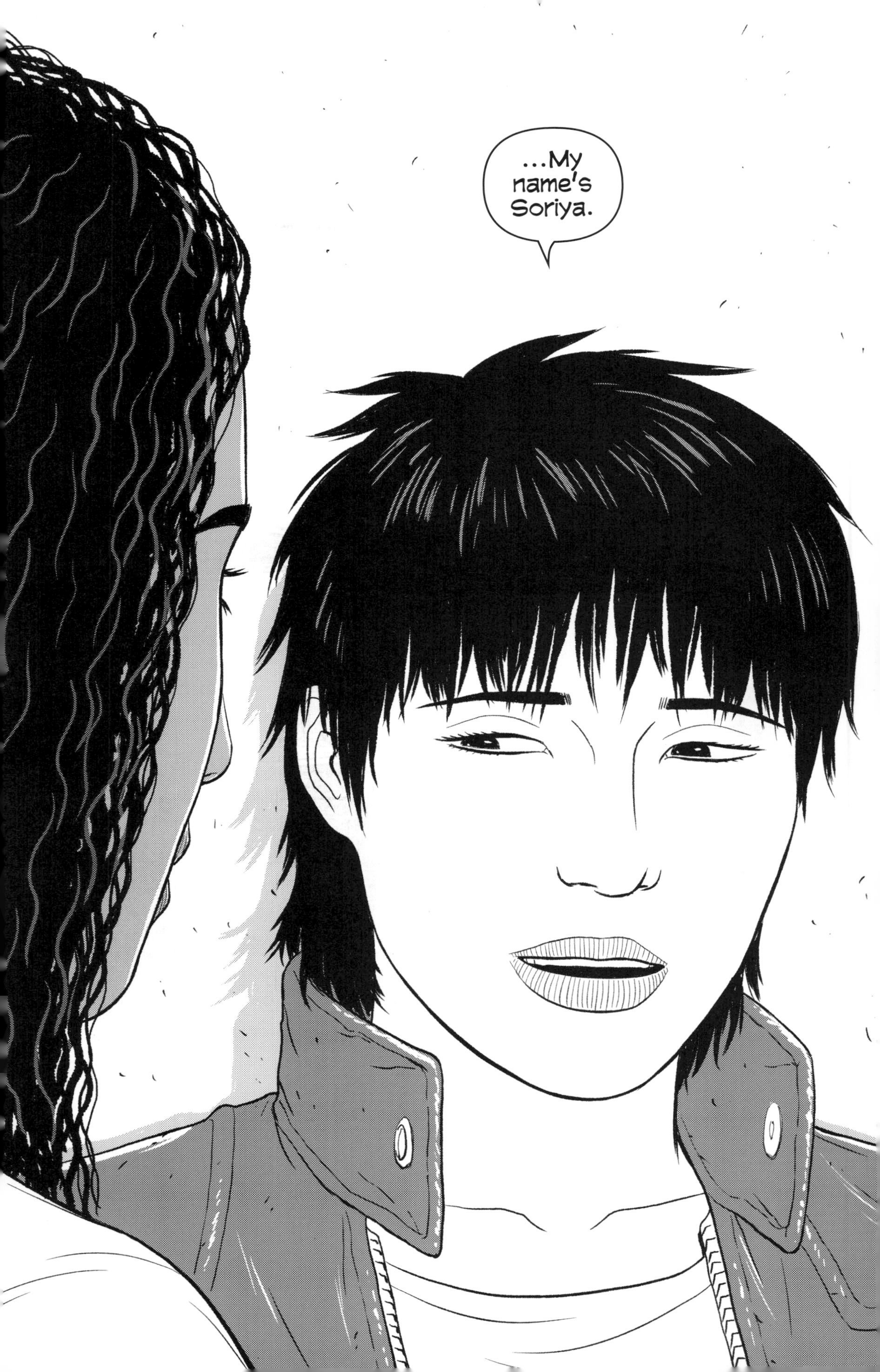
...My name's Soriya.

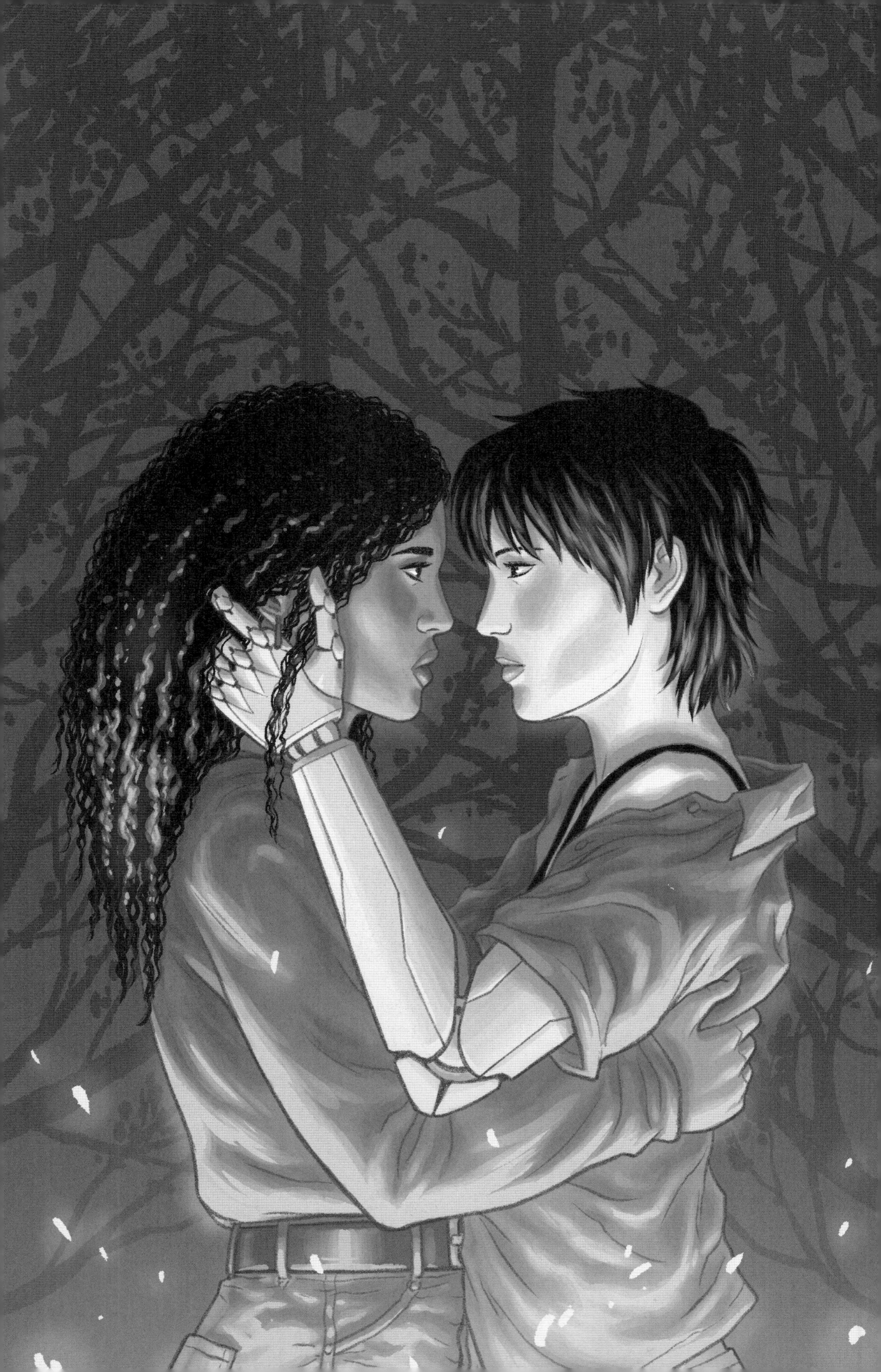

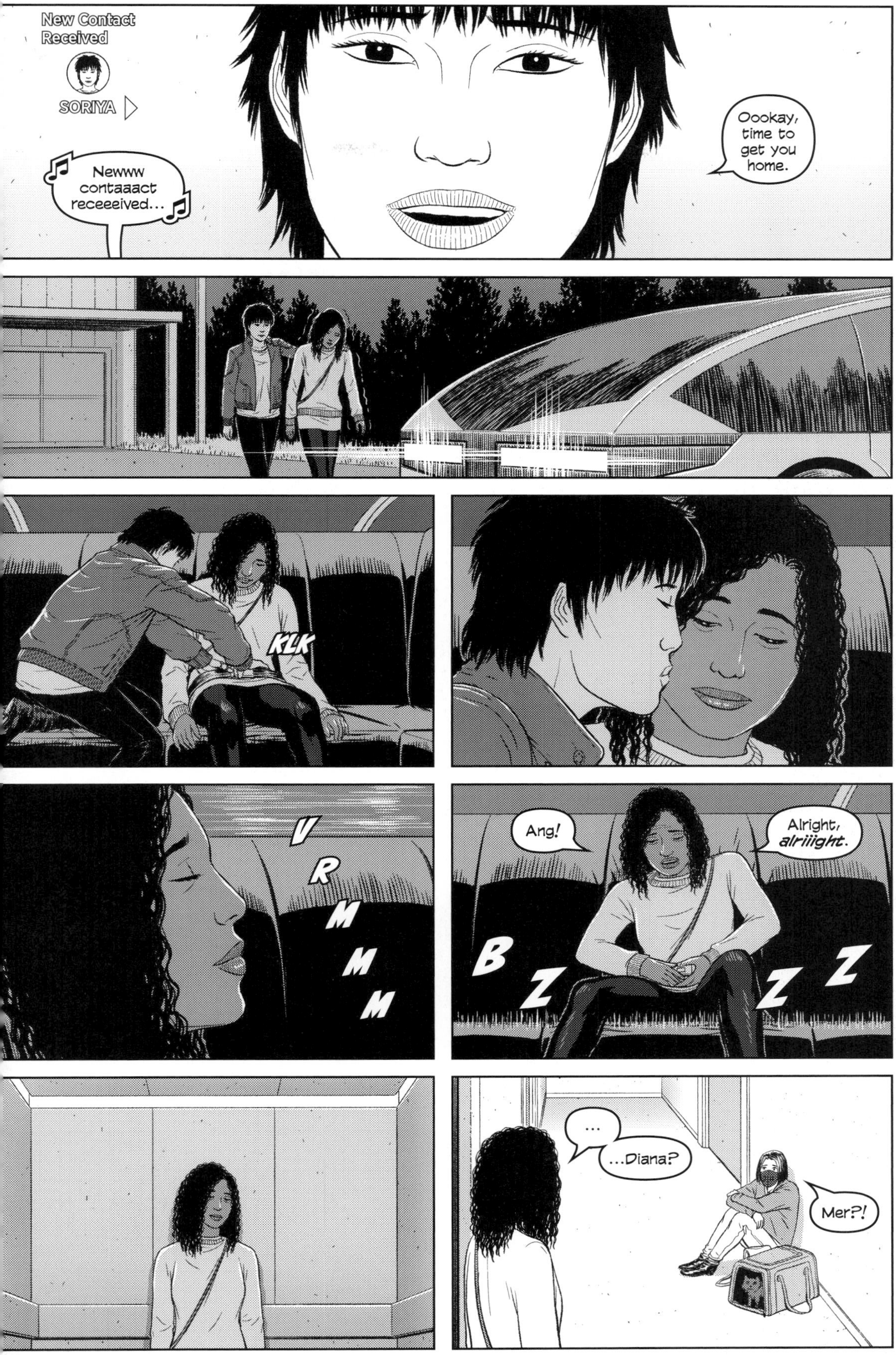
New Contact Received
SORIYA
Newww contaaact receeeived...
Oookay, time to get you home.
KLK
VRMMM
Ang!
Alright, *alriiight*.
BZZZ
...
...Diana?
Mer?!

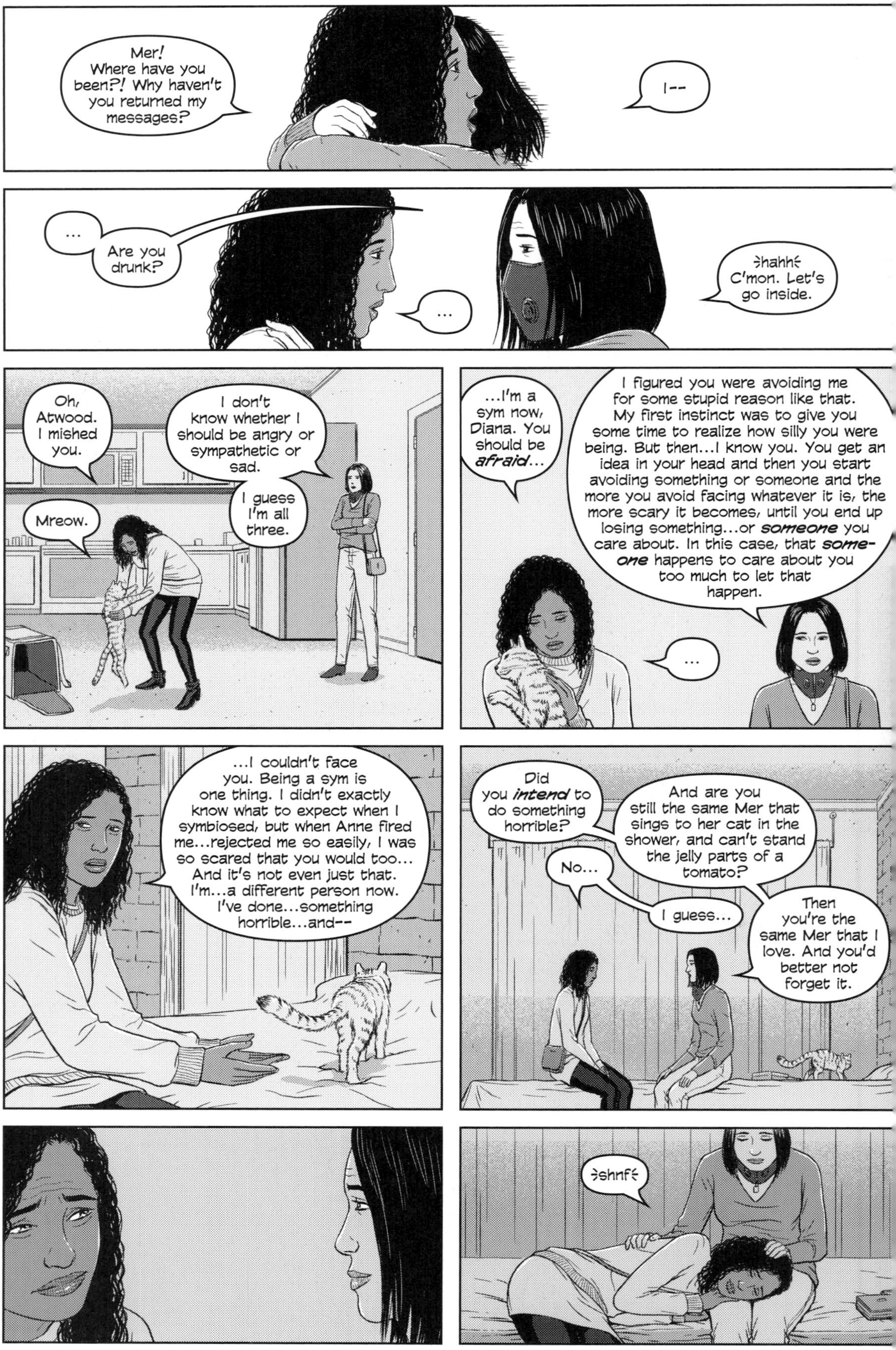

Mer! Where have you been?! Why haven't you returned my messages?
I--
...
Are you drunk?
...
≻hahh≺ C'mon. Let's go inside.
Oh, Atwood. I mished you.
Mreow.
I don't know whether I should be angry or sympathetic or sad.
I guess I'm all three.
...I'm a sym now, Diana. You should be *afraid*...
I figured you were avoiding me for some stupid reason like that. My first instinct was to give you some time to realize how silly you were being. But then...I know you. You get an idea in your head and then you start avoiding something or someone and the more you avoid facing whatever it is, the more scary it becomes, until you end up losing something...or *someone* you care about. In this case, that *some-one* happens to care about you too much to let that happen.
...
...I couldn't face you. Being a sym is one thing. I didn't exactly know what to expect when I symbiosed, but when Anne fired me...rejected me so easily, I was so scared that you would too... And it's not even just that. I'm...a different person now. I've done...something horrible...and--
Did you *intend* to do something horrible?
No...
I guess...
And are you still the same Mer that sings to her cat in the shower, and can't stand the jelly parts of a tomato?
Then you're the same Mer that I love. And you'd better not forget it.
≻shnf≺

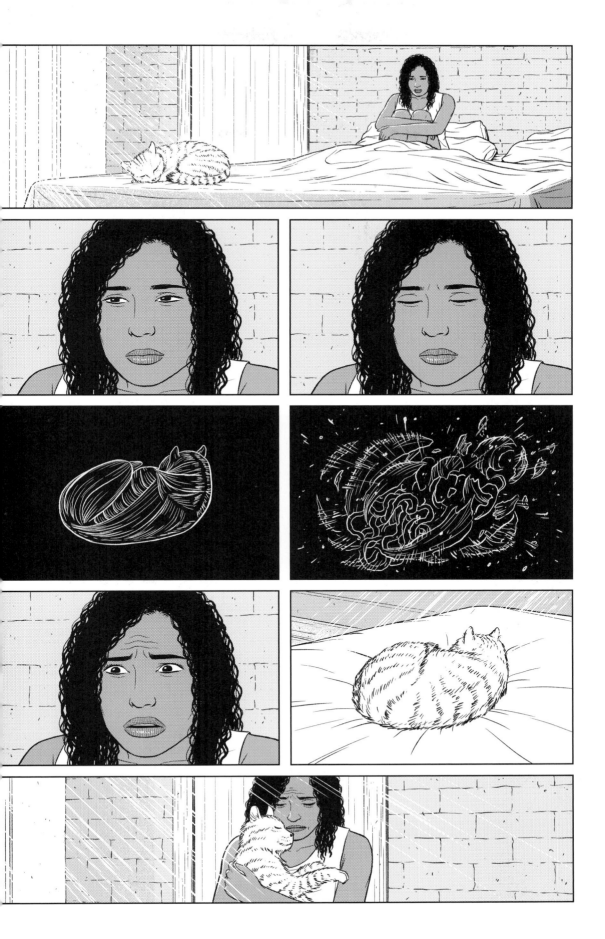

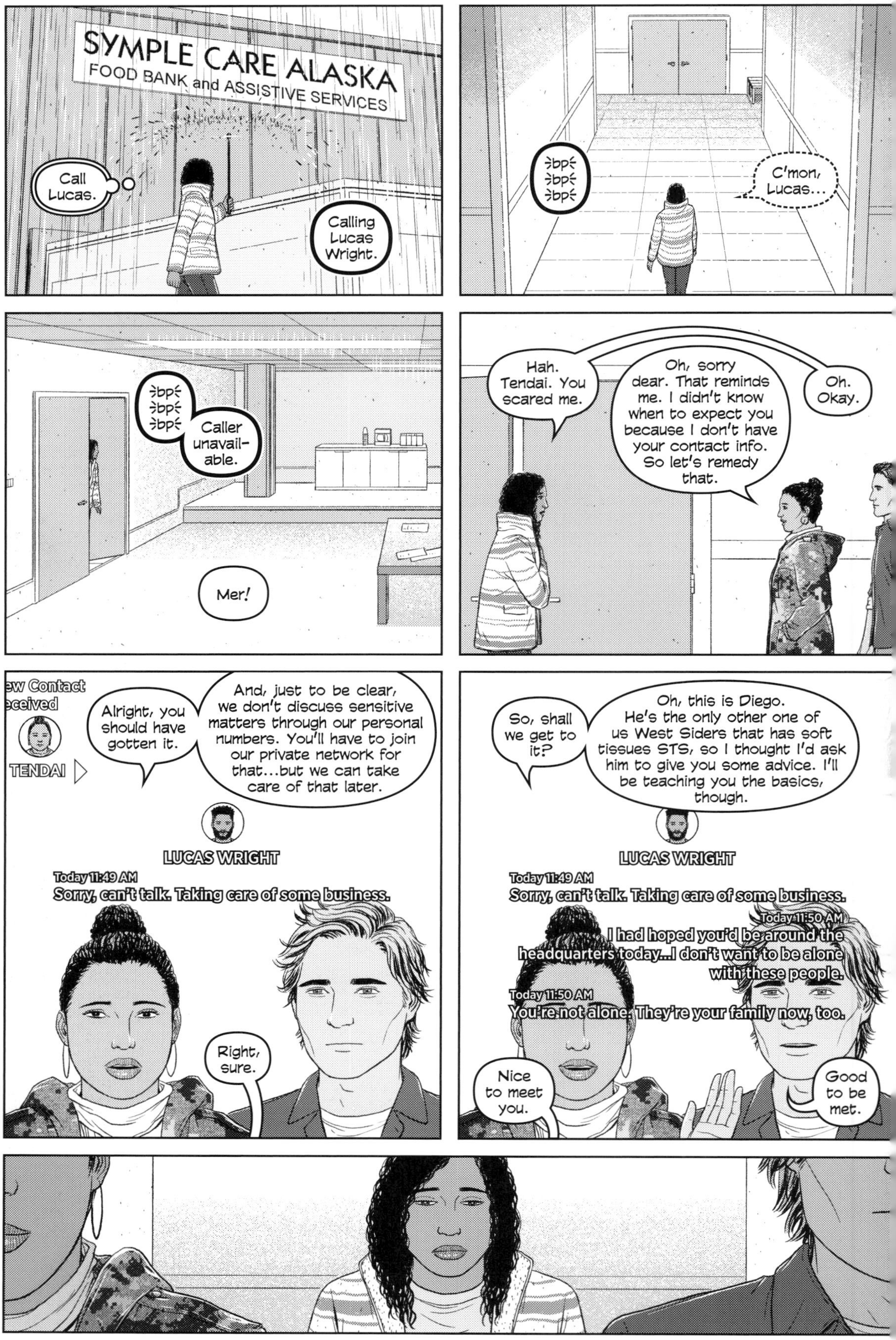
SYMPLE CARE ALASKA
FOOD BANK and ASSISTIVE SERVICES
Call Lucas.
Calling Lucas Wright.
bp bp bp
C'mon, Lucas...
bp bp bp
Caller unavailable.
Mer!
Hah. Tendai. You scared me.
Oh, sorry dear. That reminds me. I didn't know when to expect you because I don't have your contact info. So let's remedy that.
Oh. Okay.
ew Contact eceived
TENDAI
Alright, you should have gotten it.
And, just to be clear, we don't discuss sensitive matters through our personal numbers. You'll have to join our private network for that...but we can take care of that later.
LUCAS WRIGHT
Today 11:49 AM
Sorry, can't talk. Taking care of some business.
Right, sure.
So, shall we get to it?
Oh, this is Diego. He's the only other one of us West Siders that has soft tissues STS, so I thought I'd ask him to give you some advice. I'll be teaching you the basics, though.
LUCAS WRIGHT
Today 11:49 AM
Sorry, can't talk. Taking care of some business.
Today 11:50 AM
I had hoped you'd be around the headquarters today...I don't want to be alone with these people.
Today 11:50 AM
You're not alone. They're your family now, too.
Nice to meet you.
Good to be met.

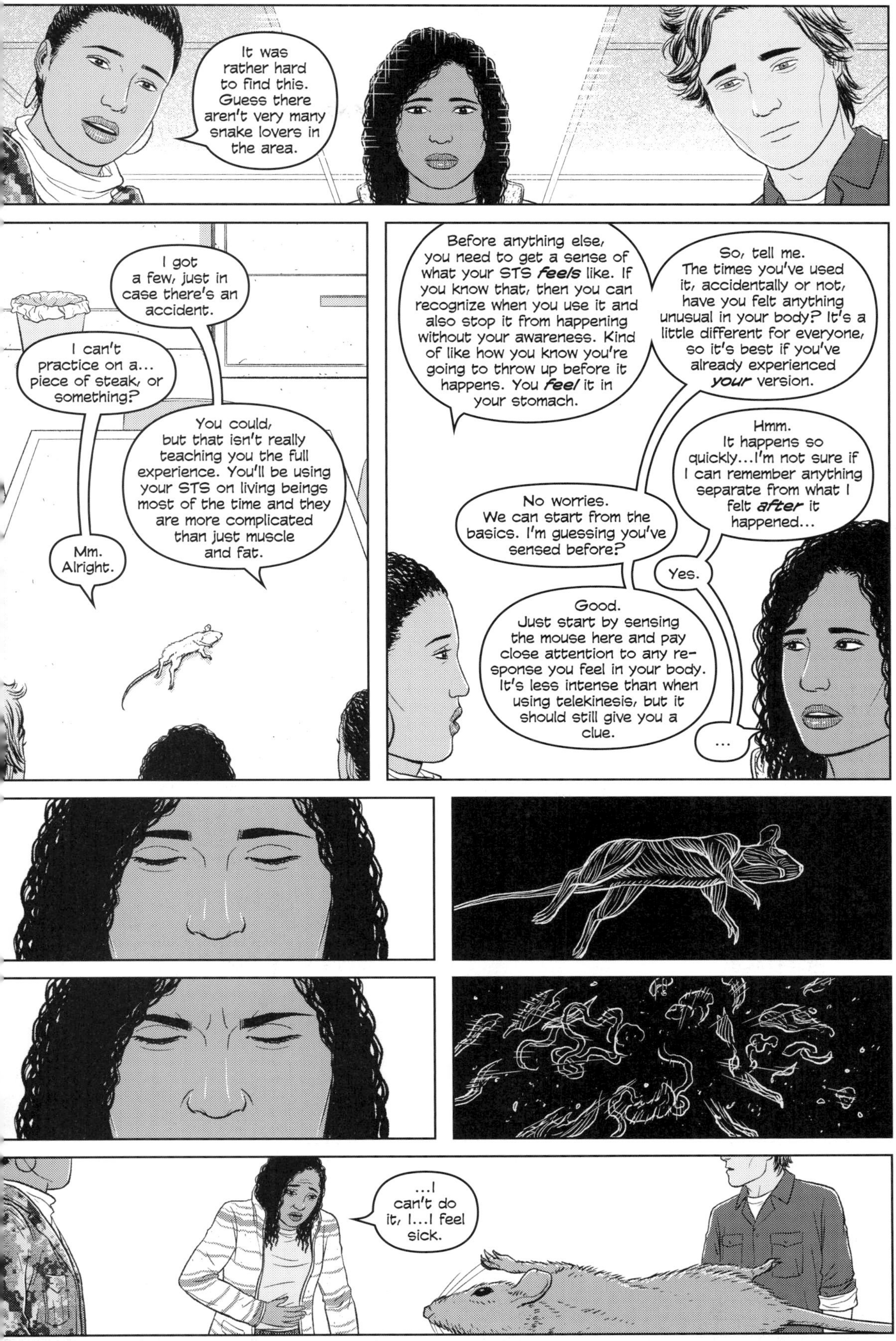
It was rather hard to find this. Guess there aren't very many snake lovers in the area.
I got a few, just in case there's an accident.
I can't practice on a... piece of steak, or something?
You could, but that isn't really teaching you the full experience. You'll be using your STS on living beings most of the time and they are more complicated than just muscle and fat.
Mm. Alright.
Before anything else, you need to get a sense of what your STS *feels* like. If you know that, then you can recognize when you use it and also stop it from happening without your awareness. Kind of like how you know you're going to throw up before it happens. You *feel* it in your stomach.
So, tell me. The times you've used it, accidentally or not, have you felt anything unusual in your body? It's a little different for everyone, so it's best if you've already experienced *your* version.
Hmm. It happens so quickly...I'm not sure if I can remember anything separate from what I felt *after* it happened...
No worries. We can start from the basics. I'm guessing you've sensed before?
Yes.
Good. Just start by sensing the mouse here and pay close attention to any response you feel in your body. It's less intense than when using telekinesis, but it should still give you a clue.
...
...I can't do it, I...I feel sick.

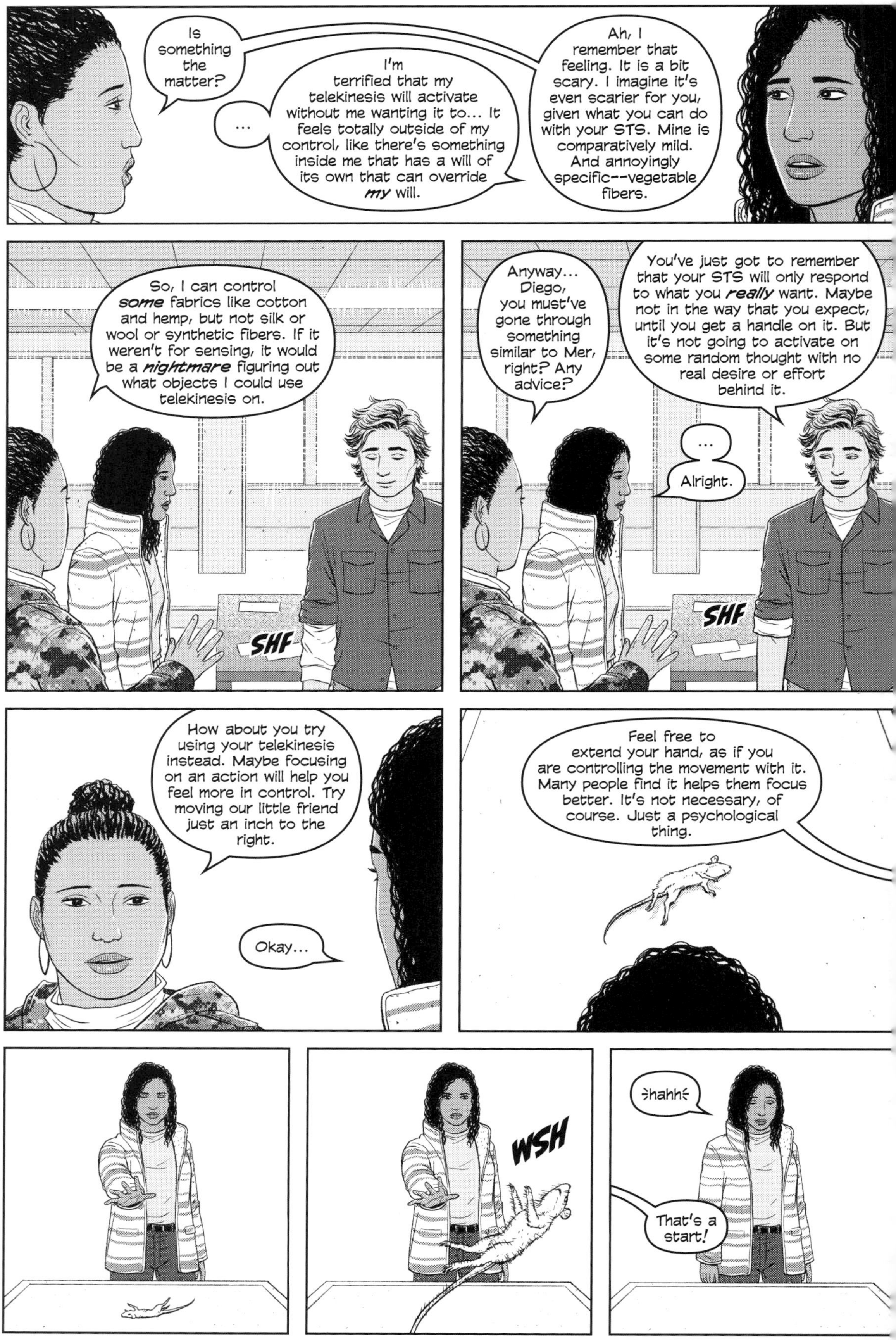
Is something the matter?
...
I'm terrified that my telekinesis will activate without me wanting it to... It feels totally outside of my control, like there's something inside me that has a will of its own that can override *my* will.
Ah, I remember that feeling. It is a bit scary. I imagine it's even scarier for you, given what you can do with your STS. Mine is comparatively mild. And annoyingly specific--vegetable fibers.
So, I can control *some* fabrics like cotton and hemp, but not silk or wool or synthetic fibers. If it weren't for sensing, it would be a *nightmare* figuring out what objects I could use telekinesis on.
SHF
Anyway... Diego, you must've gone through something similar to Mer, right? Any advice?
You've just got to remember that your STS will only respond to what you *really* want. Maybe not in the way that you expect, until you get a handle on it. But it's not going to activate on some random thought with no real desire or effort behind it.
...
Alright.
SHF
How about you try using your telekinesis instead. Maybe focusing on an action will help you feel more in control. Try moving our little friend just an inch to the right.
Okay...
Feel free to extend your hand, as if you are controlling the movement with it. Many people find it helps them focus better. It's not necessary, of course. Just a psychological thing.
WSH
hahh
That's a start!

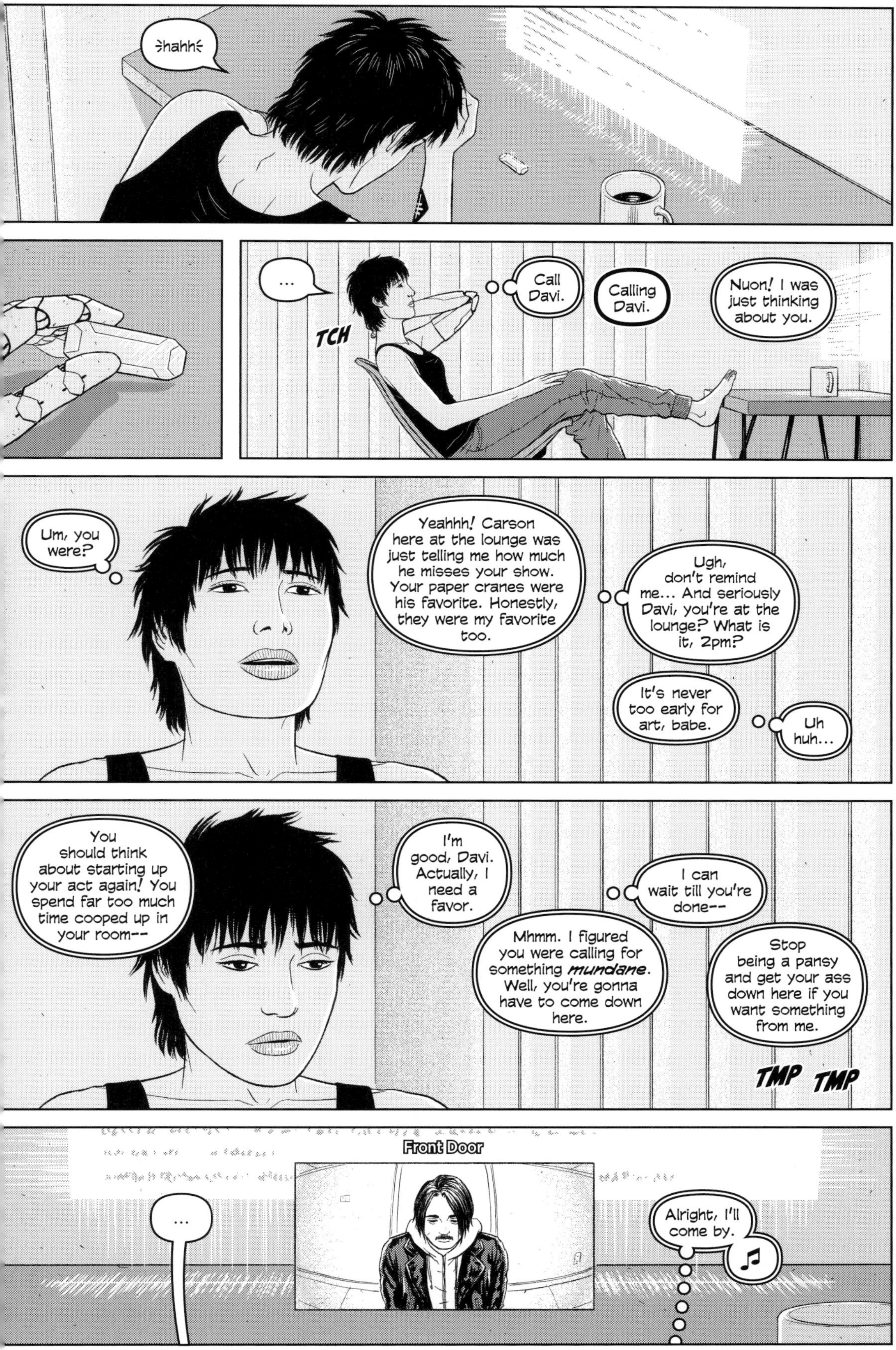

⋟hahh⋞
...
TCH
Call Davi.
Calling Davi.
Nuon! I was just thinking about you.
Um, you were?
Yeahhh! Carson here at the lounge was just telling me how much he misses your show. Your paper cranes were his favorite. Honestly, they were my favorite too.
Ugh, don't remind me... And seriously Davi, you're at the lounge? What is it, 2pm?
It's never too early for art, babe.
Uh huh...
You should think about starting up your act again! You spend far too much time cooped up in your room--
I'm good, Davi. Actually, I need a favor.
Mhmm. I figured you were calling for something *mundane*. Well, you're gonna have to come down here.
I can wait till you're done--
Stop being a pansy and get your ass down here if you want something from me.
TMP TMP
Front Door
...
Alright, I'll come by.
♫

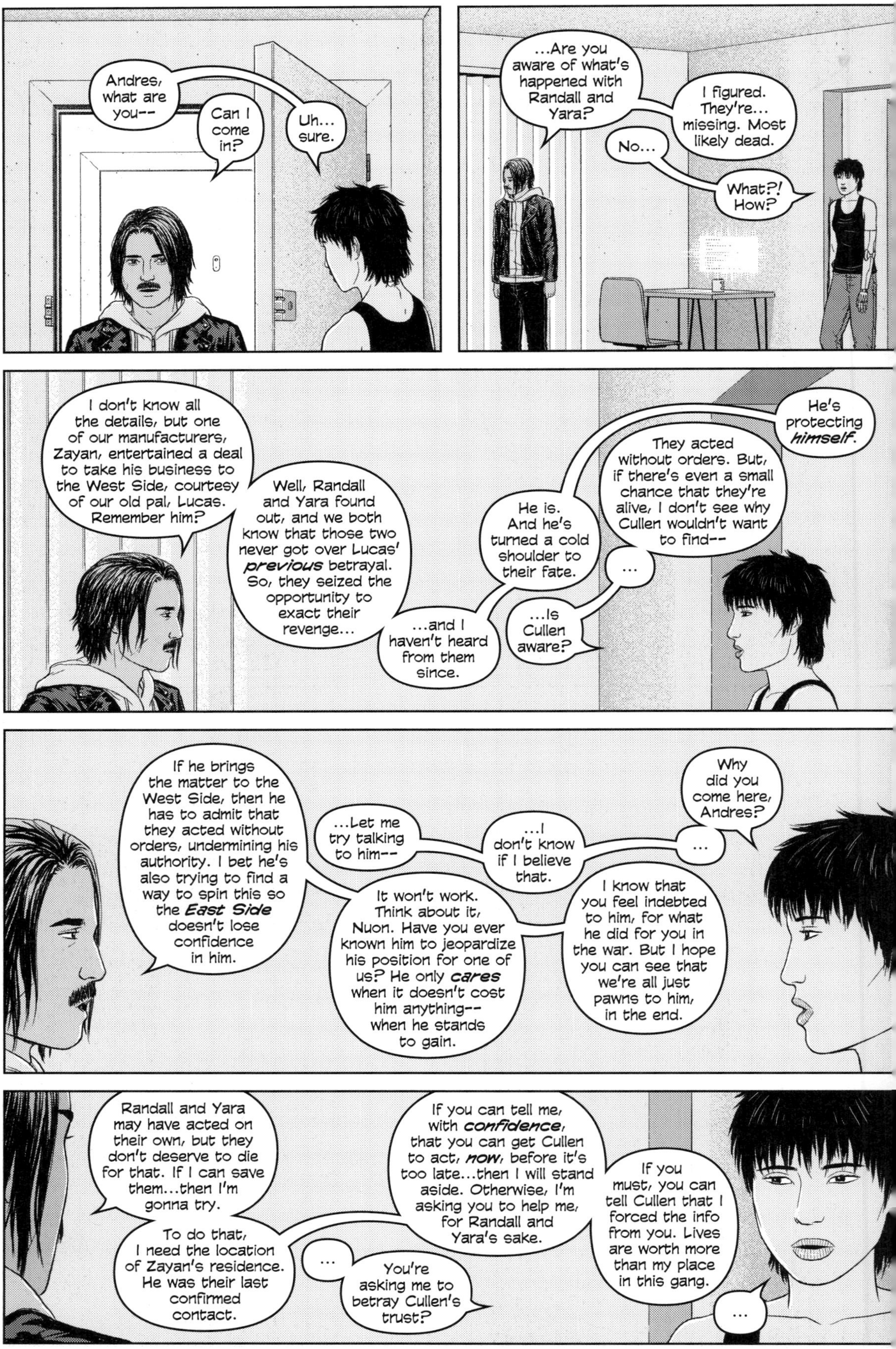

Andres, what are you--
Can I come in?
Uh... sure.
...Are you aware of what's happened with Randall and Yara?
I figured. They're... missing. Most likely dead.
No...
What?! How?
I don't know all the details, but one of our manufacturers, Zayan, entertained a deal to take his business to the West Side, courtesy of our old pal, Lucas. Remember him?
Well, Randall and Yara found out, and we both know that those two never got over Lucas' *previous* betrayal. So, they seized the opportunity to exact their revenge...
...and I haven't heard from them since.
...Is Cullen aware?
...
He is. And he's turned a cold shoulder to their fate.
They acted without orders. But, if there's even a small chance that they're alive, I don't see why Cullen wouldn't want to find--
He's protecting *himself*.
If he brings the matter to the West Side, then he has to admit that they acted without orders, undermining his authority. I bet he's also trying to find a way to spin this so the *East Side* doesn't lose confidence in him.
...Let me try talking to him--
It won't work. Think about it, Nuon. Have you ever known him to jeopardize his position for one of us? He only *cares* when it doesn't cost him anything-- when he stands to gain.
...I don't know if I believe that.
I know that you feel indebted to him, for what he did for you in the war. But I hope you can see that we're all just pawns to him, in the end.
...
Why did you come here, Andres?
Randall and Yara may have acted on their own, but they don't deserve to die for that. If I can save them...then I'm gonna try.
To do that, I need the location of Zayan's residence. He was their last confirmed contact.
...
You're asking me to betray Cullen's trust?
If you can tell me, with *confidence*, that you can get Cullen to act, *now*, before it's too late...then I will stand aside. Otherwise, I'm asking you to help me, for Randall and Yara's sake.
If you must, you can tell Cullen that I forced the info from you. Lives are worth more than my place in this gang.
...

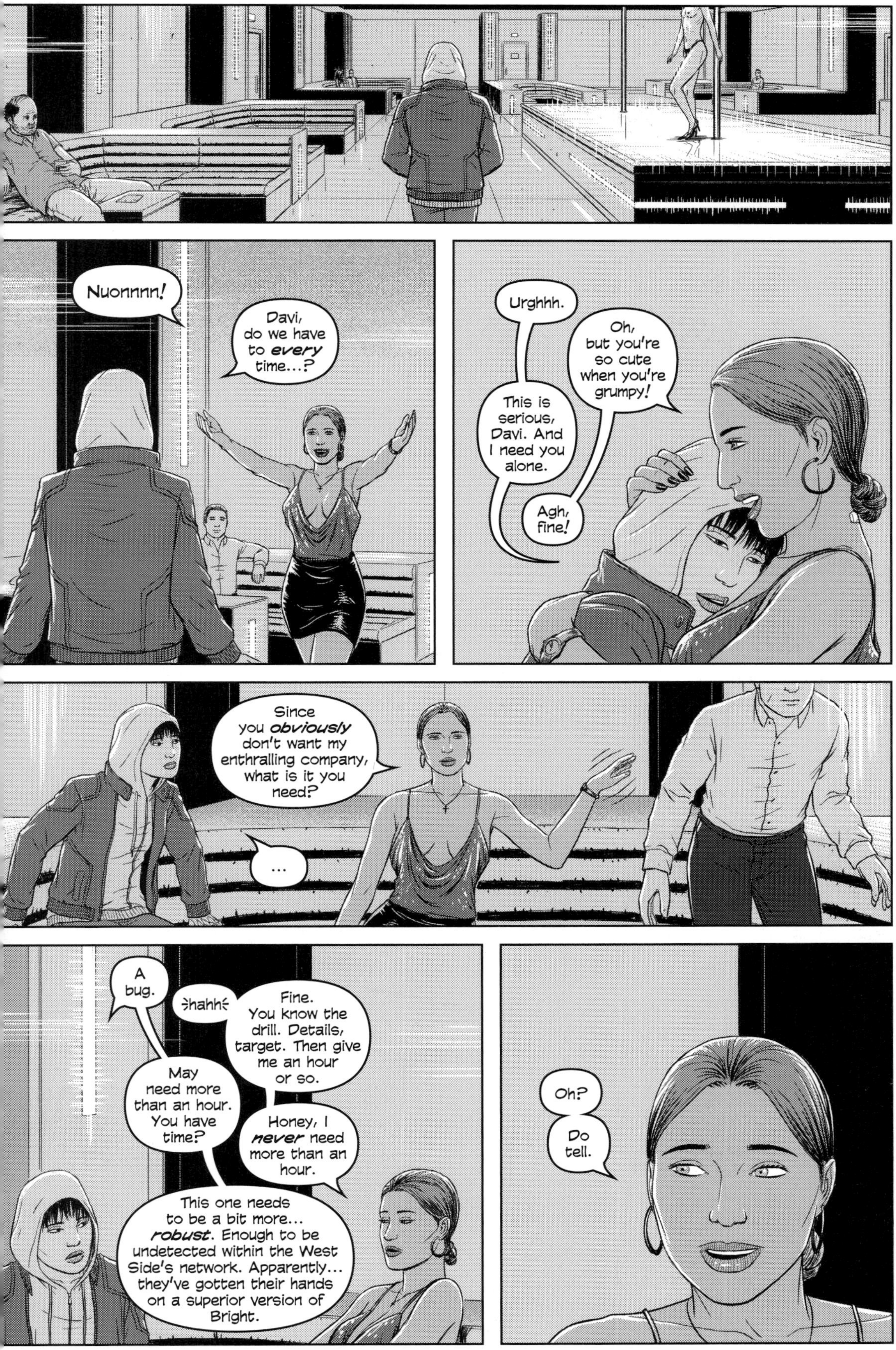

Nuonnnn!
Davi, do we have to *every* time...?
Urghhh.
This is serious, Davi. And I need you alone.
Oh, but you're so cute when you're grumpy!
Agh, fine!
Since you *obviously* don't want my enthralling company, what is it you need?
...
A bug.
≯hahh≮
Fine. You know the drill. Details, target. Then give me an hour or so.
May need more than an hour. You have time?
Honey, I *never* need more than an hour.
This one needs to be a bit more... *robust*. Enough to be undetected within the West Side's network. Apparently... they've gotten their hands on a superior version of Bright.
Oh?
Do tell.

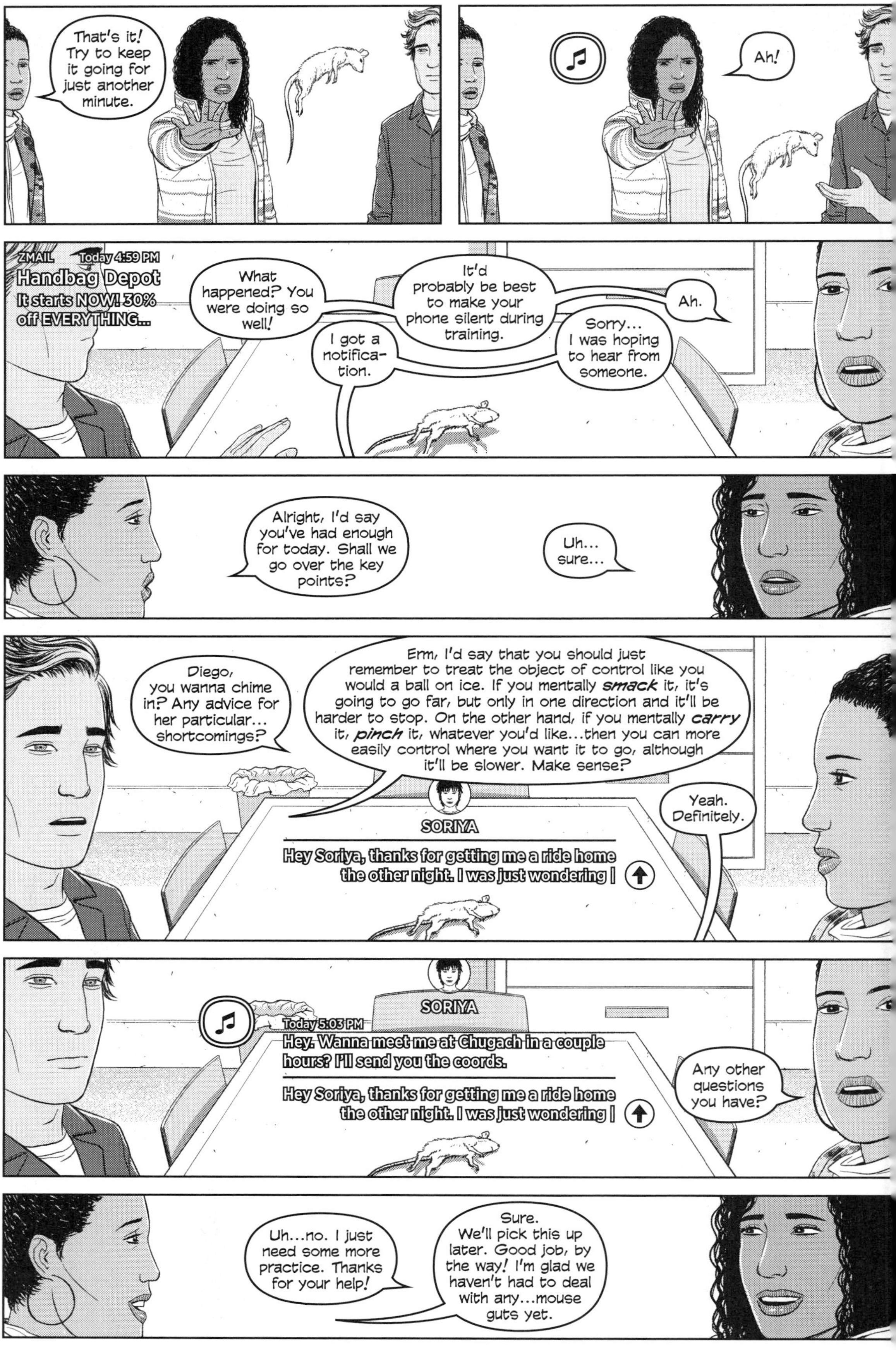

That's it! Try to keep it going for just another minute.
Ah!
ZMAIL Today 4:59 PM
Handbag Depot
It starts NOW! 30% off EVERYTHING...
What happened? You were doing so well!
I got a notification.
It'd probably be best to make your phone silent during training.
Sorry... I was hoping to hear from someone.
Ah.
Alright, I'd say you've had enough for today. Shall we go over the key points?
Uh... sure...
Diego, you wanna chime in? Any advice for her particular... shortcomings?
Erm, I'd say that you should just remember to treat the object of control like you would a ball on ice. If you mentally *smack* it, it's going to go far, but only in one direction and it'll be harder to stop. On the other hand, if you mentally *carry* it, *pinch* it, whatever you'd like...then you can more easily control where you want it to go, although it'll be slower. Make sense?
SORIYA
Hey Soriya, thanks for getting me a ride home the other night. I was just wondering |
Yeah. Definitely.
SORIYA
Today 5:03 PM
Hey. Wanna meet me at Chugach in a couple hours? I'll send you the coords.
Hey Soriya, thanks for getting me a ride home the other night. I was just wondering |
Any other questions you have?
Uh...no. I just need some more practice. Thanks for your help!
Sure. We'll pick this up later. Good job, by the way! I'm glad we haven't had to deal with any...mouse guts yet.

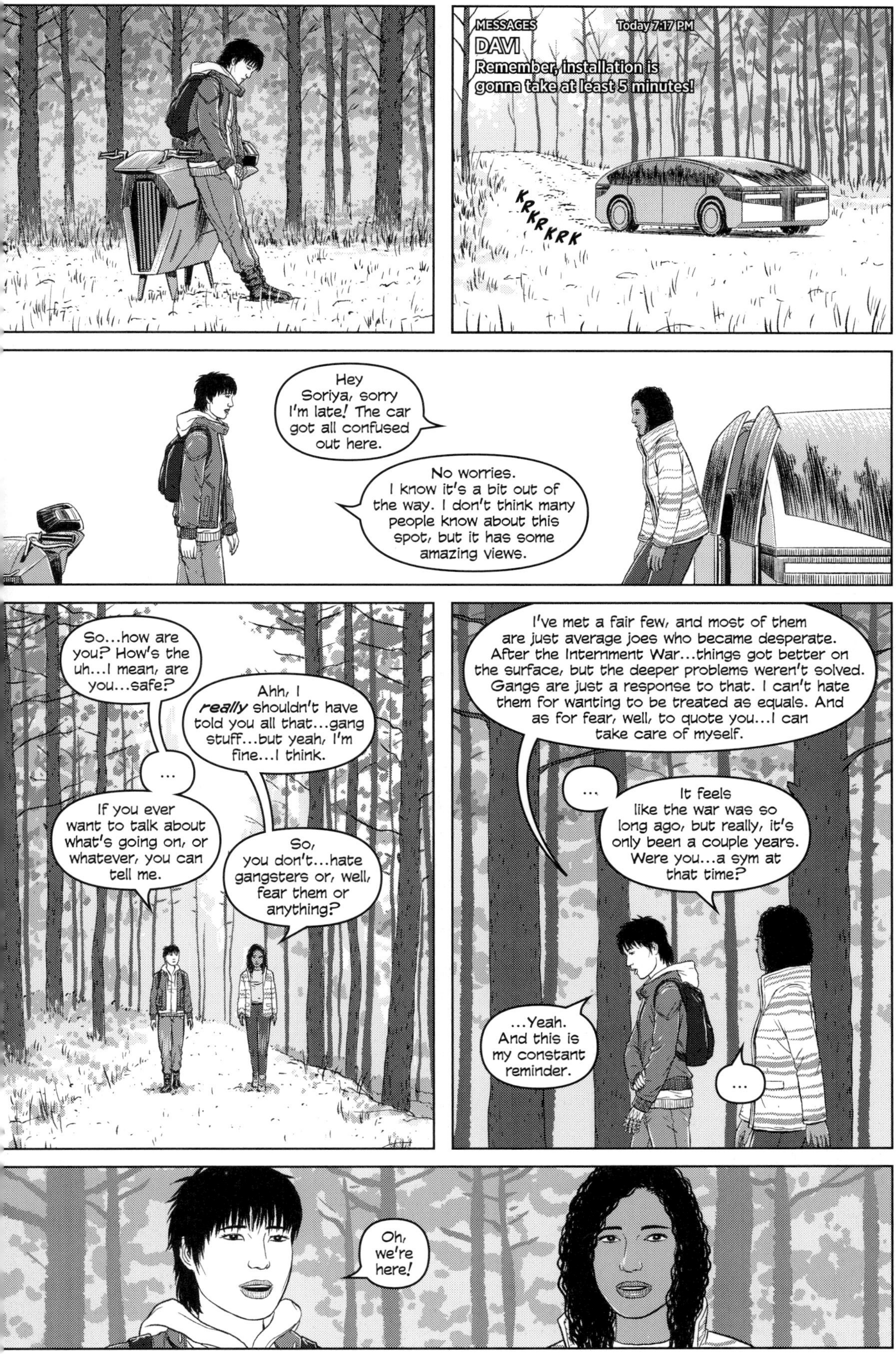
MESSAGES
Today 7:17 PM
DAVI
Remember, installation is gonna take at least 5 minutes!
KRKRKRKRK
Hey Soriya, sorry I'm late! The car got all confused out here.
No worries. I know it's a bit out of the way. I don't think many people know about this spot, but it has some amazing views.
So...how are you? How's the uh...I mean, are you...safe?
Ahh, I *really* shouldn't have told you all that...gang stuff...but yeah, I'm fine...I think.
...
If you ever want to talk about what's going on, or whatever, you can tell me.
So, you don't...hate gangsters or, well, fear them or anything?
I've met a fair few, and most of them are just average joes who became desperate. After the Internment War...things got better on the surface, but the deeper problems weren't solved. Gangs are just a response to that. I can't hate them for wanting to be treated as equals. And as for fear, well, to quote you...I can take care of myself.
...
It feels like the war was so long ago, but really, it's only been a couple years. Were you...a sym at that time?
...Yeah. And this is my constant reminder.
...
Oh, we're here!

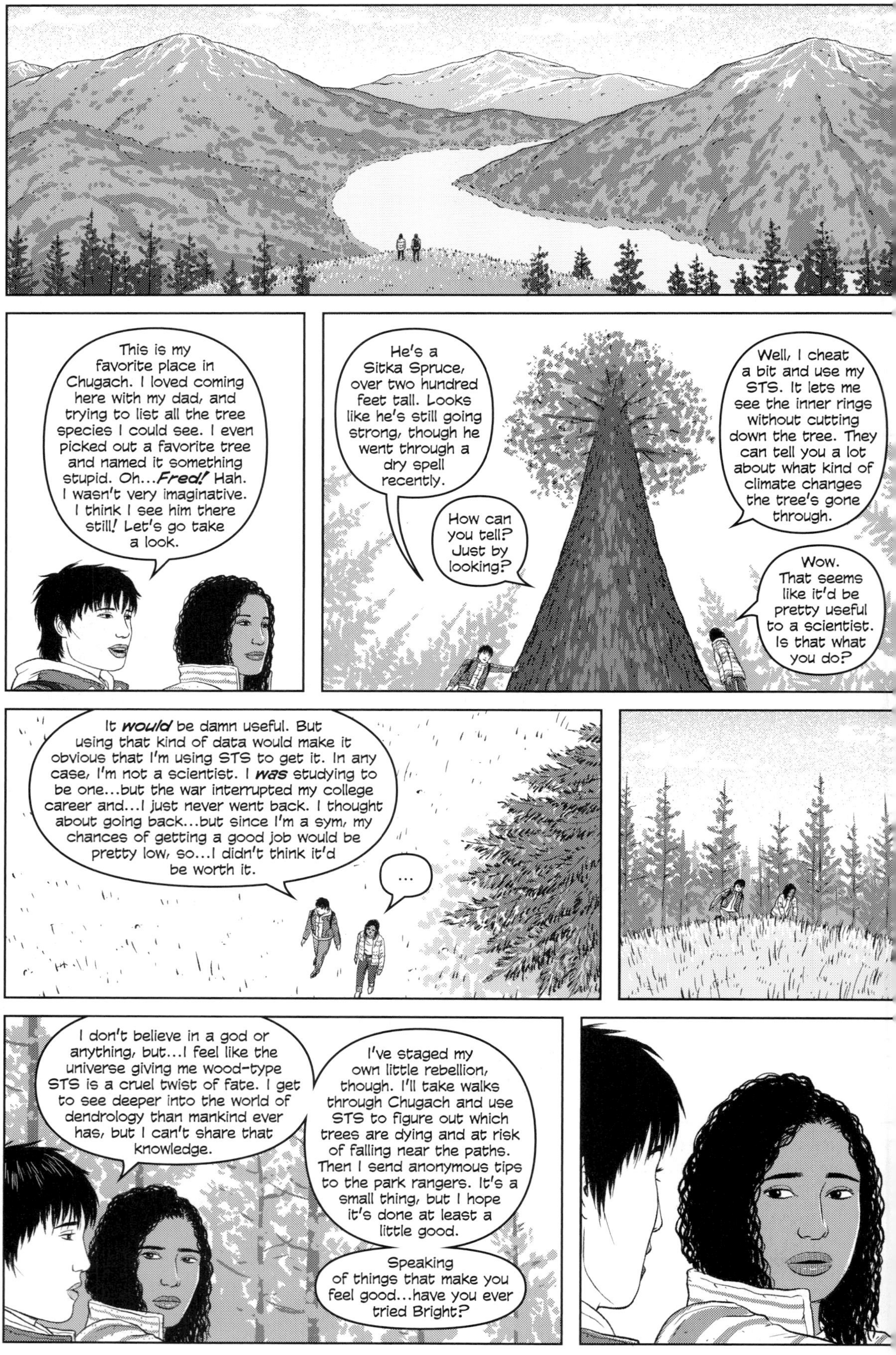

This is my favorite place in Chugach. I loved coming here with my dad, and trying to list all the tree species I could see. I even picked out a favorite tree and named it something stupid. Oh...Fred! Hah. I wasn't very imaginative. I think I see him there still! Let's go take a look.
He's a Sitka Spruce, over two hundred feet tall. Looks like he's still going strong, though he went through a dry spell recently.
How can you tell? Just by looking?
Well, I cheat a bit and use my STS. It lets me see the inner rings without cutting down the tree. They can tell you a lot about what kind of climate changes the tree's gone through.
Wow. That seems like it'd be pretty useful to a scientist. Is that what you do?
It would be damn useful. But using that kind of data would make it obvious that I'm using STS to get it. In any case, I'm not a scientist. I was studying to be one...but the war interrupted my college career and...I just never went back. I thought about going back...but since I'm a sym, my chances of getting a good job would be pretty low, so...I didn't think it'd be worth it.
...
I don't believe in a god or anything, but...I feel like the universe giving me wood-type STS is a cruel twist of fate. I get to see deeper into the world of dendrology than mankind ever has, but I can't share that knowledge.
I've staged my own little rebellion, though. I'll take walks through Chugach and use STS to figure out which trees are dying and at risk of falling near the paths. Then I send anonymous tips to the park rangers. It's a small thing, but I hope it's done at least a little good.
Speaking of things that make you feel good...have you ever tried Bright?

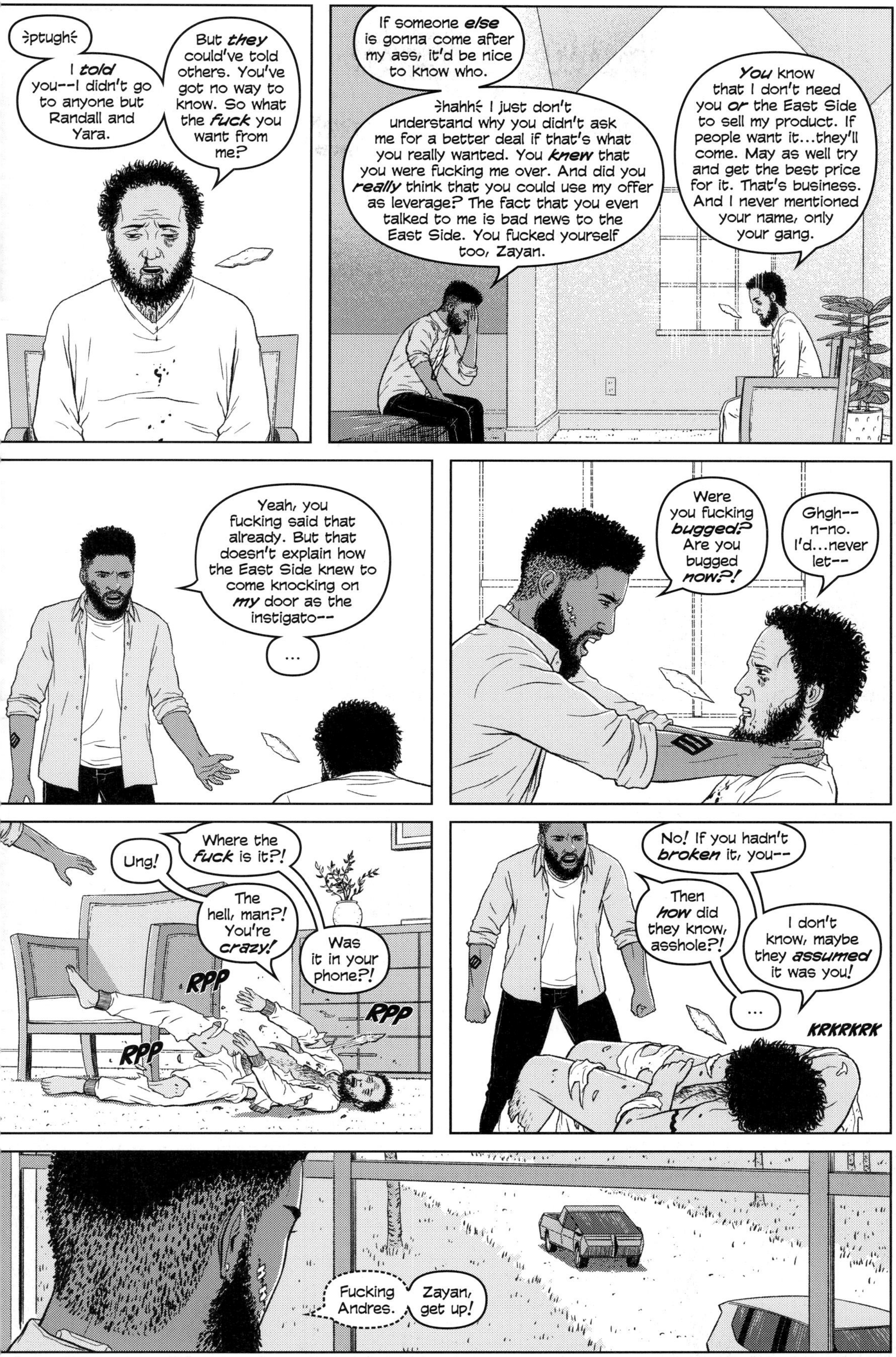

ptugh
I told you--I didn't go to anyone but Randall and Yara.
But they could've told others. You've got no way to know. So what the fuck you want from me?
If someone else is gonna come after my ass, it'd be nice to know who.
hahh I just don't understand why you didn't ask me for a better deal if that's what you really wanted. You knew that you were fucking me over. And did you really think that you could use my offer as leverage? The fact that you even talked to me is bad news to the East Side. You fucked yourself too, Zayan.
You know that I don't need you or the East Side to sell my product. If people want it...they'll come. May as well try and get the best price for it. That's business. And I never mentioned your name, only your gang.
Yeah, you fucking said that already. But that doesn't explain how the East Side knew to come knocking on my door as the instigato--
...
Were you fucking bugged? Are you bugged now?!
Ghgh--n-no. I'd...never let--
Where the fuck is it?!
Ung!
The hell, man?! You're crazy!
Was it in your phone?!
RPP
RPP
RPP
No! If you hadn't broken it, you--
Then how did they know, asshole?!
I don't know, maybe they assumed it was you!
...
KRKRKRK
Fucking Andres.
Zayan, get up!

I can sense two people in there, vaguely. Second level. Gonna have to go inside.

Wait... Holy shit, Wyatt. That's Lucas' SUV, right?

Hah. I'll be damned. Guess we won't be needing Zayan after all.

Leave the SUV to me. I brought a little *gift* for just such an occasion.

Alright. Be ready in case the asshole makes a run for it. And stay out of his telekinetic range.

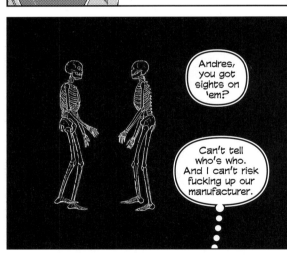

Andres, you got sights on 'em?

Can't tell who's who. And I can't risk fucking up our manufacturer.

You're coming with me, and you'd better hope that your skin is worth something to them.

VRM

What the fuck--

VRRRM

He's remoting his ride! Gonna make a jump for it!

Stop the SUV! I've got him. I--

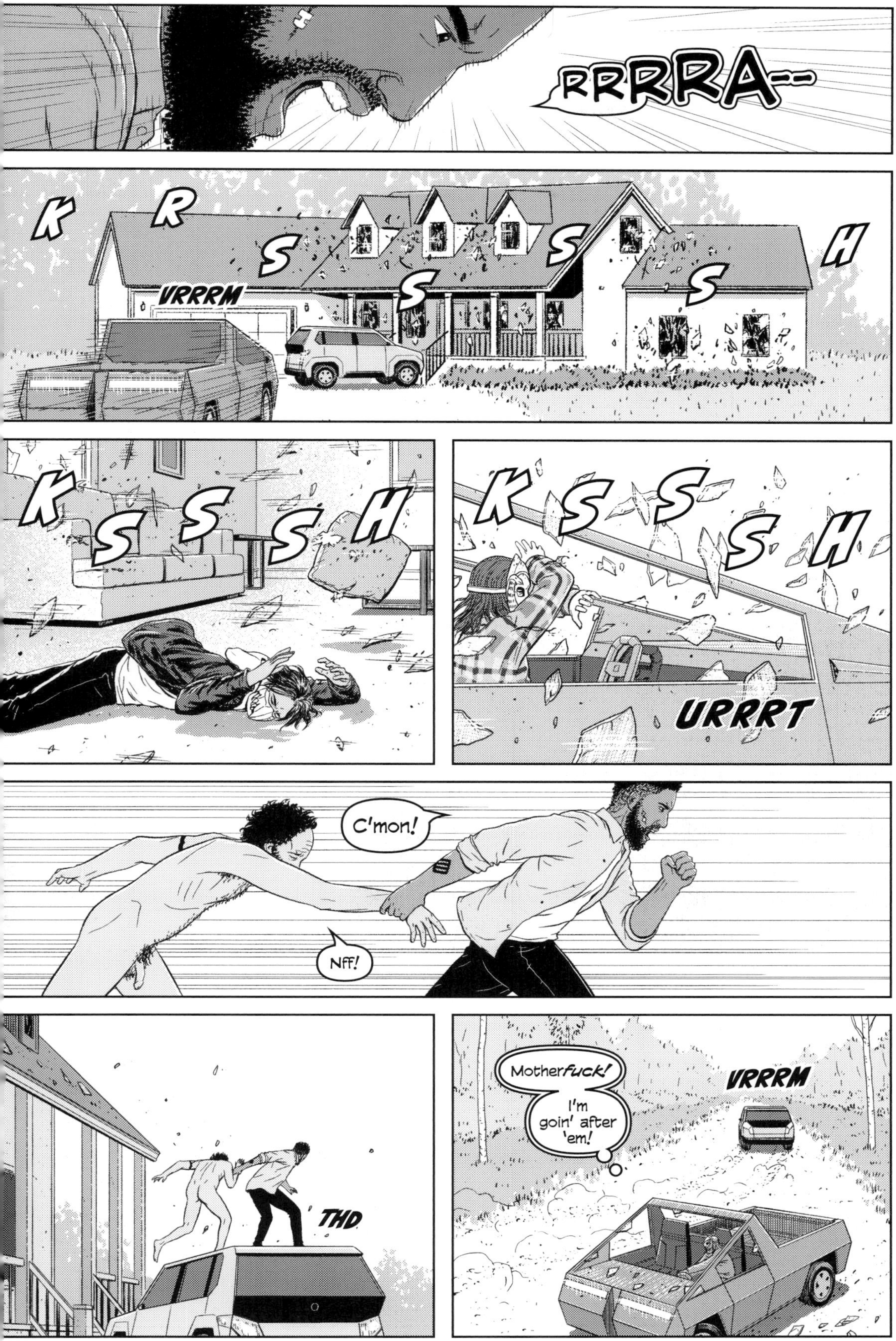
RRRRA--
K
R
VRRRM
S
S
S
S
H
K
S
S
S
H
K
S
S
S
H
URRRT
C'mon!
Nff!
THD
Motherfuck!
I'm goin' after 'em!
VRRRM

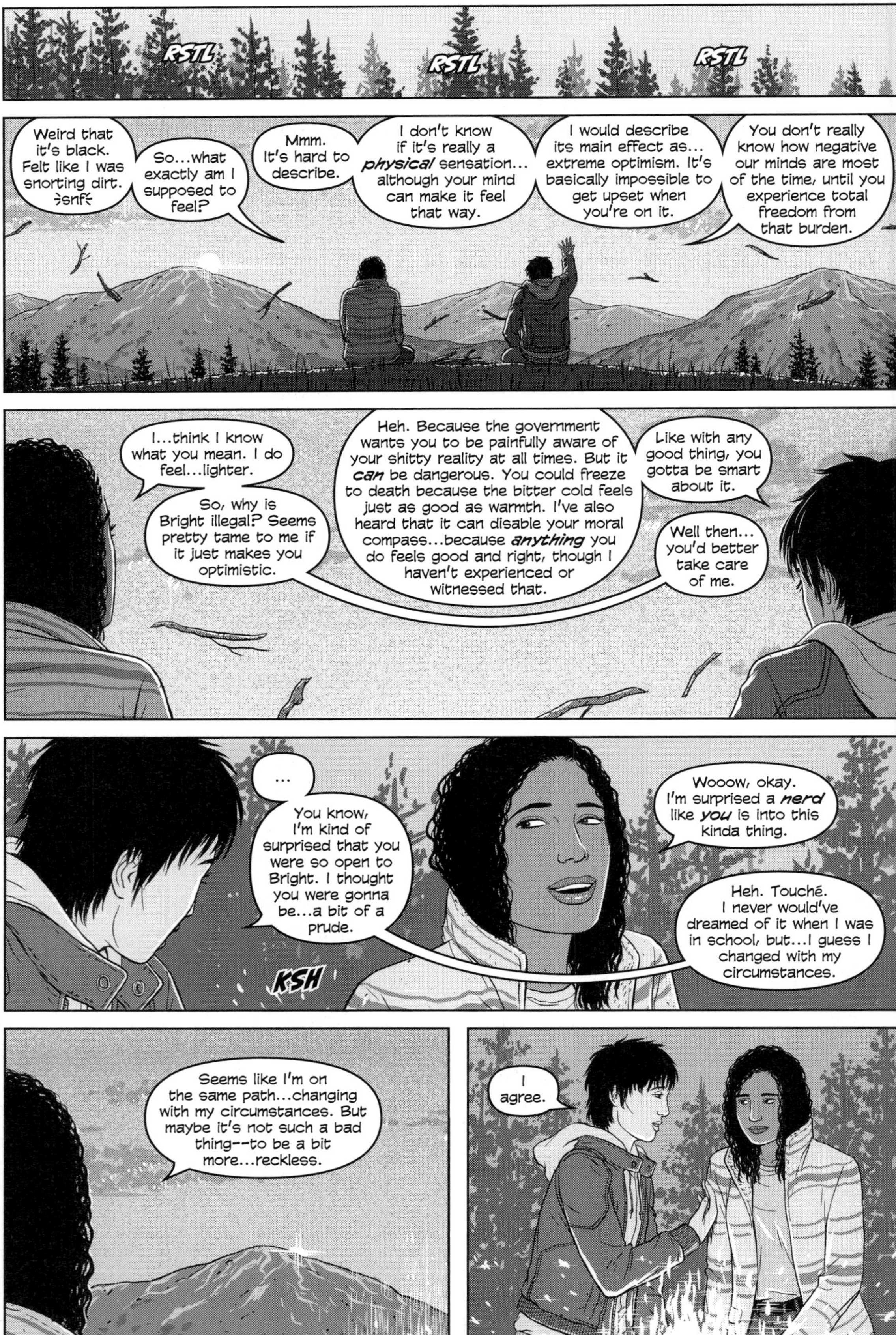
RSTL
RSTL
RSTL
Weird that it's black. Felt like I was snorting dirt. snf
So...what exactly am I supposed to feel?
Mmm. It's hard to describe.
I don't know if it's really a *physical* sensation... although your mind can make it feel that way.
I would describe its main effect as... extreme optimism. It's basically impossible to get upset when you're on it.
You don't really know how negative our minds are most of the time, until you experience total freedom from that burden.
I...think I know what you mean. I do feel...lighter.
So, why is Bright illegal? Seems pretty tame to me if it just makes you optimistic.
Heh. Because the government wants you to be painfully aware of your shitty reality at all times. But it *can* be dangerous. You could freeze to death because the bitter cold feels just as good as warmth. I've also heard that it can disable your moral compass...because *anything* you do feels good and right, though I haven't experienced or witnessed that.
Like with any good thing, you gotta be smart about it.
Well then... you'd better take care of me.
...
You know, I'm kind of surprised that you were so open to Bright. I thought you were gonna be...a bit of a prude.
Wooow, okay. I'm surprised a *nerd* like *you* is into this kinda thing.
Heh. Touché. I never would've dreamed of it when I was in school, but...I guess I changed with my circumstances.
KSH
Seems like I'm on the same path...changing with my circumstances. But maybe it's not such a bad thing--to be a bit more...reckless.
I agree.

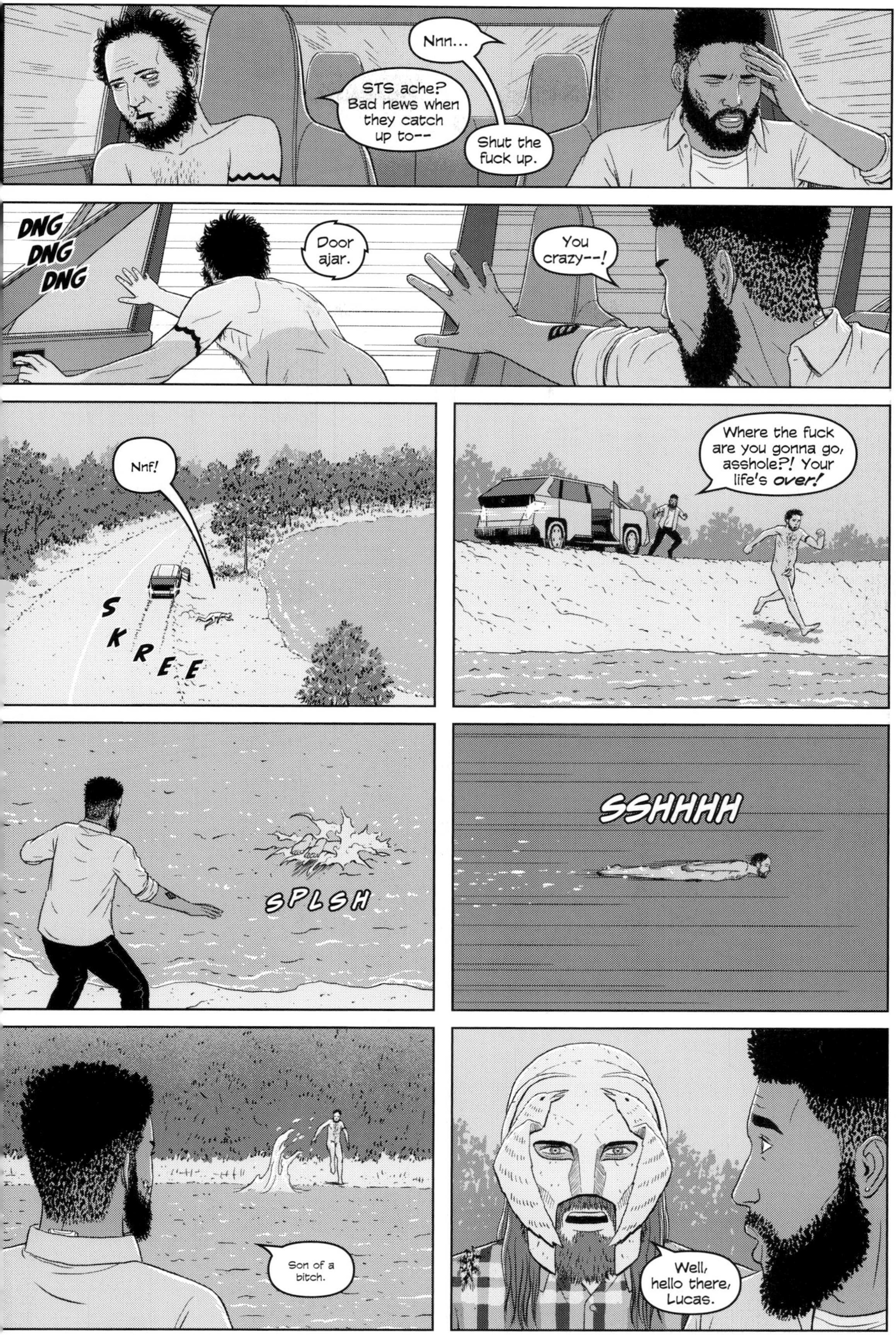

STS ache? Bad news when they catch up to--
Nnn...
Shut the fuck up.
DNG DNG DNG
Door ajar.
You crazy--!
Nnf!
SKREE
Where the fuck are you gonna go, asshole?! Your life's *over!*
SPLSH
SSHHHH
Son of a bitch.
Well, hello there, Lucas.

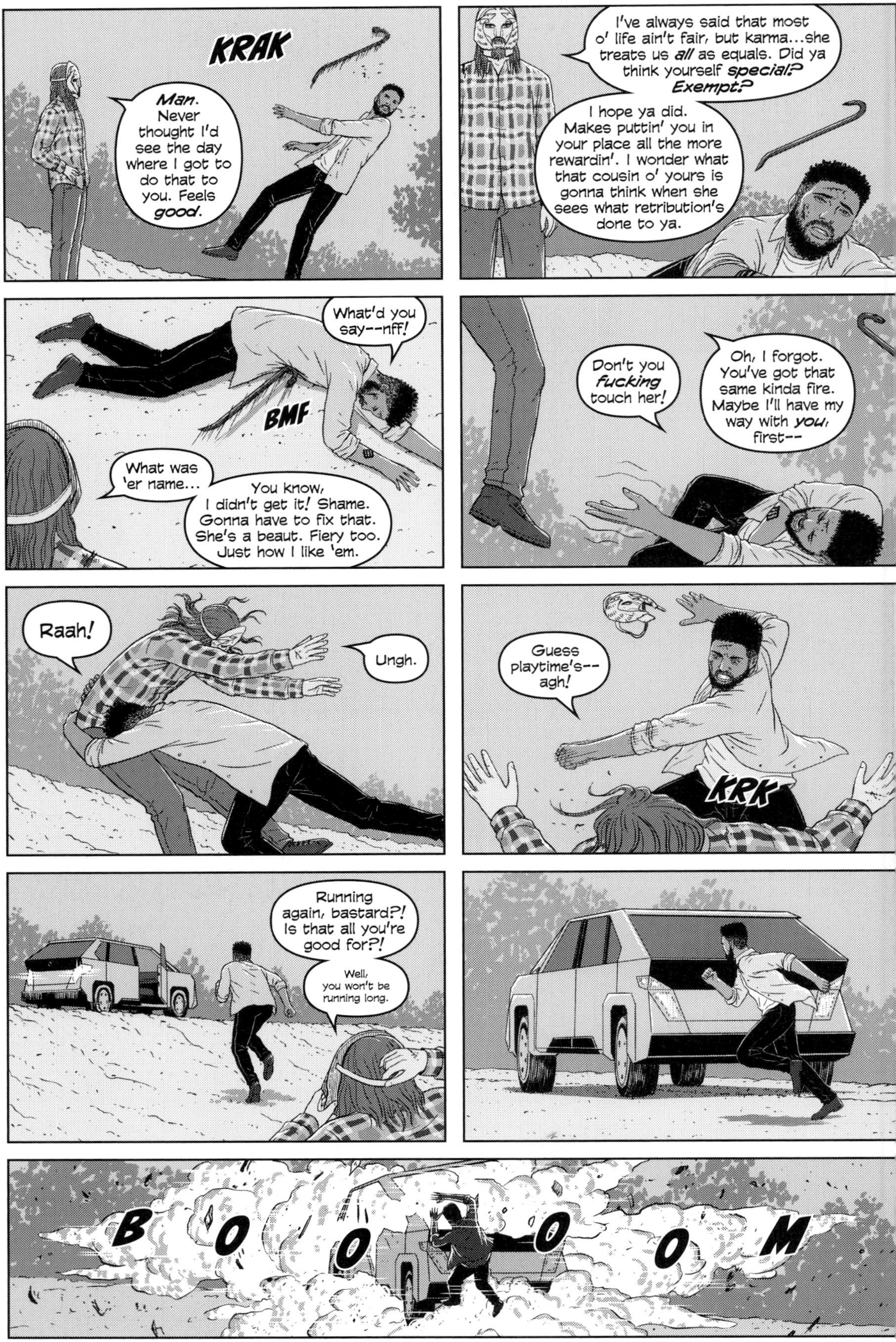
KRAK
Man. Never thought I'd see the day where I got to do that to you. Feels good.
I've always said that most o' life ain't fair, but karma...she treats us all as equals. Did ya think yourself special? Exempt?
I hope ya did. Makes puttin' you in your place all the more rewardin'. I wonder what that cousin o' yours is gonna think when she sees what retribution's done to ya.
What'd you say--nff!
BMF
What was 'er name...
You know, I didn't get it! Shame. Gonna have to fix that. She's a beaut. Fiery too. Just how I like 'em.
Don't you fucking touch her!
Oh, I forgot. You've got that same kinda fire. Maybe I'll have my way with you, first--
Raah!
Ungh.
Guess playtime's--agh!
KRK
Running again, bastard?! Is that all you're good for?!
Well, you won't be running long.
BOOOOOM

KRKL

Mmh.

≶hh≶

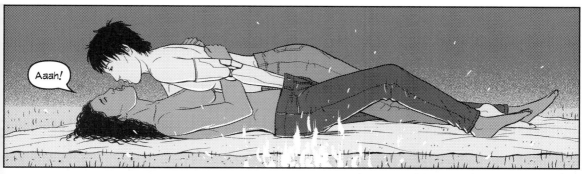

Aaah!

≶hahh≶
Do you want
me to...?

I'm
good.

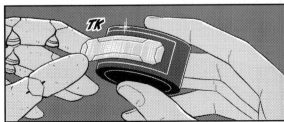

Nuons-PHN:~ nuonseng$ sudo installer -pkg /local/bd49w.pkg -blubox /
Installing bd49w.pkg... 3%

Nuons-PHN:~ nuonseng$ sudo installe
Installing bd49w.pkg... 57%

Nuons-PHN:~ nuonseng$ sudo installe
Installing bd49w.pkg... 100%
Installation complete.
Nuons-PHN:~ nuonseng$ |

Mm...?

What're you doing?

Come back to sleep.

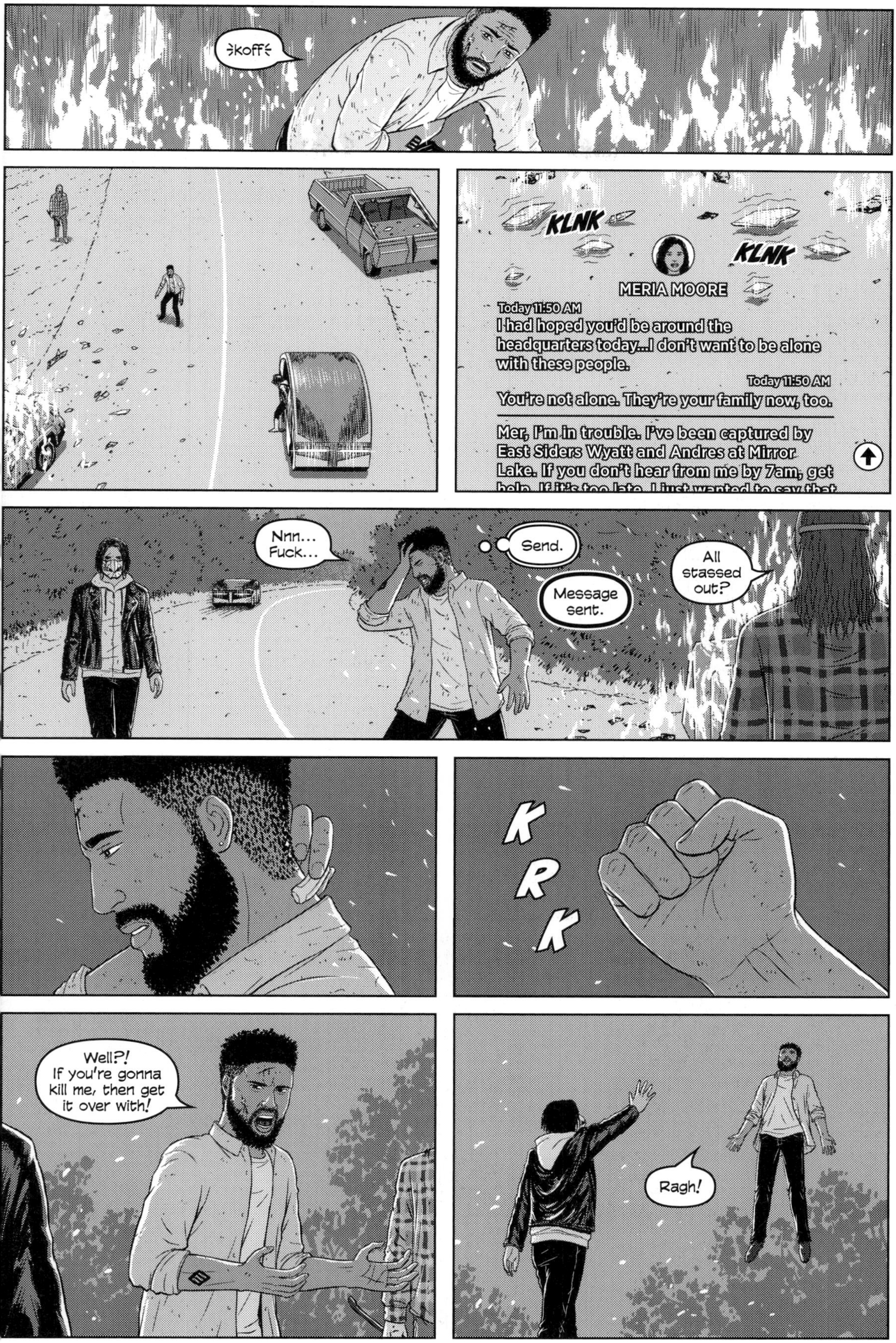

koff
KLNK
KLNK
MERIA MOORE
Today 11:50 AM
I had hoped you'd be around the headquarters today...I don't want to be alone with these people.
Today 11:50 AM
You're not alone. They're your family now, too.
Mer, I'm in trouble. I've been captured by East Siders Wyatt and Andres at Mirror Lake. If you don't hear from me by 7am, get help. If it's too late, I just wanted to say that
Nnn... Fuck...
Send.
Message sent.
All stassed out?
KRK
Well?! If you're gonna kill me, then get it over with!
Ragh!

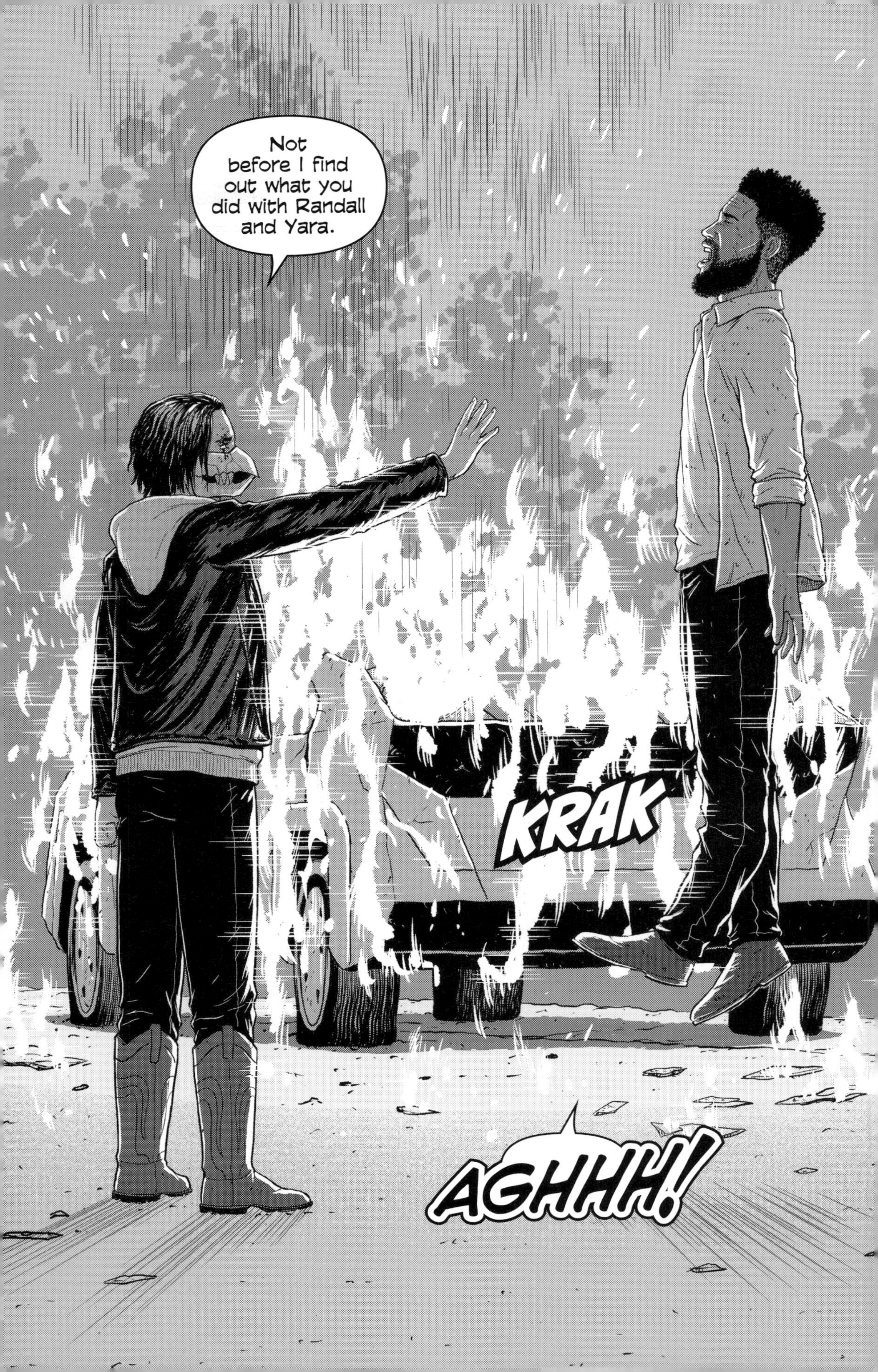
Not before I find out what you did with Randall and Yara.
KRAK
AGHHH!

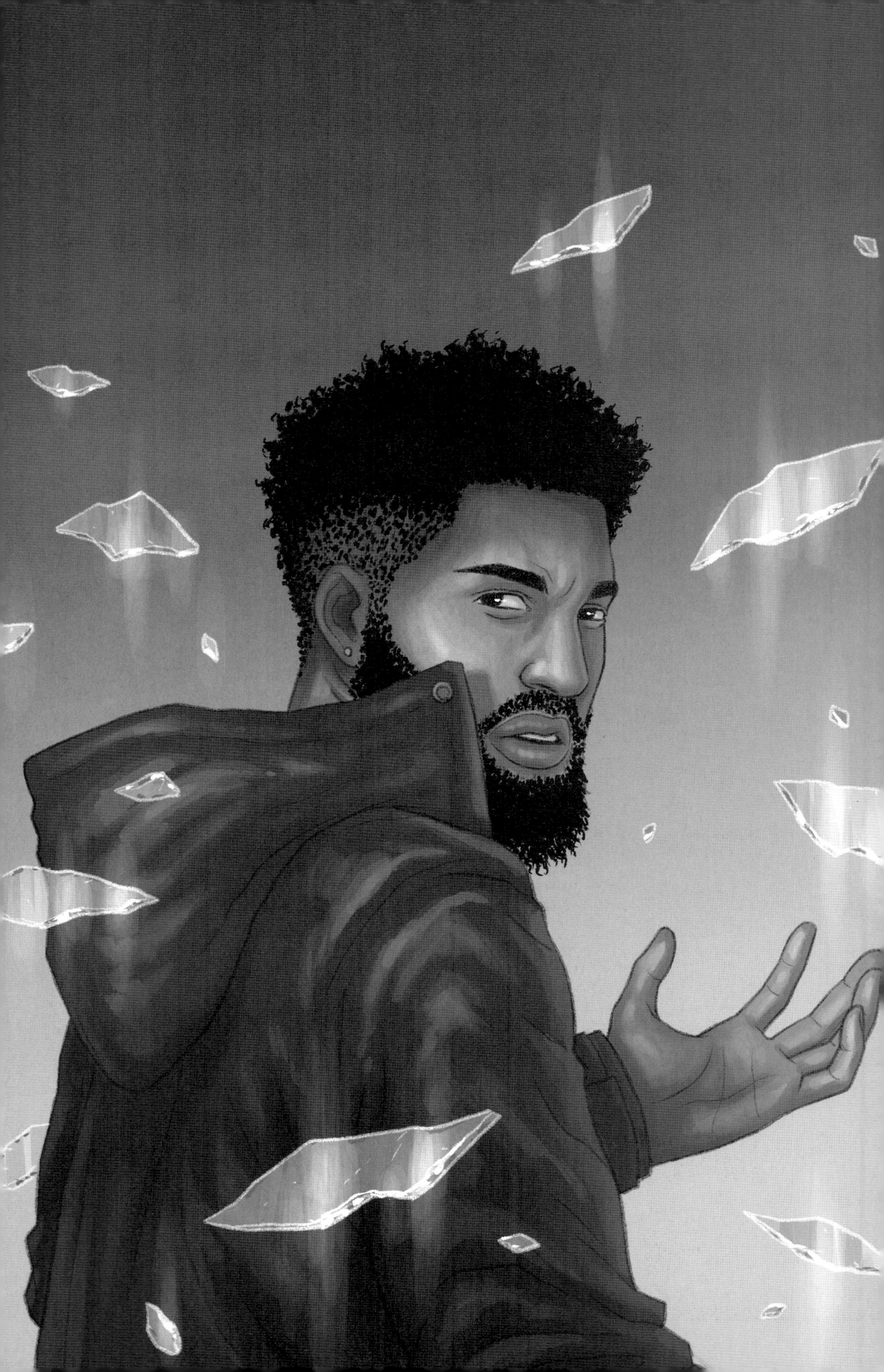

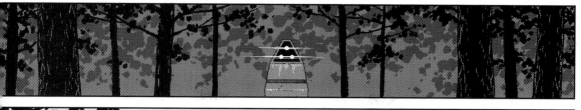

Alert!

You are camping within a no-camping zone.

It's a drog. Get dressed. Quick.

You will be issued a fine and the violation will be added to your citizen record for a period of three years. Identifying...

Identified as Nu--

KRSSH

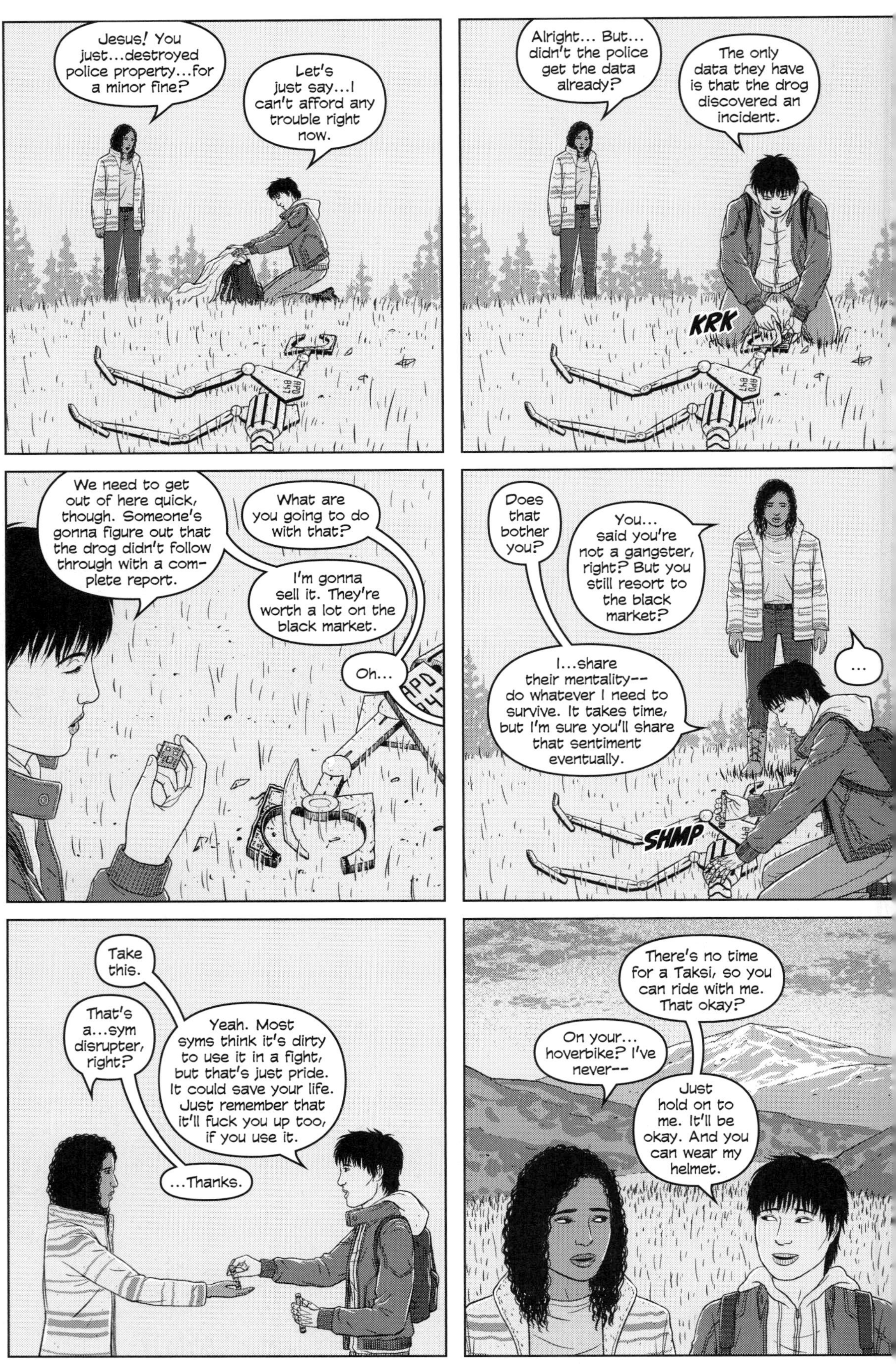
Jesus! You just...destroyed police property...for a minor fine?
Let's just say...I can't afford any trouble right now.
Alright... But... didn't the police get the data already?
The only data they have is that the drog discovered an incident.
KRK
We need to get out of here quick, though. Someone's gonna figure out that the drog didn't follow through with a complete report.
What are you going to do with that?
I'm gonna sell it. They're worth a lot on the black market.
Oh...
Does that bother you?
You... said you're not a gangster, right? But you still resort to the black market?
...
I...share their mentality-- do whatever I need to survive. It takes time, but I'm sure you'll share that sentiment eventually.
SHMP
Take this.
That's a...sym disrupter, right?
Yeah. Most syms think it's dirty to use it in a fight, but that's just pride. It could save your life. Just remember that it'll fuck you up too, if you use it.
...Thanks.
There's no time for a Taksi, so you can ride with me. That okay?
On your... hoverbike? I've never--
Just hold on to me. It'll be okay. And you can wear my helmet.

RRRHM

Not too bad, right?

Heh. Not too bad.

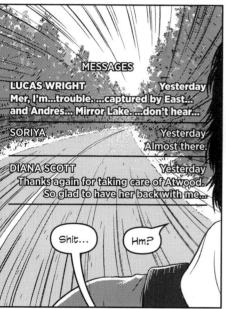

MESSAGES

LUCAS WRIGHT   Yesterday
Mer, I'm...trouble. ...captured by East...
and Andres... Mirror Lake. ...don't hear...

SORIYA   Yesterday
Almost there.

DIANA SCOTT   Yesterday
Thanks again for taking care of Atwood.
So glad to have her back with me...

Shit...

Hm?

Pull over! Please.

Everything okay?

No. Someone I know is...

KSSH

...in trouble.

LUCAS WRIGHT

Yesterday 11:34 PM
Mer, I'm...trouble. ...captured by East...and
Andres... Mirror Lake. ...don't hear from me by...
get help. If...too late, I just wanted to say that...
sorry for everything. ...know I've been selfish.
But I did miss... Hope you...forgive me.

Fuck... This message was sent almost *twelve* hours ago! The notification should have woken me up! But it looks like it got...corrupted or something...

Oh... Um, anything I can do?

Can you... drop me off somewhere? I can send you the location.

Sure. Whatever you need.

Thanks, Soriya.

Call Tendai.

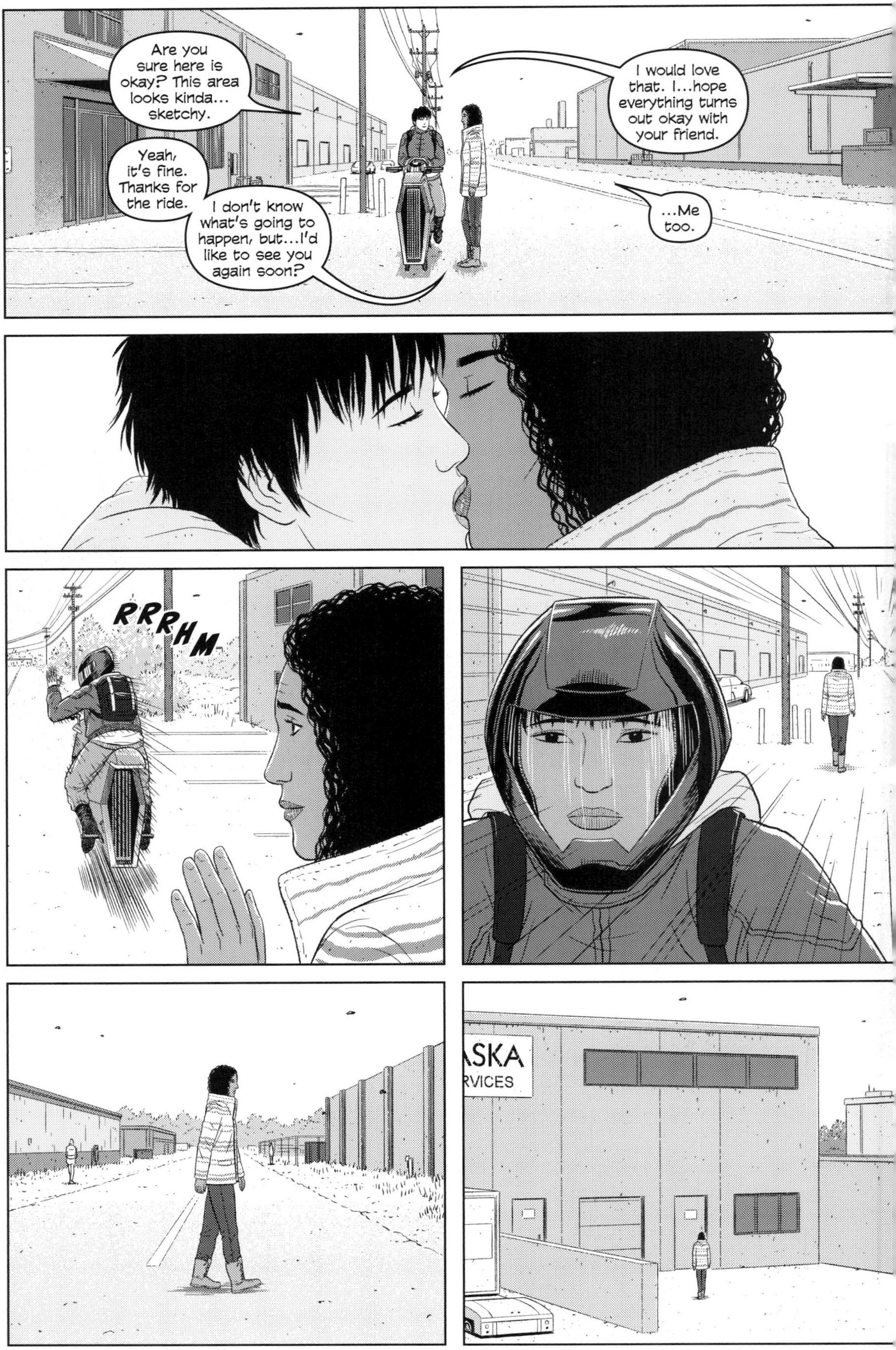
Are you sure here is okay? This area looks kinda... sketchy.
Yeah, it's fine. Thanks for the ride.
I don't know what's going to happen, but...I'd like to see you again soon?
I would love that. I...hope everything turns out okay with your friend.
...Me too.
RRRHM
ASKA
RVICES

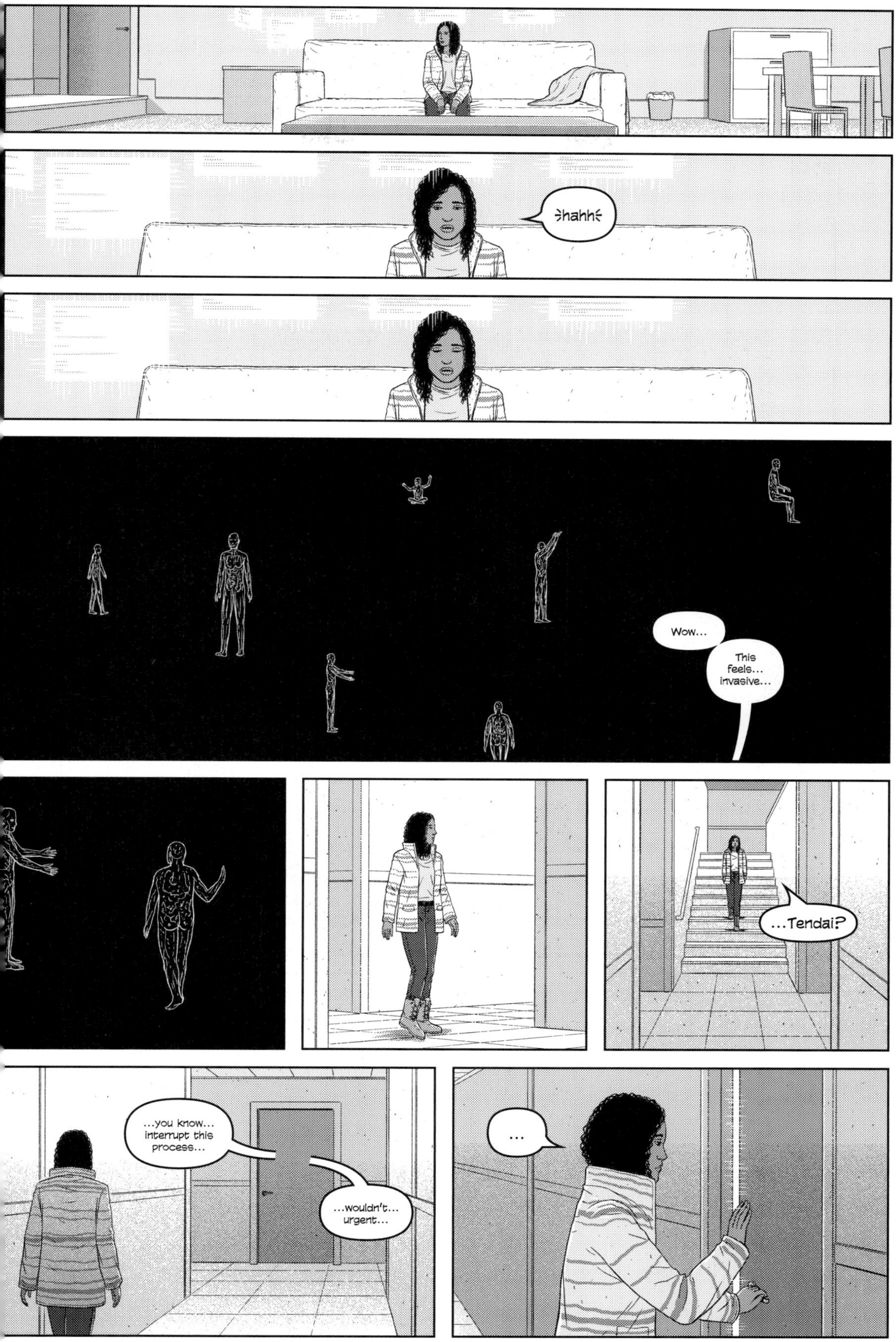
hahh
Wow...
This feels... invasive...
...Tendai?
...you know... interrupt this process...
...wouldn't... urgent...
...

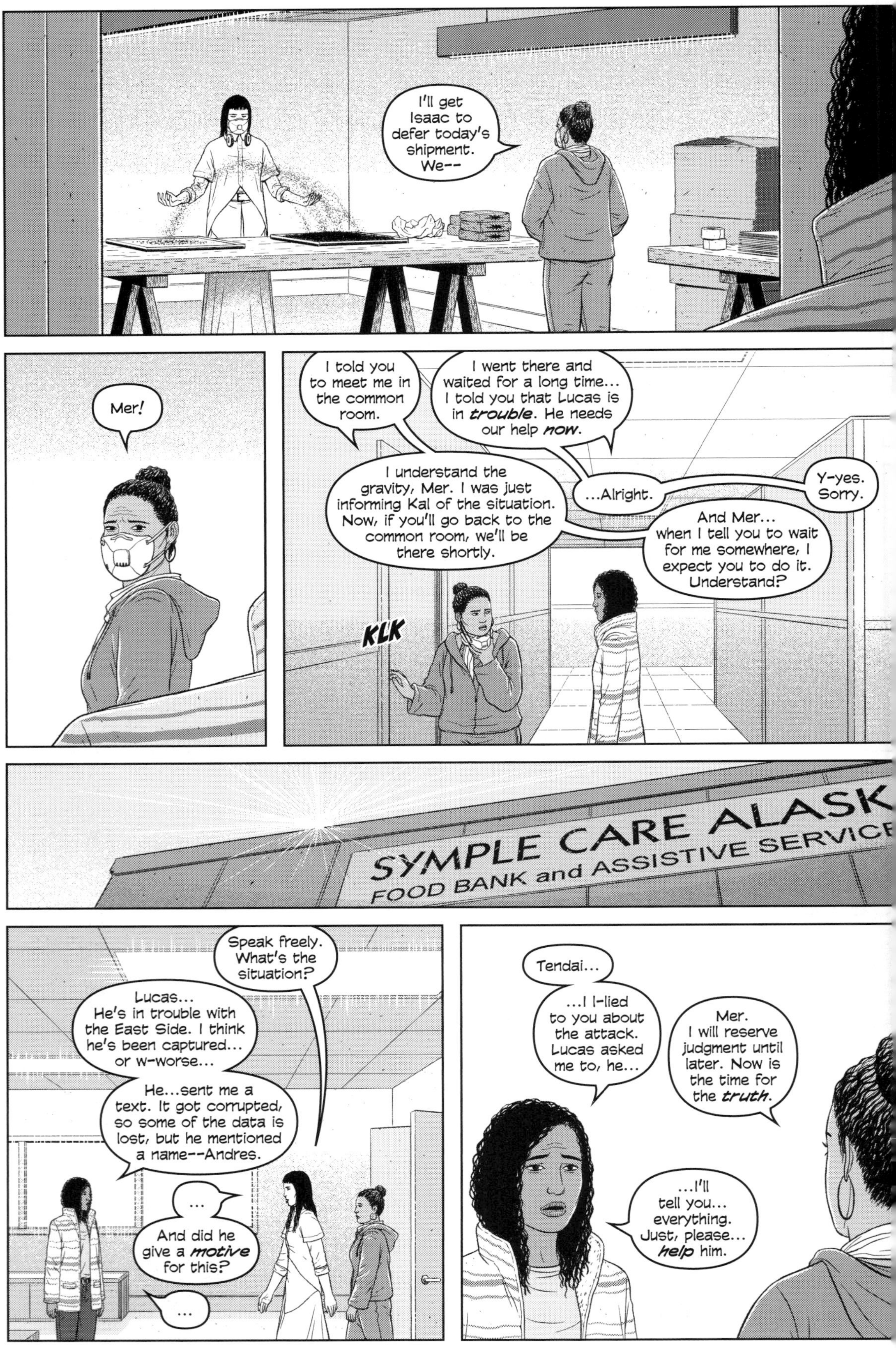
I'll get Isaac to defer today's shipment. We--
Mer!
I told you to meet me in the common room.
I went there and waited for a long time... I told you that Lucas is in *trouble*. He needs our help *now*.
I understand the gravity, Mer. I was just informing Kal of the situation. Now, if you'll go back to the common room, we'll be there shortly.
...Alright.
Y-yes. Sorry.
And Mer... when I tell you to wait for me somewhere, I expect you to do it. Understand?
KLK
SYMPLE CARE ALASK
FOOD BANK and ASSISTIVE SERVIC
Speak freely. What's the situation?
Lucas... He's in trouble with the East Side. I think he's been captured... or w-worse...
He...sent me a text. It got corrupted, so some of the data is lost, but he mentioned a name--Andres.
...
And did he give a *motive* for this?
...
Tendai...
...I l-lied to you about the attack. Lucas asked me to, he...
Mer. I will reserve judgment until later. Now is the time for the *truth*.
...I'll tell you... everything. Just, please... *help* him.

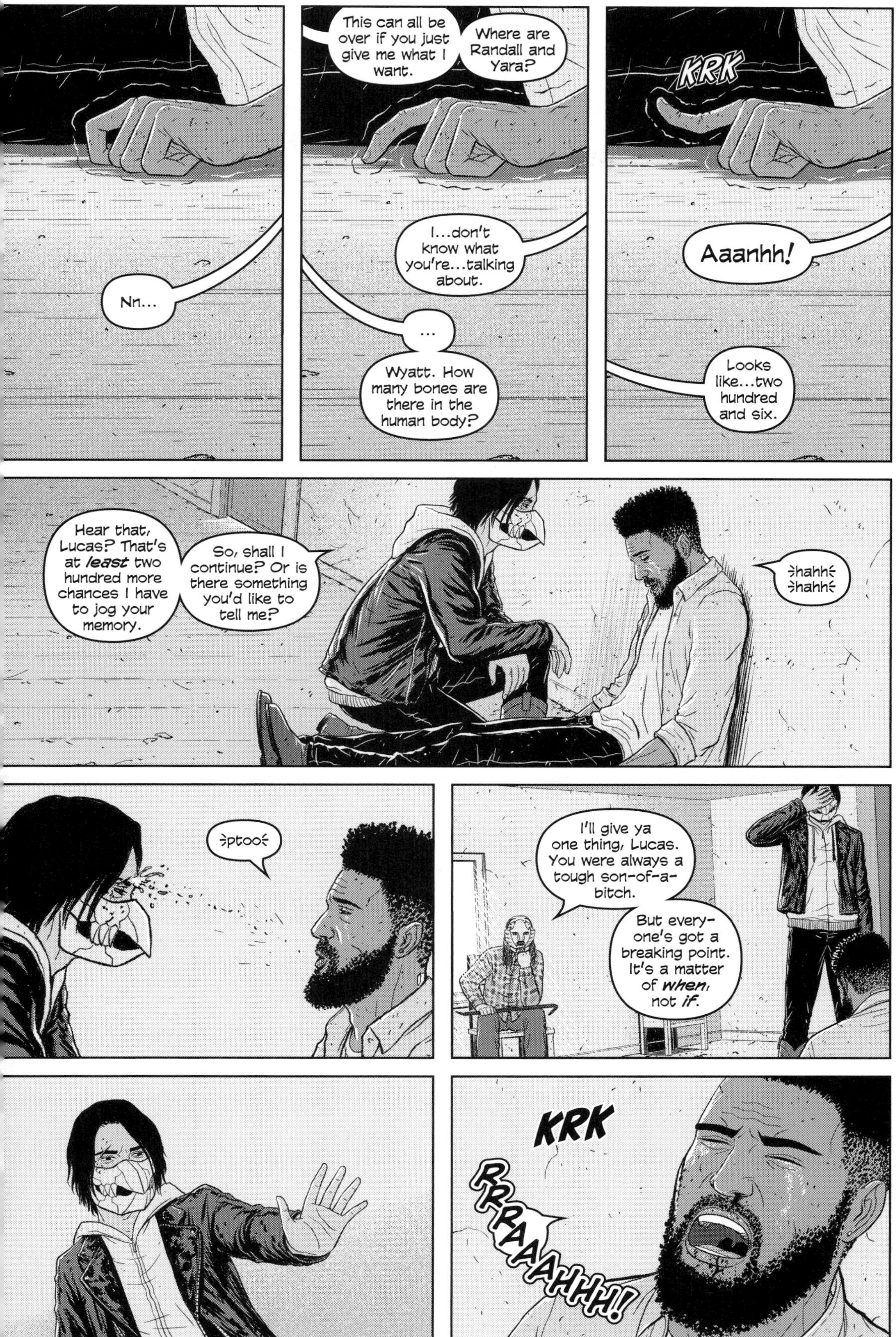
Nn...
This can all be over if you just give me what I want.
Where are Randall and Yara?
I...don't know what you're...talking about.
...
Wyatt. How many bones are there in the human body?
KRK
Aaanhh!
Looks like...two hundred and six.
Hear that, Lucas? That's at *least* two hundred more chances I have to jog your memory.
So, shall I continue? Or is there something you'd like to tell me?
hahh hahh
ptoo
I'll give ya one thing, Lucas. You were always a tough son-of-a-bitch.
But every-one's got a breaking point. It's a matter of *when*, not *if*.
KRK
RRRAAAHHH!

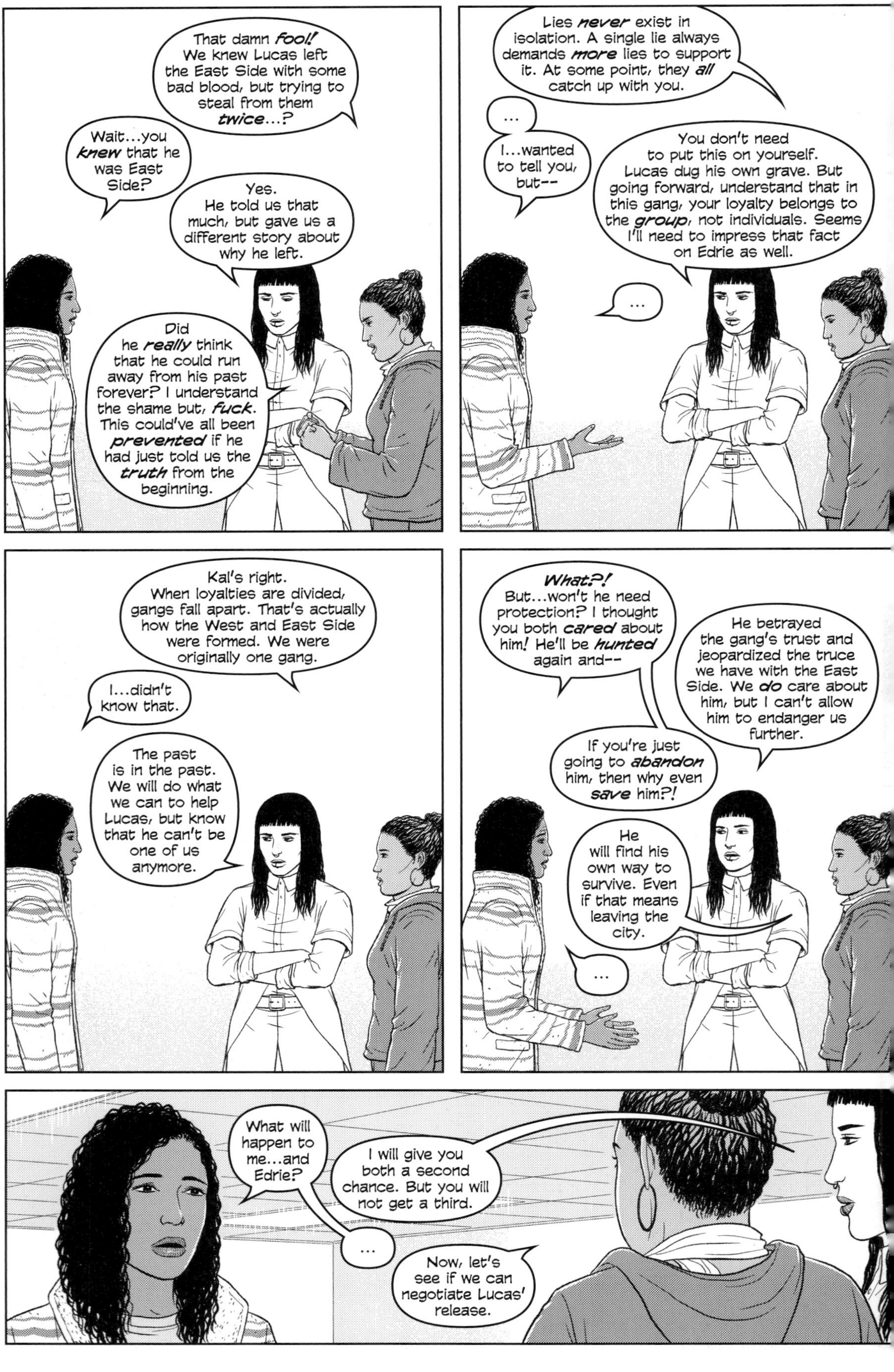
That damn *fool!* We knew Lucas left the East Side with some bad blood, but trying to steal from them *twice*...?
Wait...you *knew* that he was East Side?
Yes. He told us that much, but gave us a different story about why he left.
Did he *really* think that he could run away from his past forever? I understand the shame but, *fuck*. This could've all been *prevented* if he had just told us the *truth* from the beginning.
Lies *never* exist in isolation. A single lie always demands *more* lies to support it. At some point, they *all* catch up with you.
...
I...wanted to tell you, but--
You don't need to put this on yourself. Lucas dug his own grave. But going forward, understand that in this gang, your loyalty belongs to the *group*, not individuals. Seems I'll need to impress that fact on Edrie as well.
...
Kal's right. When loyalties are divided, gangs fall apart. That's actually how the West and East Side were formed. We were originally one gang.
I...didn't know that.
The past is in the past. We will do what we can to help Lucas, but know that he can't be one of us anymore.
What?! But...won't he need protection? I thought you both *cared* about him! He'll be *hunted* again and--
He betrayed the gang's trust and jeopardized the truce we have with the East Side. We *do* care about him, but I can't allow him to endanger us further.
If you're just going to *abandon* him, then why even *save* him?!
He will find his own way to survive. Even if that means leaving the city.
...
What will happen to me...and Edrie?
I will give you both a second chance. But you will not get a third.
...
Now, let's see if we can negotiate Lucas' release.

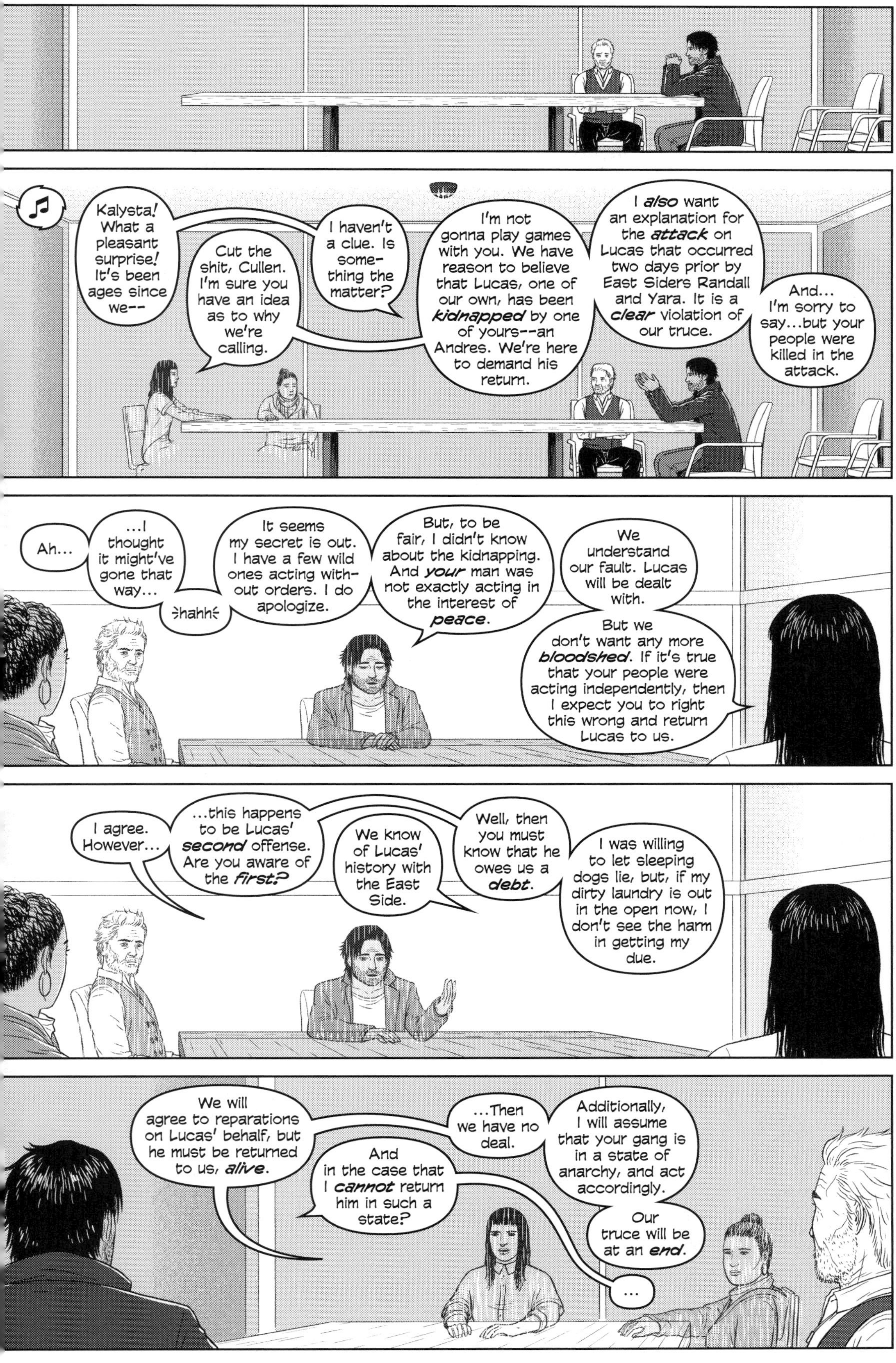

Kalysta! What a pleasant surprise! It's been ages since we--
Cut the shit, Cullen. I'm sure you have an idea as to why we're calling.
I haven't a clue. Is something the matter?
I'm not gonna play games with you. We have reason to believe that Lucas, one of our own, has been kidnapped by one of yours--an Andres. We're here to demand his return.
I also want an explanation for the attack on Lucas that occurred two days prior by East Siders Randall and Yara. It is a clear violation of our truce.
And... I'm sorry to say...but your people were killed in the attack.
Ah...
...I thought it might've gone that way...
hahh
It seems my secret is out. I have a few wild ones acting without orders. I do apologize.
But, to be fair, I didn't know about the kidnapping. And your man was not exactly acting in the interest of peace.
We understand our fault. Lucas will be dealt with.
But we don't want any more bloodshed. If it's true that your people were acting independently, then I expect you to right this wrong and return Lucas to us.
I agree. However...
...this happens to be Lucas' second offense. Are you aware of the first?
We know of Lucas' history with the East Side.
Well, then you must know that he owes us a debt.
I was willing to let sleeping dogs lie, but, if my dirty laundry is out in the open now, I don't see the harm in getting my due.
We will agree to reparations on Lucas' behalf, but he must be returned to us, alive.
And in the case that I cannot return him in such a state?
...Then we have no deal.
Additionally, I will assume that your gang is in a state of anarchy, and act accordingly.
Our truce will be at an end.
...

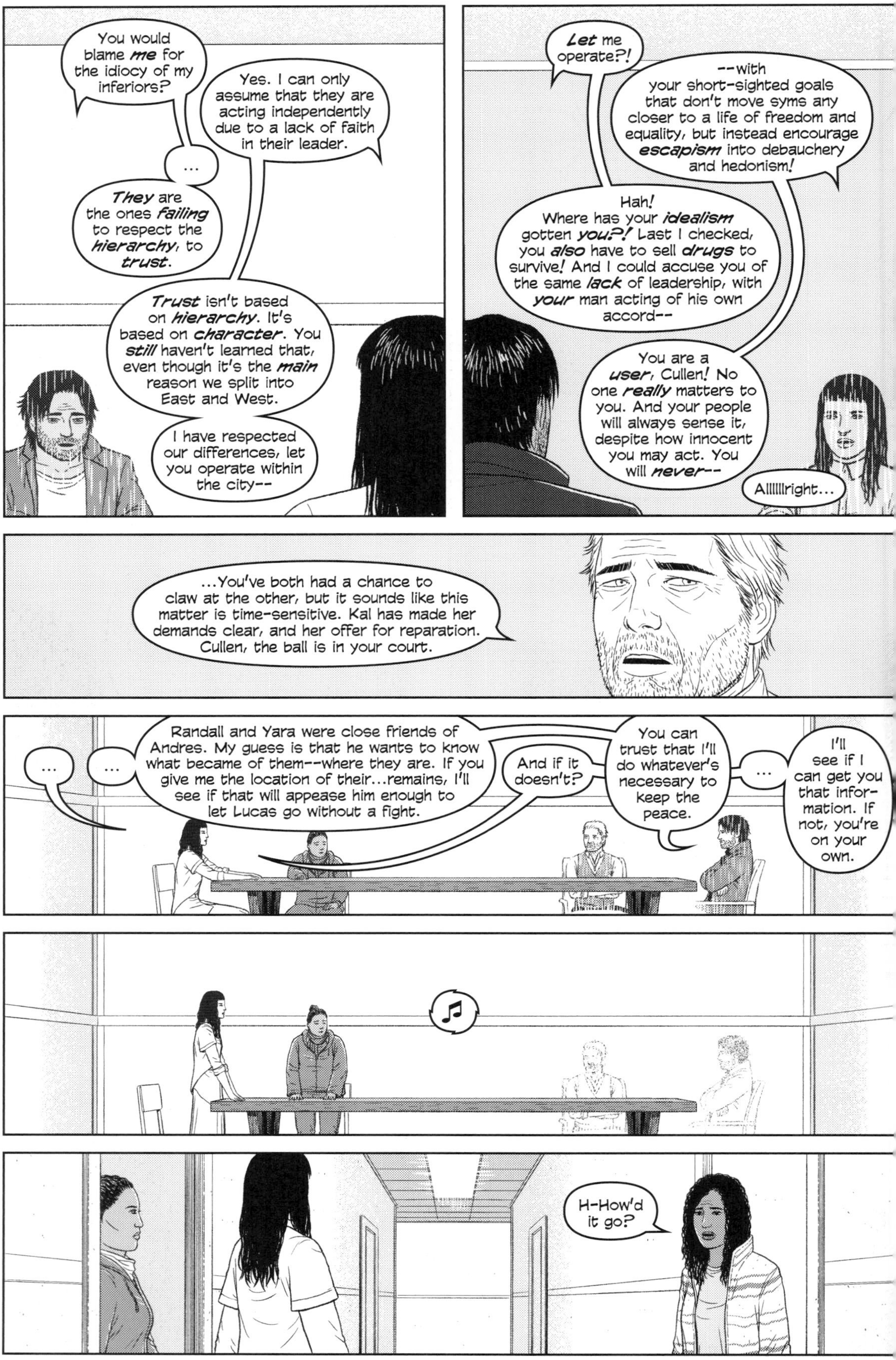
You would blame *me* for the idiocy of my inferiors?
Yes. I can only assume that they are acting independently due to a lack of faith in their leader.
...
They are the ones *failing* to respect the *hierarchy*, to *trust*.
Trust isn't based on *hierarchy*. It's based on *character*. You *still* haven't learned that, even though it's the *main* reason we split into East and West.
I have respected our differences, let you operate within the city--
Let me operate?!
--with your short-sighted goals that don't move syms any closer to a life of freedom and equality, but instead encourage *escapism* into debauchery and hedonism!
Hah! Where has your *idealism* gotten *you?!* Last I checked, you *also* have to sell *drugs* to survive! And I could accuse you of the same *lack* of leadership, with *your* man acting of his own accord--
You are a *user*, Cullen! No one *really* matters to you. And your people will always sense it, despite how innocent you may act. You will *never*--
Allllllright...
...You've both had a chance to claw at the other, but it sounds like this matter is time-sensitive. Kal has made her demands clear, and her offer for reparation. Cullen, the ball is in your court.
...
...
Randall and Yara were close friends of Andres. My guess is that he wants to know what became of them--where they are. If you give me the location of their...remains, I'll see if that will appease him enough to let Lucas go without a fight.
And if it doesn't?
You can trust that I'll do whatever's necessary to keep the peace.
...
I'll see if I can get you that information. If not, you're on your own.
H-How'd it go?

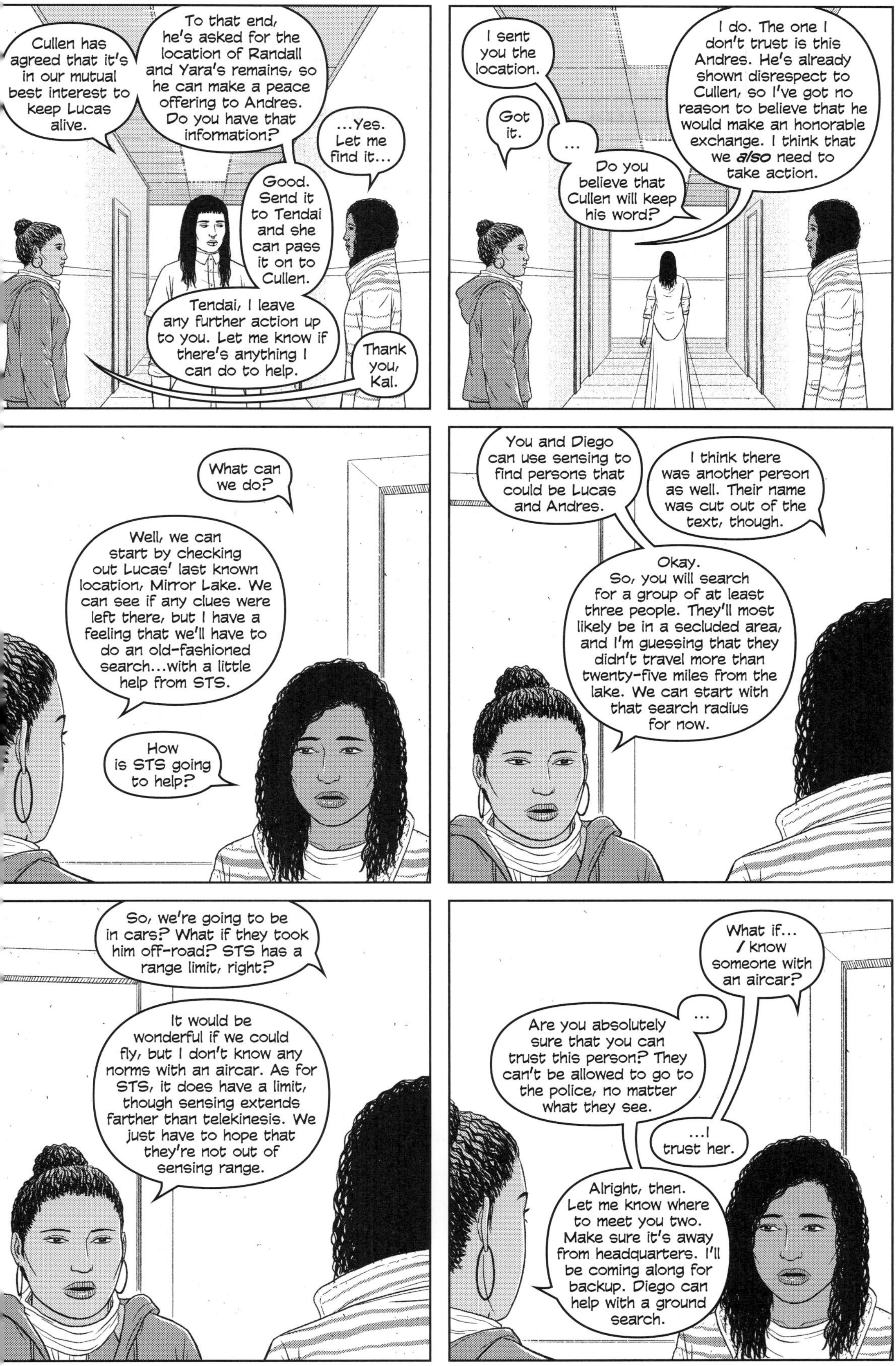
Cullen has agreed that it's in our mutual best interest to keep Lucas alive.
To that end, he's asked for the location of Randall and Yara's remains, so he can make a peace offering to Andres. Do you have that information?
...Yes. Let me find it...
Good. Send it to Tendai and she can pass it on to Cullen.
Tendai, I leave any further action up to you. Let me know if there's anything I can do to help.
Thank you, Kal.
I sent you the location.
Got it.
...
Do you believe that Cullen will keep his word?
I do. The one I don't trust is this Andres. He's already shown disrespect to Cullen, so I've got no reason to believe that he would make an honorable exchange. I think that we *also* need to take action.
What can we do?
Well, we can start by checking out Lucas' last known location, Mirror Lake. We can see if any clues were left there, but I have a feeling that we'll have to do an old-fashioned search...with a little help from STS.
How is STS going to help?
You and Diego can use sensing to find persons that could be Lucas and Andres.
I think there was another person as well. Their name was cut out of the text, though.
Okay. So, you will search for a group of at least three people. They'll most likely be in a secluded area, and I'm guessing that they didn't travel more than twenty-five miles from the lake. We can start with that search radius for now.
So, we're going to be in cars? What if they took him off-road? STS has a range limit, right?
It would be wonderful if we could fly, but I don't know any norms with an aircar. As for STS, it does have a limit, though sensing extends farther than telekinesis. We just have to hope that they're not out of sensing range.
What if... *I* know someone with an aircar?
...
Are you absolutely sure that you can trust this person? They can't be allowed to go to the police, no matter what they see.
...I trust her.
Alright, then. Let me know where to meet you two. Make sure it's away from headquarters. I'll be coming along for backup. Diego can help with a ground search.

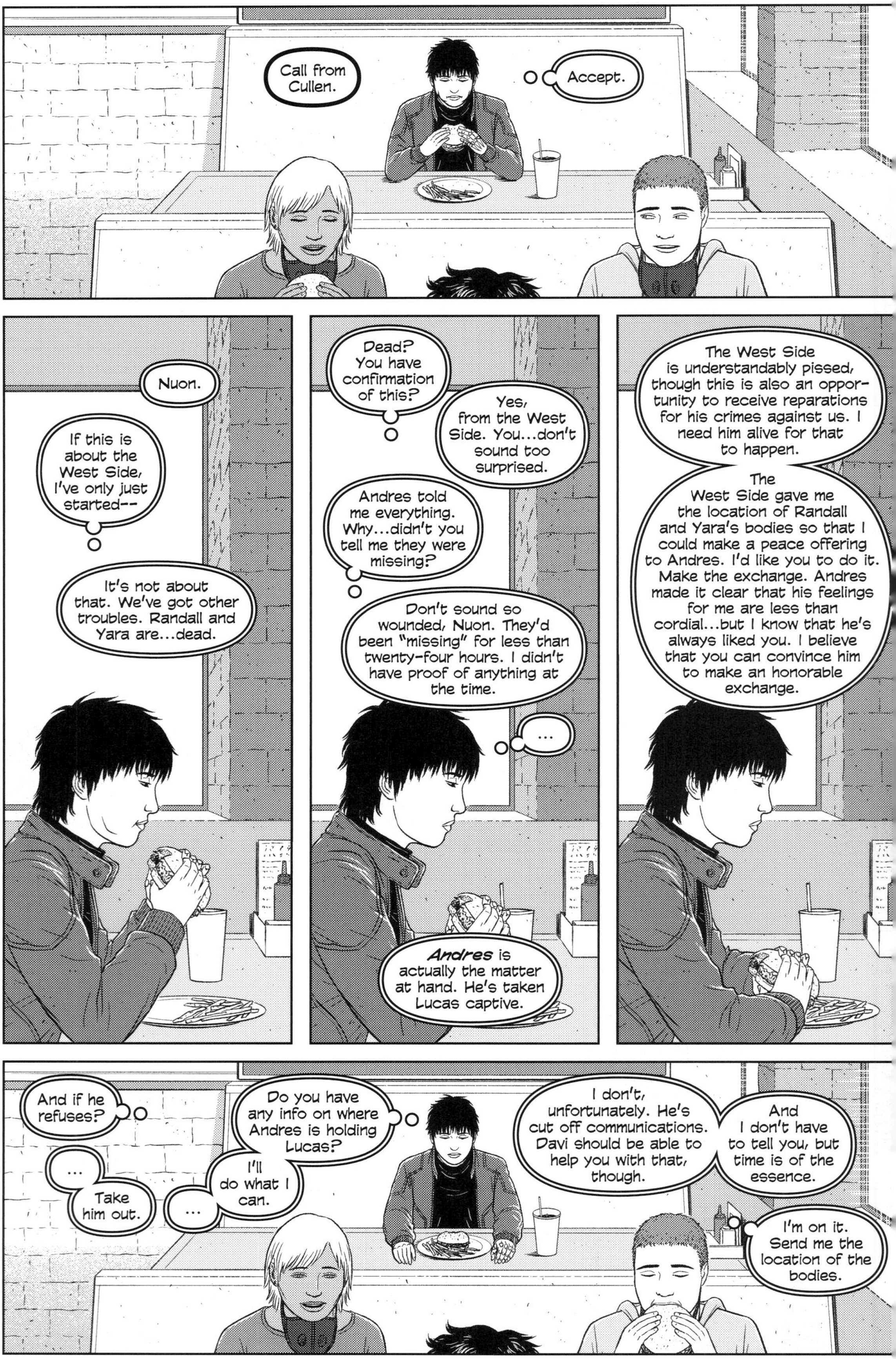
Call from Cullen.
Accept.
Nuon.
If this is about the West Side, I've only just started--
It's not about that. We've got other troubles. Randall and Yara are...dead.
Dead? You have confirmation of this?
Yes, from the West Side. You...don't sound too surprised.
Andres told me everything. Why...didn't you tell me they were missing?
Don't sound so wounded, Nuon. They'd been "missing" for less than twenty-four hours. I didn't have proof of anything at the time.
...
Andres is actually the matter at hand. He's taken Lucas captive.
The West Side is understandably pissed, though this is also an opportunity to receive reparations for his crimes against us. I need him alive for that to happen.
The West Side gave me the location of Randall and Yara's bodies so that I could make a peace offering to Andres. I'd like you to do it. Make the exchange. Andres made it clear that his feelings for me are less than cordial...but I know that he's always liked you. I believe that you can convince him to make an honorable exchange.
And if he refuses?
...
Take him out.
...
I'll do what I can.
Do you have any info on where Andres is holding Lucas?
I don't, unfortunately. He's cut off communications. Davi should be able to help you with that, though.
And I don't have to tell you, but time is of the essence.
I'm on it. Send me the location of the bodies.

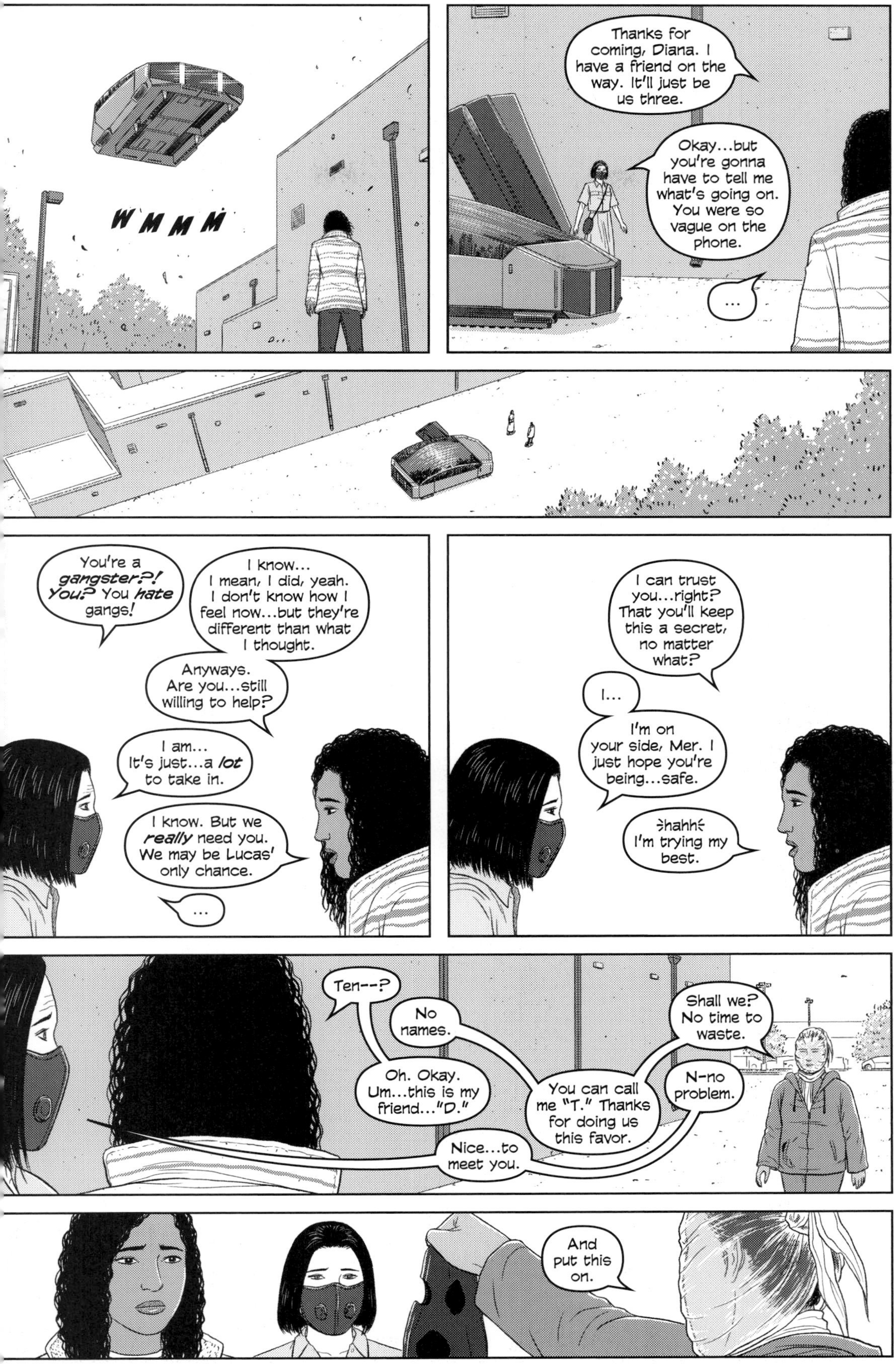
WMMM
Thanks for coming, Diana. I have a friend on the way. It'll just be us three.
Okay...but you're gonna have to tell me what's going on. You were so vague on the phone.
...
You're a gangster?! You? You hate gangs!
I know... I mean, I did, yeah. I don't know how I feel now...but they're different than what I thought.
Anyways. Are you...still willing to help?
I am... It's just...a lot to take in.
I know. But we really need you. We may be Lucas' only chance.
...
I can trust you...right? That you'll keep this a secret, no matter what?
I...
I'm on your side, Mer. I just hope you're being...safe.
hahh
I'm trying my best.
Ten--?
No names.
Oh. Okay. Um...this is my friend..."D."
Nice...to meet you.
You can call me "T." Thanks for doing us this favor.
N-no problem.
Shall we? No time to waste.
And put this on.

Thanks for meeting me on such short notice.

Of course! Anything for my favorite fellow gangster.

So, what can I do for you this time?

I need you to track down Andres.

Oh? What's he gotten himself into?

He's gone rogue... captured a West Sider.

Ooooh, exciting!

It's grave, Davi. Cullen's asked me to stop him. If I don't...it could mean war.

¿hahh¿ You scare me sometimes.

So, can you help me?

Shame. A war would liven things up around here. Our gang's become a bit *dull* if you ask me.

That depends. Is the price right? Tracking down Andres would be a little...risky.

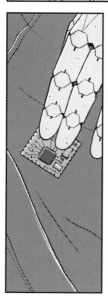

You can hack into the police network with this, right? Get access to drone footage?

Perhaps.

Well, you can keep it after you do that. Sell it or whatever.

...

Deal! You can wait in my apartment while I search the network. Shouldn't be long.

Alright.

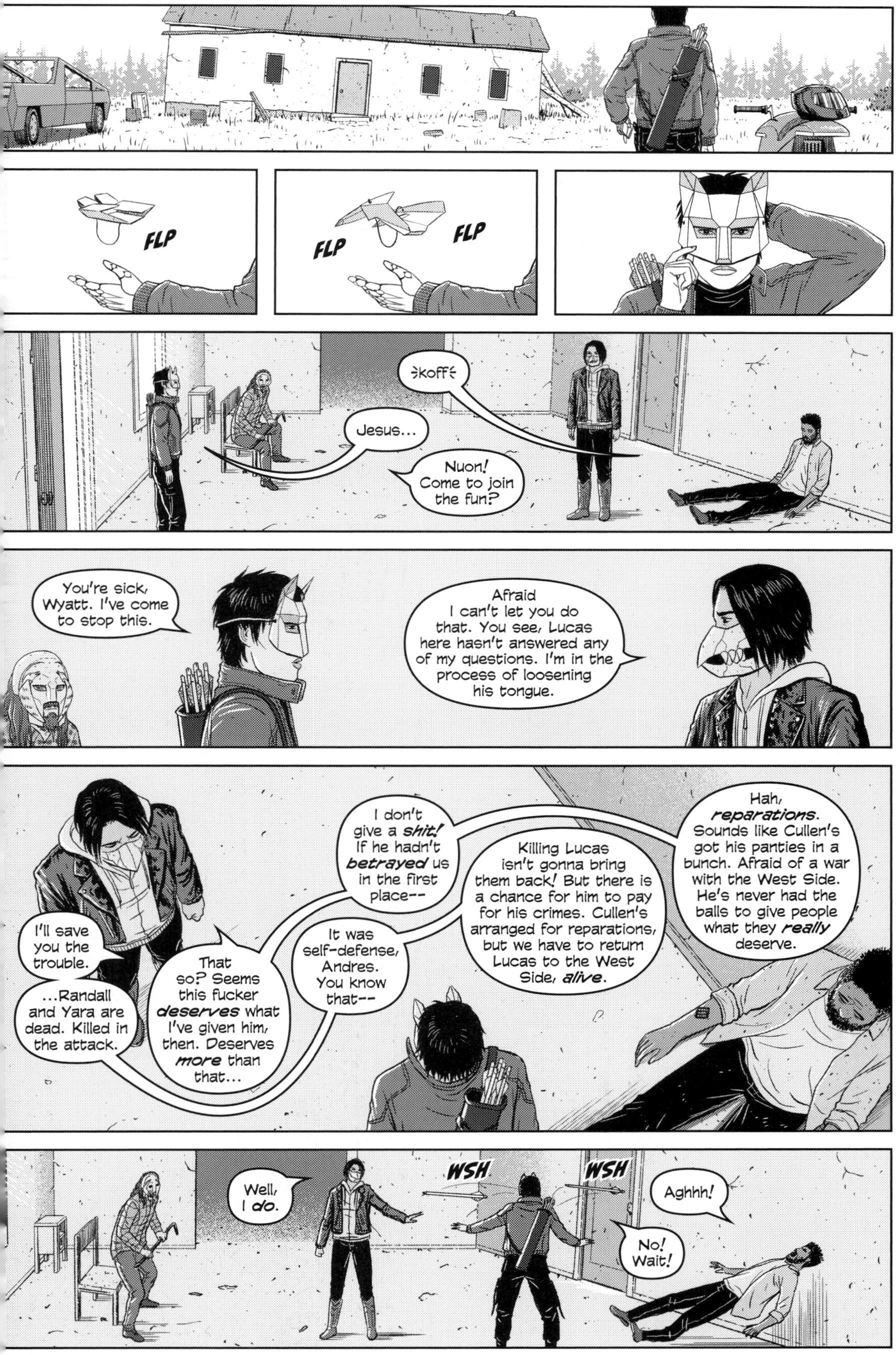
FLP
FLP
FLP
≯koff≮
Jesus...
Nuon! Come to join the fun?
You're sick, Wyatt. I've come to stop this.
Afraid I can't let you do that. You see, Lucas here hasn't answered any of my questions. I'm in the process of loosening his tongue.
I'll save you the trouble.
...Randall and Yara are dead. Killed in the attack.
That so? Seems this fucker *deserves* what I've given him, then. Deserves *more* than that...
It was self-defense, Andres. You know that--
I don't give a *shit!* If he hadn't *betrayed* us in the first place--
Killing Lucas isn't gonna bring them back! But there is a chance for him to pay for his crimes. Cullen's arranged for reparations, but we have to return Lucas to the West Side, *alive*.
Hah, *reparations*. Sounds like Cullen's got his panties in a bunch. Afraid of a war with the West Side. He's never had the balls to give people what they *really* deserve.
Well, I *do*.
WSH
WSH
No! Wait!
Aghhh!

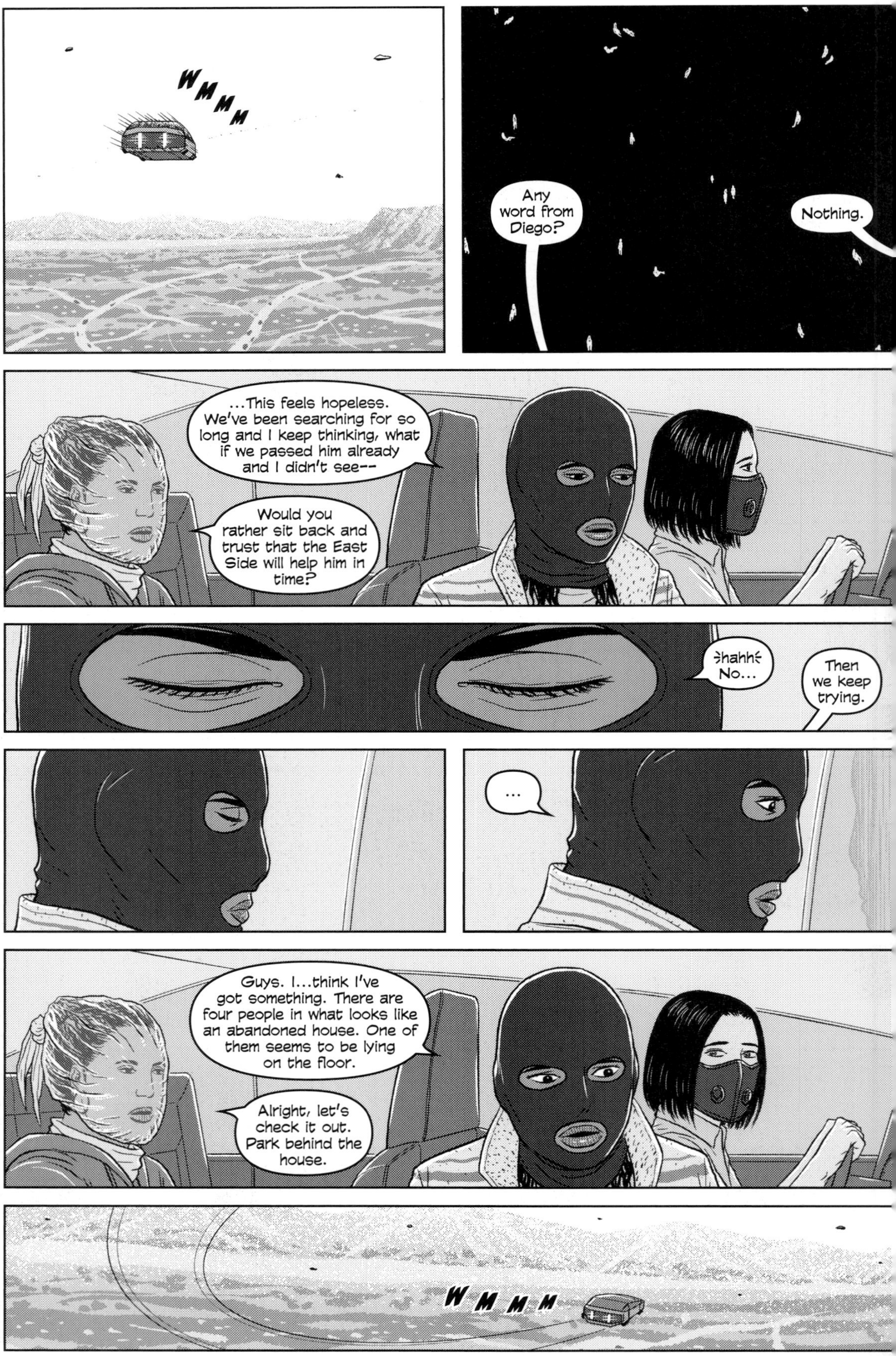
WMMM
Any word from Diego?
Nothing.
...This feels hopeless. We've been searching for so long and I keep thinking, what if we passed him already and I didn't see--
Would you rather sit back and trust that the East Side will help him in time?
hahh No...
Then we keep trying.
...
Guys. I...think I've got something. There are four people in what looks like an abandoned house. One of them seems to be lying on the floor.
Alright, let's check it out. Park behind the house.
WMMM

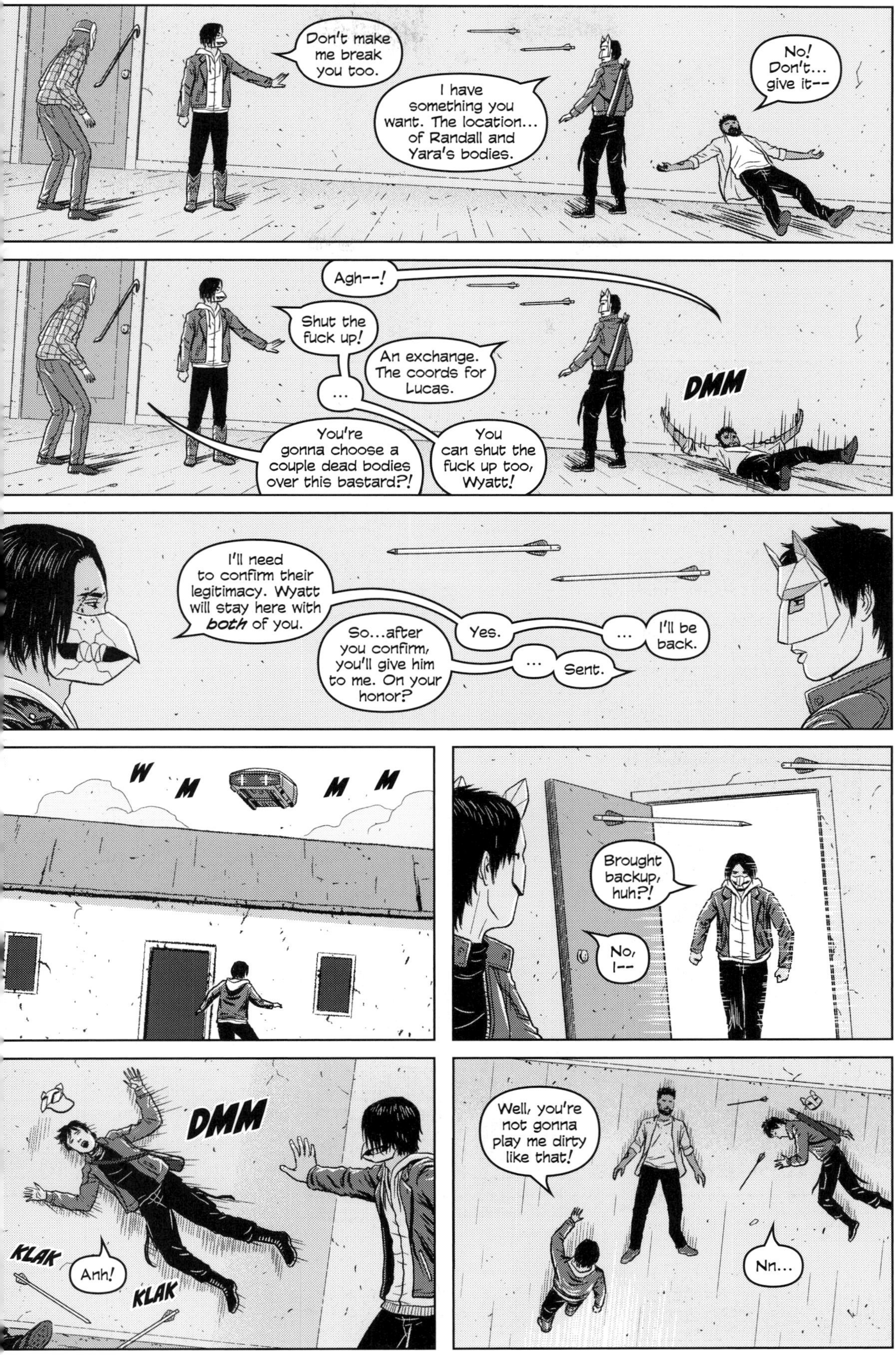
Don't make me break you too.
I have something you want. The location... of Randall and Yara's bodies.
No! Don't... give it--
Agh--!
Shut the fuck up!
...
An exchange. The coords for Lucas.
DMM
You're gonna choose a couple dead bodies over this bastard?!
You can shut the fuck up too, Wyatt!
I'll need to confirm their legitimacy. Wyatt will stay here with *both* of you.
Yes.
...
I'll be back.
So...after you confirm, you'll give him to me. On your honor?
...
Sent.
W M M M
Brought backup, huh?!
No, I--
DMM
KLAK
Anh!
KLAK
Well, you're not gonna play me dirty like that!
Nn...

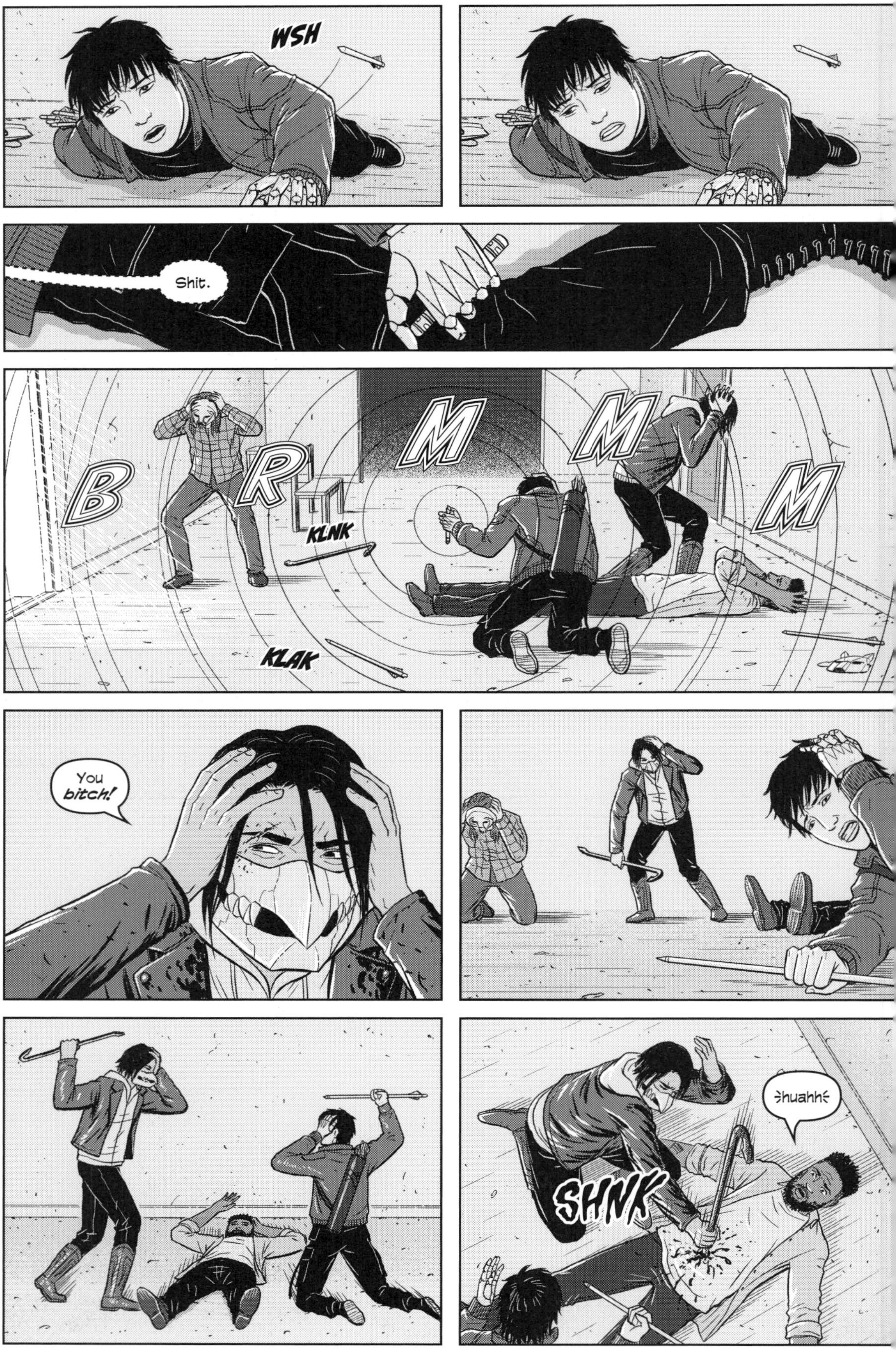
WSH
Shit.
B R M M M
KLNK
KLAK
You bitch!
huahh
SHNK

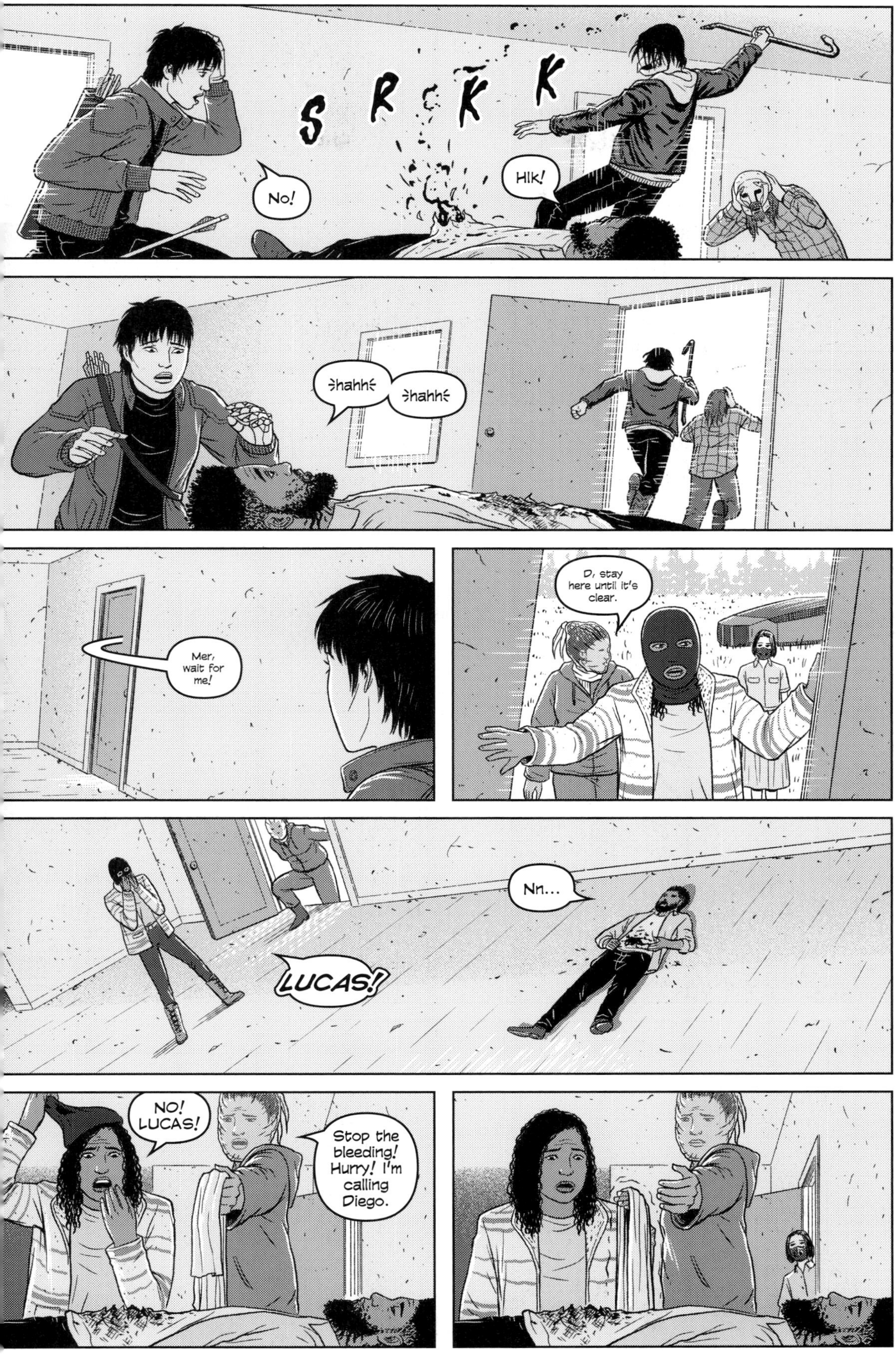
No!
S R K K
HIK!
hahh
hahh
Mer, wait for me!
D, stay here until it's clear.
Nn...
LUCAS!
NO! LUCAS!
Stop the bleeding! Hurry! I'm calling Diego.

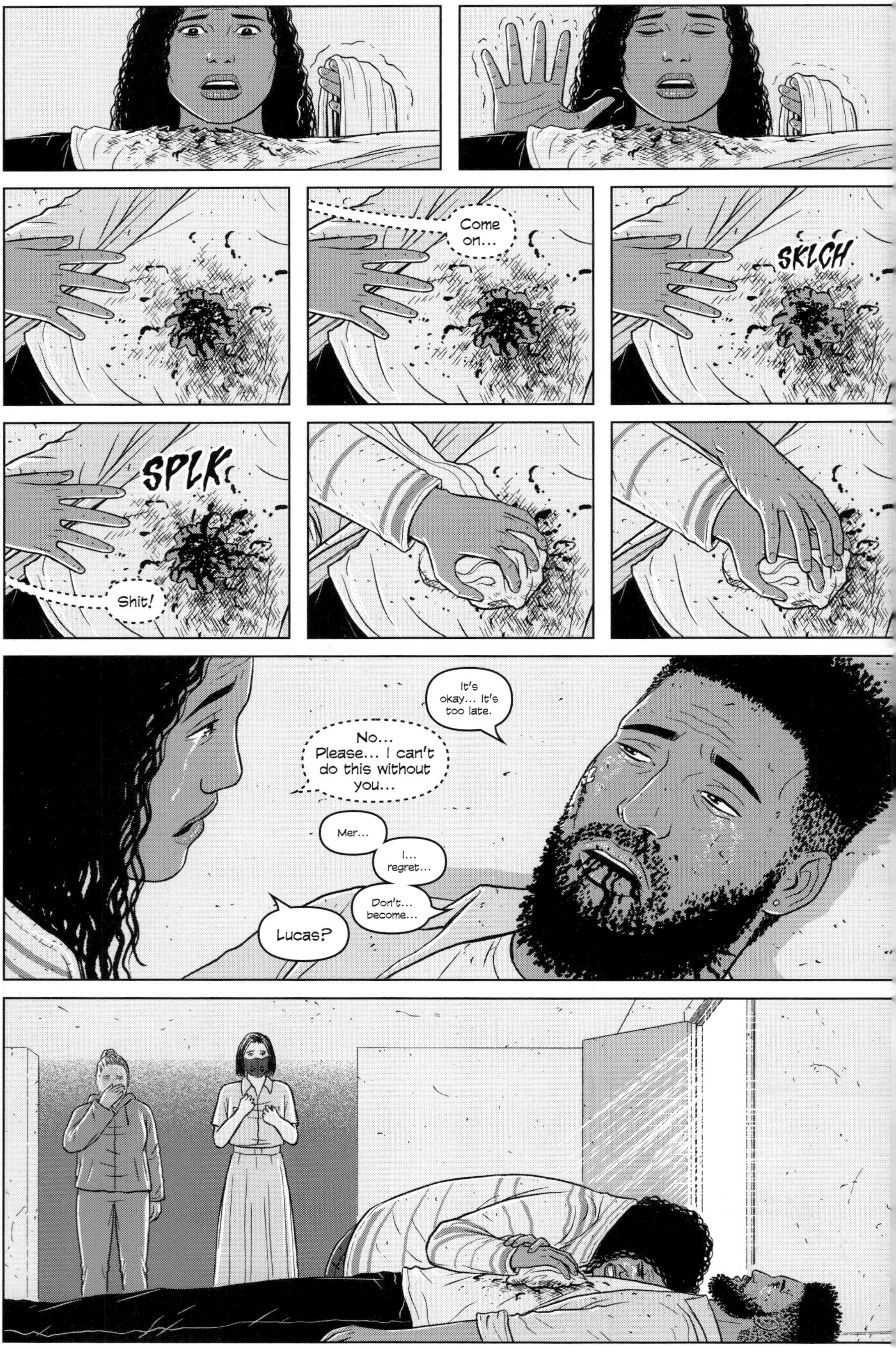
Come on...
SKLCH
SPLK
Shit!
It's okay... It's too late.
No... Please... I can't do this without you...
Mer...
I... regret...
Don't... become...
Lucas?

Alright... I think my STS is fully back now. There's definitely no sign of Nuon.

Good. I'd rather *not* have to kill her.

... Get ready to bring the truck in here.

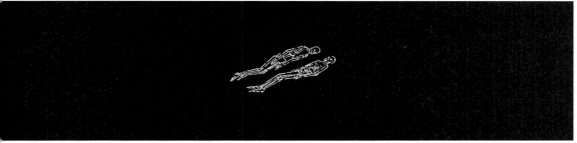

SHK

SHHP

You find 'em?

Yeah. And it looks like Lucas had an accomplice.

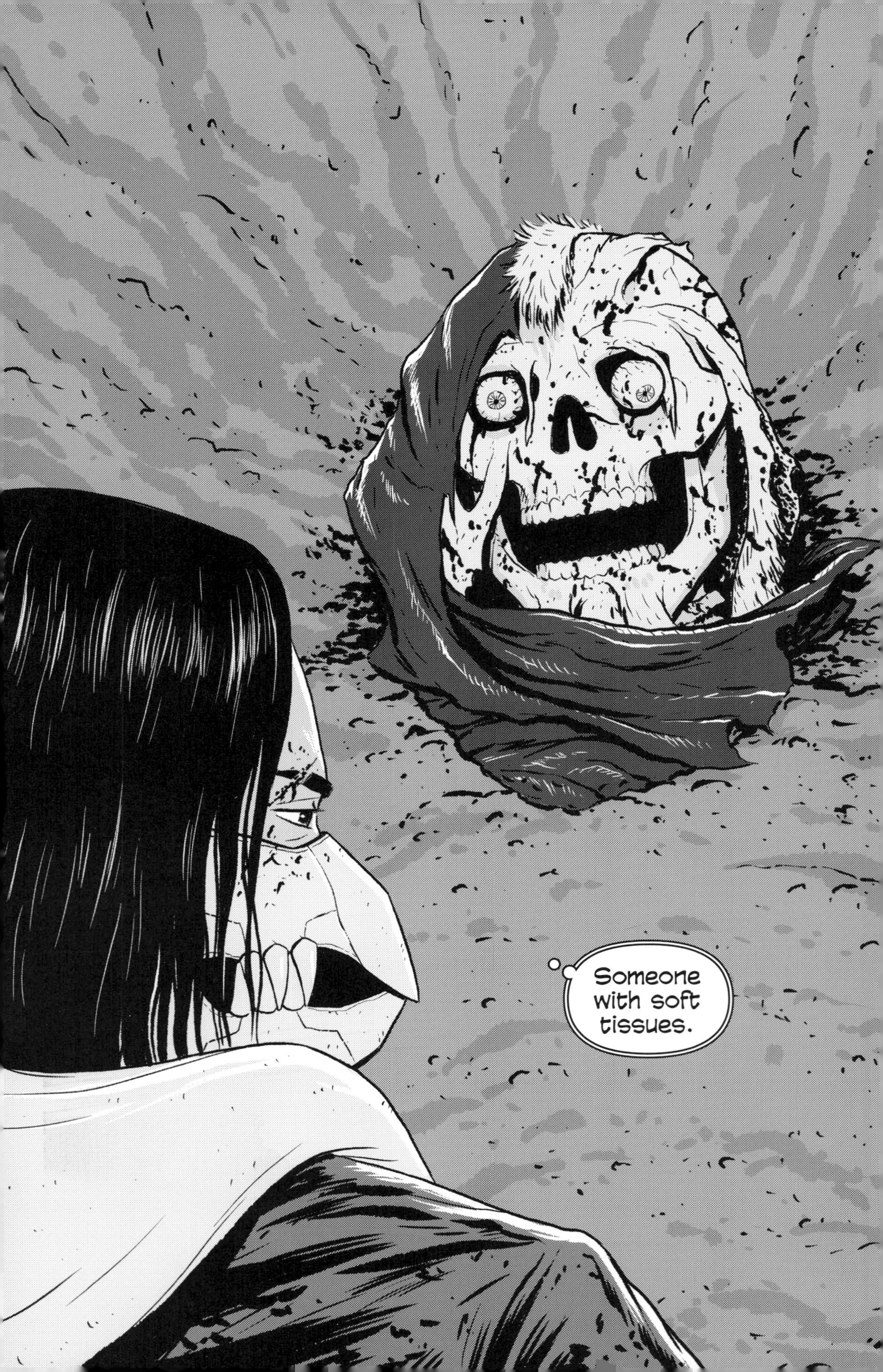
Someone with soft tissues.

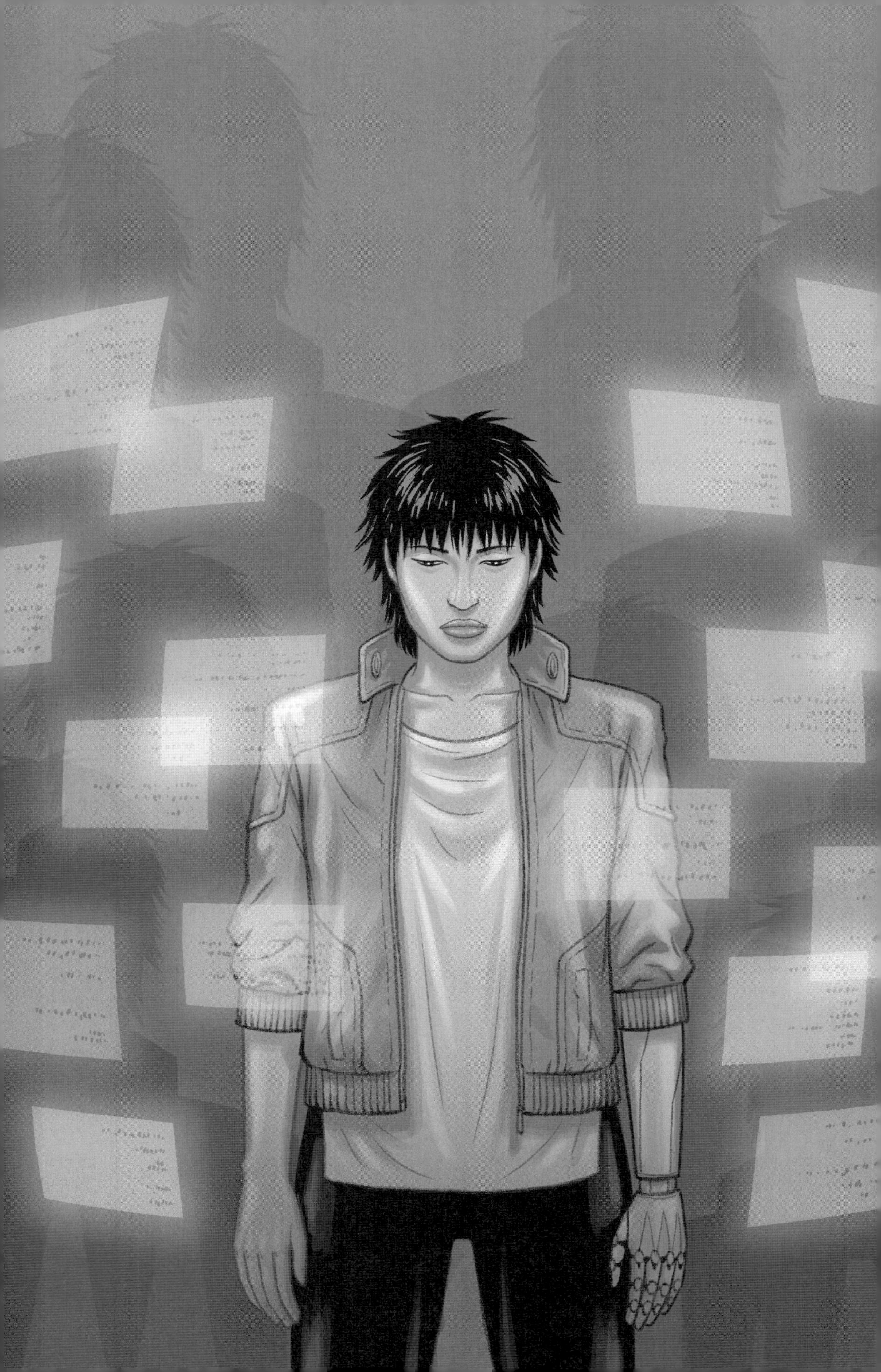

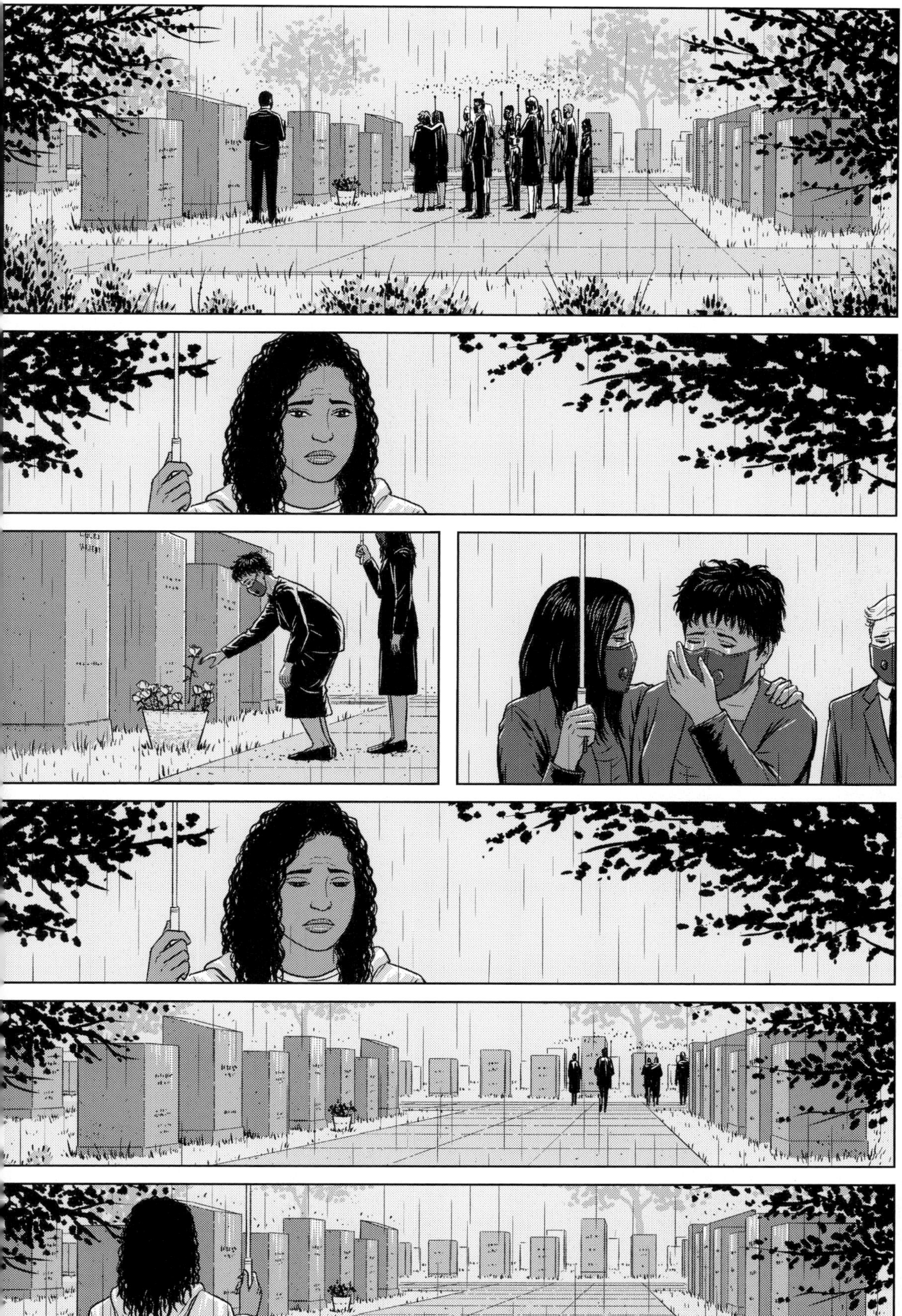

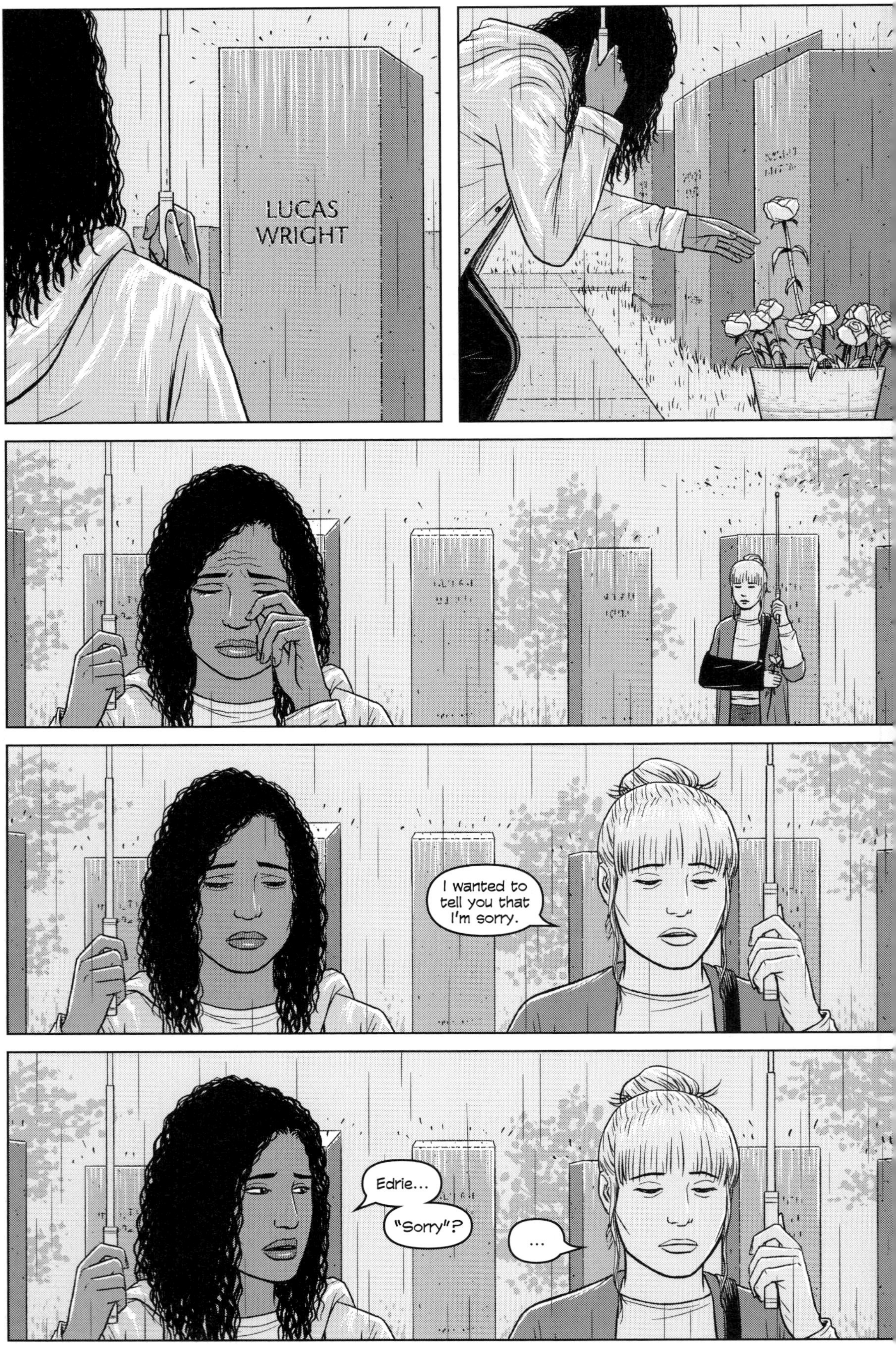
LUCAS
WRIGHT
I wanted to tell you that I'm sorry.
Edrie...
"Sorry"?
...

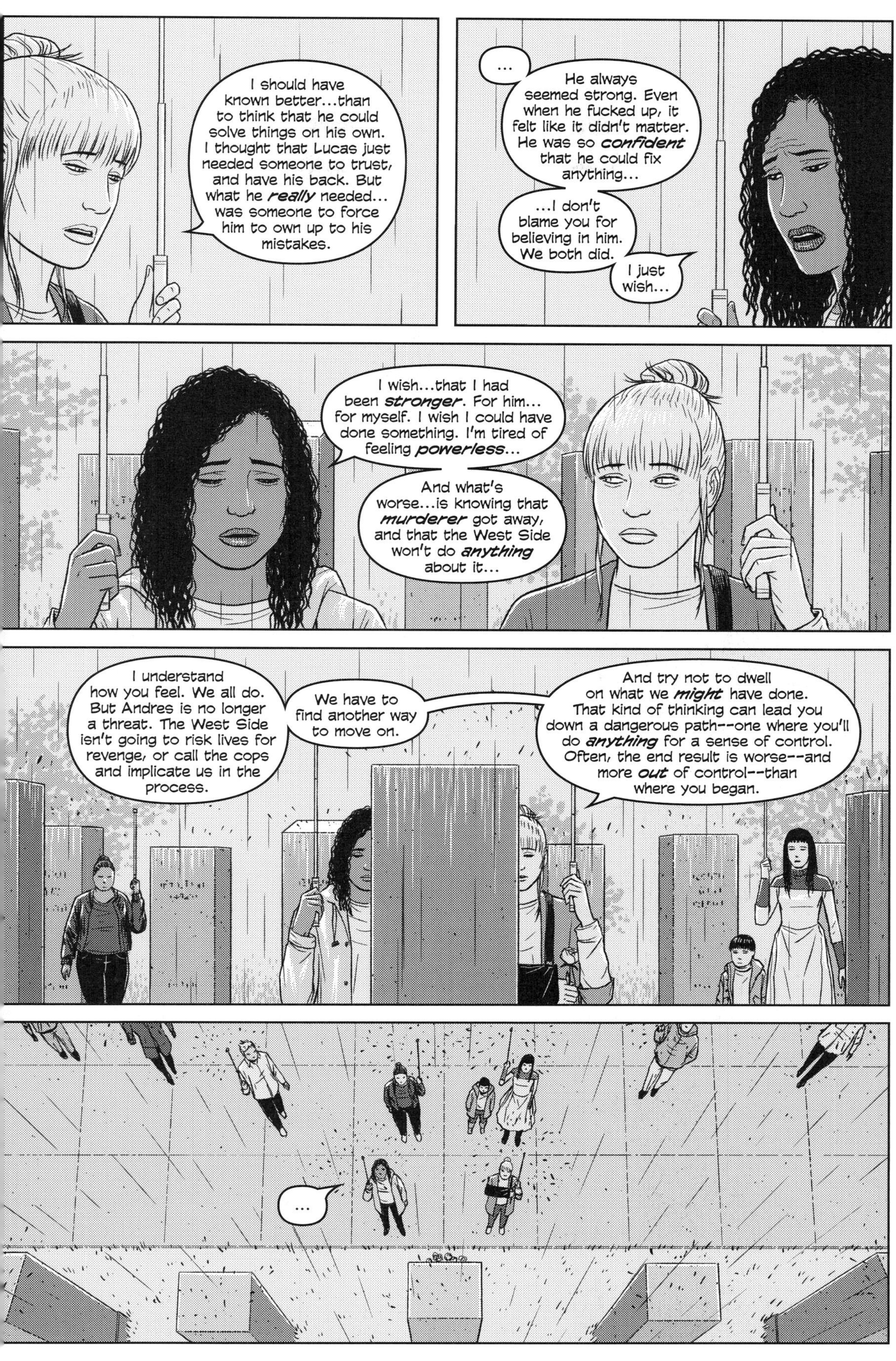
I should have known better...than to think that he could solve things on his own. I thought that Lucas just needed someone to trust, and have his back. But what he *really* needed... was someone to force him to own up to his mistakes.
...
He always seemed strong. Even when he fucked up, it felt like it didn't matter. He was so *confident* that he could fix anything...
...I don't blame you for believing in him. We both did.
I just wish...
I wish...that I had been *stronger*. For him... for myself. I wish I could have done something. I'm tired of feeling *powerless*...
And what's worse...is knowing that *murderer* got away, and that the West Side won't do *anything* about it...
I understand how you feel. We all do. But Andres is no longer a threat. The West Side isn't going to risk lives for revenge, or call the cops and implicate us in the process.
We have to find another way to move on.
And try not to dwell on what we *might* have done. That kind of thinking can lead you down a dangerous path--one where you'll do *anything* for a sense of control. Often, the end result is worse--and more *out* of control--than where you began.
...

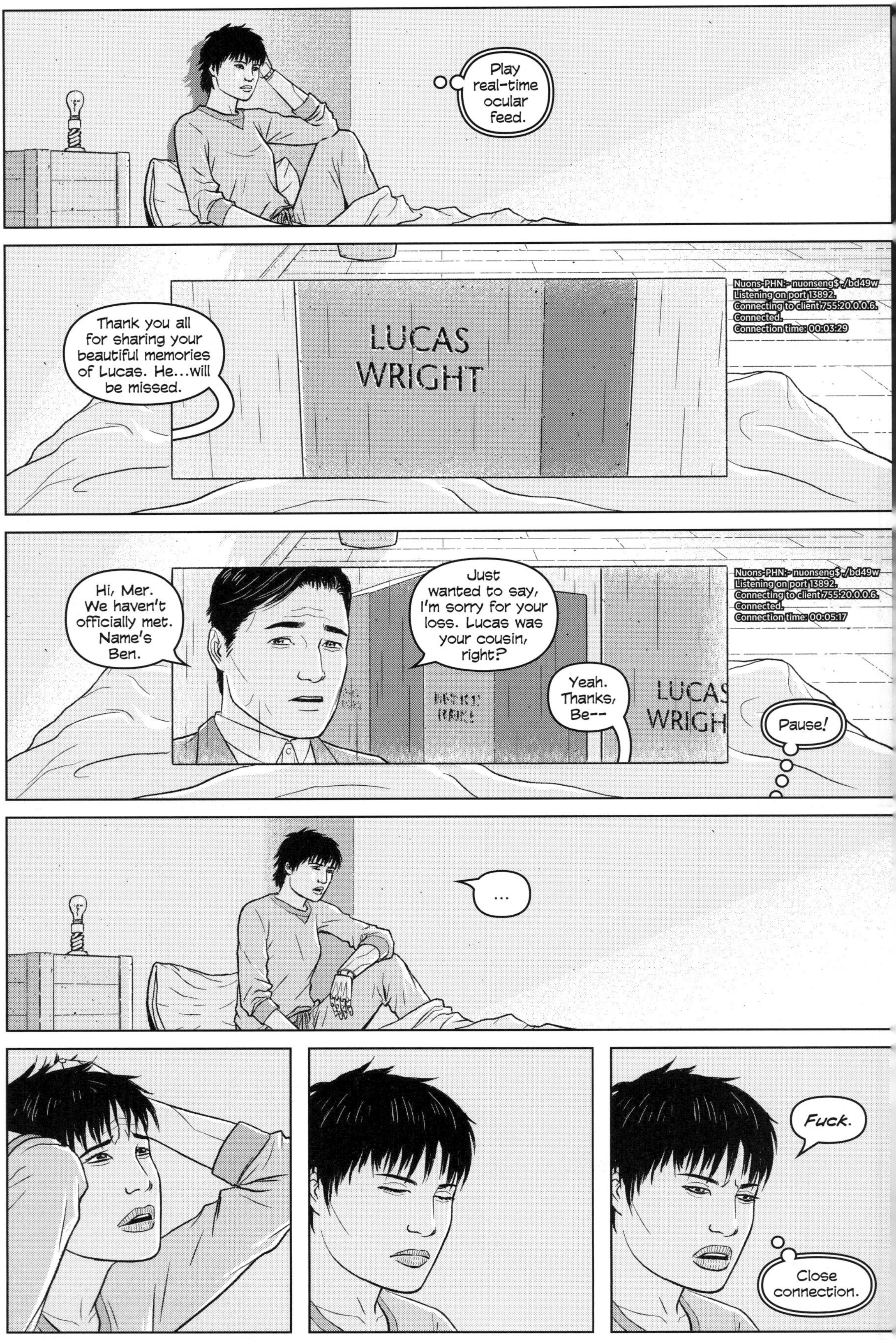
Play real-time ocular feed.
Nuons-PHN:~ nuonseng$ ./bd49w
Listening on port 13892.
Connecting to client 755:20.0.0.6.
Connected.
Connection time: 00:03:29
Thank you all for sharing your beautiful memories of Lucas. He...will be missed.
LUCAS WRIGHT
Nuons-PHN:~ nuonseng$ ./bd49w
Listening on port 13892.
Connecting to client 755:20.0.0.6.
Connected.
Connection time: 00:05:17
Hi, Mer. We haven't officially met. Name's Ben.
Just wanted to say, I'm sorry for your loss. Lucas was your cousin, right?
Yeah. Thanks, Be--
LUCAS WRIGH
Pause!
...
Fuck.
Close connection.

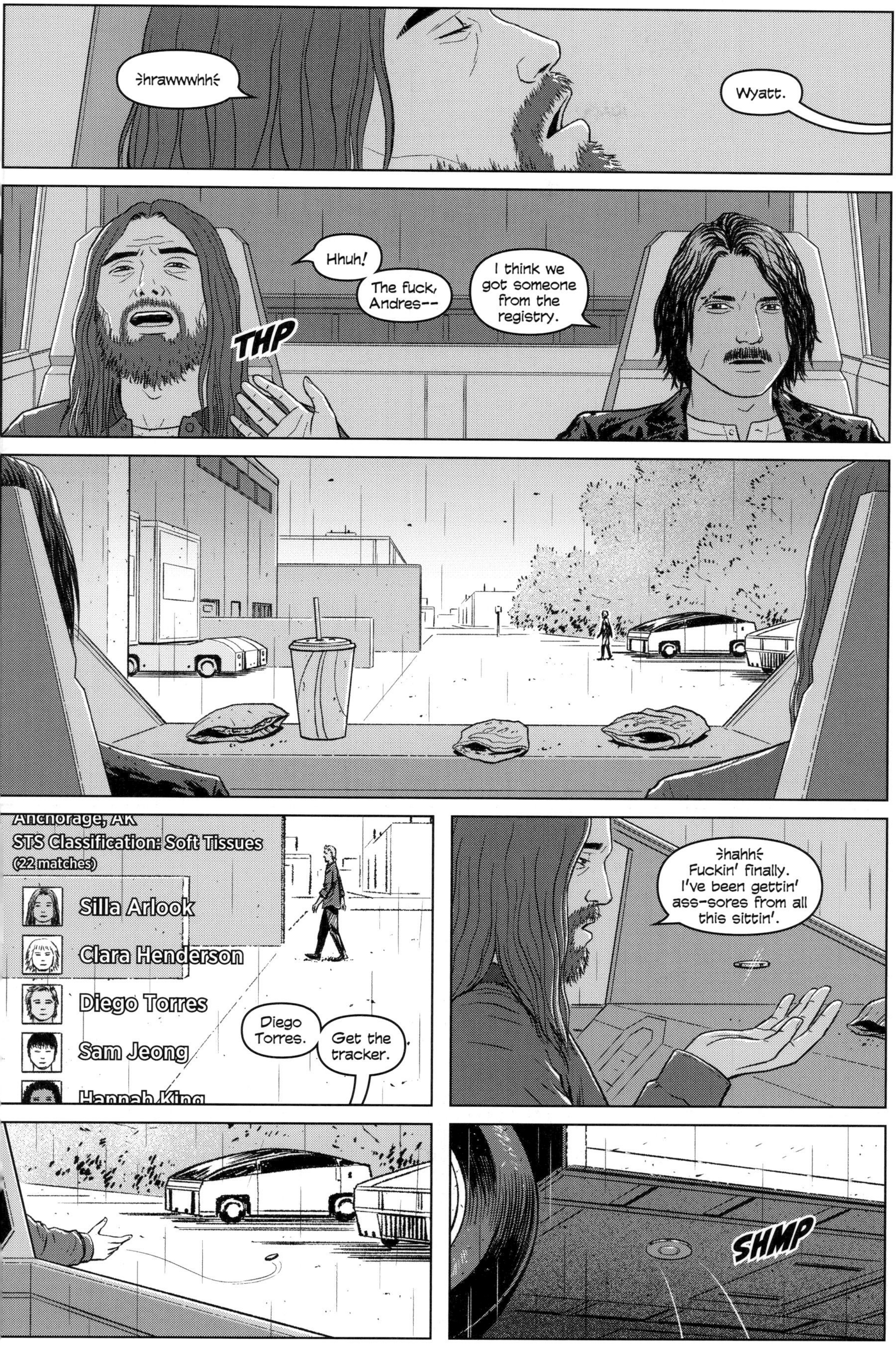

≈hrawwwhh≈
Wyatt.
Hhuh!
The fuck, Andres--
I think we got someone from the registry.
THP
Anchorage, AK
STS Classification: Soft Tissues
(22 matches)
Silla Arlook
Clara Henderson
Diego Torres
Sam Jeong
Diego Torres.
Get the tracker.
≈hahh≈ Fuckin' finally. I've been gettin' ass-sores from all this sittin'.
SHMP

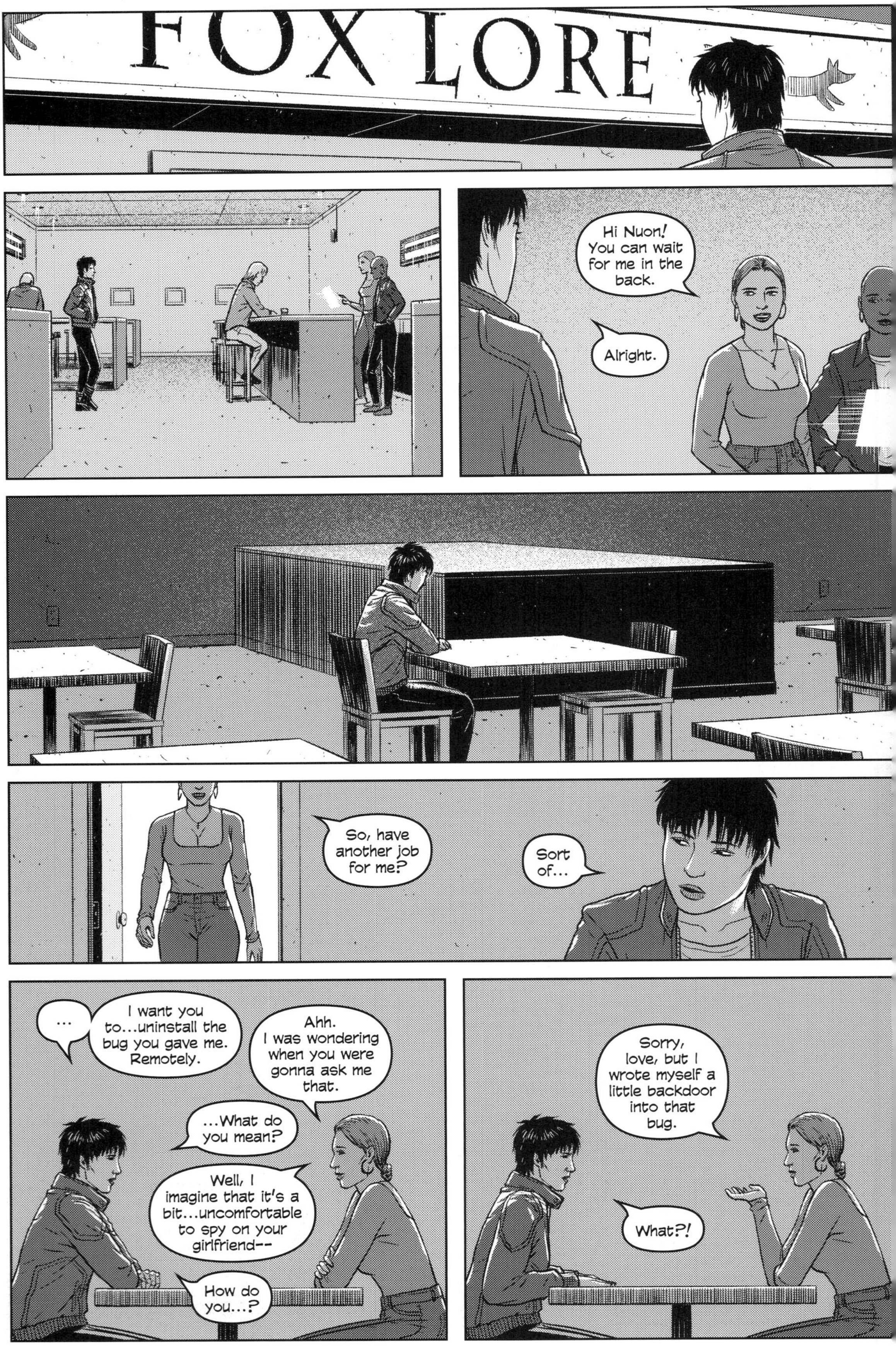
FOX LORE
Hi Nuon! You can wait for me in the back.
Alright.
So, have another job for me?
Sort of...
...
I want you to...uninstall the bug you gave me. Remotely.
Ahh. I was wondering when you were gonna ask me that.
...What do you mean?
Well, I imagine that it's a bit...uncomfortable to spy on your girlfriend--
How do you...?
Sorry, love, but I wrote myself a little backdoor into that bug.
What?!

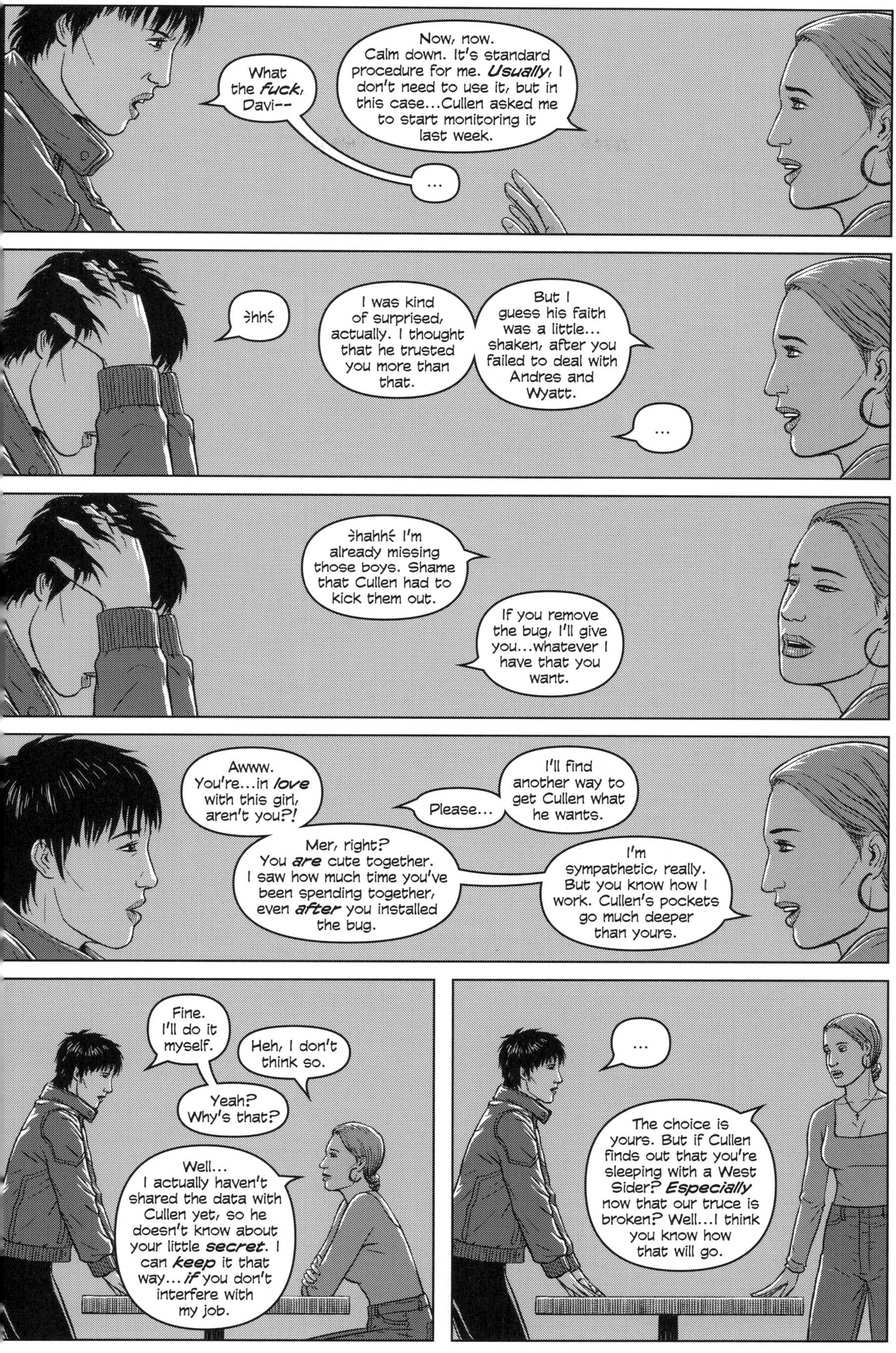
What the *fuck*, Davi--
Now, now. Calm down. It's standard procedure for me. ***Usually***, I don't need to use it, but in this case...Cullen asked me to start monitoring it last week.
...
ǂhhǂ
I was kind of surprised, actually. I thought that he trusted you more than that.
But I guess his faith was a little... shaken, after you failed to deal with Andres and Wyatt.
...
ǂhahhǂ I'm already missing those boys. Shame that Cullen had to kick them out.
If you remove the bug, I'll give you...whatever I have that you want.
Awww. You're...in ***love*** with this girl, aren't you?!
Please...
I'll find another way to get Cullen what he wants.
Mer, right? You ***are*** cute together. I saw how much time you've been spending together, even ***after*** you installed the bug.
I'm sympathetic, really. But you know how I work. Cullen's pockets go much deeper than yours.
Fine. I'll do it myself.
Heh, I don't think so.
Yeah? Why's that?
Well... I actually haven't shared the data with Cullen yet, so he doesn't know about your little ***secret***. I can ***keep*** it that way... ***if*** you don't interfere with my job.
...
The choice is yours. But if Cullen finds out that you're sleeping with a West Sider? ***Especially*** now that our truce is broken? Well...I think you know how that will go.

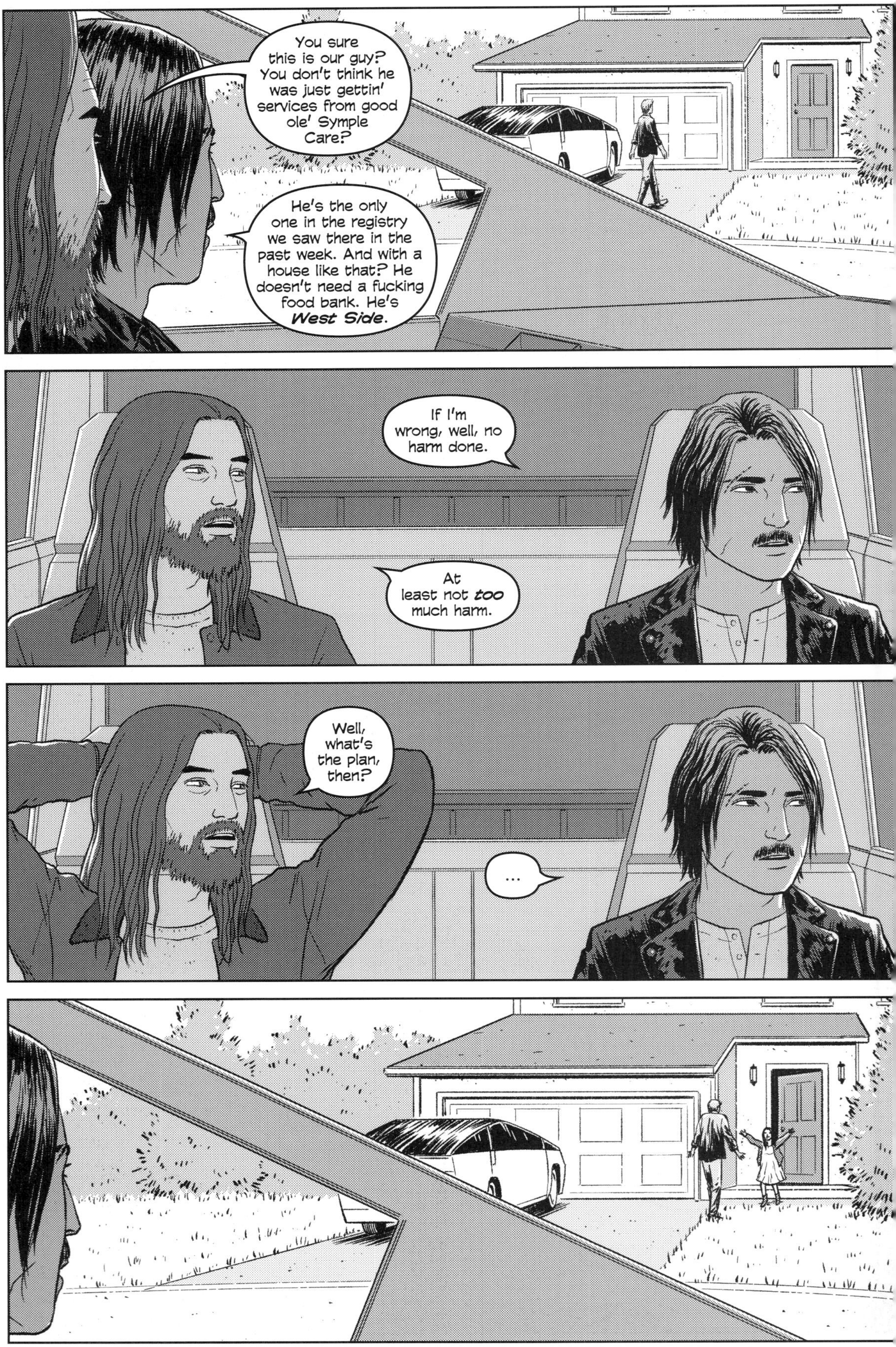
You sure this is our guy? You don't think he was just gettin' services from good ole' Symple Care?
He's the only one in the registry we saw there in the past week. And with a house like that? He doesn't need a fucking food bank. He's *West Side*.
If I'm wrong, well, no harm done.
At least not *too* much harm.
Well, what's the plan, then?
...

＝mra＝

TMP

SKLCH

Hah,
Atwood...

Why'd you
take *that* one?
There were two
perfectly good
mice--

♫ Call from
Soriya.

Accept.

Hey.
Not quite
ready for you to
come over yet.
Still have a
bunch of prep
to do.

Alright,
just checking.
Let me know if
I should bring
anything. And...
don't work too
hard on my
behalf.

Hah.
You know me.
I want it to be
perfect. Can't wait to
show you my place. I'll
let you know when
I'm ready. ♫

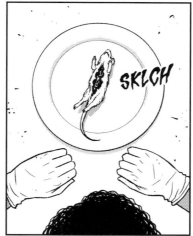

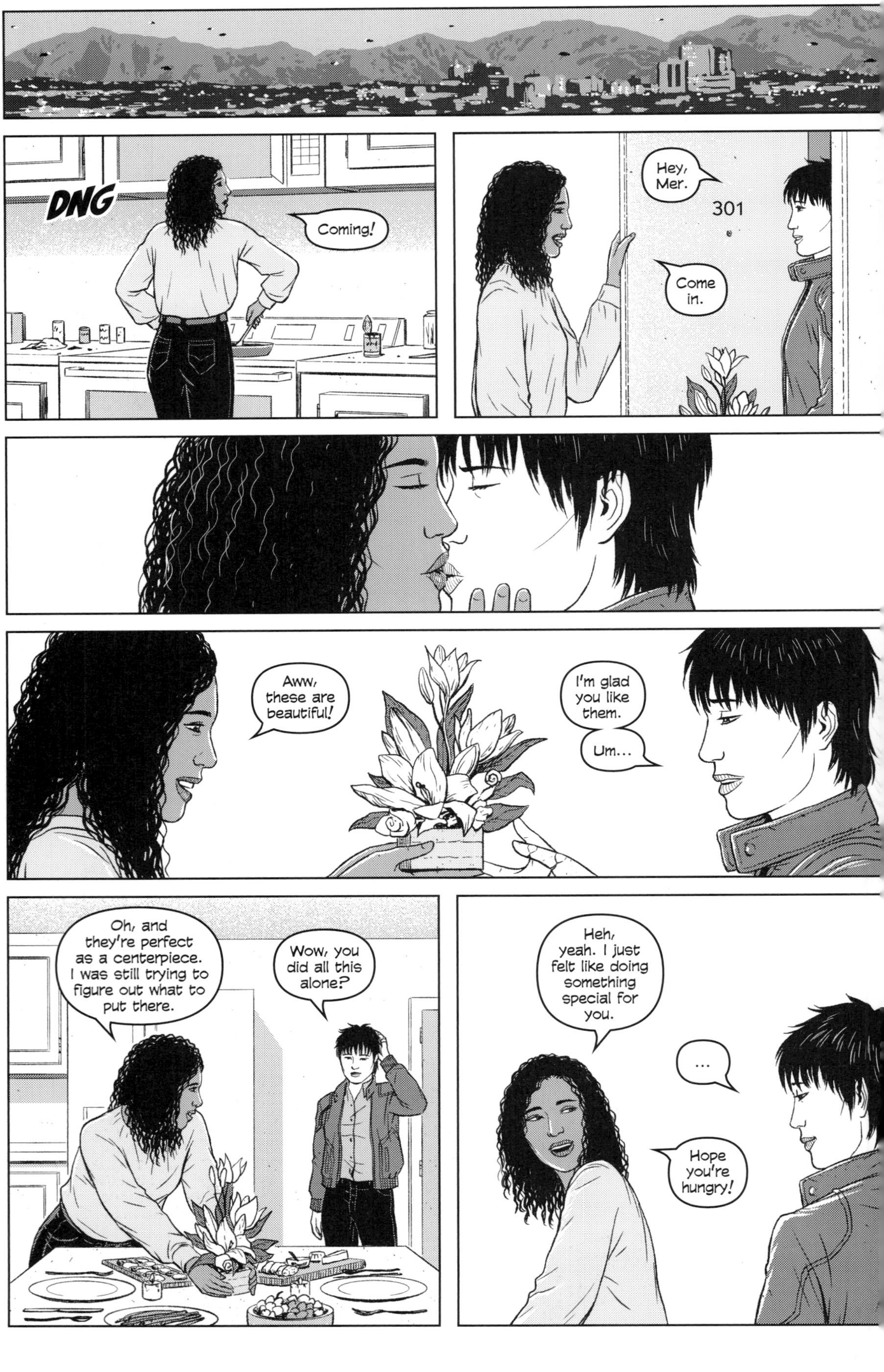
DNG
Coming!
Hey, Mer.
301
Come in.
Aww, these are beautiful!
I'm glad you like them.
Um...
Oh, and they're perfect as a centerpiece. I was still trying to figure out what to put there.
Wow, you did all this alone?
Heh, yeah. I just felt like doing something special for you.
...
Hope you're hungry!

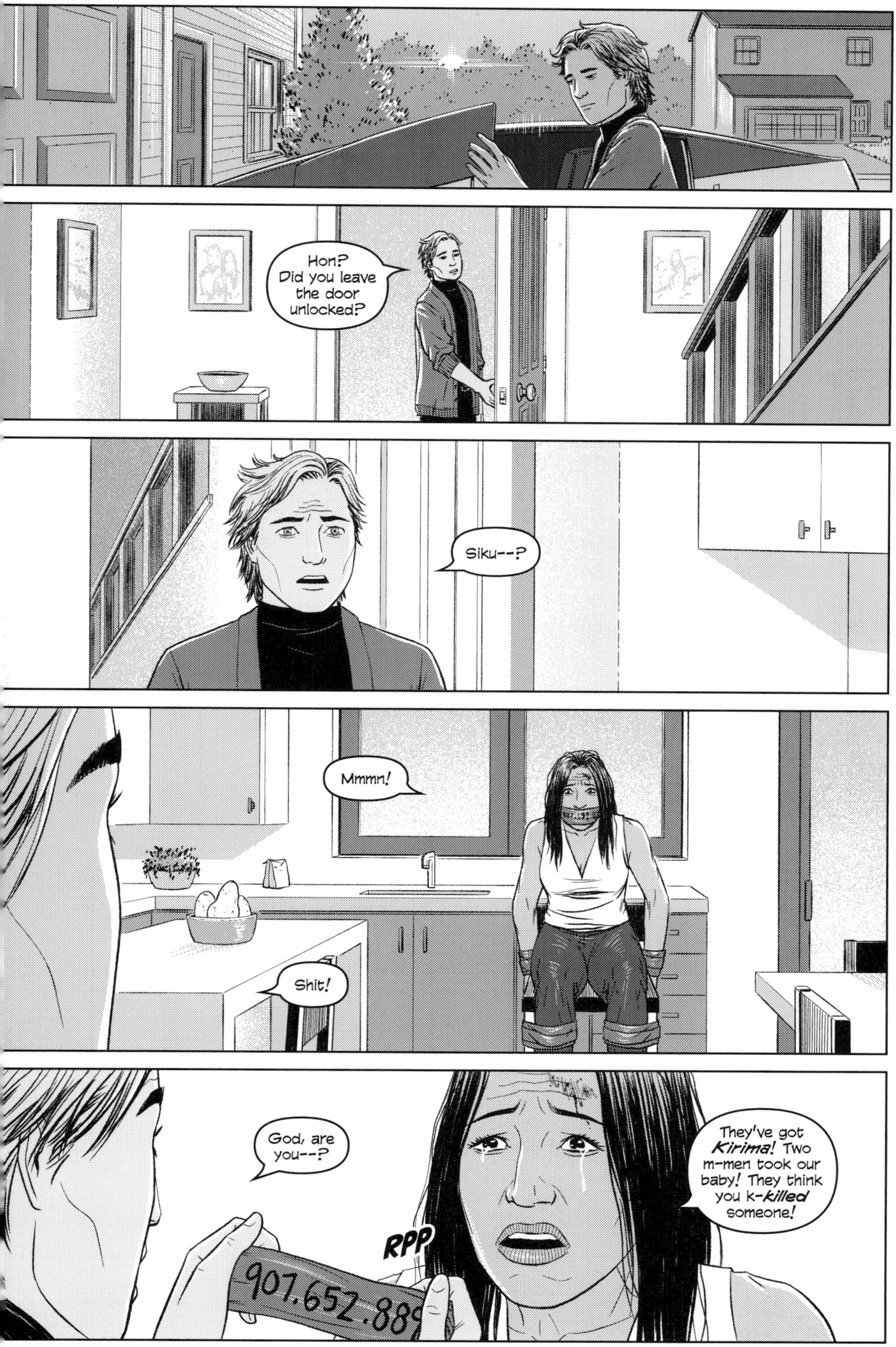

Hon? Did you leave the door unlocked?
Siku--?
Mmmn!
Shit!
God, are you--?
They've got *Kirima!* Two m-men took our baby! They think you k-*killed* someone!
RPP
907.652.889

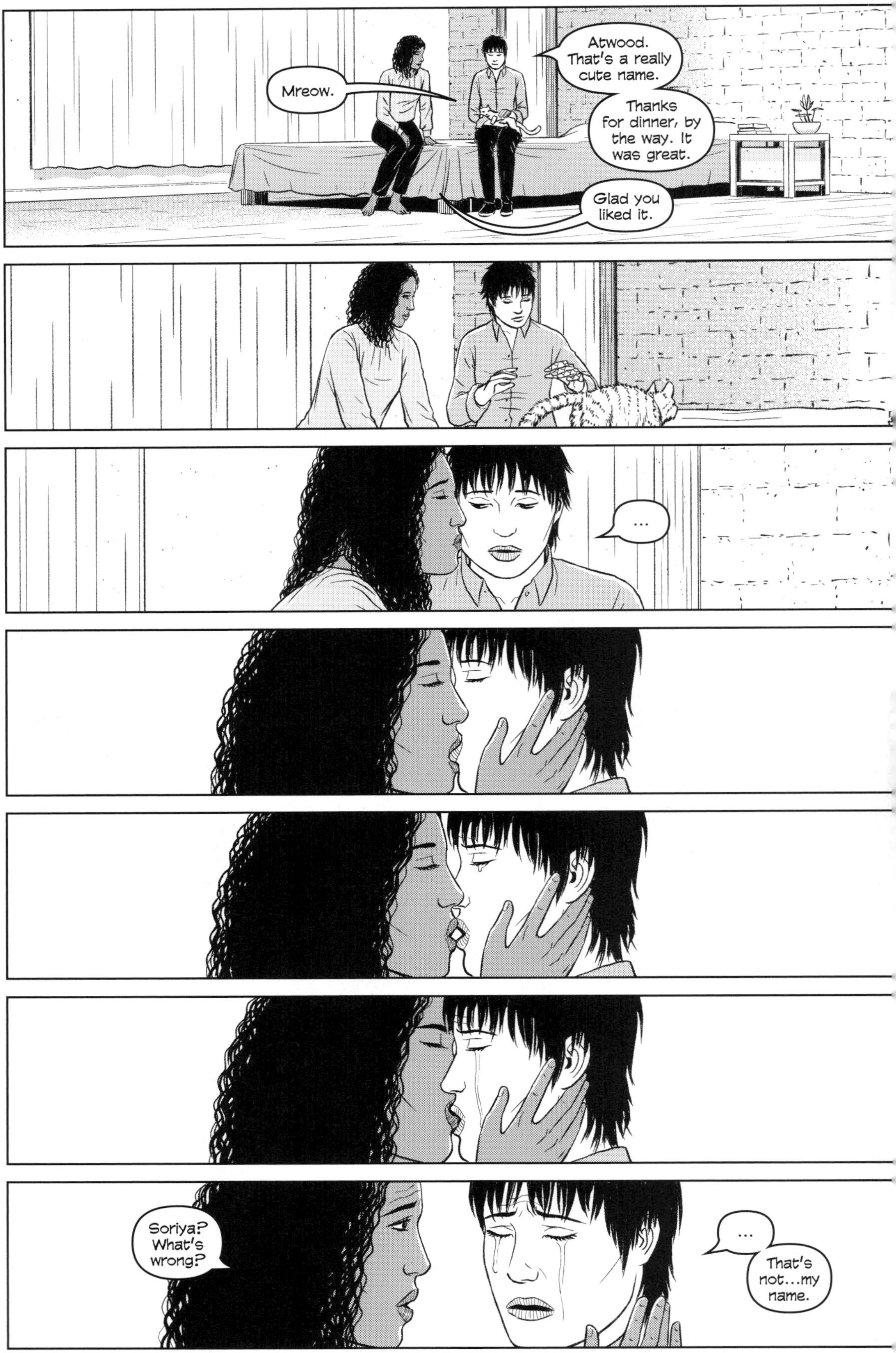
Atwood. That's a really cute name.
Mreow.
Thanks for dinner, by the way. It was great.
Glad you liked it.
...
Soriya? What's wrong?
...
That's not...my name.

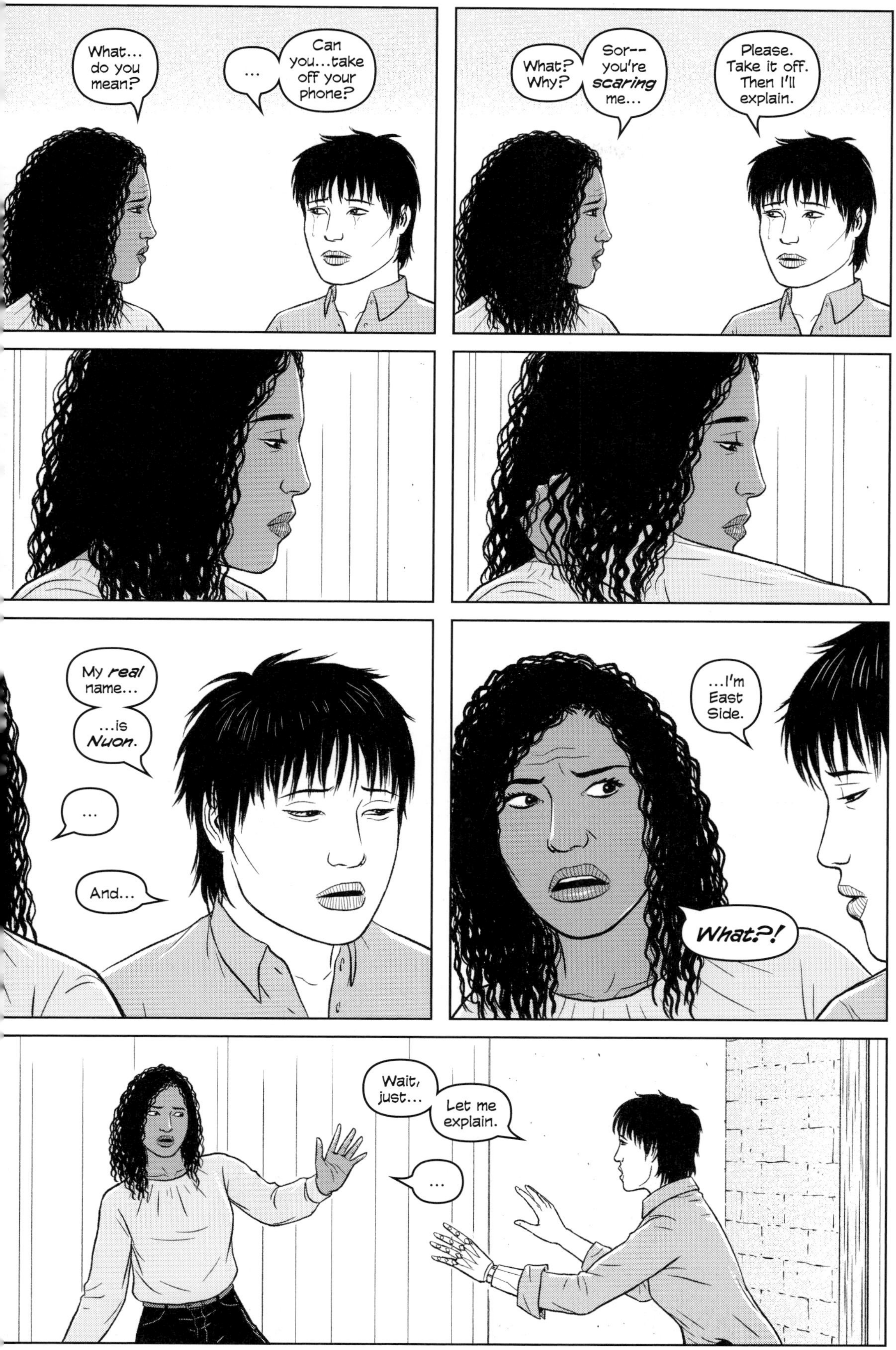

What... do you mean?
...
Can you...take off your phone?
What? Why?
Sor-- you're *scaring* me...
Please. Take it off. Then I'll explain.
My *real* name...
...is *Nuon*.
...
And...
...I'm East Side.
What?!
Wait, just...
Let me explain.
...

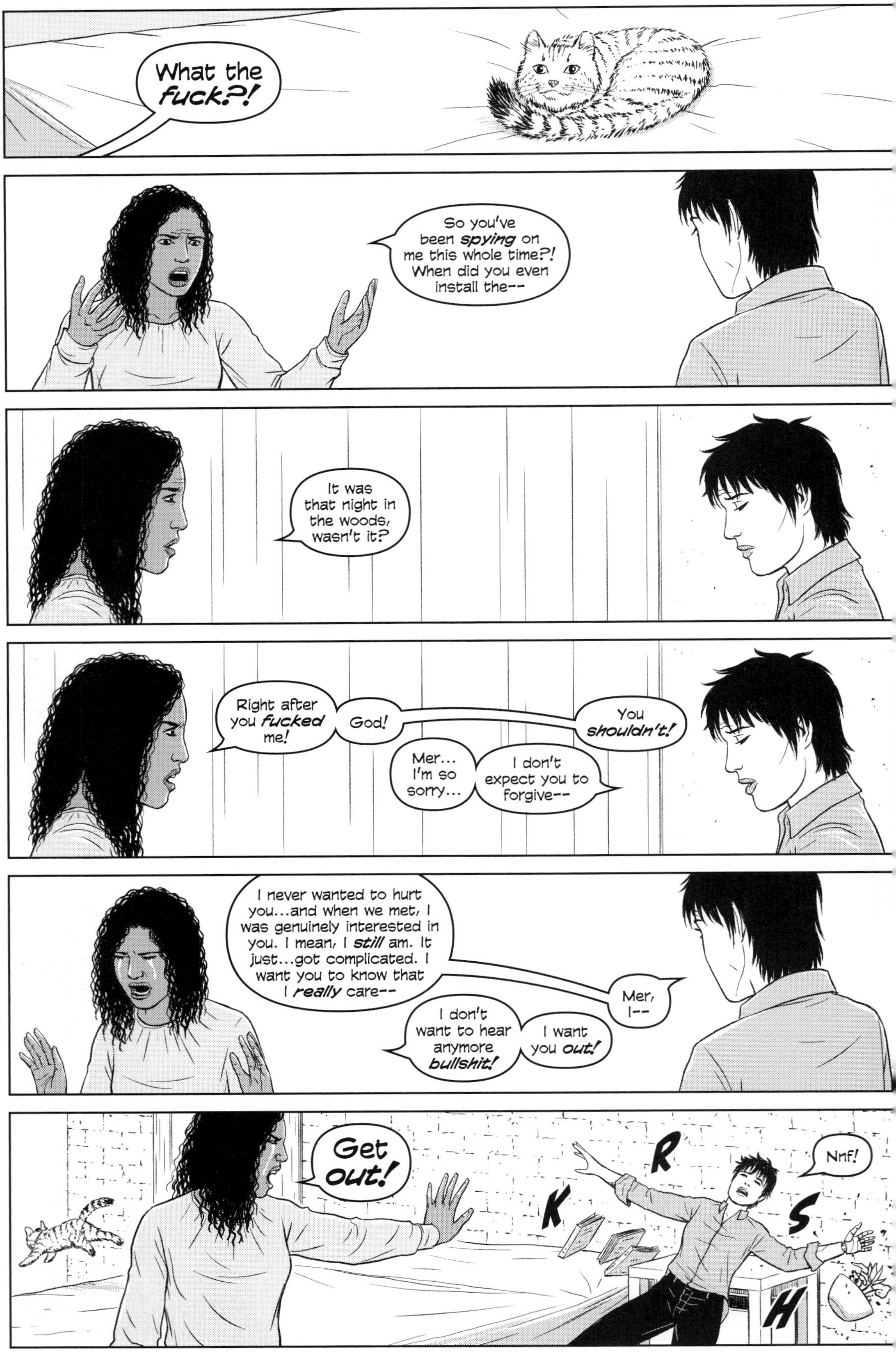

What the *fuck?!*
So you've been *spying* on me this whole time?! When did you even install the--
It was that night in the woods, wasn't it?
Right after you *fucked* me!
God!
You *shouldn't!*
Mer... I'm so sorry...
I don't expect you to forgive--
I never wanted to hurt you...and when we met, I was genuinely interested in you. I mean, I *still* am. It just...got complicated. I want you to know that I *really* care--
Mer, I--
I don't want to hear anymore *bullshit!*
I want you *out!*
Get *out!*
K
R
S
H
Nnf!

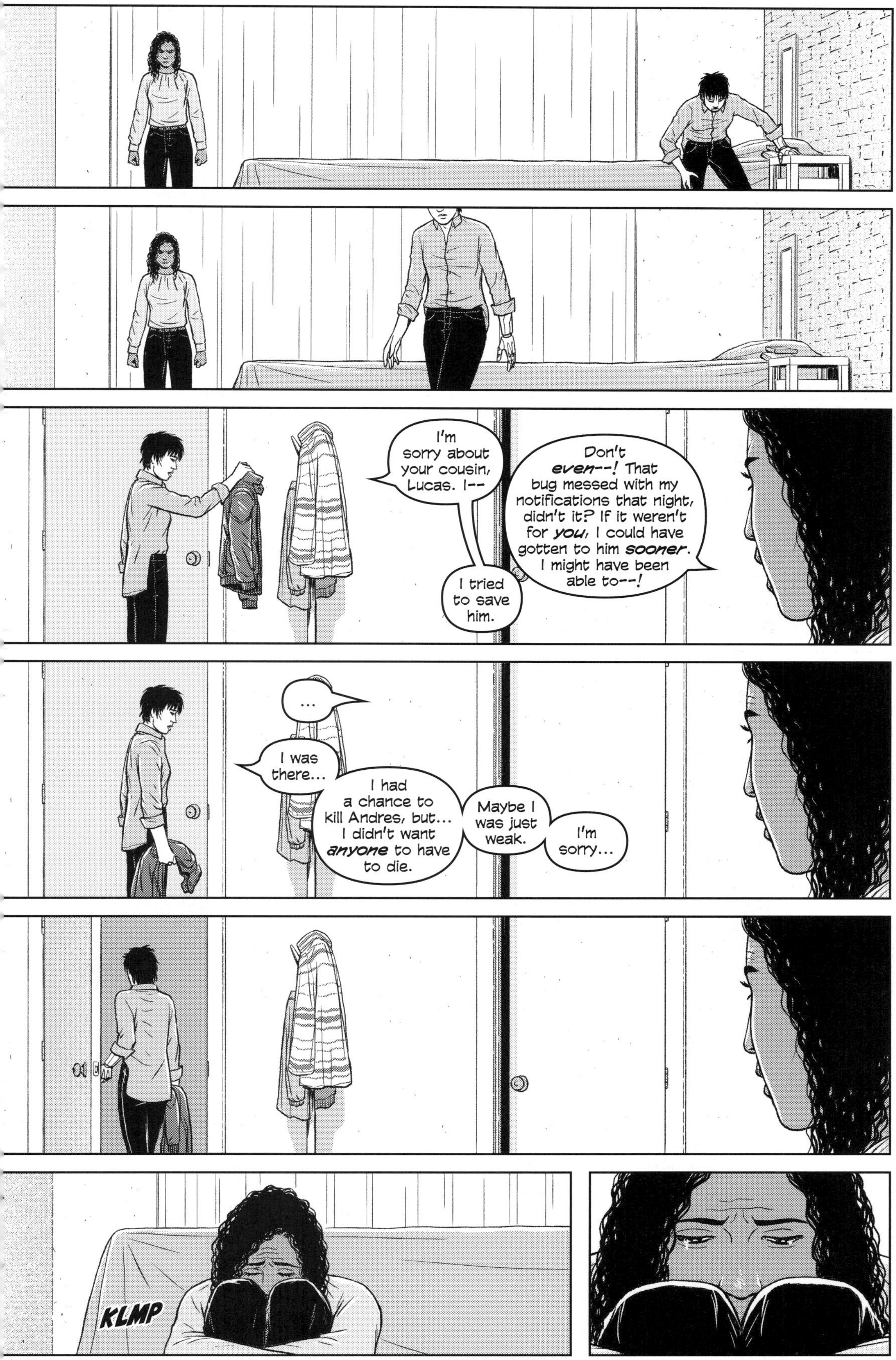

I'm sorry about your cousin, Lucas. I--
I tried to save him.
Don't *even*--! That bug messed with my notifications that night, didn't it? If it weren't for *you*, I could have gotten to him *sooner*. I might have been able to--!
...
I was there...
I had a chance to kill Andres, but... I didn't want *anyone* to have to die.
Maybe I was just weak.
I'm sorry...
KLMP

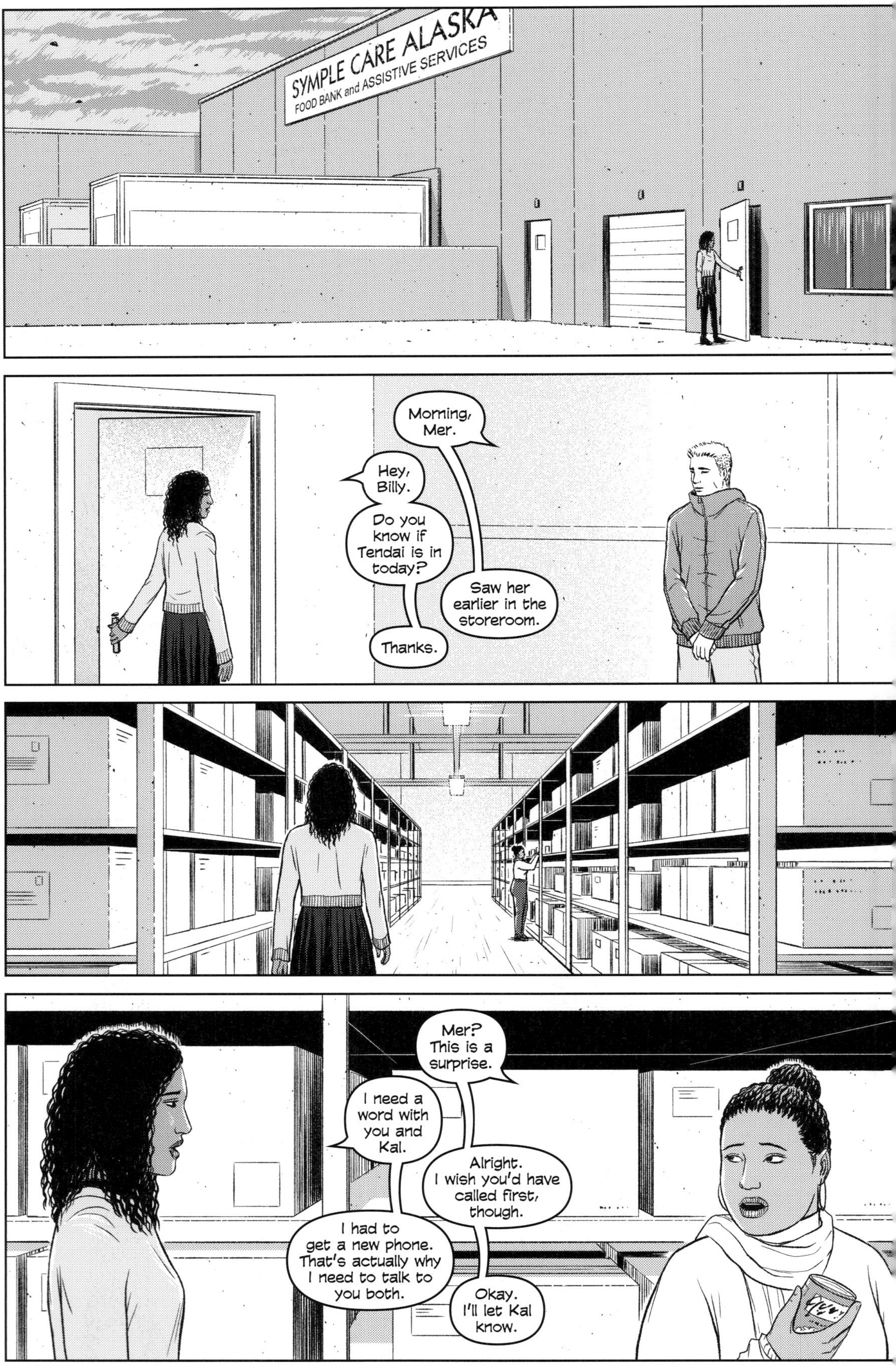
SYMPLE CARE ALASKA
FOOD BANK and ASSISTIVE SERVICES
Morning, Mer.
Hey, Billy.
Do you know if Tendai is in today?
Saw her earlier in the storeroom.
Thanks.
Mer? This is a surprise.
I need a word with you and Kal.
Alright. I wish you'd have called first, though.
I had to get a new phone. That's actually why I need to talk to you both.
Okay. I'll let Kal know.

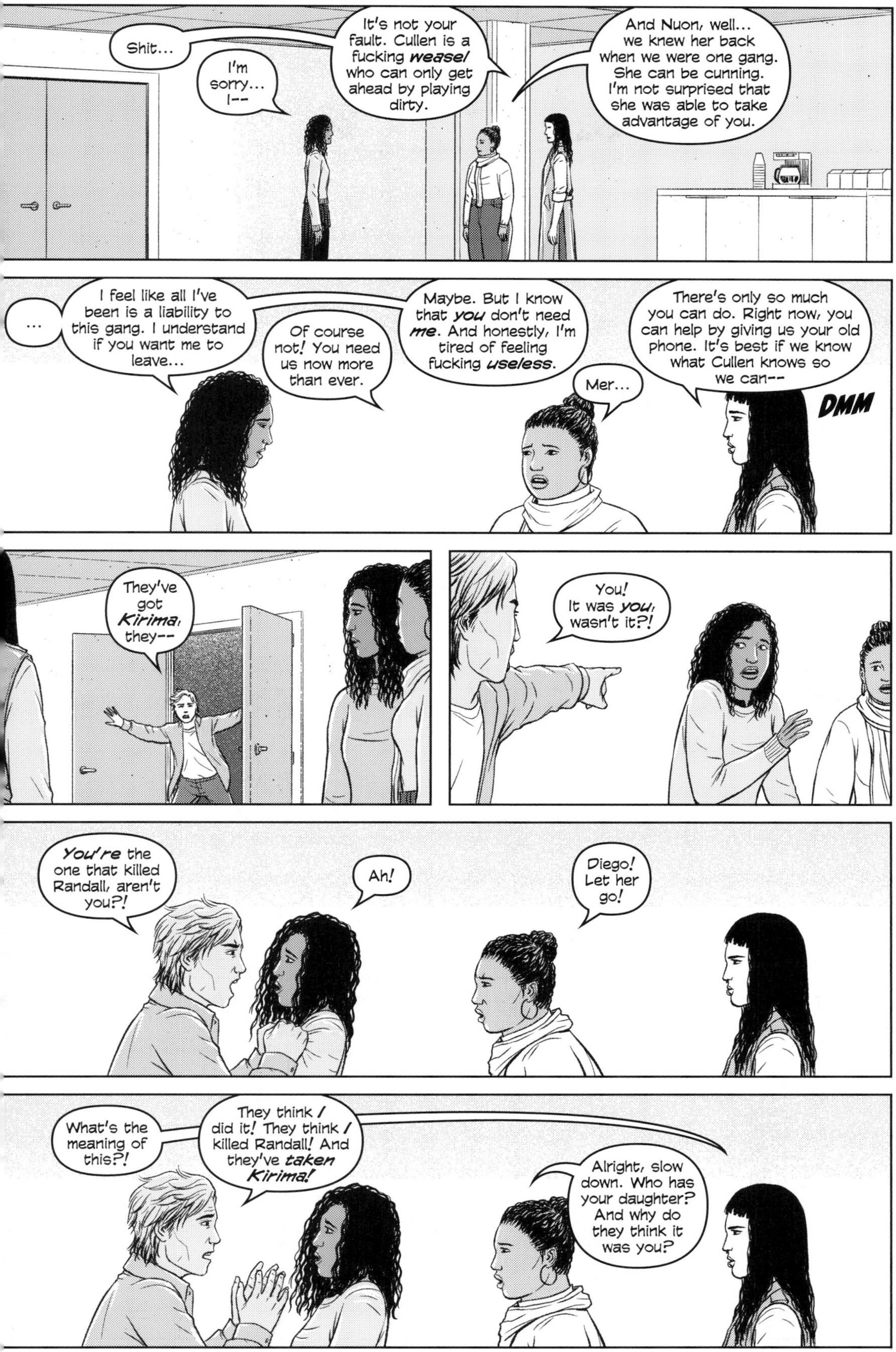

Shit...
I'm sorry... I--
It's not your fault. Cullen is a fucking *weasel* who can only get ahead by playing dirty.
And Nuon, well... we knew her back when we were one gang. She can be cunning. I'm not surprised that she was able to take advantage of you.
...
I feel like all I've been is a liability to this gang. I understand if you want me to leave...
Of course not! You need us now more than ever.
Maybe. But I know that *you* don't need *me*. And honestly, I'm tired of feeling fucking *useless*.
Mer...
There's only so much you can do. Right now, you can help by giving us your old phone. It's best if we know what Cullen knows so we can--
DMM
They've got *Kirima*, they--
You! It was *you*, wasn't it?!
You're the one that killed Randall, aren't you?!
Ah!
Diego! Let her go!
What's the meaning of this?!
They think *I* did it! They think *I* killed Randall! And they've *taken Kirima!*
Alright, slow down. Who has your daughter? And why do they think it was you?

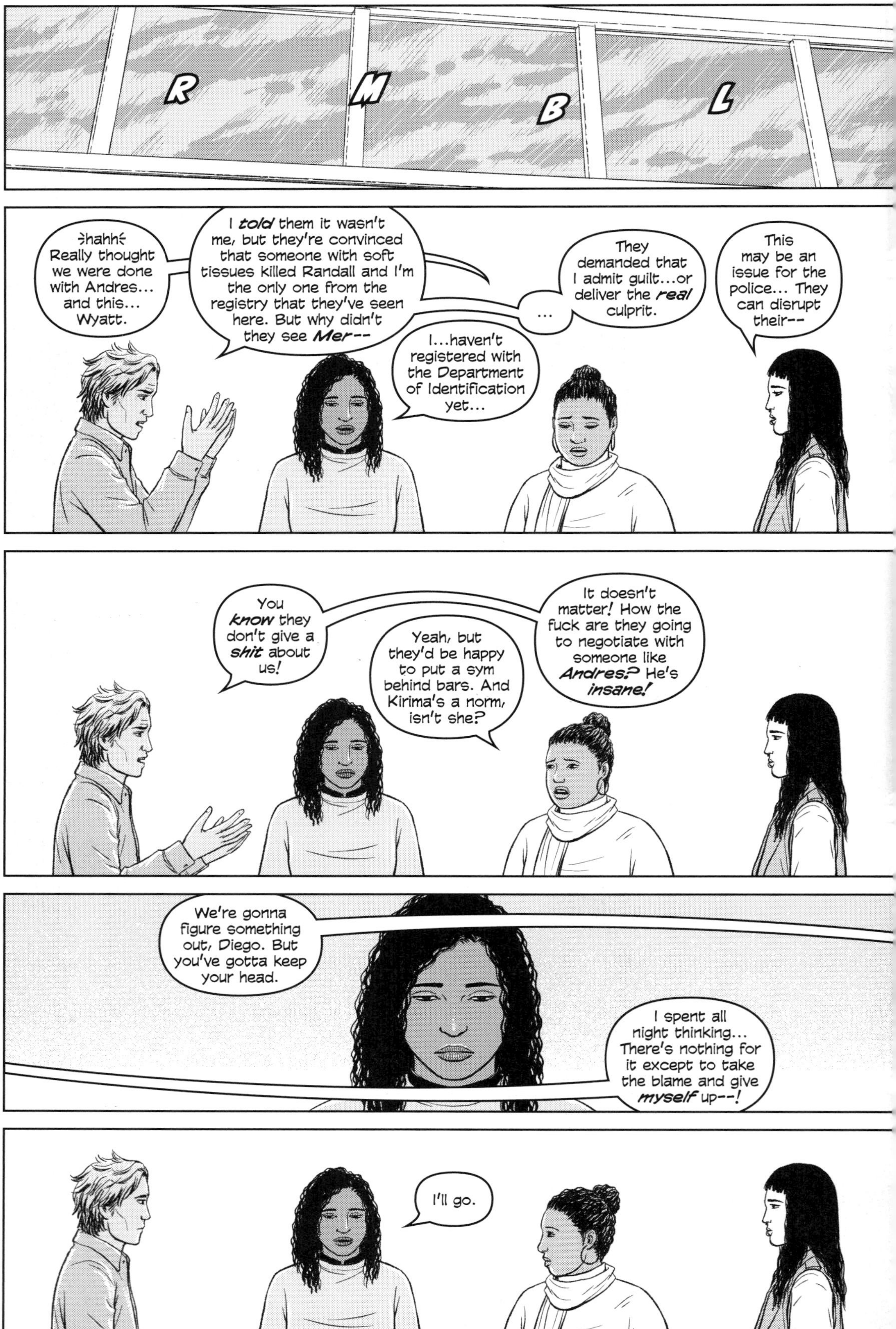
R M B L
⁓hahh⁓ Really thought we were done with Andres... and this... Wyatt.
I told them it wasn't me, but they're convinced that someone with soft tissues killed Randall and I'm the only one from the registry that they've seen here. But why didn't they see Mer--
I...haven't registered with the Department of Identification yet...
...
They demanded that I admit guilt...or deliver the real culprit.
This may be an issue for the police... They can disrupt their--
You know they don't give a shit about us!
It doesn't matter! How the fuck are they going to negotiate with someone like Andres? He's insane!
Yeah, but they'd be happy to put a sym behind bars. And Kirima's a norm, isn't she?
We're gonna figure something out, Diego. But you've gotta keep your head.
I spent all night thinking... There's nothing for it except to take the blame and give myself up--!
I'll go.

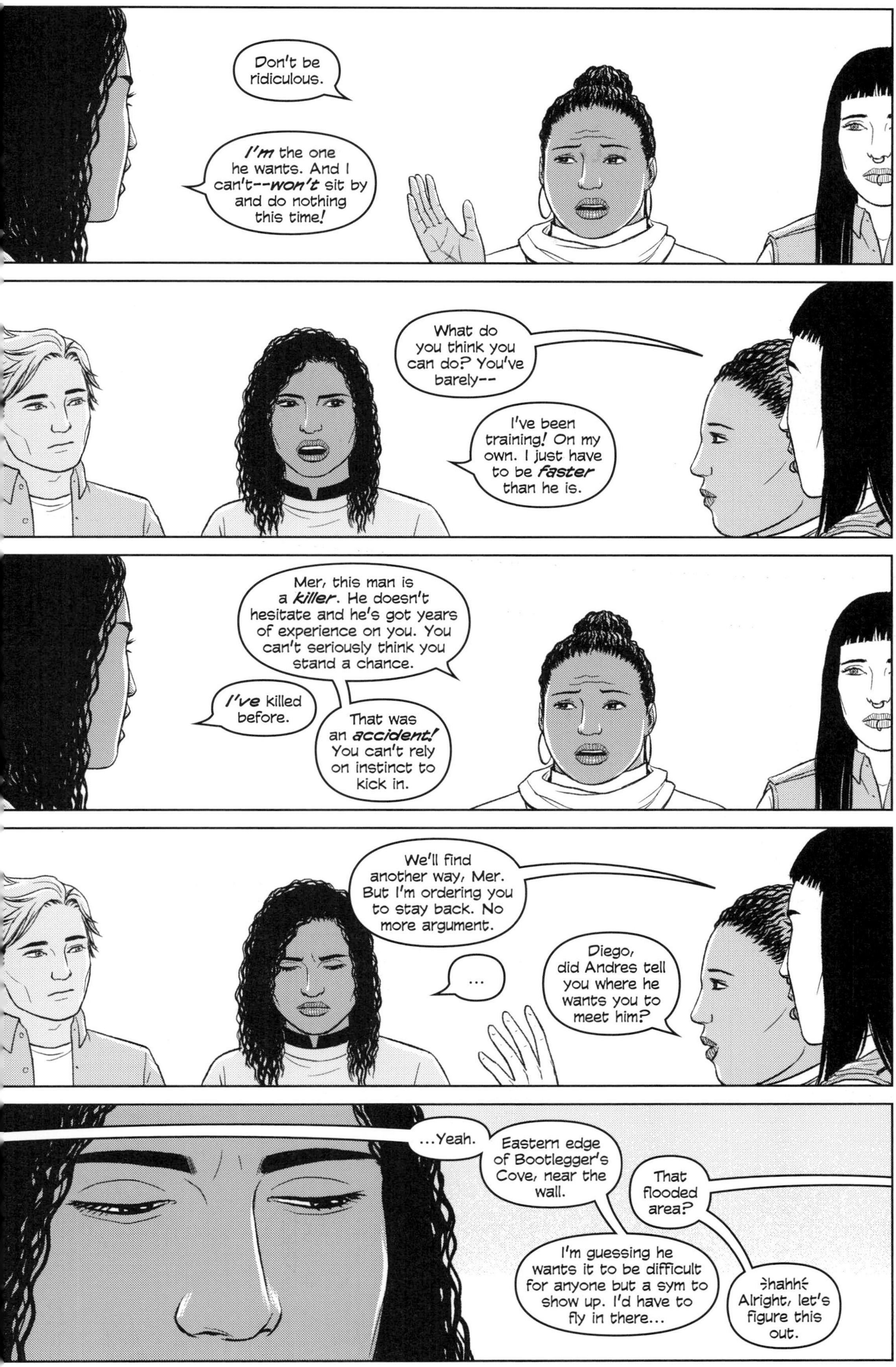
Don't be ridiculous.
I'm the one he wants. And I can't--won't sit by and do nothing this time!
What do you think you can do? You've barely--
I've been training! On my own. I just have to be faster than he is.
Mer, this man is a killer. He doesn't hesitate and he's got years of experience on you. You can't seriously think you stand a chance.
I've killed before.
That was an accident! You can't rely on instinct to kick in.
We'll find another way, Mer. But I'm ordering you to stay back. No more argument.
...
Diego, did Andres tell you where he wants you to meet him?
...Yeah.
Eastern edge of Bootlegger's Cove, near the wall.
That flooded area?
I'm guessing he wants it to be difficult for anyone but a sym to show up. I'd have to fly in there...
hahh
Alright, let's figure this out.

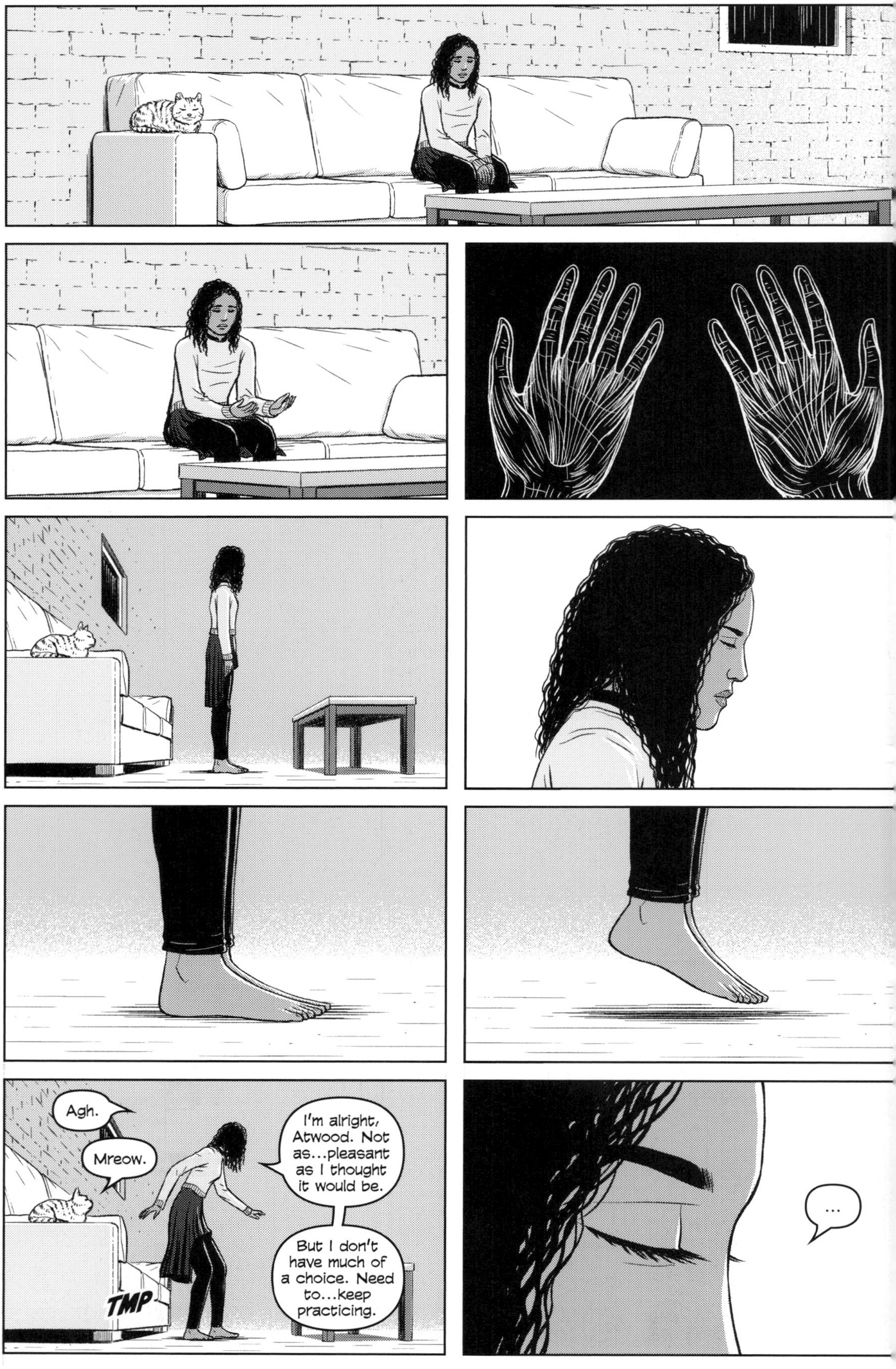
Agh.
Mreow.
TMP
I'm alright, Atwood. Not as...pleasant as I thought it would be.
But I don't have much of a choice. Need to...keep practicing.
...

KRAK

DNG

301

Hey Diana,
Thanks again for
watching Atwood. I
owe you one. I'm
writing this letter,
though, because I'm
about to c

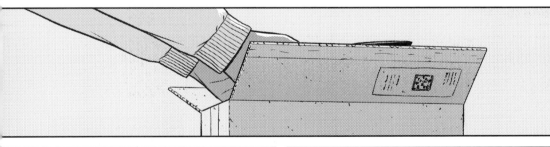

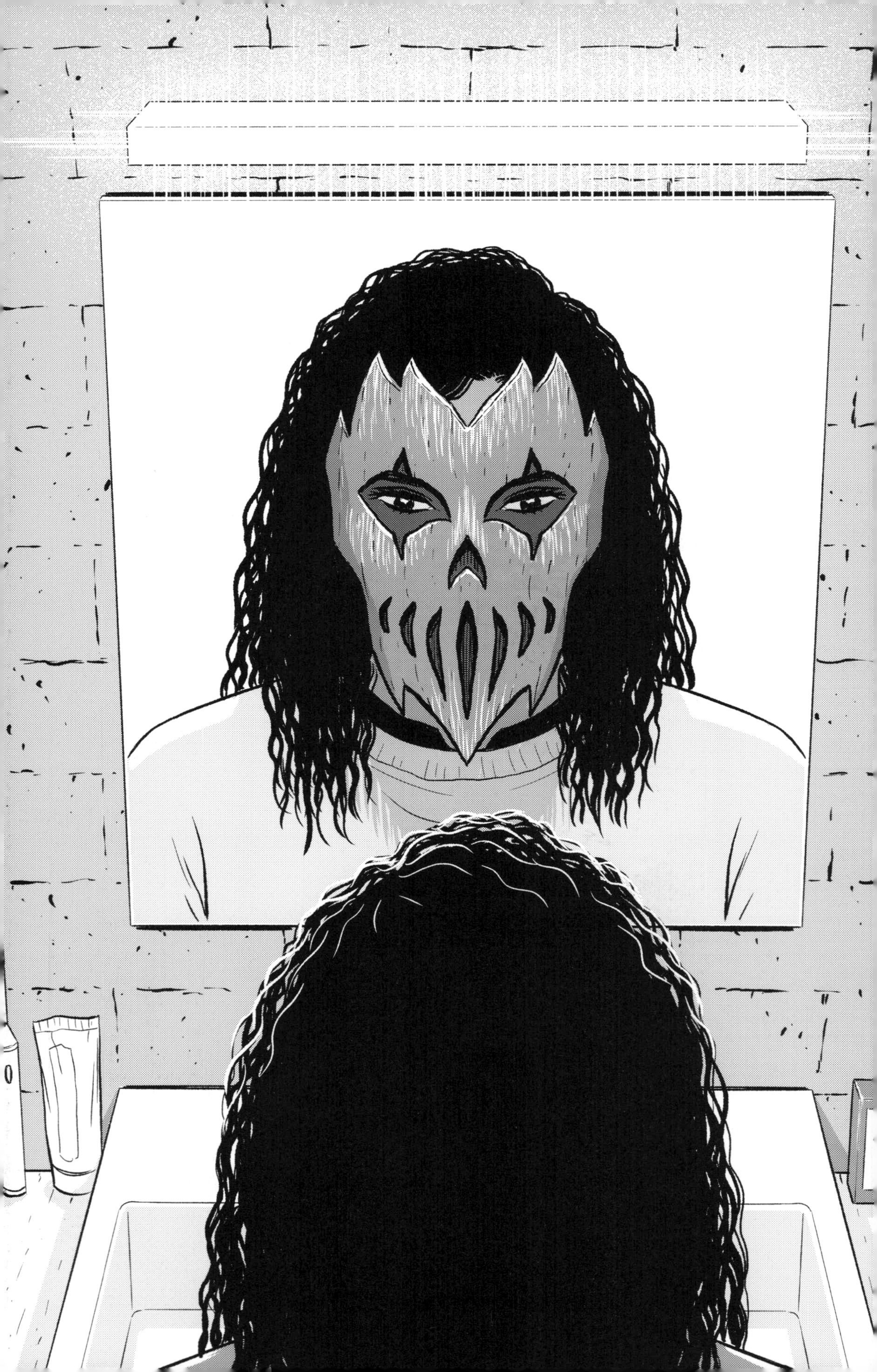

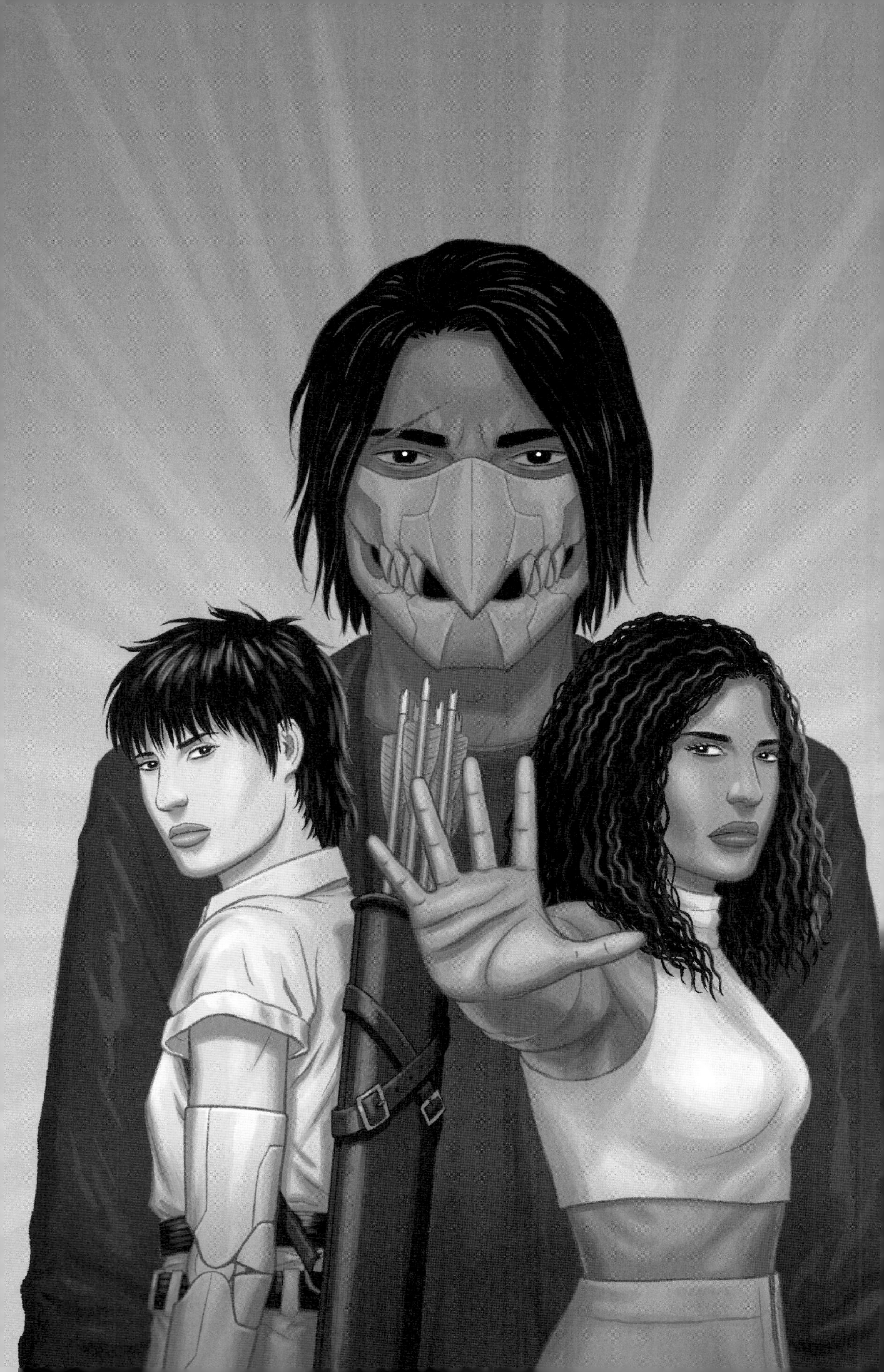

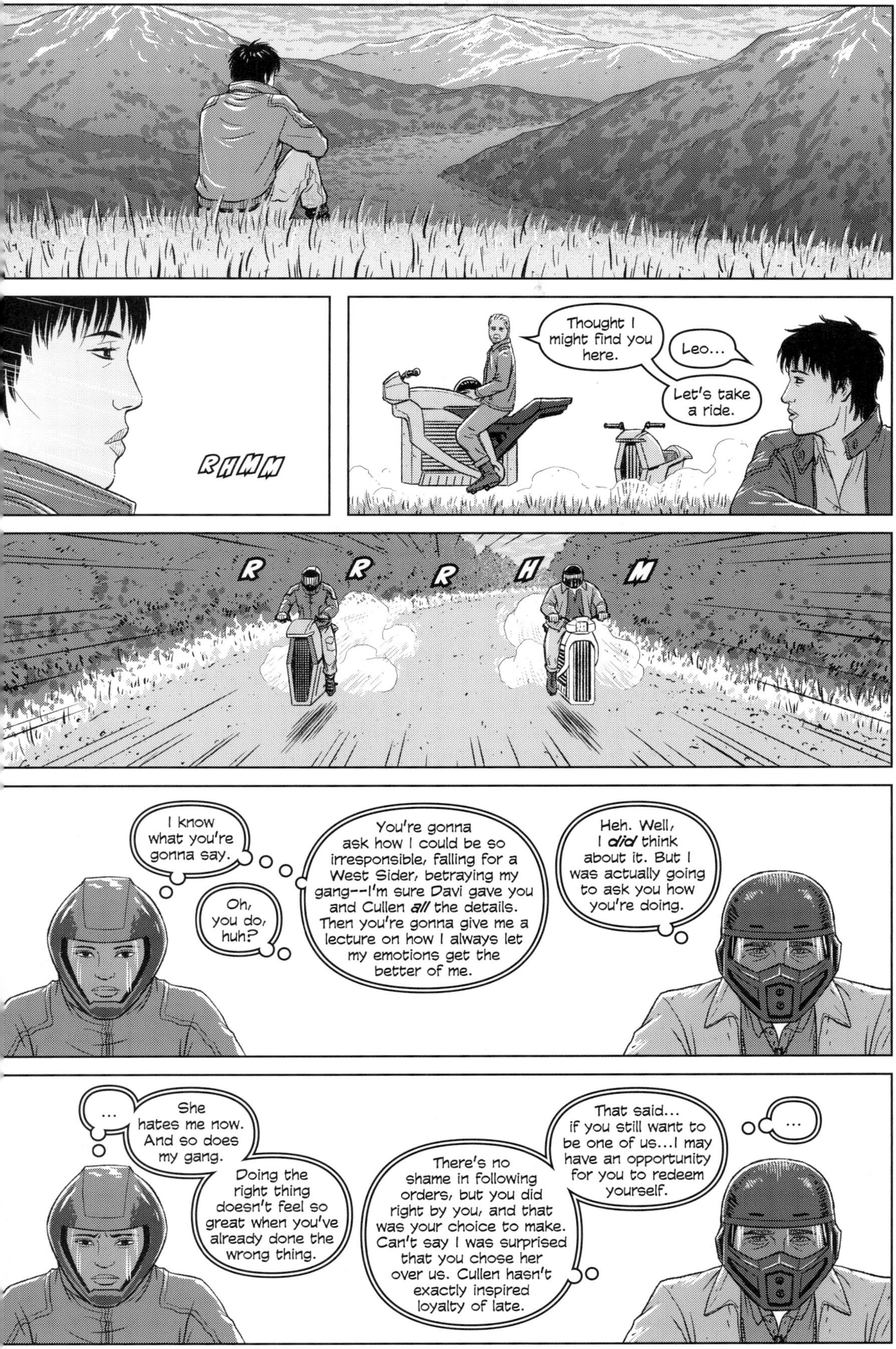
RHMM
Thought I might find you here.
Leo...
Let's take a ride.
R R R H M
I know what you're gonna say.
Oh, you do, huh?
You're gonna ask how I could be so irresponsible, falling for a West Sider, betraying my gang--I'm sure Davi gave you and Cullen *all* the details. Then you're gonna give me a lecture on how I always let my emotions get the better of me.
Heh. Well, I *did* think about it. But I was actually going to ask you how you're doing.
...
She hates me now. And so does my gang.
Doing the right thing doesn't feel so great when you've already done the wrong thing.
There's no shame in following orders, but you did right by you, and that was your choice to make. Can't say I was surprised that you chose her over us. Cullen hasn't exactly inspired loyalty of late.
That said... if you still want to be one of us...I may have an opportunity for you to redeem yourself.
...

It's about Andres. He's out for blood again.

...Why?

He believes a different West Sider killed Randall. ...He's taken their daughter hostage.

How do you know this?

Kal. She told Cullen and me when he called her to plea for a new peace deal with the West Side.

Cullen... pleaded for a new deal?

That was my handiwork. By some miracle, I convinced him to set aside his pride for the sake of the gang. But that's where the good news ends.

Kal won't consider a deal unless Cullen sends aid to stop Andres... but Cullen refuses. He believes that Andres isn't his problem anymore since he's out of the gang.

So, you want *me* to deal with Andres and claim that Cullen had a change of heart?

That's the idea. Cullen wouldn't want to deal with the shame of contradicting you.

Why me, though? I already failed once...

Truth is, no one else is gonna risk their neck for a West Sider unless Cullen orders it. But you have something to gain. This could be the difference between peace and war between the gangs. An act like that would earn back Cullen's trust.

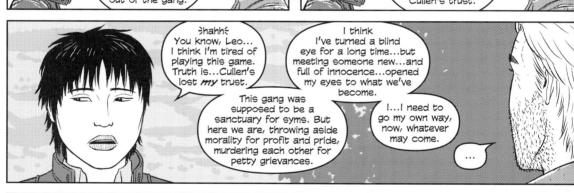

ϡhahhϟ You know, Leo... I think I'm tired of playing this game. Truth is...Cullen's lost *my* trust.

I think I've turned a blind eye for a long time...but meeting someone new...and full of innocence...opened my eyes to what we've become.

This gang was supposed to be a sanctuary for syms. But here we are, throwing aside morality for profit and pride, murdering each other for petty grievances.

I...I need to go my own way, now, whatever may come.

...

Promise... to not be a stranger?

Promise.

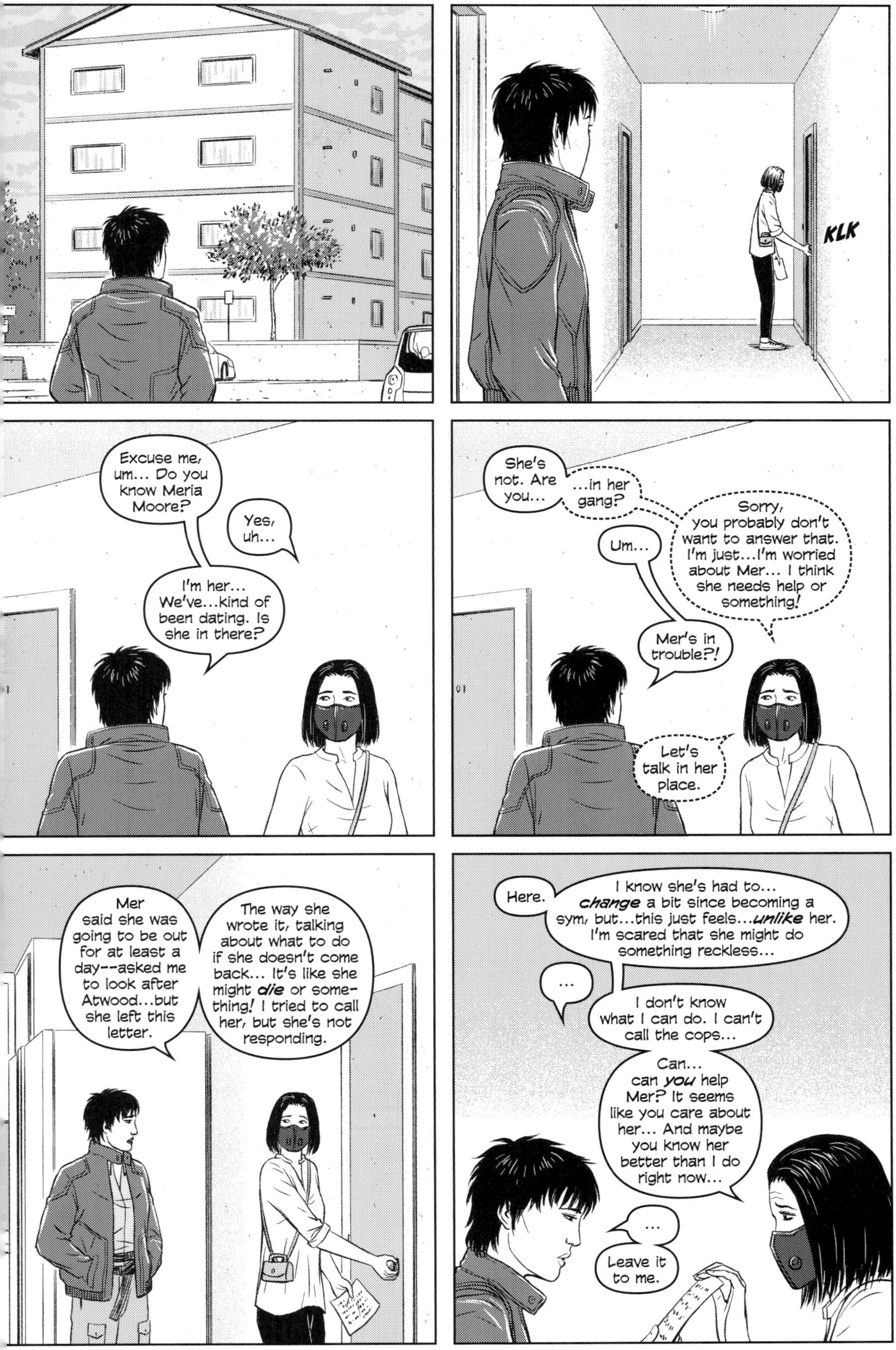
KLK
Excuse me, um... Do you know Meria Moore?
Yes, uh...
I'm her... We've...kind of been dating. Is she in there?
She's not. Are you...
...in her gang?
Sorry, you probably don't want to answer that. I'm just...I'm worried about Mer... I think she needs help or something!
Um...
Mer's in trouble?!
Let's talk in her place.
Mer said she was going to be out for at least a day--asked me to look after Atwood...but she left this letter.
The way she wrote it, talking about what to do if she doesn't come back... It's like she might *die* or something! I tried to call her, but she's not responding.
Here.
I know she's had to... *change* a bit since becoming a sym, but...this just feels...*unlike* her. I'm scared that she might do something reckless...
...
I don't know what I can do. I can't call the cops...
Can... can *you* help Mer? It seems like you care about her... And maybe you know her better than I do right now...
...
Leave it to me.

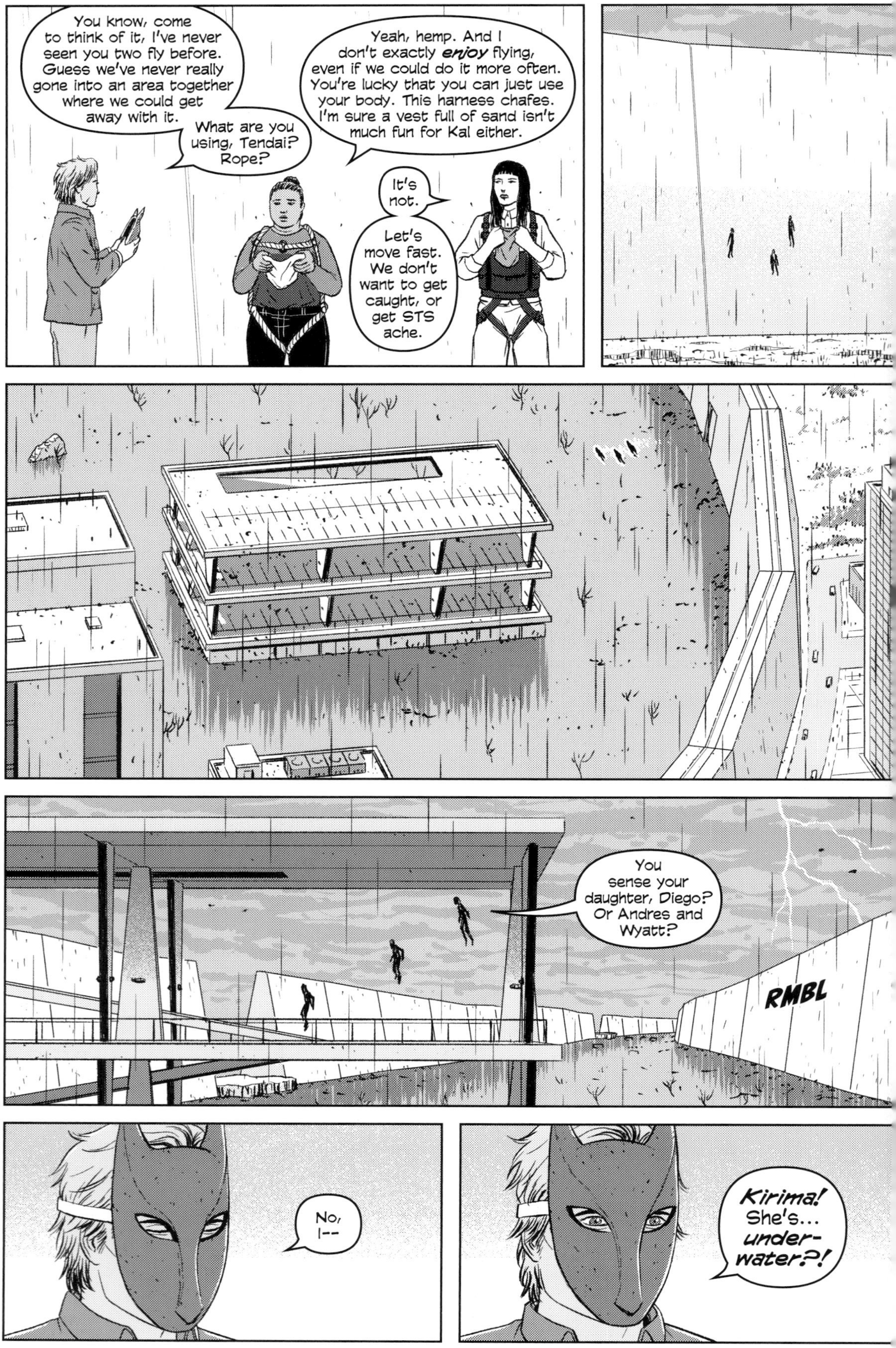
You know, come to think of it, I've never seen you two fly before. Guess we've never really gone into an area together where we could get away with it.
What are you using, Tendai? Rope?
Yeah, hemp. And I don't exactly *enjoy* flying, even if we could do it more often. You're lucky that you can just use your body. This harness chafes. I'm sure a vest full of sand isn't much fun for Kal either.
It's not.
Let's move fast. We don't want to get caught, or get STS ache.
You sense your daughter, Diego? Or Andres and Wyatt?
RMBL
No, I--
Kirima! She's... *under-water?!*

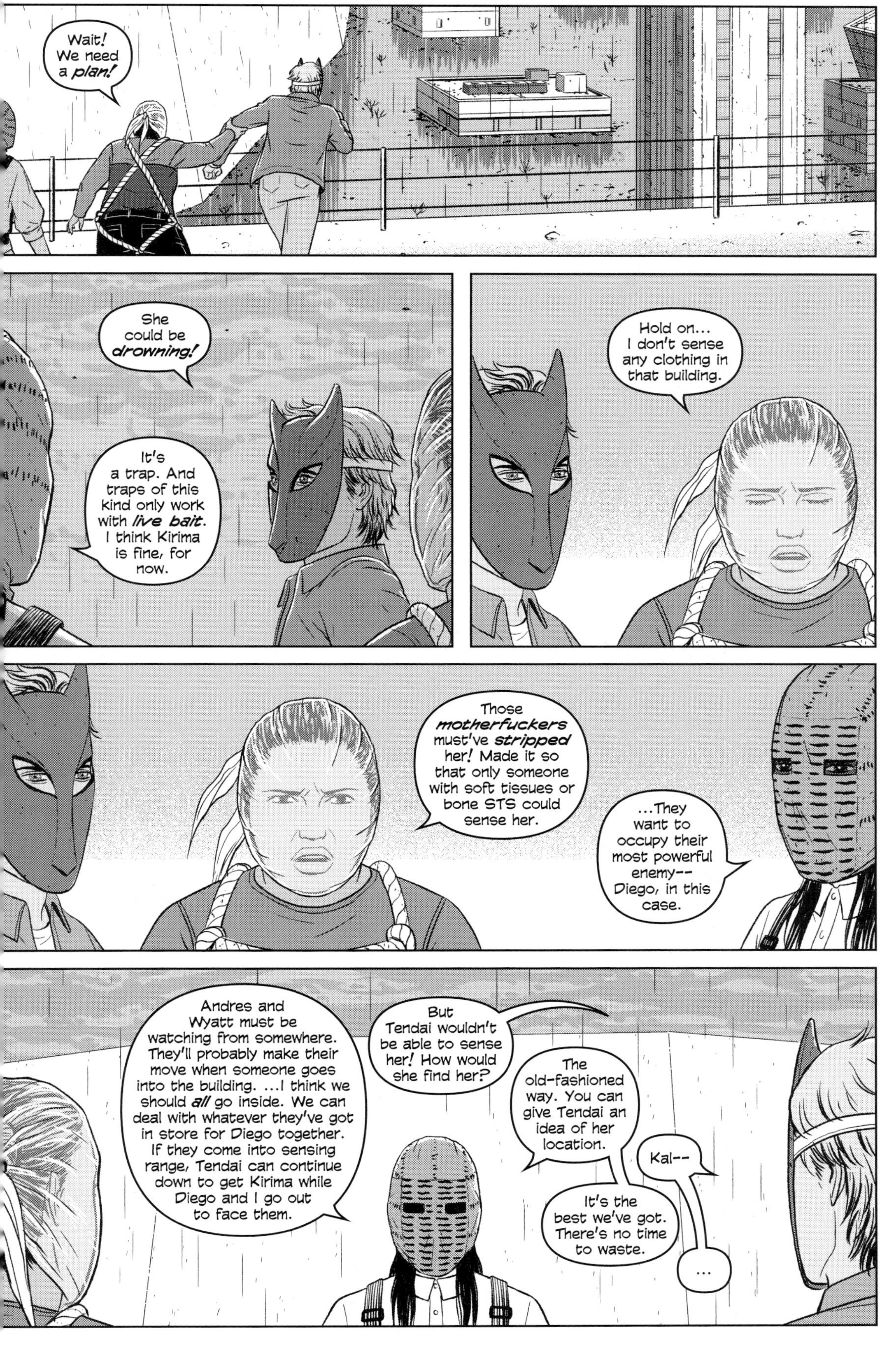

Wait! We need a *plan!*
She could be *drowning!*
It's a trap. And traps of this kind only work with *live bait*. I think Kirima is fine, for now.
Hold on... I don't sense any clothing in that building.
Those *motherfuckers* must've *stripped* her! Made it so that only someone with soft tissues or bone STS could sense her.
...They want to occupy their most powerful enemy-- Diego, in this case.
Andres and Wyatt must be watching from somewhere. They'll probably make their move when someone goes into the building. ...I think we should *all* go inside. We can deal with whatever they've got in store for Diego together. If they come into sensing range, Tendai can continue down to get Kirima while Diego and I go out to face them.
But Tendai wouldn't be able to sense her! How would she find her?
The old-fashioned way. You can give Tendai an idea of her location.
It's the best we've got. There's no time to waste.
Kal--
...

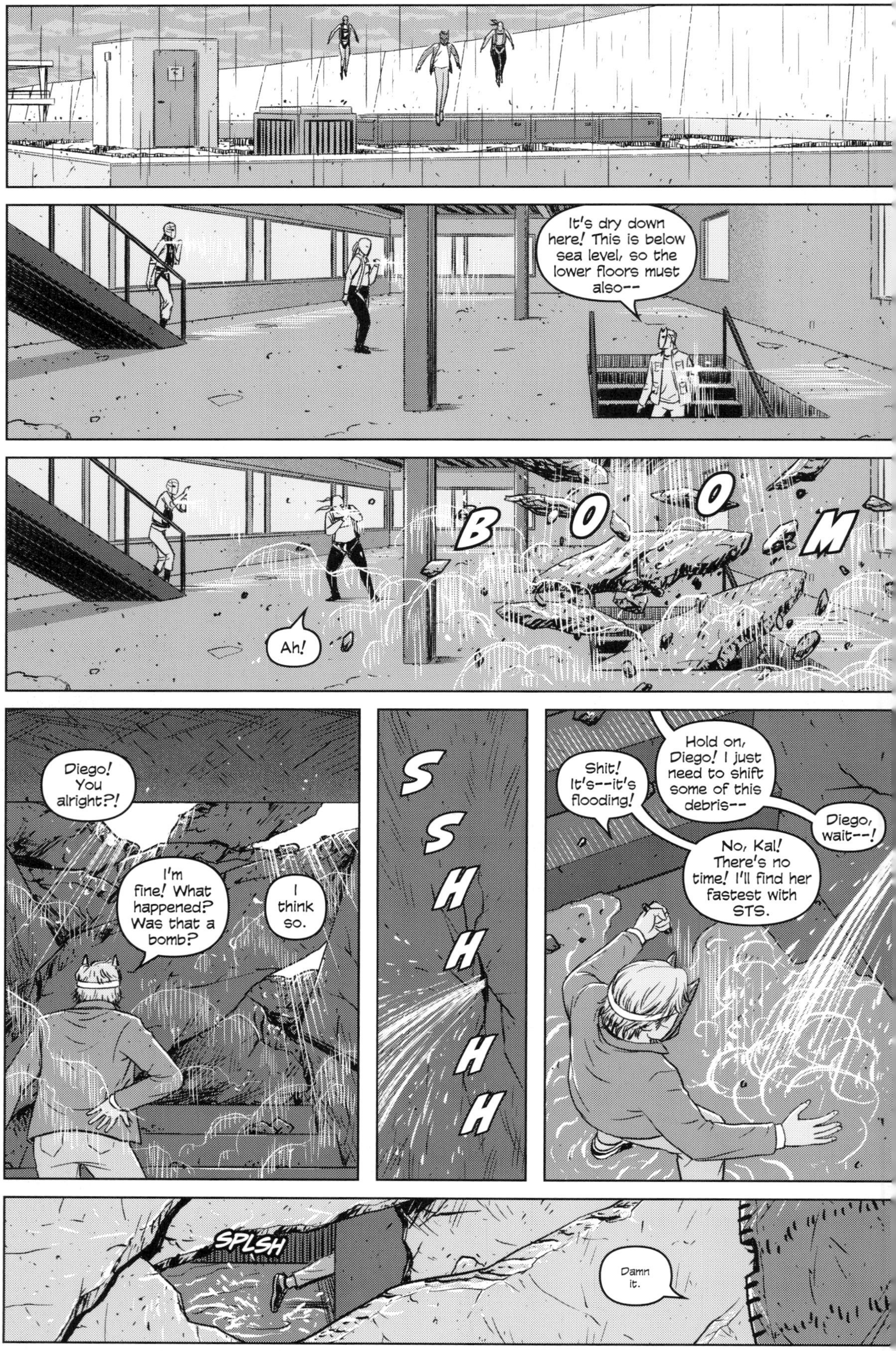
It's dry down here! This is below sea level, so the lower floors must also--
BOOM
Ah!
Diego! You alright?!
I'm fine! What happened? Was that a bomb?
I think so.
SSHHHH
Hold on, Diego! I just need to shift some of this debris--
Shit! It's--it's flooding!
Diego, wait--!
No, Kal! There's no time! I'll find her fastest with STS.
SPLSH
Damn it.

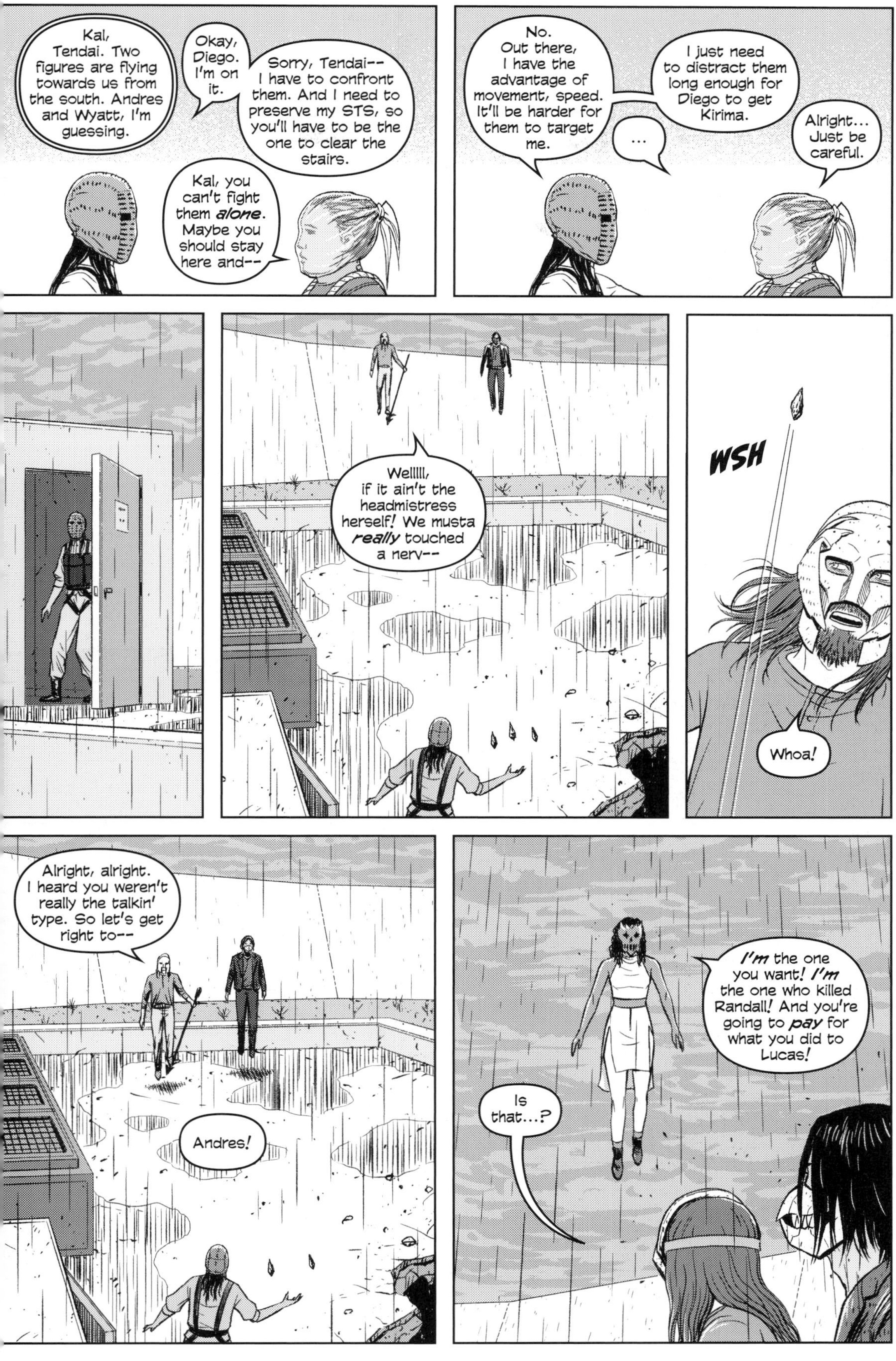
Kal, Tendai. Two figures are flying towards us from the south. Andres and Wyatt, I'm guessing.
Okay, Diego. I'm on it.
Sorry, Tendai-- I have to confront them. And I need to preserve my STS, so you'll have to be the one to clear the stairs.
Kal, you can't fight them *alone*. Maybe you should stay here and--
No. Out there, I have the advantage of movement, speed. It'll be harder for them to target me.
...
I just need to distract them long enough for Diego to get Kirima.
Alright... Just be careful.
Wellll, if it ain't the headmistress herself! We musta *really* touched a nerv--
WSH
Whoa!
Alright, alright. I heard you weren't really the talkin' type. So let's get right to--
Andres!
I'm the one you want! *I'm* the one who killed Randall! And you're going to *pay* for what you did to Lucas!
Is that...?

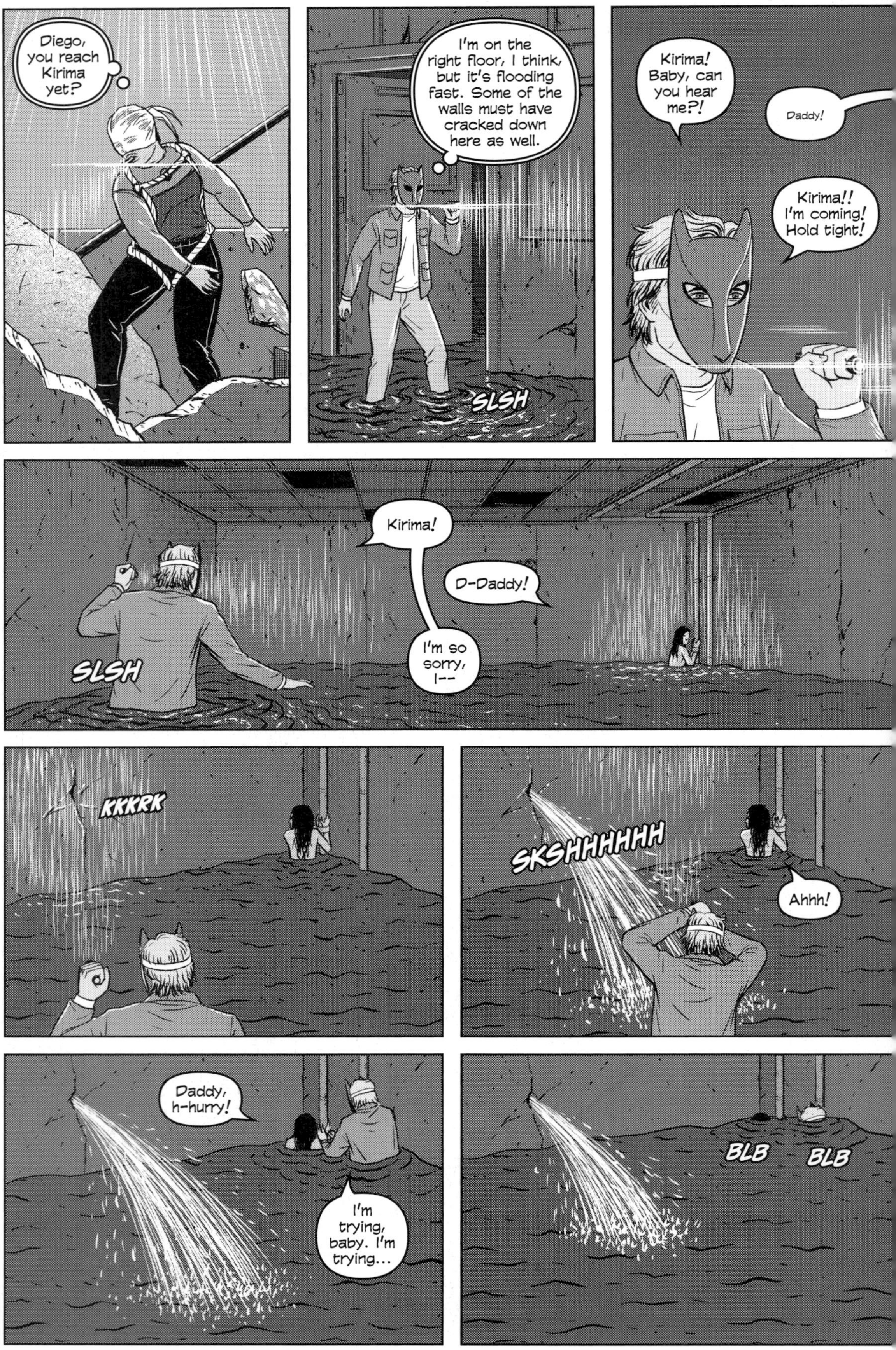

Diego, you reach Kirima yet?
I'm on the right floor, I think, but it's flooding fast. Some of the walls must have cracked down here as well.
SLSH
Kirima! Baby, can you hear me?!
Daddy!
Kirima!! I'm coming! Hold tight!
Kirima!
D-Daddy!
I'm so sorry, I--
SLSH
KKKRK
SKSHHHHHH
Ahhh!
Daddy, h-hurry!
I'm trying, baby. I'm trying...
BLB
BLB

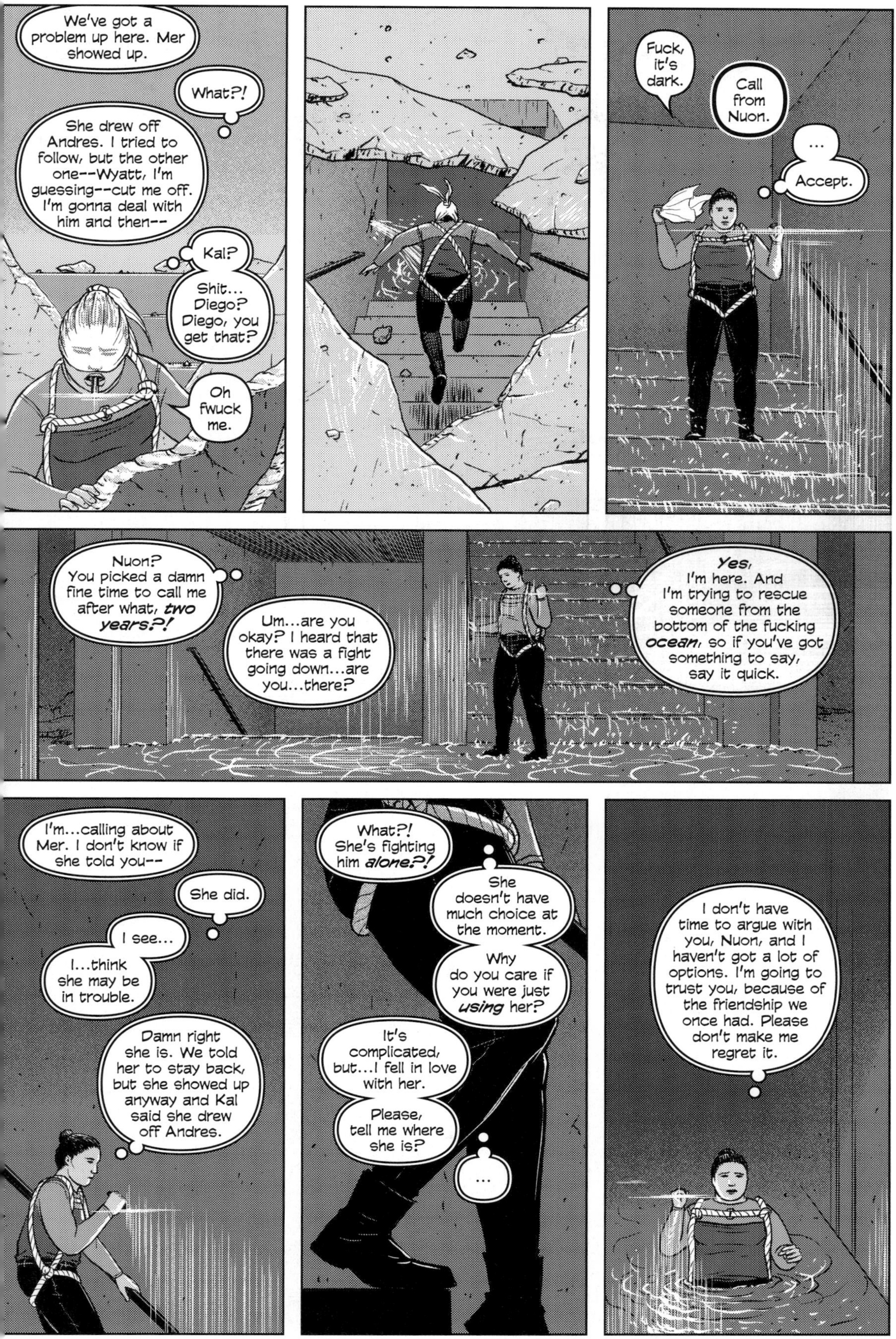
We've got a problem up here. Mer showed up.
What?!
She drew off Andres. I tried to follow, but the other one--Wyatt, I'm guessing--cut me off. I'm gonna deal with him and then--
Kal?
Shit... Diego? Diego, you get that?
Oh fwuck me.
Fuck, it's dark.
Call from Nuon.
...
Accept.
Nuon? You picked a damn fine time to call me after what, *two years?!*
Um...are you okay? I heard that there was a fight going down...are you...there?
Yes, I'm here. And I'm trying to rescue someone from the bottom of the fucking *ocean*, so if you've got something to say, say it quick.
I'm...calling about Mer. I don't know if she told you--
She did.
I see...
I...think she may be in trouble.
Damn right she is. We told her to stay back, but she showed up anyway and Kal said she drew off Andres.
What?! She's fighting him *alone?!*
She doesn't have much choice at the moment.
Why do you care if you were just *using* her?
It's complicated, but...I fell in love with her.
Please, tell me where she is?
...
I don't have time to argue with you, Nuon, and I haven't got a lot of options. I'm going to trust you, because of the friendship we once had. Please don't make me regret it.

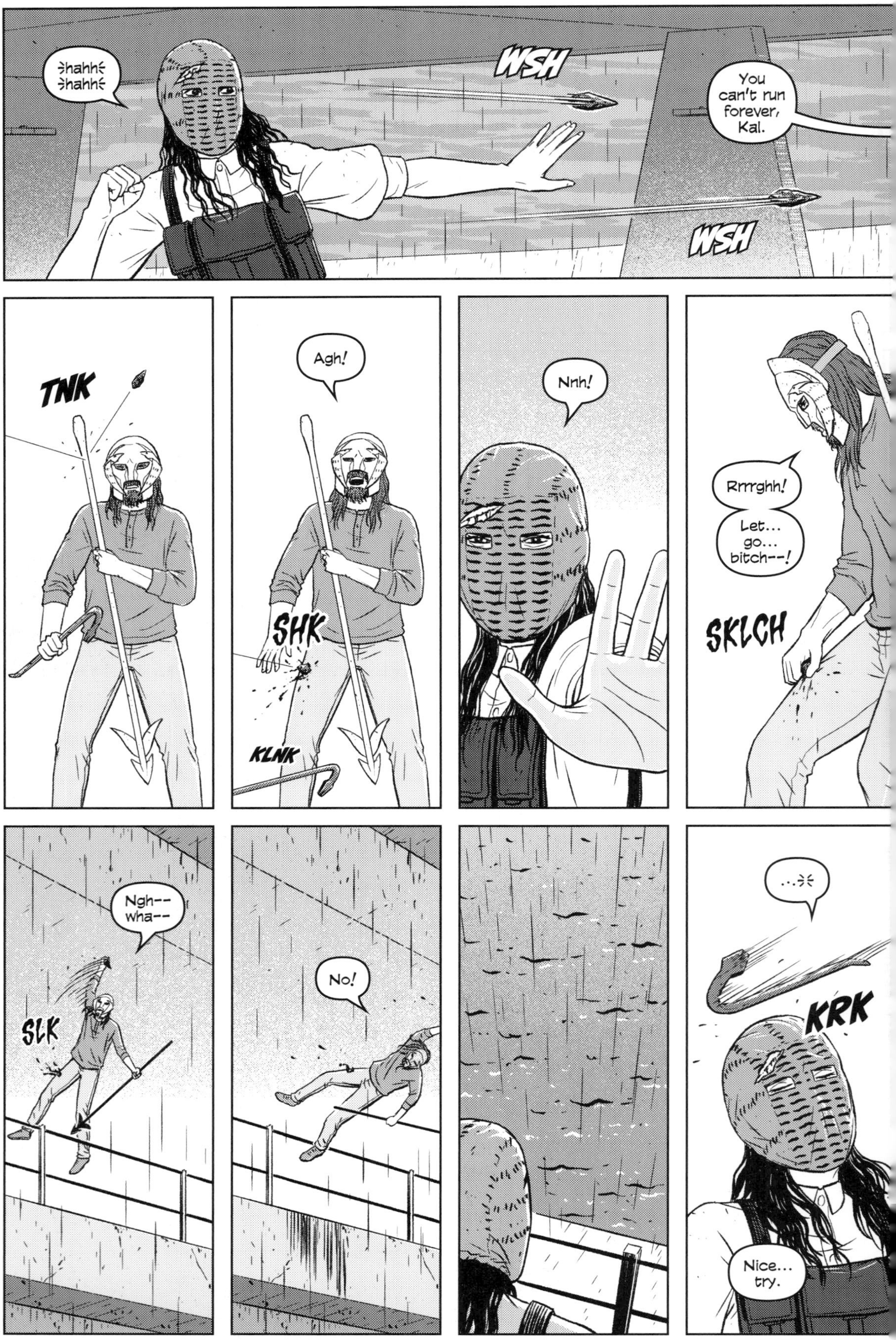

hahh
hahh
WSH
You can't run forever, Kal.
WSH
TNK
Agh!
SHK
KLNK
Nnh!
Rrrrghh!
Let... go... bitch--!
SKLCH
Ngh-- wha--
SLK
No!
...
KRK
Nice... try.

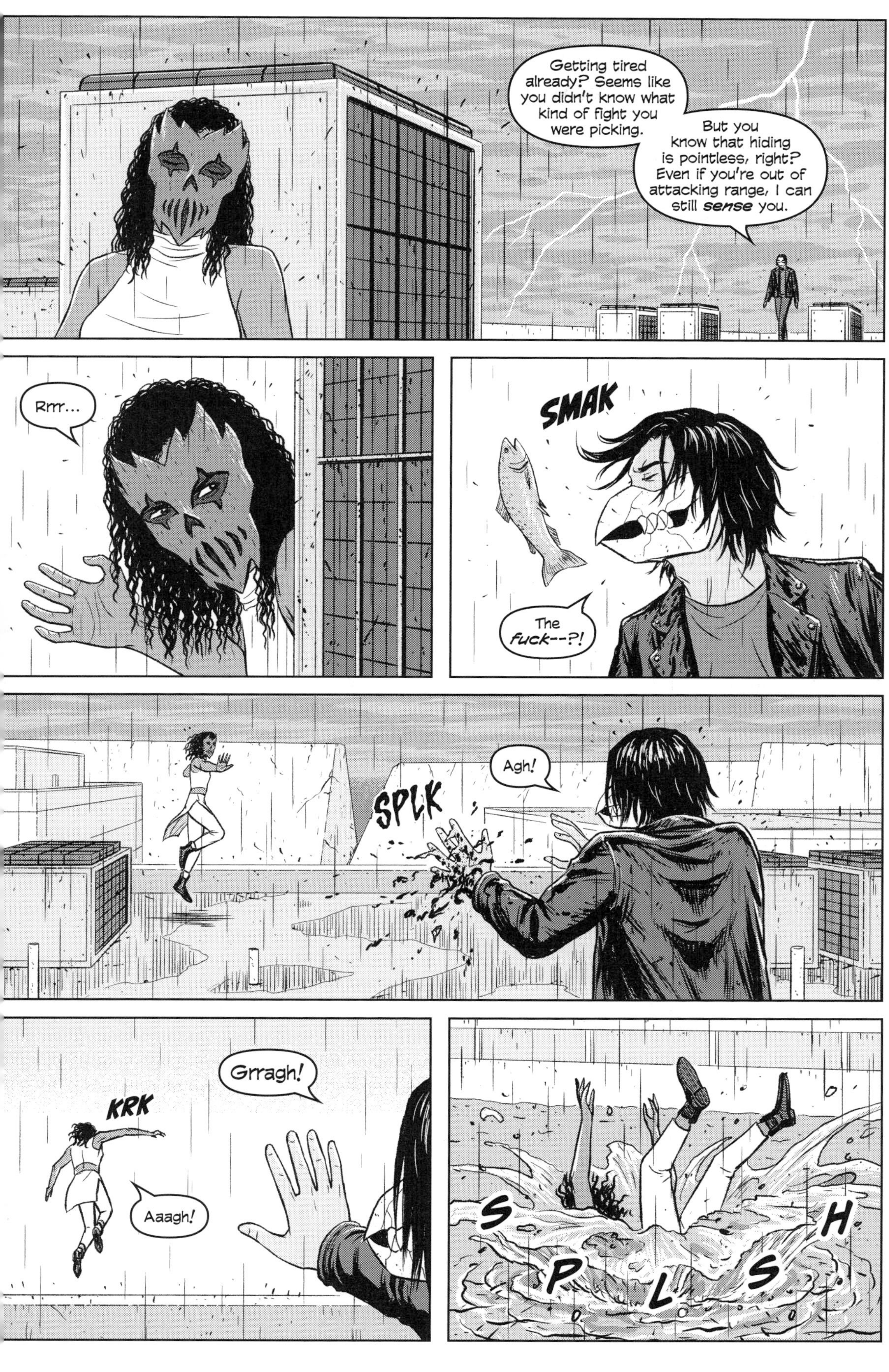
Getting tired already? Seems like you didn't know what kind of fight you were picking.
But you know that hiding is pointless, right? Even if you're out of attacking range, I can still *sense* you.
Rrrr...
SMAK
The *fuck*--?!
SPLK
Agh!
KRK
Grragh!
Aaagh!
SPLSH

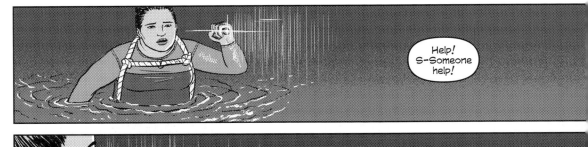

Help!
S—Someone help!

Kirima!

Help!
Daddy's stuck!
He c—can't breathe!

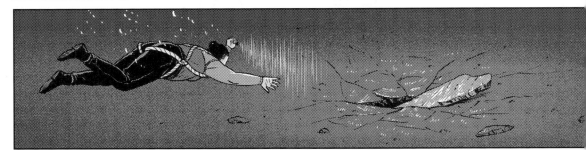

SHHF

W
R
B
L

≶hagh≶
≶hahk≶

≶huu≶

Ungh... This a *migraine* or...?

Fuck!

Raah!

Jesus, she's-- Wait--

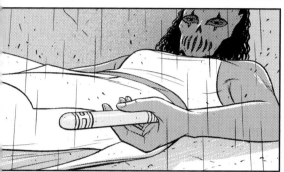

Another fucking sym disrupter?

Ah--!

Now, that's no fun.

KRK

Agh!

T H D

Wait just a sec. Let me get a look at 'er.

Make it quick.

Well, I'll be. It *is* the little bird!

SHK

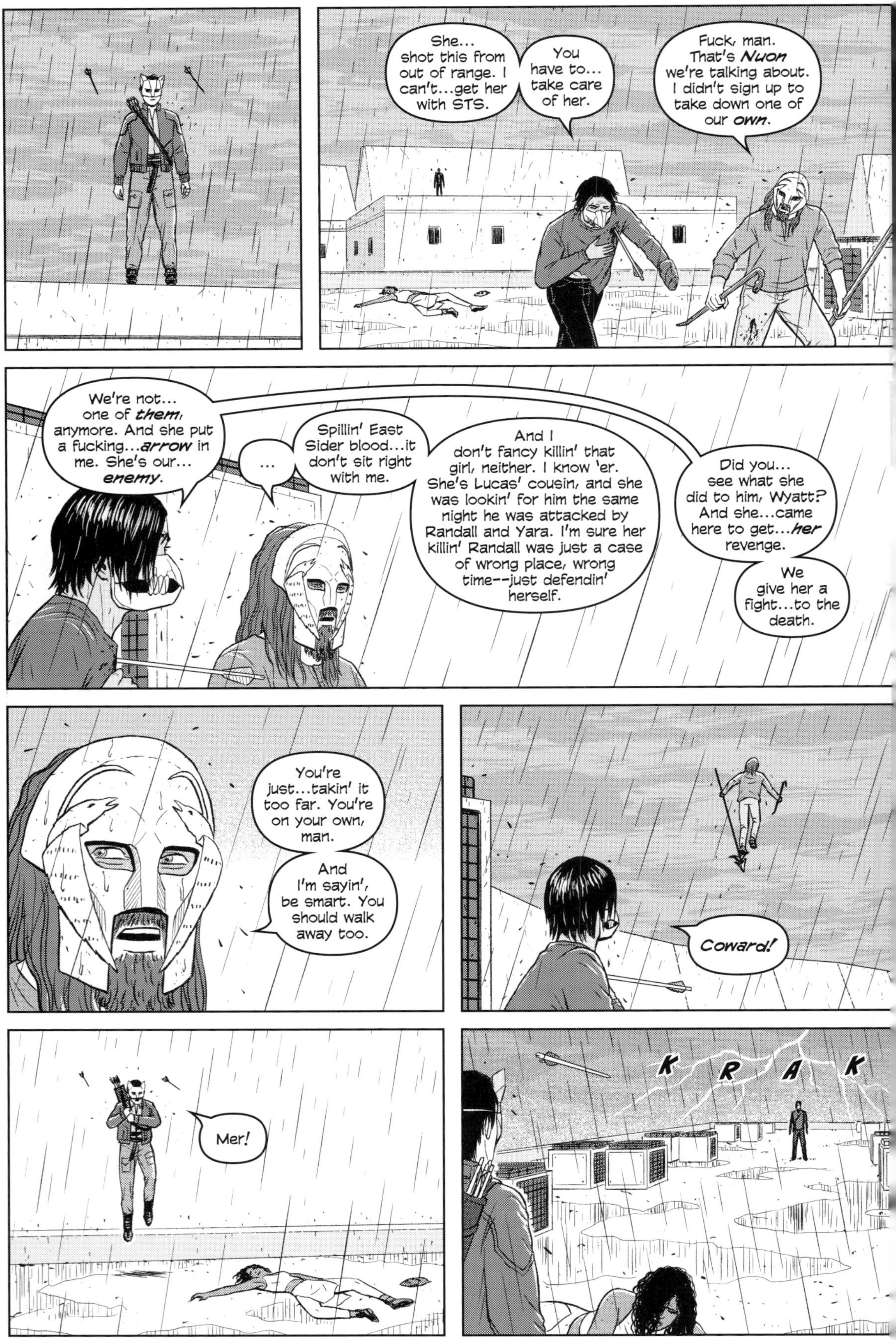
She... shot this from out of range. I can't...get her with STS.
You have to... take care of her.
Fuck, man. That's Nuon we're talking about. I didn't sign up to take down one of our own.
We're not... one of them, anymore. And she put a fucking...arrow in me. She's our... enemy.
...
Spillin' East Sider blood...it don't sit right with me.
And I don't fancy killin' that girl, neither. I know 'er. She's Lucas' cousin, and she was lookin' for him the same night he was attacked by Randall and Yara. I'm sure her killin' Randall was just a case of wrong place, wrong time--just defendin' herself.
Did you... see what she did to him, Wyatt? And she...came here to get...her revenge.
We give her a fight...to the death.
You're just...takin' it too far. You're on your own, man.
And I'm sayin', be smart. You should walk away too.
Coward!
Mer!
K R A K

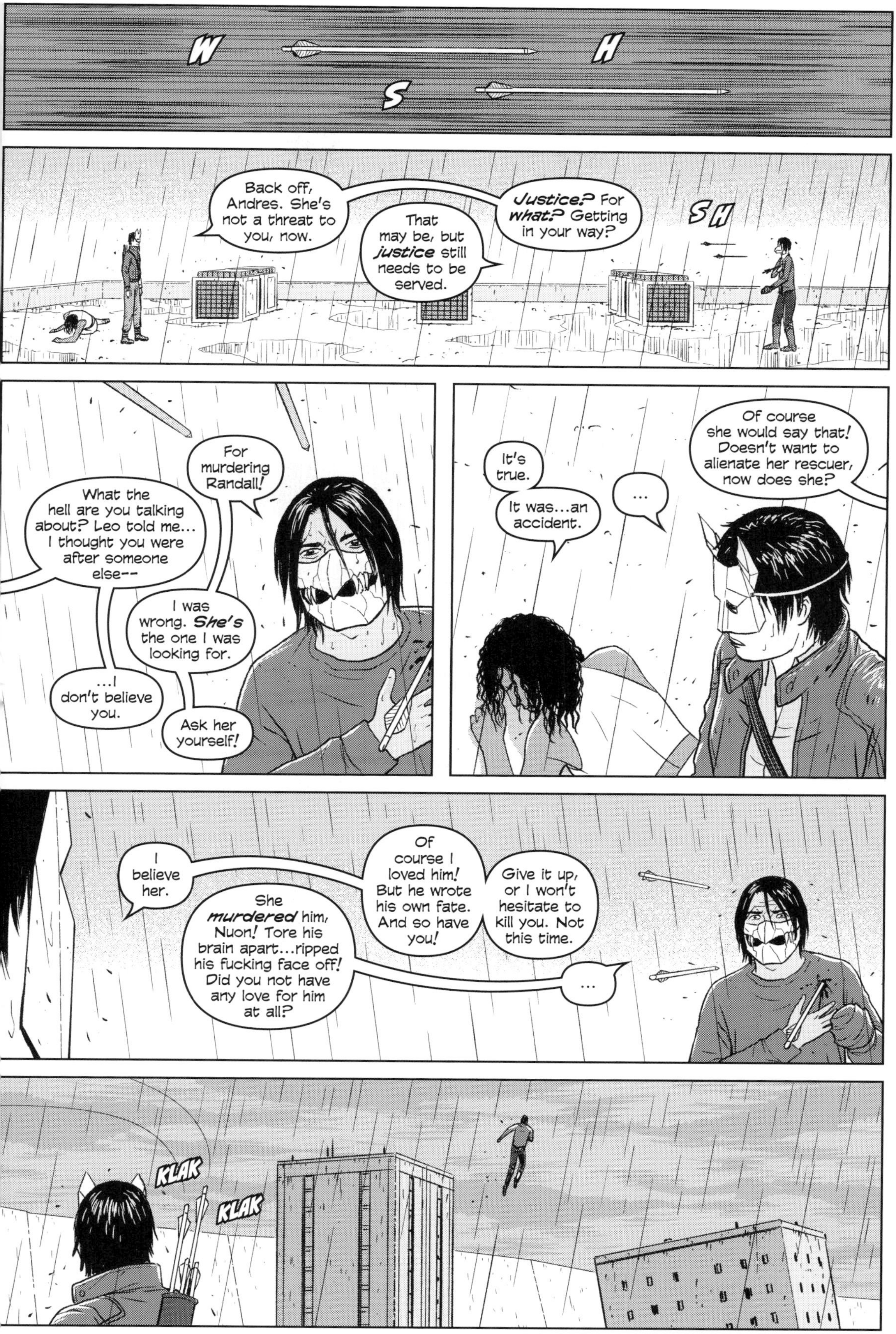
W
H
S
Back off, Andres. She's not a threat to you, now.
That may be, but justice still needs to be served.
Justice? For what? Getting in your way?
SH
What the hell are you talking about? Leo told me... I thought you were after someone else--
For murdering Randall!
I was wrong. She's the one I was looking for.
...I don't believe you.
Ask her yourself!
It's true.
It was...an accident.
...
Of course she would say that! Doesn't want to alienate her rescuer, now does she?
I believe her.
She murdered him, Nuon! Tore his brain apart...ripped his fucking face off! Did you not have any love for him at all?
Of course I loved him! But he wrote his own fate. And so have you!
Give it up, or I won't hesitate to kill you. Not this time.
...
KLAK
KLAK

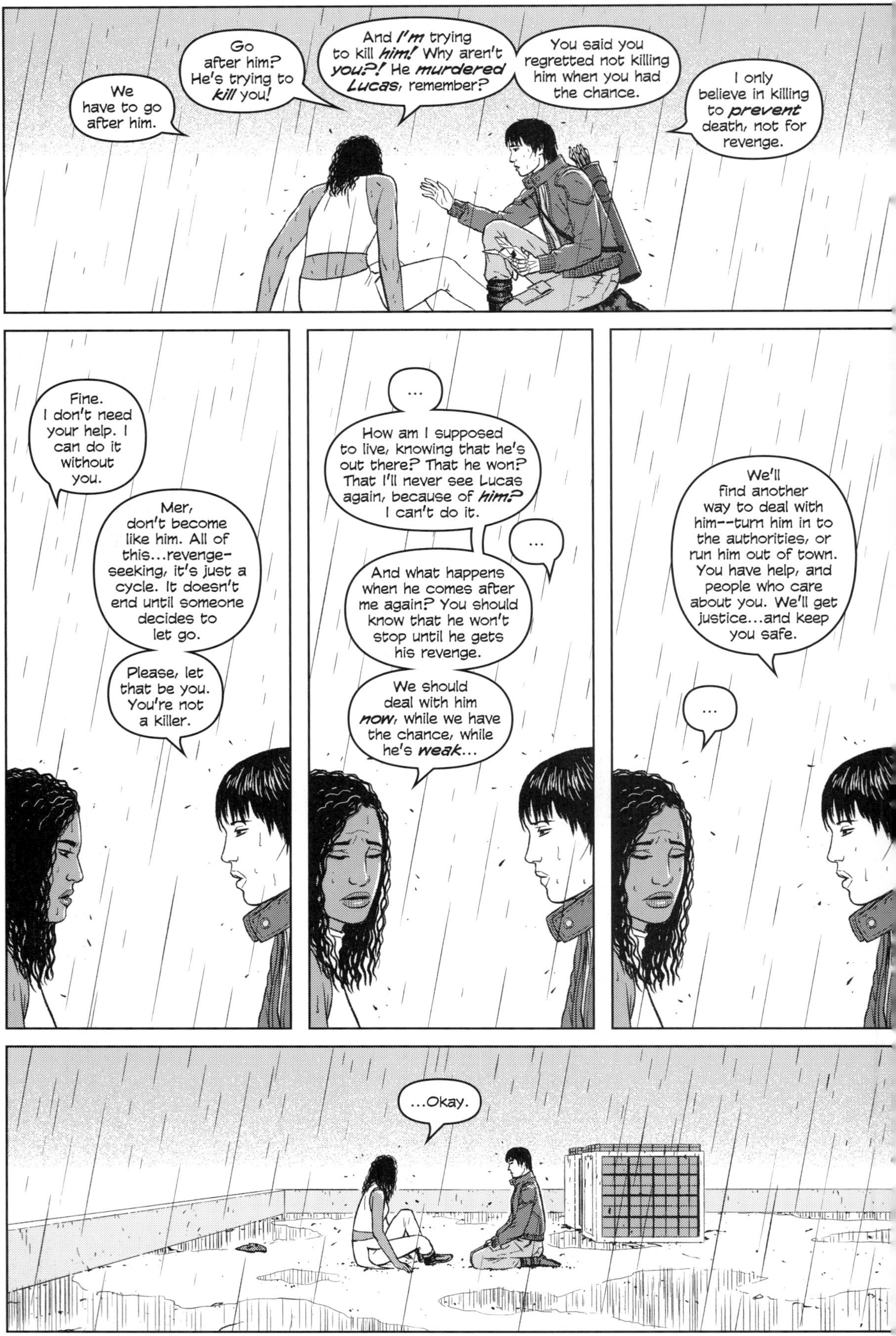

We have to go after him.
Go after him? He's trying to kill you!
And I'm trying to kill him! Why aren't you?! He murdered Lucas, remember?
You said you regretted not killing him when you had the chance.
I only believe in killing to prevent death, not for revenge.
Fine. I don't need your help. I can do it without you.
Mer, don't become like him. All of this...revenge-seeking, it's just a cycle. It doesn't end until someone decides to let go.
Please, let that be you. You're not a killer.
...
How am I supposed to live, knowing that he's out there? That he won? That I'll never see Lucas again, because of him? I can't do it.
...
And what happens when he comes after me again? You should know that he won't stop until he gets his revenge.
We should deal with him now, while we have the chance, while he's weak...
We'll find another way to deal with him--turn him in to the authorities, or run him out of town. You have help, and people who care about you. We'll get justice...and keep you safe.
...
...Okay.

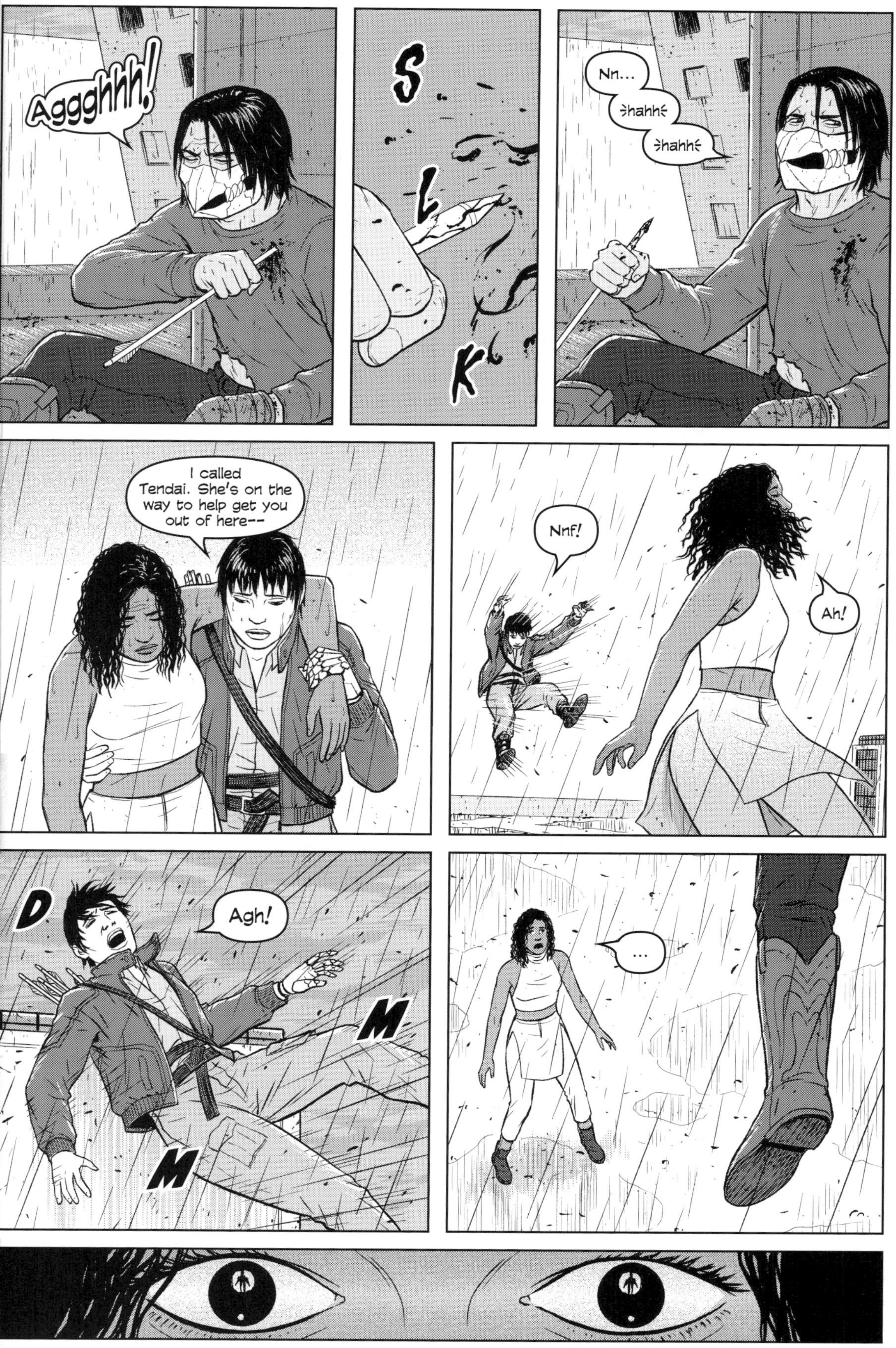
Aggghhh!
S
L
K
Nn...
hahh
hahh
I called Tendai. She's on the way to help get you out of here--
Nnf!
Ah!
D
Agh!
M
M
...

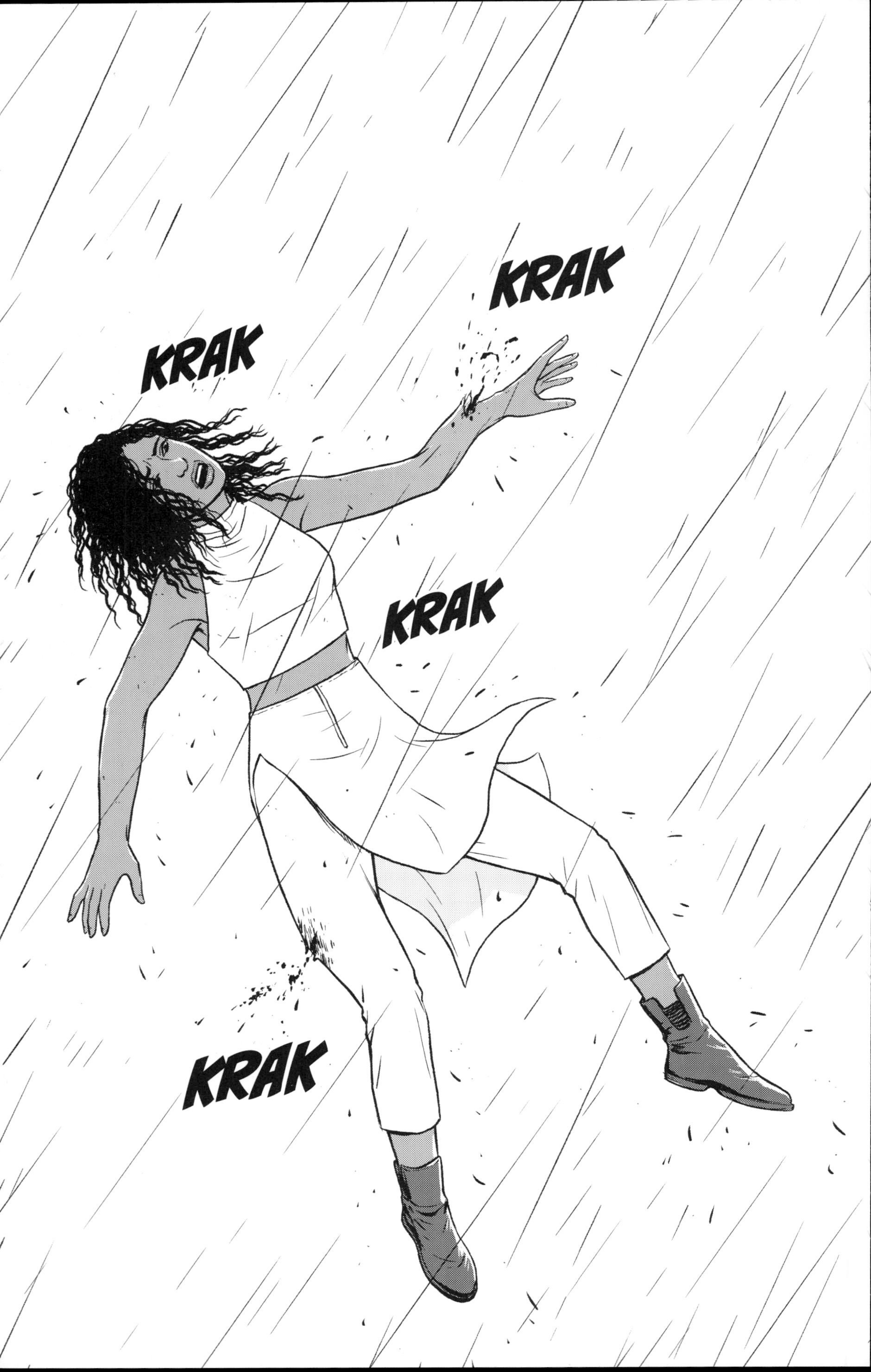
KRAK
KRAK
KRAK
KRAK

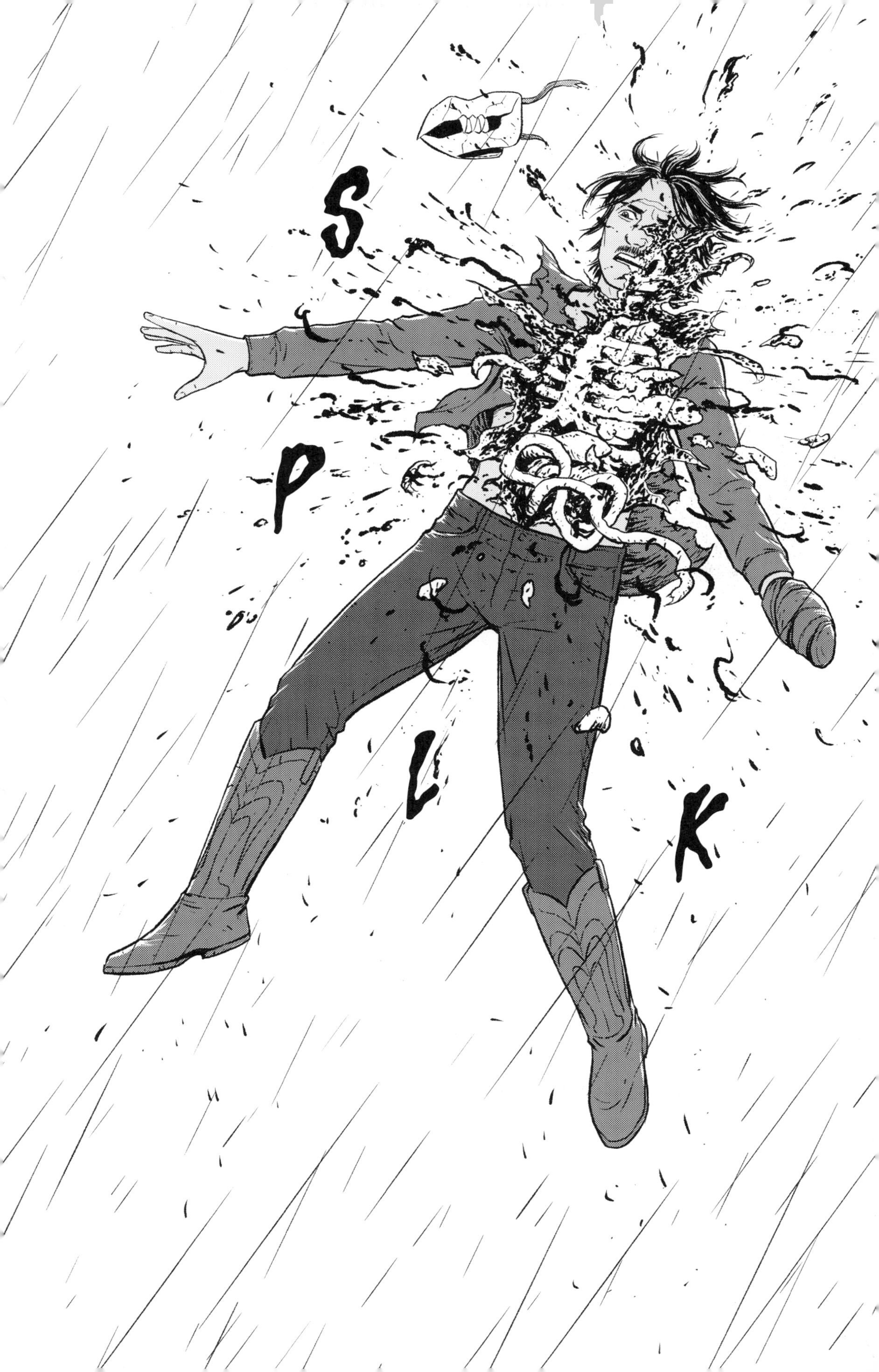
SPLK

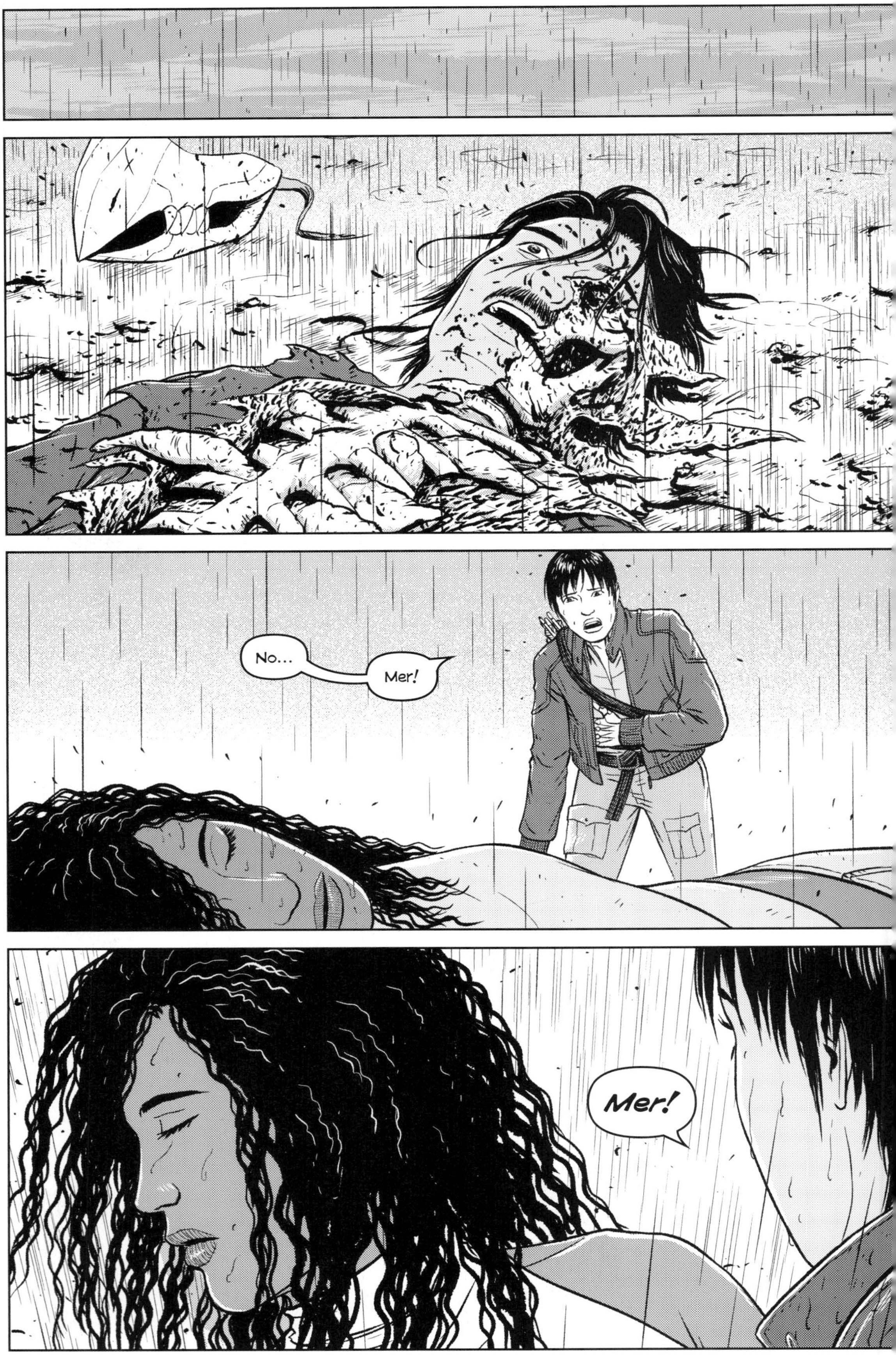
No...
Mer!
Mer!

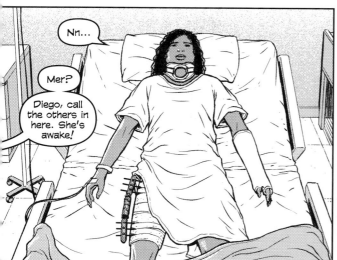

Nn...

Mer?

Diego, call the others in here. She's awake!

Tendai...

Oh, sweetheart... I'm here.

You're all... here...

Of course we are.

...

Oh, hon--

My arm... I can't feel it, I...

...

Andres... he did...quite a number on you...

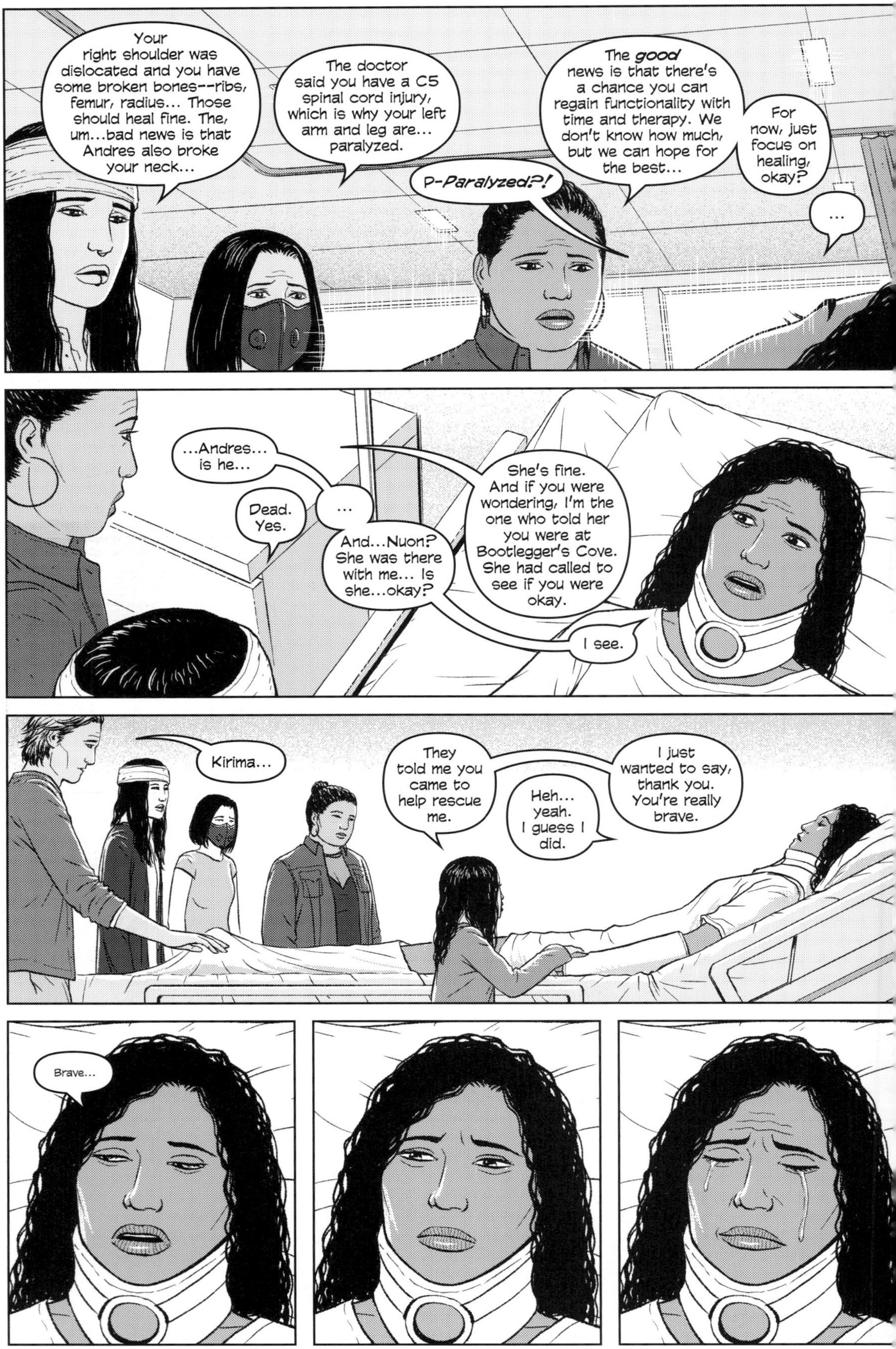
Your right shoulder was dislocated and you have some broken bones--ribs, femur, radius... Those should heal fine. The, um...bad news is that Andres also broke your neck...
The doctor said you have a C5 spinal cord injury, which is why your left arm and leg are... paralyzed.
P-*Paralyzed?!*
The ***good*** news is that there's a chance you can regain functionality with time and therapy. We don't know how much, but we can hope for the best...
For now, just focus on healing, okay?
...
...Andres... is he...
Dead. Yes.
...
And...Nuon? She was there with me... Is she...okay?
She's fine. And if you were wondering, I'm the one who told her you were at Bootlegger's Cove. She had called to see if you were okay.
I see.
Kirima...
They told me you came to help rescue me.
Heh... yeah. I guess I did.
I just wanted to say, thank you. You're really brave.
Brave...

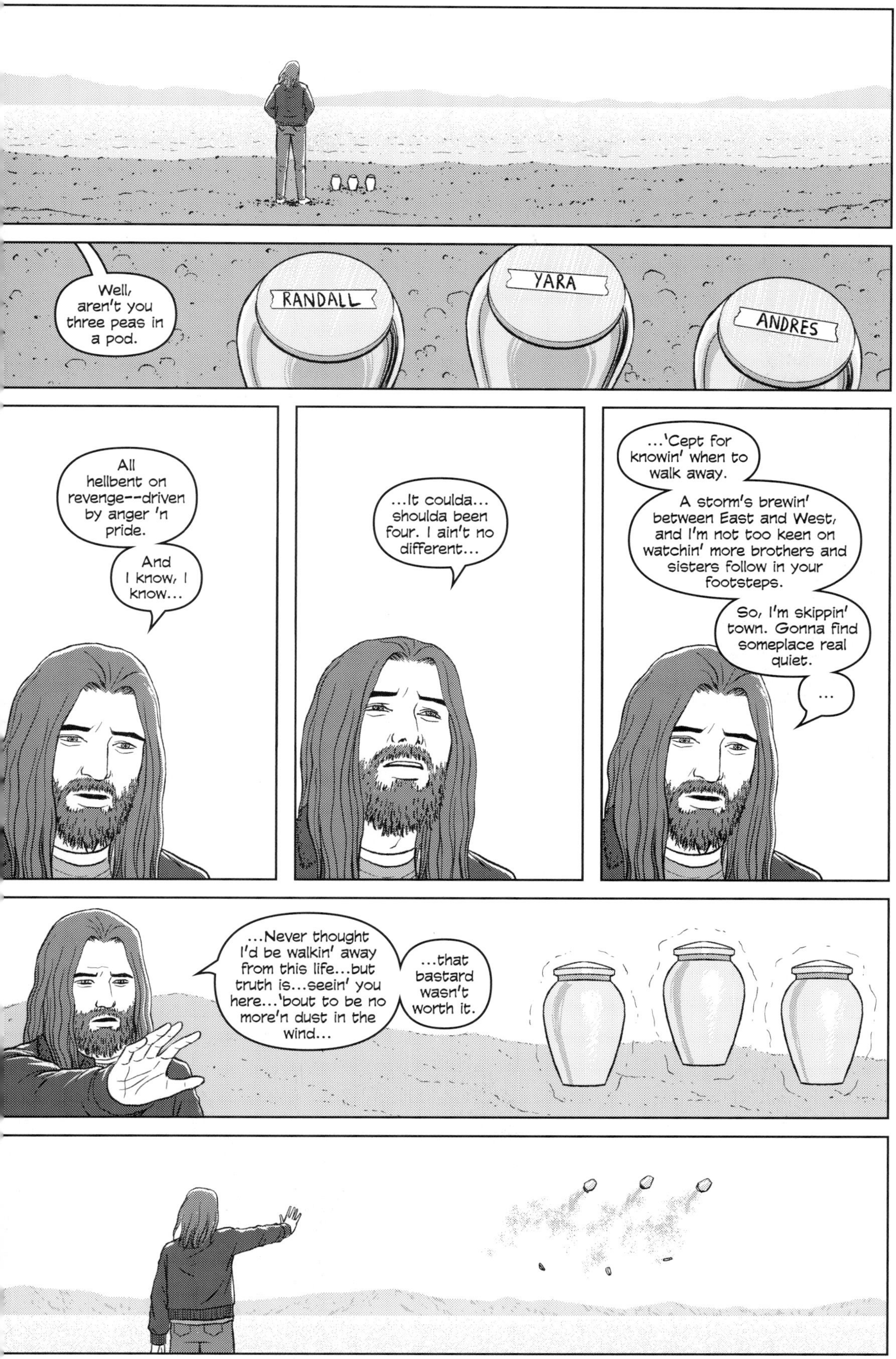

Well, aren't you three peas in a pod.
RANDALL
YARA
ANDRES
All hellbent on revenge--driven by anger 'n pride.
And I know, I know...
...It coulda... shoulda been four. I ain't no different...
...'Cept for knowin' when to walk away.
A storm's brewin' between East and West, and I'm not too keen on watchin' more brothers and sisters follow in your footsteps.
So, I'm skippin' town. Gonna find someplace real quiet.
...
...Never thought I'd be walkin' away from this life...but truth is...seein' you here...'bout to be no more'n dust in the wind...
...that bastard wasn't worth it.

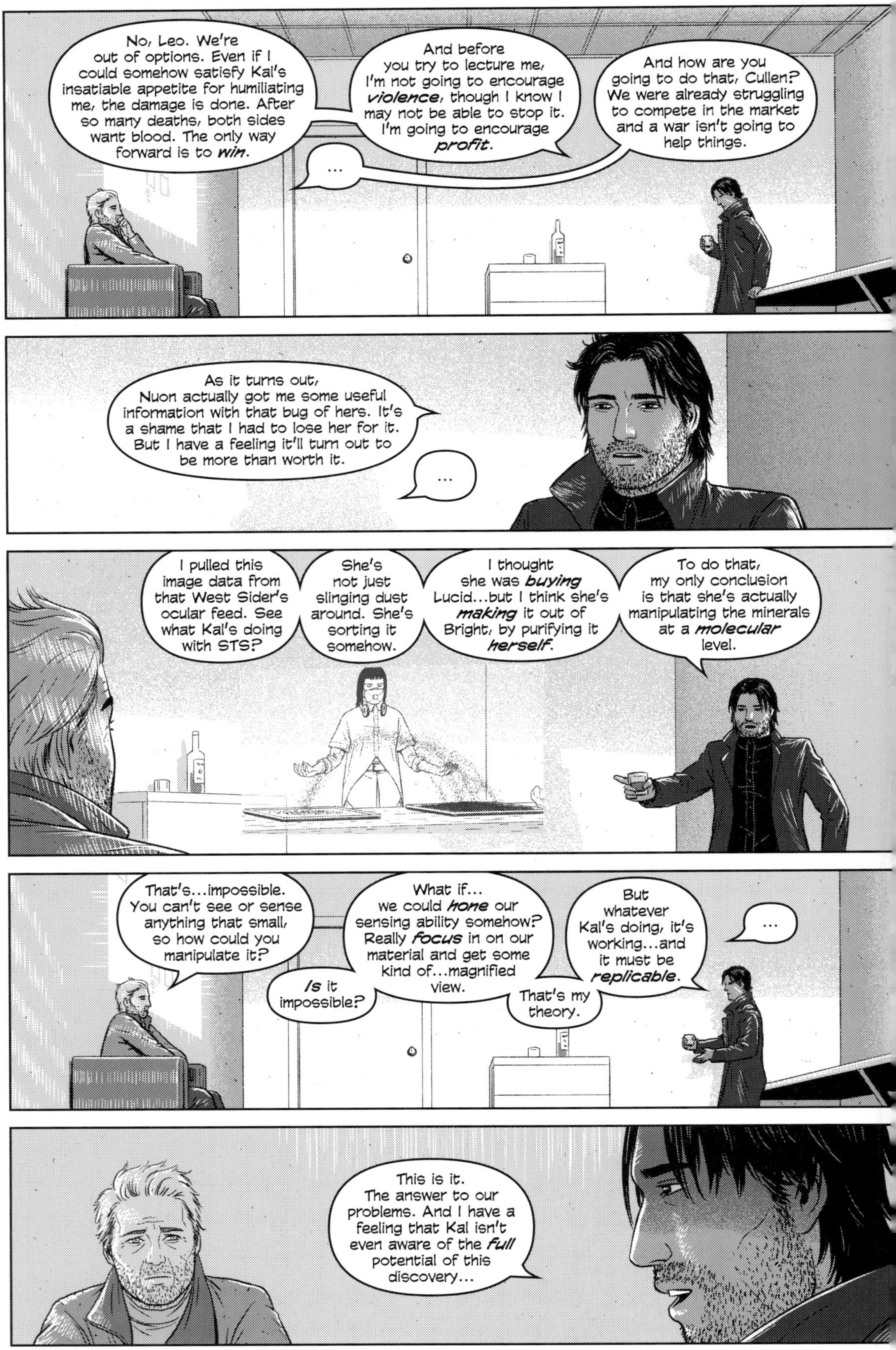
No, Leo. We're out of options. Even if I could somehow satisfy Kal's insatiable appetite for humiliating me, the damage is done. After so many deaths, both sides want blood. The only way forward is to *win*.
...
And before you try to lecture me, I'm not going to encourage *violence*, though I know I may not be able to stop it. I'm going to encourage *profit*.
And how are you going to do that, Cullen? We were already struggling to compete in the market and a war isn't going to help things.
As it turns out, Nuon actually got me some useful information with that bug of hers. It's a shame that I had to lose her for it. But I have a feeling it'll turn out to be more than worth it.
...
I pulled this image data from that West Sider's ocular feed. See what Kal's doing with STS?
She's not just slinging dust around. She's sorting it somehow.
I thought she was *buying* Lucid...but I think she's *making* it out of Bright, by purifying it *herself*.
To do that, my only conclusion is that she's actually manipulating the minerals at a *molecular* level.
That's...impossible. You can't see or sense anything that small, so how could you manipulate it?
Is it impossible?
What if... we could *hone* our sensing ability somehow? Really *focus* in on our material and get some kind of...magnified view.
That's my theory.
But whatever Kal's doing, it's working...and it must be *replicable*.
...
This is it. The answer to our problems. And I have a feeling that Kal isn't even aware of the *full* potential of this discovery...

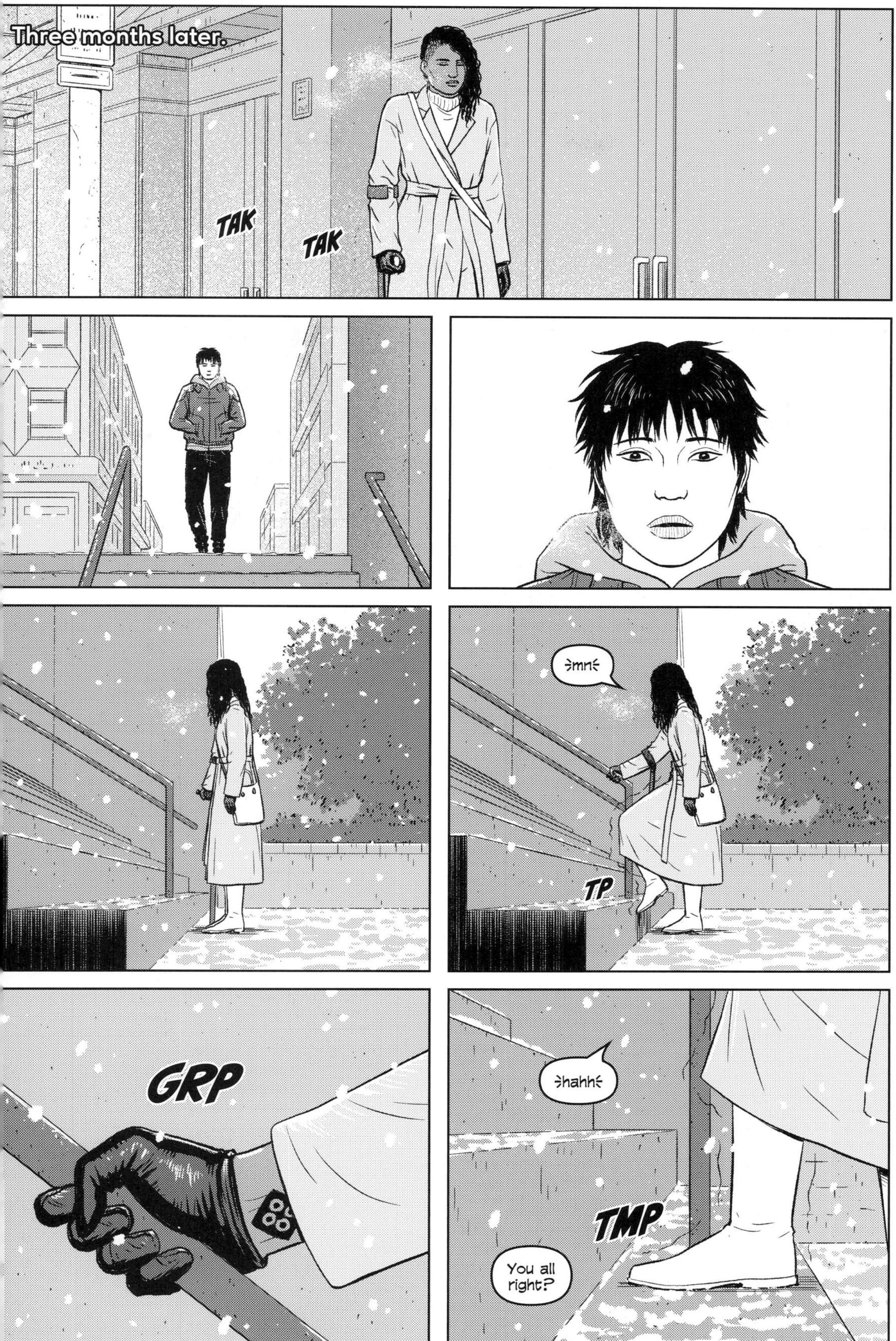
Three months later.
TAK
TAK
mn
TP
GRP
hahh
TMP
You all right?

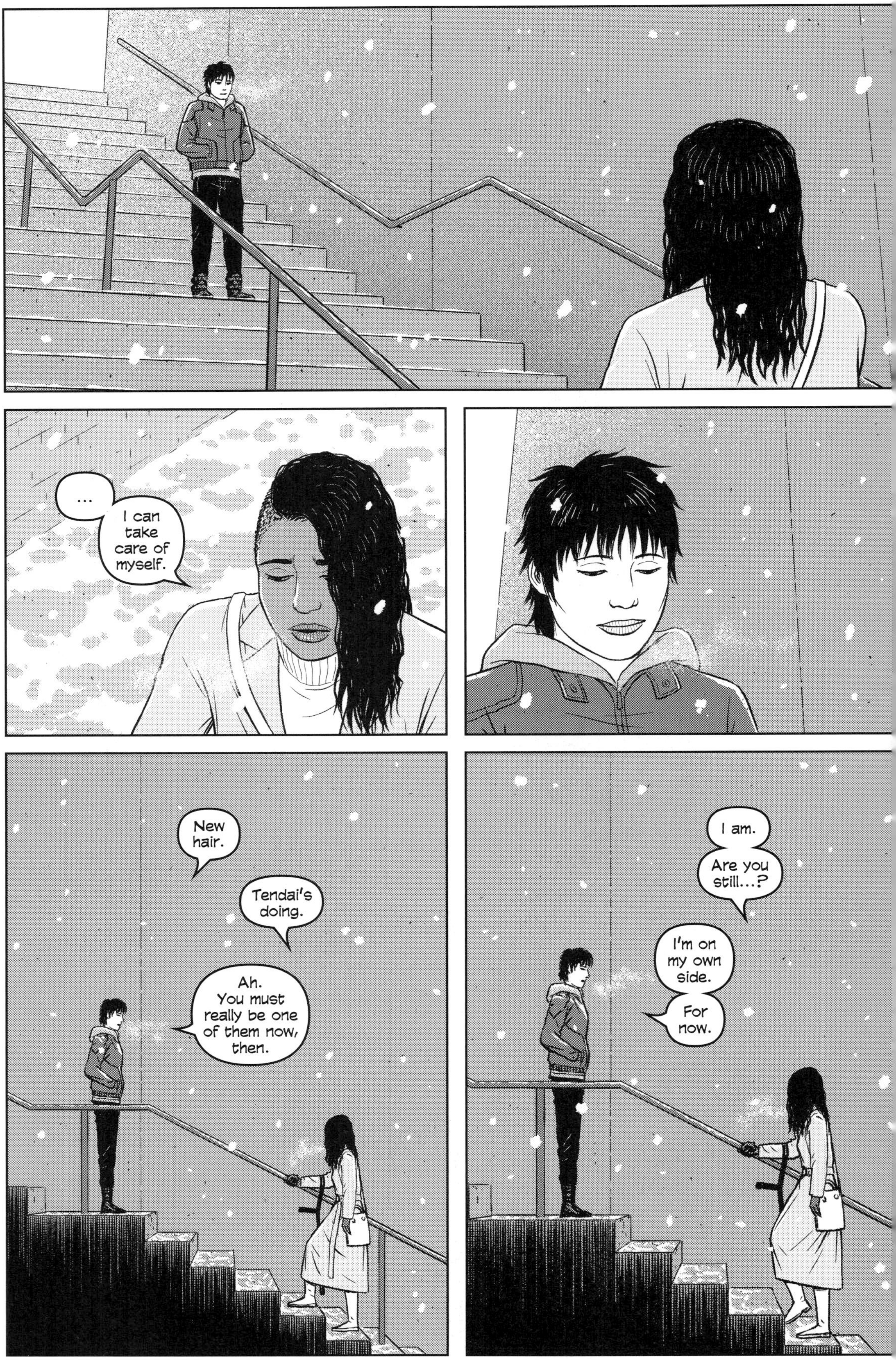
...
I can take care of myself.
New hair.
Tendai's doing.
Ah. You must really be one of them now, then.
I am.
Are you still...?
I'm on my own side.
For now.

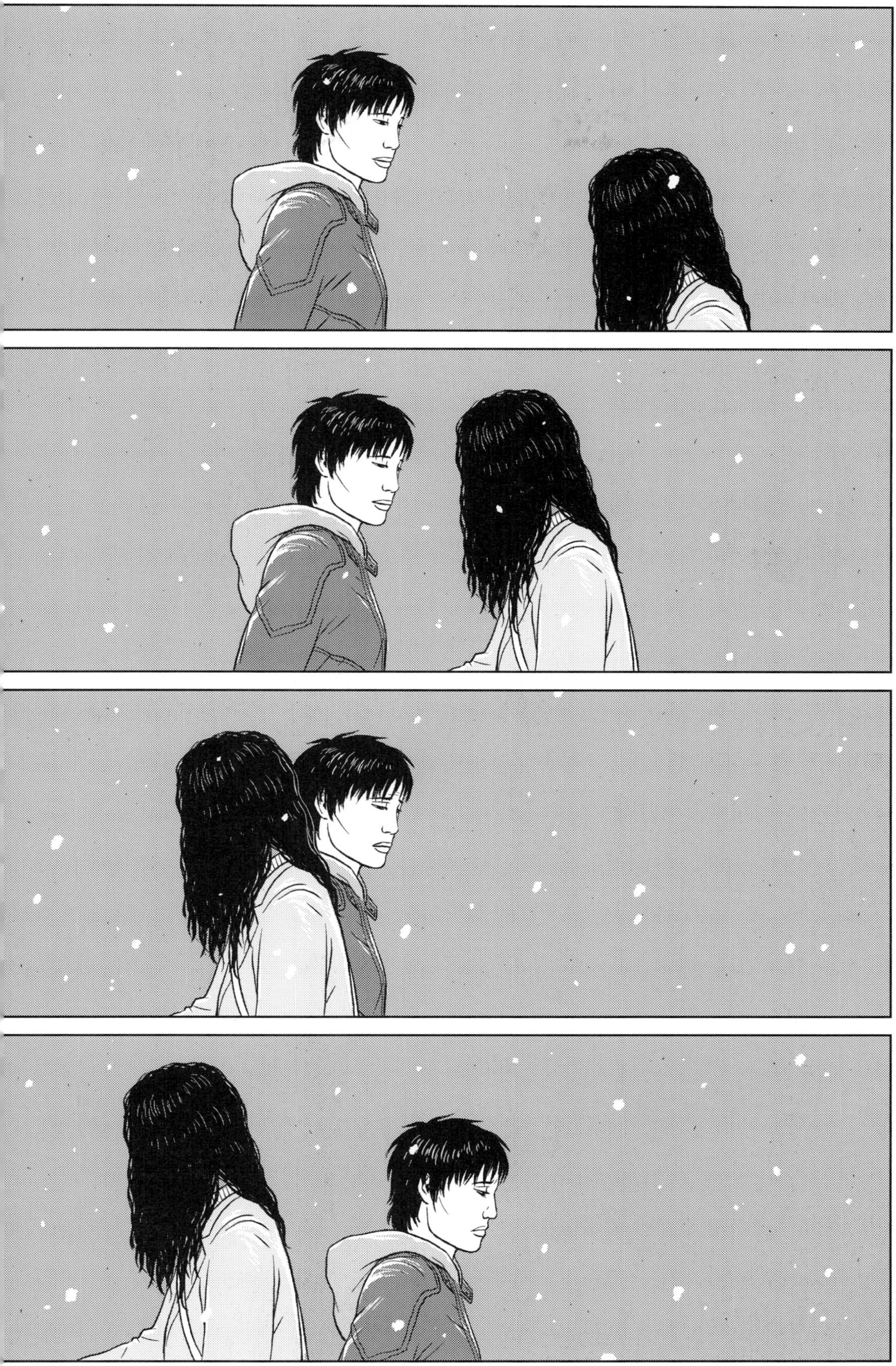

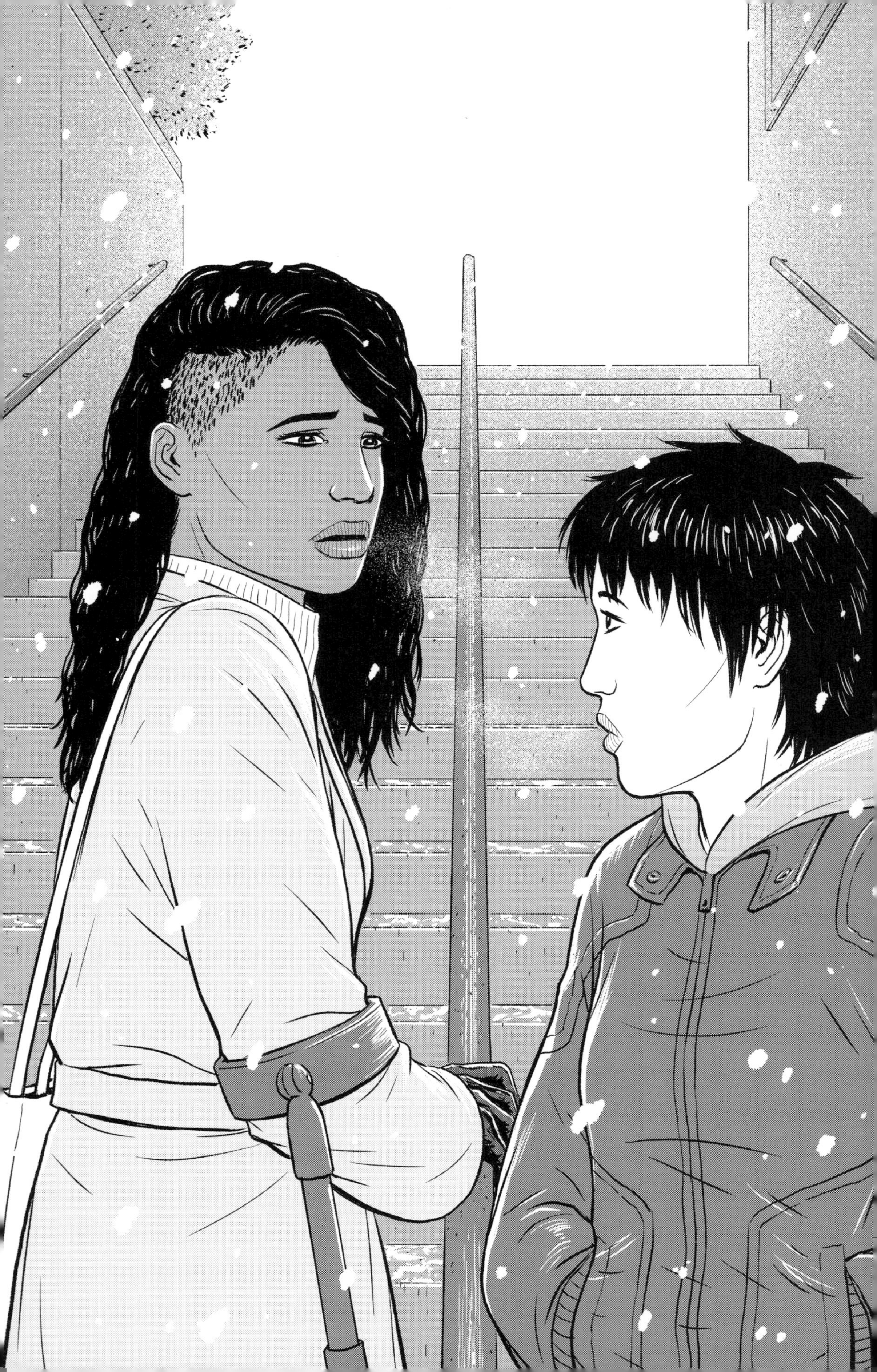

JONATHAN LUNA

co-created and illustrated ETERNAL EMPIRE and ALEX + ADA (Image Comics) with Sarah Vaughn, and THE SWORD, GIRLS, and ULTRA (Image Comics) with his brother, Joshua Luna. He also illustrated *Spider-Woman: Origin* (Marvel Comics), written by Brian Michael Bendis and Brian Reed, and wrote and illustrated STAR BRIGHT AND THE LOOKING GLASS (Image Comics).

Jonathan was born in California and spent most of his youth in Iceland and Italy as a military child. He returned to the United States in his late teens.

Writing and drawing comics since he was a child, he graduated from the Savannah College of Art and Design with a BFA in Sequential Art.

He currently resides in Northern Virginia.

www.jonathanluna.com

LAUREN KEELY

is an artist and writer living in Northern Virginia. She lives and breathes all things magical and aspires to share that love with the world.

This is her first comic book series.

www.laurenkeely.com